ACCLAIM FOR THOMAS F. MONTELEONE'S
THE RESURRECTIONIST!

"Thomas F. Monteleone hasn't lost his chops. . . . A sly blend of political thriller and horror novel."
—*San Francisco Sunday Examiner & Chronicle*

"Fascinating . . . twists and turns into a roller-coaster conclusion."
—*Roanoke Times*

"Kicks into overdrive in chapter one and accelerates from there. A wild, dazzling, daring ride into the heart of millennial fever."
—F. Paul Wilson, author of *The Select* and *The Keep*

"What a plot. What terrific characters. What a fascinating idea! I had an awful lot of fun with this one . . . and the basic concept—terrific!"
—Whitley Strieber, author of *Communion* and *Breakthrough*

"Powerful."
—*Science Fiction Chronicle*

"Monteleone raises interesting questions regarding personal r̶e̶s̶u̶r̶r̶e̶c̶t̶i̶o̶n̶ and the power of faith . . . pushes all the ̶̶̶̶̶̶̶̶̶̶̶̶̶̶̶̶̶̶̶̶̶̶̶̶"
—*Publishers Weekly*

D1413324

THE
RESURRECTIONIST

THOMAS F. MONTELEONE

WARNER BOOKS

A Time Warner Company

WARNER BOOKS EDITION

Copyright © 1995 by Tall Shadows Ltd.
All rights reserved.

Aspect® is a registered trademark of Warner Books, Inc.

Cover design by Don Puckey
Cover illustration by Phil Heffernan

Warner Books, Inc.
1271 Avenue of the Americas
New York, NY 10020

Visit our Web site at
http://pathfinder.com/twep

Ⓦ A Time Warner Company

Printed in the United States of America

Originally Published in Hardcover by Warner Books.

First Paperback Printing: January, 1997

10 9 8 7 6 5 4 3 2 1

THE
RESURRECTIONIST

ONE

Flanagan

Aboard Flight 957

Screw the bastards'?" said Larry Constantino in a whisper touched with alarm. "Is that what I just heard you say, Tom?"

"You heard me right," said Thomas Flanagan, the popular Republican senator from Maryland. "Screw. The. Bastards. Which word didn't you understand?"

"But they're your *constituents*. They think you're their representative."

"What is this, Larry? A tenth-grade Civics class?"

"You can't just *lie* to them, at least not now. . . ." Constantino looked at his friend, then around the cabin to see if anyone was paying attention to them.

Tom stretched out in his first-class seat on Flight 957 out of Washington National. He was scheduled to land in Miami around 8:00 P.M. It had been a long day, and he desperately needed to catch an hour's nap before facing the press at the airport and then limoing off to the National Governors' Convocation at the Miami Beach Hyatt Regency.

A little sleep would be nice, but he knew he wouldn't be getting any as long as he had Larry sitting next to him. Aide-de-camp, campaign manager, confidant, and all-around best friend, Lawrence Constantino had served him for fifteen years with the dedication of Gunga Din. They had yet to nail down the major points of his impending speech to the governors, but Larry would get the job done because he was the best in the biz and because he was a major pain in the ass.

Tom looked over at the slightly overweight Constantino, who'd just kicked in the door to his forties. Larry was dressed in a stylish dark suit with a tie that made just the correct fashion statement. His Greek heritage touched his features in all the right places making him good-looking but not movie-star handsome. He balanced a notebook computer on his lap, where Tom's speech awaited on a paper-white screen.

"Well . . . ?" nudged Larry. "What're you going to tell the governors?"

"Well *what?* I tell them I've got a plan to get plenty of new jobs created in all their states, and they'll love me. I tell them the truth—that I'm gonna kick all their silly state agencies off the gravy train, and they'll throw their desserts at me en masse!"

"But you *don't* have a plan. You can't lie. Some smart-assed reporter will call your bluff."

"Look, Larry, these governors don't give a damn what I really think of all those *non*-issues we've been using to smokescreen the *lumpen.* Abortion. Prayer in the schools. Whether or not you can buy a *Penthouse* at the corner Seven-Eleven. They don't really care!"

"I know that, Tom. Keep your voice down. Take it easy."

Tom instantly reined himself in. No way he wanted any of the common men back in steerage hearing his true feelings on *anything.* Even the Secret Service goons in first class weren't privy to his sincerest opinions.

"They want to know they'll still be dipping their beaks in the federal trough. They want some more of that funny money to throw at anybody who yells loud enough. They want real answers from me and a real commitment. I don't see how I can do anything *but* lie."

Larry considered this, then typed out a few lines on his keyboard. "All right, say it like this: your state-aid package is still being fine-tuned and that the details can't yet be discussed. That doesn't make you such a bare-assed liar."

Tom smiled. "Even though I am?"

"Even though you are." Larry sighed, shook his head, typed in another line.

"That's your problem, Larry," said the senator. "Even after all this time, you still want things to be on the up-and-up."

"That's so bad?"

"Of course it's not *bad*—just impossible. C'mon, Larry, you know we can't tell the scuttlefish what's really going on! Besides, they really don't want to know. As long as they've got plenty of sitcoms and ballgames to watch, as long as they get to slink off for two weeks a year to the beaches or the theme parks, and still make their bills every month, they're happy."

"Thomas Jefferson would have you hanged."

Tom Flanagan chuckled softly. "Larry, Larry . . . you're so naive sometimes. Jefferson was the architect of a democracy."

"Yeah, so?"

"What we have here is an oligarchy, remember? A plutocracy, if you want to get right down to it."

Larry nodded, returned his attention to his keyboard. "Okay, what about the Immigration Act? You got some heat on our position when it came up in Phoenix. I'm not sure I like the way the changes have been worded here. Look . . . "

Tom looked at the words scrolling on the notebook. He didn't really care what they wrote for him about the pending legislation on the control of allowing aliens into the country. He would say whatever would get him the highest "coefficient of approval," to quote the current knowledge-meisters. He recalled what the combine at *Time* had written about his appearance in Phoenix and mouthed an appropriate response to Larry, who incorporated it into his latest draft of the speech. Tom had always hated speech-writing; he'd never picked up that gift you needed to catch the subtleties, to create just the right nuance for just the right audience.

"Okay," said Larry. "I'll get this printed out and let Sydney give it a final polish before we get to the hotel. He might pick up something we've overlooked."

Tom watched his friend cable into a small inkjet printer on the tray table. Several keystrokes later, sheets of his speech began rolling out of the two-pound device in twelve-point Helvetica. Amazing how the technology just kept getting better.

Larry Constantino watched over his toys like a fussy mother. He'd always been a gadgeteer, even when they'd been in college. Tom remembered the battery-powered page-turning gizmo Larry ordered from the back of some magazine. It was supposed to let him read his textbooks while he lounged in his dorm room bed. Plainly a piece of shit, it never worked right, but that never deterred Larry from trying almost every contraption offered on late-night television.

Tom checked his watch.

(God, this flight is going on forever ... I need a little sleep.)

He could blame Valerie for his exhaustion, but it had been his decision to take that little detour from Chicago out to New York City where she was staying with the crew from her latest film. Under the guise of an impromptu appearance at the Hard Rock Cafe as a campaign/publicity stunt, he'd used the opportunity to log a few hours with his Hollywood mistress.

(And now I'm paying for it. This old age thing is going to be a bitch. . . .)

Tom smiled and looked past Larry to the darkened window beyond which the night rushed past them at 600 miles per hour. There were so many people out there, down there. So many people he'd never meet, never know, and yet here he sat, soaring above them like some demigod whose whims or suspicions could twist and wrench their lives into whatever pitiable shape he chose. Some men might quail at the prospect of such power, but Tom Flanagan had lusted after it from the first day he sipped from the cup of political influence. There was nothing like the rush you could get from knowing you were turning a wheel that would in turn move a million others. Not even sex. There was truly nothing to compare. Nothing. They said it took a special kind of man to want to be the president of the United States, and Tom Flanagan had always known he was special, that he was destined for something great. The time was almost at hand when—

Larry's notebook computer leaped into the air as the jet-liner dropped through an air pocket. The FASTEN SEATBELTS light chimed on, and Tom expected an intercom announcement about turbulence. Larry grabbed his precious computer before it tumbled to his feet, and the plane pitched hard to the right, sending brandy snifters, champagne glasses, and coffee cups in all directions.

TWO

Flanagan

And then, just like that, Senator Thomas Flanagan was sitting there in his wide-body seat listening to the words all air passengers never hope to hear.

Ladies and gentlemen, this is your captain speaking— we are experiencing a major system malfunction. Please prepare for an emergency landing as soon as possible.

The jetliner began dropping at a sickening angle; its engines protesting and its metal skeleton groaning from excessive demands.

Sweat, not the perspiration which appeared on cue under the TV studio lights, but real *sweat*, tinged with the acid of his fear, oozed from him as he white-knuckled the armrests under his palms. The intimacy of the first-class cabin had become suddenly claustrophobic. The air was spiked with tension riding the edge of panic.

The flight attendant, a young, slightly effeminate man named James, was trying to speak evenly, giving final instructions before impact. His words did little to hide his panic as the vestiges of professionalism surrendered to the finality of their descent.

Listening numbly to the request to bend forward and grasp his ankles, Tom looked into the slack, pale face of Larry Constantino.

"God help us, Tom," muttered Larry. "We've got—"

They were yanked violently to the left as the fuselage lurched across the night sky, tilting and suddenly plummeting downward with all the grace of a rock falling off a cliff.

The cabin inflated with screams. Loose papers flew around their heads like maddened gulls.

(I'm going to die.)

The thought assaulted Senator Tom Flanagan with its bleak, simple truth. It hammered him like a cheap piece of tin, leaving him flat and cold.

(You're going to hit the ground at more than three hundred miles per hour, and the hands of gravity and all the laws of motion are going to twist this piece of shit plane into something ugly. . . .)

Tom blinked his eyes and realized he was leaning forward, staring at his fingers as though, infantlike, he were discovering them for the first time.

One of the engines was screaming like a Valkyrie, struggling against the plane's dive into the dark pool of night. Somewhere below them stretched the deadly murk of the Florida Everglades.

"Tom . . ." Larry Constantino's voice reached for him.

"Hang on," said Tom, "we're going to make it!"

"Ever the politician!" shouted Larry, fighting to be heard over the painful whine of the engines.

The nose of the plane shot upward as if on a string, then dipped again with a roller-coaster drop. A chorus of screams from the passengers filled the coach—a Gregorian chant of terror. The fuselage began vibrating and the cabin filled with a horribly loud chuddering sound. The shaking became so violent Tom would've sworn the seats were separating from the bolts anchoring them to the floor. Their downward path steepened, leaning to the left, as though threatening to slip into a barrel roll.

(How much *more* can we drop?)

Tom looked into the inked-in square of window by his seat. No way to tell where they were in relation to the ground, or when the impact might come. . . .

The *waiting* for that inevitable moment was tearing through his gut with a serrated edge. It *had* to be worse than the actual event happening, Tom thought with a curious detachment. Probably be instantaneous, almost—a few seconds of hideous noise and motion and pain . . . and then nothing.

(But this fucking *waiting* was going on forever! What was it like for those poor bastards being carted off to be hanged or beheaded . . . ?)

Suddenly the jetliner's nose veered up and to the right as the engines whined with a final burst of power. The right wing buckled, and there was the sound of metal actually being *torn*, and the image of a huge piece of paper being ripped slowly in half stuck in Tom's mind. A new chorus of screams rose up to fill the jagged air of the cabin.

"Jesus!" yelled Larry Constantino, then fumbled for the barf bag stuffed somewhere in the elastic pocket of the seat-back in front of him. Oddly, Tom was reminded of the first time he and Larry had gotten drunk together at Georgetown, and how his friend couldn't keep down some cheap apple wine called Boar's Head. Larry had asked him for help that night because he was scared and because Tom was his friend.

Larry's hands had become puffy, white mittens with no control or dexterity. As the bile of fear and nausea frothed out of him, he began to cry.

Tom turned to help him, but realized he could do nothing. Larry was blue-white and waxy like a sheet of fax paper. He was going to die and he couldn't handle it any longer.

The fuselage dropped again as though the wires suspending it had been abruptly cut—that was the wing separating, breaking loose, and sending them downward with ever-increasing acceleration.

It wasn't until that moment that Tom realized he would *never* see Valerie again . . . that he'd never see his college-age son, Chip, get his diploma or his daughter Kiley and her new baby, or—

God's hammer struck the plane, coming up beneath the fuselage like the hard, flat indifference of an anvil's face. The last thing Tom remembered was being pulled forward with such force he could feel his *bones* being yanked out of their soft flesh.

THREE

Flanagan

Senator Thomas Flanagan was wet and terribly cold. . . .

But he was *alive*.

The sensations and the concept came to him slowly, as though passing down a tunnel of great distance, but closing the span inexorably. He seemed to be suspended in some vast sea of darkness—an astronaut hanging against the endless night of the mind's inner space.

He blinked his eyes, but saw nothing.

(Blind?!)

(Jesus, anything but that.)

Since he was a little kid, it was one of those things he'd always been freaked about—his eyes and going blind.

Concentrating, he could feel his arms, his hands. His somatic sense was coming back, slowly but intact. He touched his face and it felt wet, slippery.

(Am I bleeding?)

He ran his hands over his face. Everything felt fine. No blood, just water, sweat.

He was okay. . . . He would live. He would see his children . . . Valerie . . . everybody.

Looking up, he laughed at the sight of the stars, and even though the sound of his voice seemed weak and fragile, it was a *good* sound, a happy sound.

(Larry . . .)

Where was Larry? He'd been sitting right beside him.

Larry?

Did he call out his friend's name? Or had he merely thought of it?

(Got to get it together a little better. Where am I? Just exactly what the fuck is going on here?)

"Larry . . . where are you, buddy? Larry . . . !?"

The sound of his own voice was oddly comforting, making everything more real. He tried to listen for a response, but his ears were ringing, buzzing. He could hear himself through the bones of his skull, not his eardrums.

Take it easy. Stay calm and concentrate.

Although he had no time sense, no awareness of its passage or duration, he began to feel better. He knew now he was still strapped into his jetliner seat, tilted at a severe angle to the ground.

But the ground was somewhere *below* him in the murk. Tom rested in the branches of a dead tree. The seat had somehow been ripped loose from the cabin's floor as the fuselage broke apart and had been caught by the tree like a line drive in a center fielder's glove.

As he hung there, wondering how high up he might be, he began to hear the mosaic soundquilt that described the aftermath of the plane's impact: the crackle and snap of scattered fires, the pained calls of survivors . . . and an eerie overlay of animal growls and bird calls. And all of this underscored by a million-insect chorale.

The Everglades.

(Great. Just great . . .)

They'd gone down in the living room of every predator and hungry bug in Florida. . . .

Humid air seemed to cling to him as his vision continued to improve, aided by an almost-full moon and the fires. Tom focused on the gnarled terrain not more than ten feet below him.

Nothing down there but swamp water—an organic soup of slime and bacteria.

(Looks great. Can't wait to sink my tailored cuffs and Bostonian wingtips into that shit. . . .)

He fumbled with the seat belt clasp with his left hand while he used his stronger right hand to gain a firm purchase on the side of the seat. Just ease down. No sense dropping like a rock.

But it didn't work that way.

As soon as he pulled on the flat metal clip of the seat belt, he felt like he was being *ripped* from the embrace of the cushions by an unseen hand. No chance to grab for anything.

He fell like a skydiver in freefall—but briefly. Then the cold slap of Everglades ooze. Tom Flanagan sank into the thick clutch of the swamp, silk suit clinging to him like some hideous marine creature. His mouth had been open, ready to scream, when the water sludged into him. He could feel it sealing up his ears, nose, and eyes. . . .

Pushing upward, he burst from the vileness like a sub-launched Polaris. The rank frog-smell of the air rushed into him with honeysuckle sweetness, and Jesus!—it had never smelled so *good*!

His gag reflex kicked in; he staggered and weaved in the chest-high water like a club fighter ready to take a fall. His vision wavered, finally cleared. His hair felt wet and heavy against his skull and for some reason it really bugged him. He'd never realized how much he'd become attached to his blowdryer.

Postcrash sounds gradually seeped back to him. People crying out. Fires still crackling. Bugs and critters still singing.

Tom walked forward, with no idea where he was going. Something was burning up ahead, and it drew him like a beacon. Maybe a hundred yards distant lay a piece of a seat or a section of the cabin. The mud at his feet sloped upward, and the swamp gradually receded from him. Ahead the burning debris rested on higher ground. He slogged onward. There were people huddled near the smoldering pieces of the wreckage.

As he pushed closer to the shoal, he was amazed by the scatter of rubble—clothing, food trays, pieces of luggage, toys, cushions, paper, and countless chunks of metal. A girl of maybe ten walked up to him, crying in short bursts.

"Mister, you gotta help us!" Her baggy ESPRIT sweat-shirt was stained an ugly brown and her jeans were scorched on the left side, but she looked uninjured. She reached out to take his hand and guide him forward.

"I will, honey . . ." he heard himself saying.

She pulled him into the midst of the final pieces of so many lives, past the stilled bodies to a young-looking man leaning against the stump of a dead tree. He was dressed casually, a typical Florida vacation ensemble of polo shirt and cotton pants. Leaning up against a tree, he breathed with much effort, his eyes staring off at some unseen land-scape.

"My daddy's hurt," she said.

Tom kneeled down and touched the guy's arm. He didn't react.

"Where's it hurt?"

"My legs . . . can't move 'em. Feels like they're on fire."

As he stared at the man, Senator Tom Flanagan realized how utterly helpless he was in the face of real horror. All the bullshit speeches and all the slick deal-making and glad-handing was crap right now. He'd always thought the power of his office could get him through anything, could open the doors and smooth the ways, and grease the wheels of *any* goddamned machinery, any goddamned where . . .

But as he hunkered down next to this poor bastard with no feeling in his legs, he realized that all his power and influ-ence wasn't much of anything on the grand scale.

"Are you a doctor?" The man's voice sounded weak, forced.

Tom shook his head. "No, I'm sorry, I'm not."

(Christ, I'm not even a lawyer . . . !)

"My wife . . . ? Where's my wife? She was sitting across the aisle from Sally and me . . ."

"I don't know," said Tom, standing up. "I'll try to find someone who can help you."

"Don't go, mister!" The girl named Sally grabbed his dangling arm, her grip hard, desperate.

How could he tell her he *had* to go, to just get away from the mirror of pain that revealed to him the complete *fake* that he was.

That old Golding novel he'd read as a kid, *The Lord of the Flies*, was so dead on, wasn't it? We can be so smooth and civilized—as much as we damn well please—but just rip off our clothes and get us away from our fax machines and televisions and wine coolers for a couple of minutes and we're back to the Paleolithic, so fast you'd never see the rock that bashed your head even coming. All the sizzle and glitz of Washington was light-years away right now. He was just a clumsy shell-shocked guy with no real skill other than how to talk out of both sides of his mouth.

(Keep it up—you're doing a great job. . . .)

He staggered off, staying to the high ground. The air held him in its humid cloak, and the night stretched into an endless plain of twisted dreams and lives. He couldn't imagine that so much *stuff*, so many people, could have been crammed into the plane. A numbness gradually overwhelmed him; he couldn't have pushed himself without the emotional shutdown.

(Too much . . . too much of everyfuckingthing . . .)

He kept telling himself he was looking for Larry Constantino. His campaign manager had been sitting right *next* to him, for God's sake.

(So where the hell was he now?)

Using his fractured sense of direction, Tom tried to cover the crash site in an ever-widening circle, calling out Larry's name. He walked for what could have been hours or only minutes. The only thing that kept him going was the need to find out what happened to Larry. They'd been sitting right next to each other. He couldn't have just disappeared.

(And by the way: where the hell were the rescue teams?)

Above him, the dark sky remained mute and empty. No search planes or choppers, not even swamp skimmers or powerboats on the water. Nothing but a monotone litany of pain and death being offered up to the night.

His legs were starting to feel like rubber, and his left knee kept sending out little spikes of pain like there was an icepick or something jabbing away in there at his ligaments. Maybe he'd been hurt when he fell out of the tree? Maybe he should stop the aimless wandering and sit down before he did something that might cripple him for life.

(Yeah, right . . . how can you even think like that with all these poor suffering bastards all around you? Get going, you pussy. . . .)

His hair had dried out and it felt like straw when he ran his hand through it. He knew he didn't look very much like the powerful, on-the-rise, white-knight political savior the *Washington Post* liked to describe.

(You're just like everybody else out here. . . .)

Tom stood as straight as he could, tried to gather up whatever strength and dignity he had left. Compared to most of the people around him, he was a lucky stiff. That he could even consider wimping out on Larry was absurd, and it made him feel like a shithead to know that it had even entered his thinking. He was—

The chuddering sound of engines and rotors fell out of the sky. Looking up, losing his last thought, Tom could see the piercing beams of searchlights playing erratically across the swamp. Finally, they'd been found. All around him, people who'd been dazed and slack were suddenly coming back to life. The air filled with screams and shouts as everyone who could stand or run around waving their arms had started doing so.

Tom watched them silently, knowing he had to find Larry Constantino before anybody else did. He just *had* to.

The sound of other engines filled the air. Searchlights pinpointed pockets of activity, smoke, and fire. Tom wandered through the wreckage, looking in spots less likely to harbor survivors. If Larry was dead, Tom knew he had to be the one to face Sophia and tell her she'd lost her husband. That was nobody's job but Tom's, and he knew he had to be able to say he'd been with him till the last of it. . . .

(Yeah, even if it was bullshit. . . .)

Pushing on through the smoke-tinged air, he approached a section of the fuselage that had listed over halfway. Tom could see through the jagged cross section of the cabin several seats and overhead storage racks still intact. Still strapped into one of the seats, eyes open, sat Larry Constantino. His carefully trimmed hair remained neat, his classic red power-tie centered between the folds of his suit jacket. He displayed an expression of mild surprise as his hands gripped the armrests with white-knuckled determination.

"Larry!" yelled Tom, as he closed the distance to him. "Migod, I've been looking all over for you! You okay . . . ?"

Larry continued to stare slack-jawed in his direction, but said nothing.

Dead men never do.

Tom grabbed his friend by the shoulder, shook him hard. "C'mon, Larry . . . talk to me, man. . . ."

His words were an afterthought. Something that needed to be said, even though he knew Larry Constantino was beyond ever hearing them. Tom looked at his friend, trying to figure out what had killed him. He looked so at ease. No sign of violence or trauma. Heart attack, maybe?

Without thinking about it, he unbuckled the body from its seat. It was hard to imagine he'd never be talking to him again, never hear that funny laugh of his, or argue sports or . . .

The dead weight of the body caught him off guard as he tried to ease his friend from the seat and get him to the ground. This was going to be harder than—

As the body slumped forward, Tom suddenly saw what had killed his friend. Instead of falling into his arms, Larry Constantino kind of slid forward on the jagged piece of metal that had skewered the back of his seat and entered his lungs and heart. Just deep enough to not break through his chest and discolor his white oxford shirt, but room to spare to gut him like a pig. A few inches to the side and it would have been Senator Tom Flanagan lanced neatly by a lethal piece of the hull instead of poor Larry Constantino.

(Aw, Jesus . . . all the blood . . .)

The back of Larry's suit and the airline seat's fabric had been stained a deep red-black.

Tom had to forcefully yank his friend's body off the barbed end of the wreckage. He heard something tear, something give way. Finally the corpse fell free, pulling Tom down to the soft earth with it. Fighting back the tears, he couldn't stop staring at Larry's ruined back. It was impossible, yet he was handling his stilled flesh like a store mannequin. This couldn't be happening. This body that had been his friend. What had happened to Larry?

There was a part of him dealing with it. Accepting it, realizing the depth of the tragedy and relating it to all the death he'd already seen that night. But there was another part that was having none of it. You didn't survive a goddamned plane crash in the Everglades and get used to it this fast. . . .

No way.

Nobody should get away that easy.

Larry Constantino had been the most decent human being he'd ever met. To see him lying on the dark earth was the hardest thing he'd ever have to believe and accept and then get up and go on with the rest of his life.

(Do something!)

But there was nothing he could do. It was long over; the flies and all the million other bugs were already starting to show interest in his best friend.

(No!)

Swatting the insects away, he kneeled down and touched Larry's shoulder, ran his hand down the tailored jacket until it fell into the canyon-wound.

Cold. Sticky. Pungent.

His stomach lurched, but Tom kept his hand inside the laceration. He had no idea what he was doing, or why. It was just something he was doing.

(Don't move. . . .)

A wave of dizziness washed over him, but it wasn't nausea. This was something he'd never felt before. It was like a chord being struck in the pit of his being. A . . . a *resonance*. He felt as if a giant tuning fork had been struck, and the tuning fork was *him*.

Involuntarily, he leaned back to steady himself, and as his hand left the wound, the sensation left him. Instantly. Like throwing a switch in a power station.

And the *absence* of the feeling was worse.

(What the hell *was* that . . . ?)

Blinking his eyes, he leaned forward, inched his fingers ahead until he again touched the place in Larry's back where the wreckage had pierced him.

(Why am I doing this?)

Again, as he touched the wound, the . . . resonance returned. Tom Flanagan's fingers began tingling, and he could feel warmth emanating from the hole in his friend's back. No, not warmth—*heat*. And it wasn't coming from the wound.

It was coming from his *fingers*.

(No, that's impossible. . . .)

But it wasn't. He could feel the heat. He was causing it, making it. There was something inside, boiling up, spilling out of him. Something the color and texture of anger, the sharp edge of pain and frustration. It was a force that geysered up from deep in the wellspring of Tom Flanagan's soul.

A force of will.

A will to power.

A powerful force.

It was all these things. It was none of them.

It was something he'd never known lay coiled within the darkness of his being, and yet when it revealed itself, he was not surprised. Instead, he looked into the calm eye of its soul-storm and faced the force without fear, without doubt. It was like standing at the edge of a vast pit while unknown winds slapped you around. The sense of the power and the danger assaulted him, excited him. The white noise of the universe hummed in his skull. Somehow, he'd tapped into a trunk line to one of life's main generators—he knew this, and he did not fear it.

(Do it. Go on! Push . . .)

Without really knowing why, only that he must, Tom Flanagan eased his fingers deeper into the drying blood within the wound.

Above him, the *whumping* rotor of a helicopter grew louder. An intrusive sound, punctuated by the probing finger of its searchlight. As it passed over him, Tom felt outrage.

(The dumb bastards . . . ! Not now!)

He hunched over, into the moonshadows and away from the offending light. He willed himself in touch with the sensations cresting over him.

Closing his eyes, he imagined himself standing at the edge of a bottomless canyon, leaning out, forward, held there by winds of time. It was as if his hands were melting now, heating up, sinking deeply into the ruined flesh that had been his friend. There was a rhythm building within him. Like a low-amperage current, he felt it synching up with his pulse, his lifeline.

There was no pain, no fear, only a belief—that there was an engine revving, somewhere beyond his senses, but threatening to burst free of its moorings to burn free in our world.

Deeper he plunged his hands into Larry's back. The sensation was almost erotic as he violated the sacred space of his friend's viscera. The amperage increased, the sounds and color of the world evaporated under the withering heat of this pure experience.

Heat.

Light.

Life.

The idea/images flashed through him—lightning strokes against the dark landscape of his soul.

And Tom Flanagan reached down, endlessly down, into the black vein of experience and flesh that had been his friend, and like a dredge on a harbor bottom, he sifted and seined and clutched for those vital fragments that had defined the gestalt entity known as Larry Constantino.

It felt as though Tom's hands had become plastic—elongated tentacles uncoiling, stretching along the helical ladders of memory and time and space.

And finally, he touched that magic engine at the heart-spring's center, that place where all things are known and defined within us, and he massaged the cold core, and made it spark.

Then pulse . . .

And finally burn again.

(Larry . . . ?)

Withdrawing his hands slowly, they commenced their million-light-year journey across the blasted escarpments of a lifetime.

(Larry . . . C'mon, guy . . . I've got you now.)

Somehow, he knew. Tom Flanagan knew where he'd been, what he had done.

As his hands cleared the ugly slash across Larry's back, he could feel the flesh already closing, like a hungry mouth, gulping down big chunks of life, storing it up for the next time. He could hear it sealing itself shut, healing from the deepest inside layers all the way out.

Leaning back, he slowly felt the world crawl back to him. The damp, fetid air, the ratcheting blades of a copter descending nearby, and the cacophony of human joy and pain that rose up to meet it—everything blended together. Tom Flanagan roughly grabbed the shoulder of his friend, tugged him up and over.

He looked down at the face and saw that the eyes no longer stared into eternity. In fact, they were closed.

But only for an instant. He watched as the lids quivered, fluttered once, then lifted to reveal a pair of eyes so dark they could have been Greek olives.

"Tom! Are you okay?" said Larry Constantino. "Christ . . . What happened?"

FOUR

Barrero

It was going to be a long night for the staff at Keller Memorial General Hospital in West Palm Beach. Dr. Estela Barrero had been fumbling with the clasp of her pearls, the perfect accent to her black Halston ensemble, when she and other hospital staff were beeped about Flight 957. Not that she so much wanted to attend another one of the chief of staff's dinner parties, but hospital politics and protocol almost demanded that she at least make an appearance at all of Dr. Hansen's functions. Tonight, the party broke up early as many of the guests ran for their cars.

She glided her BMW 535csi south along the coastal highway. The road stretched black as the night, black as the anxiety that was tightening its grip upon her. Estela tried not to think about the mayhem she would be greeting when she reached the ER, but there was no escaping it. Any night in a metropolitan hospital emergency room assaulted you like a street punk with its immediacy and its coppery smell of blood. The endless procession of domestic fight injuries, gunshot wounds, stabbings, broken limbs, kitchen accidents, staircase tumbles, and automobile victims were routine. But a plane crash . . .

Oh, yes . . . a fine and special carnage. A panorama of pain and suffering that elevated the word "trauma" to divine status. As chief resident in ER, Estela shouldered the brunt of all decision-making, and that meant Administration ignored her when things went smoothly and dragged her up on the carpet whenever things fucked up. Experience had taught her that tonight would slap her face with myriad decisions, all needing to be made quickly and efficiently, and she knew some of hers would be correct and some would be disasters.

Her hands were gripping the leather-padded wheel just a little too tightly, and she tried to will some of the growing tension away. Part of the price you paid to be a physician these days—there was just so much to know, so much to read, more than any one doctor could ever hope to know. No wonder everybody had to specialize. She knew that, accepted it, but sometimes had some problems dealing with it.

Looking through the sloping windshield, the road snaked away from her into the endless night ahead. To her left, over the water, a big ugly moon mocked her, kept pace with her sleek vehicle. It made her think of the times she'd taken moonlight drives with Antonio down this same stretch of road, and he would tell her how the moon looked so big because it was some kind of optical illusion. He'd explained it over and over and she'd never understood it anyway. She smiled when she thought back on how exasperated he used to get sometimes.

Something dark and furry scuttled onto the roadway, pinned by her lights for an instant, its eyes wide with fear. She swerved the wheel, felt a *thumpthump* as she nailed it, whatever it had been. Her stomach roiled, and she felt herself getting weepy. It was at times like this that she missed Antonio the most. When she was feeling low or anxious, or angry, he'd always been there to listen or to give support, or even to just argue with her so the tension could shake itself loose.

Antonio. *Mi vida, mi amor,* she used to call him. . . .

Two years. Has it really been two years already?

Estela shook her head, tried to concentrate on her driving. Two years ago she'd been working the graveyard shift when the paramedics showed up with Antonio. He'd been driving on the interstate when a drunk in a Cherokee careened across the median strip and caught him head-on. His little sports car folded up like a cheap accordion and it took them three hours to cut him out of the twisted metal, and it was far too late.

Mi amor ... So young and brilliant. She didn't want to think of her fiancé packaged up and lodged beneath the earth somewhere, forever cold, forever dark. It was impossible. That couldn't be her Antonio. He was somewhere else, he *had* to be. But she knew she'd never see him again; it was one of those things she just simply *knew* and tried to never think about.

But God, how she *missed* him!

His elitist sense of humor that had both infuriated and charmed her, his clear analytical way of seeing the world, his curiosity, and his incredible enthusiasm. What a unique character he'd been. She missed his raging egomania, his kindness, his flashes of self-righteous anger. He'd always seemed to be excited about whatever he was doing as if he were twelve years old and he'd just discovered it and it was simply the most wonderful thing in the world—no matter what it might have been.

I'll always love you. . . .

Blinking away another tear, Estela registered the approaching sign for her exit. Keller Memorial lay just beyond the hill and the next off-ramp. She fingered the pearls at her neck, feeling suddenly foolish for showing up at the hospital in her evening wear. But there'd been no time to change into the pale green scrubs of her profession. There was a sense of security, if not an actual anonymity wearing those silly-looking pajamas. She didn't know why, but she usually didn't want anyone to really know her when she had to do her job. It was better to just be another doctor on the assembly line.

And it *would* be an assembly line tonight. She'd heard the newscasts—the plane had gone down with 227 people on board and at least half of them had probably survived. Although the word "survived" was a relative term. The mangling the human body could endure during the tremendous G-forces of a jetliner crash were horrifying. Skin flayed or scorched to a black crisp, bones jellied, limbs shredded and sheared off, the list of atrocities as endless as the possibilities.

Stop thinking about it. There'll be plenty of the real thing soon enough.

A few more turns and the restricted parking area of Keller Memorial loomed before her headlights. Mel, the security guard, nodded her through the gate, and she slipped into her space with the automatic moves of something long practiced. Estela jumped from the car and ran toward the staff entrance. Another security guard waved her into ER. Like the backstage of a theater before opening night, everyone was running in different directions, last-minute precautions being shouted in several languages, the air almost sizzling with tension.

No one seemed to even notice her evening fashions as she reached the door to the physicians' lounge and lockers. Keying in her security code on the digital lock, she waited until the door clicked open with a loud snap. The scrub room was eerily quiet and empty with its pale green walls and cold fluorescents as she slipped out of her clothes and hung them carefully in her locker. As she pulled on her scrubs, she almost smiled at their soft familiarity.

Yes, the thought slipped efficiently through her mind. This is what is right for you. You are a doctor and it feels just right.

Estela stopped at the sinks to pull her long auburn hair from her face. She secured it in a Spanish bun, looking like a peasant girl in an El Greco portrait. As she washed up antiseptically, she realized she hadn't cleaned her makeup from her face. Too late to worry about it now. . . .

Entering the emergency room, she approached the nurses' station, which fronted her office like a castle's crenelated wall. Mary Sturgeon, her head nurse, looked up from her work and smiled.

"Welcome back, Doctor Barrero," she said. "I didn't think we'd be seeing you so soon."

Estela returned the smile. She liked Sturgeon's warmth and openness; it was a big asset in a place as grim and often depressing as ER. "I'd do anything to get out of one of Hansen's parties!"

"I'm sure our fearless leader would be glad to hear that," said a painfully familiar voice to her left.

Turning, Estela looked up to see Larry Geldorf, one of the other residents on the staff. No matter what was going on, he always had a kind of leering smile on his face, and his dark eyes were always in the act of undressing her.

"Hello, Doctor Geldorf," she said coolly. "Any word on when the first casualties will be getting here?" She took several steps toward her office.

"Already on their way." Geldorf started walking with her.

She stopped when she reached her door. "Excuse me, Doctor," she said without looking at him. "I'm going to be very busy this evening."

Geldorf stopped at the door, looked in at her. "Did you have to break a date tonight?"

"What?" She had reached her desk, looked back at him with as fierce a glare as she could muster.

"Hey, sorry, Doc! I was just trying to see if I still had a shot, that's all."

"The only shot I'd ever give you is one to the back of your head," she said without changing her expression. Then: "Don't you have any work to do?"

"Okay, boss," he said. "I know when I'm not wanted."

As he closed the door behind his ungracious exit, the phone rang.

"Doctor Barrero . . ." she said.

"Estela, we've got some priorities tonight," said a rough voice.

"Hello, Doctor Hansen," she said. "What's going on?"

"Chopper coming in any minute with Senator Flanagan and some of his staff. They were on Flight 957. . . ."

She nodded. "Hurt bad?"

"Don't know," said Hansen. "Just be ready for him, and give this your personal attention."

"All right, Ted. I will."

Before she could say anything, the chief of staff had clicked off the line. Theodore Hansen would never win any awards for manners, but he was a hell of a surgeon.

Estela slowly replaced the receiver to its cradle and stood up. So Thomas Flanagan was going to be making an unexpected call on them. . . . The young senator from Maryland was the Republican Party hopeful for the next presidential race, and was seen often enough on TV to be familiar to Estela, even though she did her best to ignore politics. He was a good-looking man with an engaging smile—that was all she knew about him, and if he was like the rest of his crowd, that was all she'd ever *want* to know.

She shook her head slowly. The senator was a "priority" according to her boss. What about the rest of the survivors of Flight 957? To Estela, every human life was a priority. There was nothing special about Senator Thomas Flanagan.

FIVE

Flanagan

Larry Constantino stared at him, waiting for an answer. "Tom, hey, you okay?"

"I think so. . . ." (Oh, I'm okay, Larry old buddy, but what about you? Have you been okay for the last hour or two? You know, while you sat here like a cored apple? Where've you been, man?)

Larry sat up, rubbed his hands together. His face revealed confusion and anxiety, with more than a touch of the awestruck. He shouted above the roar of the chopper engines, "Where are we? What happened?"

Tom gave him a quick synopsis. He left out some of the, shall we say, grittier details for several reasons: Larry probably wouldn't believe that he'd been dead or . . . brought back from that state of being (or should that be non-being?); and also because Tom himself wasn't yet ready to accept what he'd seen, what he'd somehow assisted like some half-witted midwife who did not really comprehend the process into which she'd been thrust. He kept trying to divert his own thoughts away from the whole thing. Ambivalence, fear, and outright hysteria all capered at the threshold of his thoughts. He needed to ground himself in far simpler realities to get through the immediate trauma of the crash and what followed. Could it be possible that he had somehow hallucinated the whole thing? Was he indeed conscious of himself at this moment? Was he dreaming everything? Could anything be so convenient?

"God, I feel so weird, Tom. What the fuck's happening to me?"

"You'll be all right," said Tom. He was kneeling at his friend's side, his knees sinking into the soft, damp earth. He was soaked through and he smelled like a frog farm.

(Yeah, no problem, old buddy! You've just been brought back from the end of time . . . but don't worry about it, man. You've just been having a bad day.)

"Yeah, we made it, didn't we?!" Larry Constantino stood up, wobbling like a man with too many martinis in his gut. Tom steadied him, tried to ignore the black-red stain across the back of his friend's suit jacket. Impossible, of course. The mark was a major reminder, a proof, really, that he'd been skewered and drained of his blood like a piece of kosher beef, and had been as dead as a bug on your windshield.

"Something's not right," said Larry. He looked like a little boy who had just opened his bedroom closet, disappointed to find the monster not there. "Something's wrong, Tom . . . terribly wrong."

"I know," said Tom. He wanted to reassure him, to put his hand on his friend's shoulder, but hesitated as the memory of the last time he'd touched Larry came rocketing back to him. He blinked back stinging tears, fought the icy grip along his spine. The sounds of approaching helicopters and swamp skimmers reached him, gave him a handgrip, something he might use to hoist himself back to the world of the familiar. He seized on the black engine noise, got lost in it.

"I keep feeling like something terrible's going to happen." Larry's voice honed to a shrill, fragile edge.

"It already did—we crashed in the Everglades, for Christ's sake!"

Larry Constantino looked at him with eyes as blank and cold as ball bearings. "No, but something's happened to me!

I can feel it! But I don't know what it is, Tom! But whatever it is, it's not over yet!"

"What do you mean," said Tom. "Of course it's not . . ."

"Huh? Do you understand what I'm talking about? Can you feel it, too?"

Tom looked at his friend—he looked so helpless, so vulnerable. There was no way he could ever tell him what madness, what totally impossibly madness, the two of them had already passed through.

"Come on! We've got to get moving!" Tom yelled over the din of the chopper's engine. He gestured at the copter, which had just touched down to disgorge rescue workers wearing fluorescent orange vests and helmets. People were waving their arms, crying out frantically, as the men fanned out to gather up the survivors.

Larry Constantino stood there, taking in the panoramic view of the crashsite, then looked back at the shard of the fuselage from which they'd emerged. The immense scope of the accident only now had begun to register in him. Tom could read the dazed comprehension in his friend's eyes, and he knew Larry was asking himself the same question that every survivor would ask: how the hell did this happen, and how did I get through it alive?

A flash of orange in Tom's peripheral vision made him turn to his left; two rescue workers were jogging toward them. As Larry also turned around to assay their approach, Tom again saw the hideous stain across the back of his friend's jacket. The ugly mark stared back at him like some kind of deviant Rorschach, a psychological trigger, a communiqué from the flipside of reality that screamed its message at Tom Flanagan, that told him perhaps he had fallen down the black well of insanity and would never return. The bloodstain was not only a frightening reminder of how much fluid the human body contained, but also a testament to the utterly impossible event Tom had ushered into being.

Larry Constantino stood before him, smiling weakly at the rescue workers, who pulled up in front of them, panting like horses after a race.

"You two all right?" asked the man carrying emergency medical gear in each hand. They both wore flight helmets with the visor flipped up. They were young, but they had the look of veterans—vigilant, prepared, confident.

"We're okay," said Tom.

(Oh, yeah, if you only knew how okay we are . . . !)

One of the rescuers looked at Tom with an expression he had become accustomed to. He was a large, broad-chested guy with a red beard and longish hair. He looked like he should be lumberjacking in Oregon. "Excuse me, sir, but are you Senator Flanagan?"

Tom nodded, fighting the sudden urge to reach out and shake the man's hand. Talk about conditioned responses, this was disgusting, although Dr. Pavlov would be proud. When a politician sees a potential voter, his glad-hand springs into action. Cute, Tom. Very cute.

"Yes," he said after an awkward pause, "and this is my campaign manager, Larry Constantino."

"We had an alert to keep an eye out for you, sir," said the red-bearded man. He fumbled with a small black box clipped to some rings on his vest, thumbed it on, and spoke into his helmet mike. "This is Delta Tango Niner! We've found Senator Flanagan! . . . Affirmative . . . Yeah, he's okay! . . . Yessir, he's okay, too! . . . Roger, we copy that . . . We'll be bringing them in . . . Delta Tango Niner, out."

Red Beard's partner was already ushering Larry toward the chopper. "Let's go, Senator," said the big man. "You've got a lot of people waiting for you."

Tom gestured at the chaos surrounding them. "We're okay, we can wait. What about some of the others?"

Red Beard smiled. "We've got people crawling all over this swamp, sir. Don't worry about them. We've got priority orders from the Secret Service, Senator. They want you outta here ASAP, so we're gonna do just that!"

Tom nodded, felt his shoulders slump. As he let the lumberjack guide him across the bank to the landing shoal, he could feel his strength leaking away from him like helium in a forgotten party balloon.

They climbed aboard and let the crew strap them into some functional, but not at all comfortable, fold-down seats. Looking over at Larry, Tom could see him getting lost in his own thoughts, as though he were rewinding and replaying something vastly important, something totally compelling. He nudged him gently. "What're you thinking about?"

Larry blinked, shook his head. "The crash. I . . . don't remember the crash at all. Do you?"

Tom paused before answering as the chopper suddenly lurched upward into the approaching dawn, leaving their stomachs earthward for an instant. The ratcheting blur of the rotors made conversation more challenging, but not impossible.

"The crash," prompted Larry again, once the aircraft was tilted forward and leaning toward a safe harbor.

"Not really. There was all this shit flying around the cabin, and the noise—I can remember the people screaming, the engines screaming . . ."

"But do you remember us hitting the ground? Do you remember what happened at that moment or when the plane started breaking up?"

"No, not really," said Tom, and that was the truth. "Why?"

"Because it's weird, Tom. It must have happened so fast, so goddamned fast, that we were knocked out instantly . . . I mean, I didn't feel a thing! The impact, the sound of the cabin cracking open, nothing! What about you?"

Tom summarized his adventure in the seat, in the tree, getting dunked in the swamp. He carefully related his search for his friend, how he found him after a long walk.

Larry nodded, considered the narrative. "This is getting weirder and weirder. . . ." he said after a moment.

"Why? What do you mean?" Tom did not look at him, but let his gaze drift out into the blackness beyond the open bay doors.

"When you were out cold," said Larry, "did you remember any of that? Did you have any . . . any dreams?"

Tom shook his head. "Nothing. No, I was just out of it. Don't remember anything."

Larry shifted his position, made sure he was staring into his friend's eyes.

"I do," he said. "I goddamned well do."

"Larry, what's the matter with you?"

Constantino hunched his shoulders, stretched his arms nervously. "I don't know, but listen, okay?"

Tom nodded, said nothing.

"I remember feeling like I was floating, like a balloon, like a fairy or something in a cartoon, you know? Just kind of drifting up and down, real gentle like. And I was not that high up in the air, just higher than the trees. I was looking down and even though it was dark—dark as hell—I could see everything!"

"Everything?"

"Yeah, I mean like the whole world. I was looking down at the whole world, and I could somehow see everything. But most of all, I could see the swamp, I could see where we'd crashed. I saw all the broken pieces and the little fires and the bodies, Jesus, the bodies were everywhere, Tom! And junk, just pieces of junk scattered all over the place like somebody's trashcan got knocked over and the dogs tore the crap out of it. . . ."

Tom nodded. He knew the tableau intimately. He sat, listening as Larry continued.

"And this is the . . . the weirdest part. I saw you down there, Tom! Yeah, I saw you wandering around like some bum and I even heard you calling for me. I heard you, man! I'm telling you, when you were telling what you did, I felt my skin crawl, Tom! Because I saw you! I saw you do exactly that."

(Yeah, my friend, I'm sure you did. I don't know how you saw me, but I know you did.)

"Some kind of ESP, maybe. . . ." Tom offered up the phrase weakly. He knew Larry wasn't asking for an explanation, rather, his friend just needed to let off some of the pressure of his experience before the jammed valve in his memory ruptured.

"I don't know," said Larry. "But listen, it gets weirder. So I'm floating above everything, right, and then I see you walk up to where we were when I woke up, remember?"

"Okay, sure. Go on."

(But don't tell me what comes next. Please don't tell me.)

Larry nodded, swallowed. The sound of the chopper blades suddenly seemed hollow, distant. An insulated envelope was enclosing them, sealing them up in a prison of their own device. ". . . And I can see that piece of the plane, busted open with some seats still in there. And then I see you, Tom, and you walk up and into the piece of the wreckage and you're looking at me, Tom! You're looking at me sitting in this seat. . . ."

(Shut up, Larry . . . just shut your face, man. I already know what you see. . . .)

Larry Constantino had shifted in his seat to look at Tom. There was a quietly couched terror lurching behind his eyes. Tom understood the man's feelings of revulsion far better than Larry did himself. He felt sorry for the poor guy, but there was no way he could ever explain to him what had happened.

". . . Tom, are listening to me?!" Larry's voice peaked.

"Yeah, of course I am. Go on, what happened then?"

"You walked up to me and I kind of looked over your shoulder, and I could see myself, Tom, and I was dead!"

"You were what?" Tom tried to play out his part as innocently as possible.

"Tom, I was dead, man. Really dead. And it was weird, I mean, as soon as I could see myself, and I *knew* I was dead, I started to like float up, only faster, like I was this balloon and you had suddenly let go of the fucker, and there I went, drifting away from you. I started screaming at you, Tom, to turn around, to see me, for Christ's sake, and to somehow maybe, to *do* something, you know . . . ?"

(Oh, I did something, all right.)

". . . but you never heard me, you never turned around. I think you were moving closer to me in my seat, but I couldn't really tell . . . 'cause I just kept floating up until you got real small, and everything looked like toys, and then I looked away from it . . . and I looked up. I don't know why, but I did, and I saw that I was floating into this long dark tunnel. God, it was so long, Tom! It was like it was endlessly long, but there was this bright light, like an explosion it was so bright, at the end of it. And I could feel myself moving up and along this tunnel. It was weird, but it wasn't scary, not really. At one point I looked back down toward the ground, and you know what?—It was gone! Yeah, when I looked down, it was just that endless tunnel only it was receding away from me, it was going away, like I'd been traveling through the damned thing forever . . . and then I looked back up and I could see a . . . a shape kind of standing at the end of the tunnel. . . ."

"A shape? What kind of shape?" Tom had been listening with his eyes squeezed shut, his shoulders all pulled together. He hadn't realized it, but he had been as tensed up as he could be.

"You mean a man? Was it a man you saw?"

Larry tried to smile, but did an awful job of it. His expression was that of a man trying to be dashingly brave and humorous, but he looked plain sad. "Yeah, I think so. It was a manlike shape. I couldn't see a face or anything like that, but it looked like somebody standing at the end of the tunnel, and I had the feeling he was waiting for me."

"How did you feel?" said Tom. "I mean, were you in pain, were you afraid?"

"Nah, no pain. Nothing. I kind of felt good . . . like at peace, and all that. But, you see, I knew I was dead, and I knew that should be bothering me and because it wasn't, well *that* kind of bothered me, you know what I mean? That I wasn't really worried or pissed that I was dead."

Tom smiled at his friend. Larry, usually so slick and in command of his language, sounded clumsy, unsure, almost like a little boy.

"And then what?" said Tom as the chopper suddenly yawed to the port side as it began to angle downward. The maneuver reminded him of the final plunge of the big jetliner, and he felt himself reaching out for anything he could find just to hang onto it.

"Oh, Jesus, feel that?" yelled Larry. "Remind you of anything?"

"You bet your ass, partner!" said Tom, nudging his friend in the ribs. "So what happened? You were telling me—"

"Yeah, well it went on like that for a while, like I was drifting, floating, getting closer to the shape at the end of the tunnel, but not close enough to see anything real clear, and then I felt the bottom just let go, and I was falling like I was made of lead or something. The tunnel had walls and I was just flying past them like I was going down a greased chute.

And then I was scared, you know, and then just when I felt like I couldn't go any faster, like I couldn't stand what it was going to feel like when I hit bottom, whenever that was, I . . . I felt somebody holding my arms, and I blinked my eyes and there you were, looking at me."

Tom swallowed hard as the banking turn of the chopper leveled off, erasing the gut-churning sensation it had caused. He stared straight ahead, tried to sound casual. "Hell of a dream," he said.

"I know, but it doesn't feel like a dream."

"Why not?" Tom turned to see a rescue worker scrambling back through a hatchway toward them.

"Because dreams start to feel dumb and weird and not real the longer you're awake from it, you know? But this one doesn't, Tom. It seems more and more real."

Tom Flanagan forced himself to chuckle. "But you know that's bullshit, Larry. You were knocked cold. I found you. I saw you!"

"Yeah," said Constantino, sounding unconvinced.

The rescuer suddenly appeared in front of them, and the noise of the rotors and the controlled chaos of the flight abruptly began churning around them. The man in the orange coveralls and helmet looked as young and eager as a campaign volunteer fresh from his polly-sci classes.

"Senator!" the young man yelled above the racket. "We're coming in to Keller Memorial! The heliport is on the roof. Hang on, sir, both of you, and we'll have you out of here in a minute!"

Tom waved in assent to the man, who moved off toward the chopper's belly doors. The craft swung from side to side as it steadied itself for the final drop to the roof of the hospital. He felt something grabbing his sleeve, pulling hard. It was Larry Constantino's hand, holding him like a carpenter's clamp. "Tom, are you listening to me?"

"Of course I am . . . Larry, take it easy, we're almost down. Everything's going to be fine."

"I'm not worried about this damned helicopter!" he yelled above the groan of the engine. "Tom, I'm not stupid! Don't treat me like I am."

"Larry—"

"I've read about this stuff, Tom! This near-death experience business . . . ! Tom, you have to tell me what happened down there!"

"What do you want me to tell you?" Tom's voice teetered on the edge of control. He didn't want to sound like he was getting emotionally charged up, but it was all he could do to hold on. Larry was scaring him, plain and simple. Scaring the hell out of him.

Larry drew a deep breath, held on to it, like it might be his last. "I want you to tell me if I was dead down there, Tom! What happened to me? Did I die?"

"If you were dead, how am I talking to you now?"

"Don't give some politician's non-answer, man! This is your 'mangler' you're talking to, Tom. Give it to me straight—did anything weird happen down there?"

Tom turned to face his friend squarely. Summoning up all the energy needed to create his most sincere expression. "Larry, I wouldn't lie to you," he said, feeling a sharp *ping* at the core of his conscience. "*Nothing* happened, do you hear me? Nothing happened."

"You swear?"

"You were knocked cold. I pulled you out of the seat, and by the time I got you to the ground, you were looking at me . . . I swear."

Larry Constantino stared at him, at his eyes actually, as though he were searching for some telltale sign in the liquid depths that might betray his friend's words. He finally nodded softly.

"I believe you," he said, and the words pierced Tom as hideously as that piece of fuselage had skewered his friend.

The chopper bobbed up and then down one final time as its landing gear kissed the roof of the hospital building. The keening death of its rotors was accompanied by the scurrying of its crew. Its bay doors rattled open to reveal a horde of hospital and media personnel. The rescue workers unstrapped them, lifted them, and offered them up to the torrent of flashing lights and helping hands.

And as Tom and his friend were lowered onto waiting wheelchairs, the sea of journalists parted to let them pass. He gave them the obligatory thumbs-up and the gritty campaign smile, but he carried the sins of Cassius and Judas in his heart.

He felt exhausted, but worse, Senator Thomas Flanagan felt abused, used up, as though the universe, or the malign thug who runs it, had decided it was finally finished toying with him.

Closing his eyes against the din surrounding him, he felt himself falling into that vacuum of unanswered prayers and broken promises.

SIX

Barrero

While humming "Tomorrow" from *Annie*, Dr. Estela Barrero tightened the final suture on a woman's thigh laceration. The wound was one of several major ones along both lower extremities. The victim had survived Flight 957's crash landing, but had been attacked by a small alligator while she lay semiconscious in the swamp.

Talk about having a bad day, thought Estela with an inward smile, this lady was way up there on the all-time list. She was not being disrespectful; if she couldn't keep her sense of humor intact, especially in the face of an endless night of Grand Guignol, she was in serious trouble.

"How's it going, Doctor?" asked Mary Sturgeon, the head nurse in Keller's emergency room. Without waiting for a reply, she moved off to direct an aide wheeling a gurney with a new patient into the treatment queue.

Estela followed her to the end of the room. "We've just gotten started and I'm already on edge," she said. "No sleep tonight, Mary."

"So who needs sleep!? Isn't that something for interns?"

Estela smiled and moved to the next gurney. Her smile slipped off her face like cheap mask when she focused on the victim lying before her—a small girl of perhaps six or seven. She lay there like a broken Christmas angel, long blond hair wet and twisted under her neck. She was unconscious, all extremities bound by inflatable splints, an IV snaked into her like the probing tendril of some obscene plant. Quickly, Estela scanned her admittance chart: fractured limbs, punctured lung, suspected concussion, possible internal injuries.

"Anybody know if we've got X-rays on this one?" She looked around the room as white and pale green-clad staff weaved and dodged amongst each other, an unrehearsed choreography that suggested more than the barely controlled chaos it was.

Mary materialized next to her with a clipboard. "X-rays on the way, boss. Do you want to get started without them, or shall we take a look at the next one?"

"How long before I get a film report?"

"Radio's got everybody on overtime," said her nurse. "You know there's got to be a logjam down there."

Estela shrugged, shook her head. She stethoscoped the little fallen angel. Despite the puncture, her breathing was steady. Vitals were still good. If there wasn't some horrible internal problem, the girl would pull through.

"All right. We'll come back as soon as I've got film." Estela leaned down and kissed the little girl's forehead. "Don't worry my little *dulzura*, I won't forget you. . . ."

Turning around she regarded the next gurney, which barely contained the body of a dark-skinned man, who could have been a Latin American Indian or perhaps a native Caribbean. He'd suffered severe head and facial injuries, and they hadn't cleaned him up very well before getting him into ER. Dried blood and swamp slime had combined to give him a terrifying aspect. A resident leaned over him, administering cardiopulmonary resuscitation.

"He's been getting ABC," said Mary, referring to the textbook CPR techniques. "Still no go. . . ."

Estela nodded. "Get me some counter-shock over here!"

·The familiar rattle of the mobile electro-defibrillation unit signaled its approach behind her. The MED technician placed his paddles on the dark man's chest. *Zzzap!* The involuntary bucking and warping of the body and then nothing. . . .

"Again!" Estela screamed.

The tech acknowledged with a second 300-watt jolt, but the body on the gurney remained unresponsive.

Estela stood mutely for an instant, feeling the familiar panic-laced distention of time pull her like a piece of warm taffy. So many thoughts and emotions pierced her in that instant. She knew that if there were not hundreds of people to be attended, she would give this man more time, more of a chance to climb back from the black well of oblivion, but there was no time, no second chances. The decision screamed to be made like the main switch in a power station. Estela was the hand on that lever and demanded it to be thrown.

Snapping back to real-time, she stared directly at the tech holding the shock paddles. "He's gone," she said. "Thank you, for trying."

The tech said nothing as he packed up his equipment and wheeled off to the next crisis. Estela covered the man's face with his sheet and signaled a nurse to move the gurney out of the treatment area. Turning to the next victim, an older man who was being examined by two young interns, she quietly moved in between them.

"How's it going here, Doctors?"

"Pretty good," said the taller, sandy-haired young man. "Lacerations, hematoma, nothing broken."

Estela nodded, sensing a break that would allow her to get back to the little girl with the blond hair. With new crash victims arriving every few minutes, the level of activity and the amount of human traffic in the emergency room was reaching absurdist levels. Literally elbowing her way through stands of people, Estela felt herself losing patience, felt her frustration quotient rising. Finally, she found Mary Sturgeon, who had a stack of X-rays under one arm.

Before Estela could say anything, Mary was handing her sheets of film. "I know, Doctor Barrero. Here she is—the little girl."

"Current status?"

"She's holding her own, but I don't want to say for sure."

"I need to get a look at these right away," said Estela, pushing a loose strand of auburn hair from her face. She was perspiring heavily and her businesslike hairdo was starting to come undone.

Mary Sturgeon stood by waiting for instructions. She looked harried, but still in control.

Estela placed the X-ray film on a wall viewer. The internal injuries she suspected were revealed. Broken ribs had pierced some vital organs. They would have to stop the hemorrhaging into the peritoneal area as soon as possible. She turned to give Mary a set of instructions that would get the girl into emergency surgery when a commotion at the far end of the ER distracted her. Turning toward the ambulance bay, she was shocked to see a crowd of people surging through the opening—police, dark-suited men, photographers. They surrounded two gurneys the paramedics were trying to wheel through the entrance area.

What the hell was going on? For a moment, confusion held her in check, then she remembered Dr. Hansen's message about Senator Flanagan. . . .

Moving quickly, she threaded her way through the chaos and into the center of the herd.

"Who's in charge here?!" she said loudly, almost screaming. So loud she half-startled herself.

No wonder the mob of media and Secret Service turned as one, staring at her in shocked silence.

"This is an emergency room!" she said sternly. "No place for a circus like this! Now, *who* is responsible?"

A thirty-ish man in a government-issue dark suit emerged from the pack. Flashing his credentials, he identified himself as "Kenyon."

"Get all these people out of here so we can get our jobs done, Mr. Kenyon."

The Secret Service man nodded to his lackeys, who began ushering everyone back through the entrance doors. Interns moved in behind them and began wheeling the two gurneys to a secured, screened-off area that Dr. Hansen had declared necessary for Senator Flanagan. Estela recognized the senator from his numerous appearances on television. Being groomed as the next Republican presidential candidate required a high profile, and Flanagan had learned his repertoire of tricks very well. Even as he was being carted off, he continued to wave to anyone who looked his way, punctuated by occasional thumbs-up signs.

As Estela was about to turn back to Mary Sturgeon and her current patient, someone grabbed her by the arm from behind. "Excuse me, Doctor Barrero?"

She wheeled around quickly, still flushed from her confrontation with the media mob. The man facing her was one of Hansen's underlings. A deputy administrator or some such title, but she couldn't remember his name. He was wearing a seersucker suit and a bow tie.

"Yes, what is it?" she snapped. "I'm very busy right now."

"I'm sure you are. Don't know if you know me— Charles Peake . . . from Doctor Hansen's office."

"What do you want, Mr. Peake?"

"Well, Doctor Hansen wanted me to make sure you took care of Senator Flanagan as soon as he arrived." His voice was flat, measured. It had the underlying smirk of authority, of absolute authority.

"I'll get to him as soon as I finish with my current patient," said Estela. "I had a cursory look at him when he just came in. He doesn't look like he's in any immediate danger."

She moved to walk past the administrator and he stepped sideways to forcibly block her path.

"What's the matter with you!" she said in a half-shout. "Didn't you hear what I said?"

"That's not the problem, Doctor." Peake smiled. "I don't think you heard what *I* said."

Estela repressed the urge to push the man in the chest and run past him. He looked like a weasel, and she sensed he was enjoying his vested authority just a little too much. "I'll take care of the senator as soon as I finish with my current patient," she said evenly.

Peake leaned into her, spoke out of one side of his mouth in a sneering whisper: "Listen, Barrero, if you don't get your ass over to Flanagan's bed immediately, you're out of a job. That's a direct quote from the Boss Man."

The stinging shock of Peake's message calmed her instantly. Most of the time she kept herself removed from the seething cauldron of political stews because she loathed the aroma of their presence. But when it was thrown in her face with such graceless aplomb, she knew she was playing with something far more powerful and dangerous. Such forces could not only keep her from working at Keller Memorial, but probably anywhere else north of the Rio Grande.

"All right," she said softly. "How silly of me to think that all of the lives we're trying to save here have equal value."

Peake continued to smile.

"Lead the way," said Estela.

She followed him through the curtains of a temporary ward area that had been set up like flimsy theater sets. Several agents surrounded the gurneys of Flanagan and his aide. Upon first glance neither one of the men appeared to be in bad shape, and she hoped she would not have to carry on the facade of extreme care with a couple of government trick ponies for very long. A smoldering resentment that could easily erupt into a full-scale loathing for Hansen's kiss-ass posturing and cheap muscle-man tactics, but she knew this was not the time to deal with it.

A small team of residents and nurses had already assembled, no doubt upon the directive of Dr. Hansen. "All right, let's keep it moving," said Estela. "Get the clothes off these two, and get me some prelims!"

Everybody started moving at the same time as Estela advanced on Flanagan. Even though his hair was plastered down and he was covered with grime, he had a rugged handsomeness that was always referred to as All-American. He lay there unconcerned as a male nurse cut him out of his clothes, not even sparing his boxer shorts with the Warner Bros. Studio logo patterned all over them. He looked at her and enacted a small smile. It unnerved her a bit, and she hoped it didn't show.

"I'm Doctor Barrero," she said, trying to sound as professional as possible. "Can you give me a damage report, Senator?"

"I think I'm fine," he said. She noticed he spoke without the media-trained inflections she expected. He sounded tired. "I spent a lot of time walking around the crash area. I feel okay, just wiped out."

"We're going to run a full slate of tests, just to make sure," she said as she stethed his chest, checked his pulse.

"I think you might want to check Mr. Constantino, too. My campaign manager was unconscious at one point," said Flanagan.

Estela nodded, a tight little smile playing at her lips. "Oh, we will. Don't worry about a thing, Senator."

"Tom," he said softly. "Please call me Tom."

She pretended to not hear the comment as she turned and dispensed orders to her attending staff. She could not help notice that Flanagan's aide, Constantino, was staring at her with dark, wide eyes. A nurse had just finished slipping an open-backed gown over the man and she too was staring at Estela.

"Doctor," she said. "Can you take a look at this?"

"What is it? What's going on?" said Constantino, his voice on edge.

"Just relax," said Estela as she opened the back of the gown to see what looked like a recently healed laceration. Soft, pink flesh almost gleamed under the overhead lights. Below the left shoulder blade, directly above the left lung was a six- to seven-inch scar almost an inch wide. It was an ugly signature to a past trauma of significant proportion. Estela touched the scar tissue; it was very warm.

"When did this happen?" she asked the man.

"When did *what* happen?" he asked nervously. "What're you talking about, Doc?"

It was impossible that the man would not know what she was talking about; perhaps he was in a mild state of shock. Estela described the severe scarring to Constantino, and he looked at her in total amazement.

"Honest to God, Doc . . . I don't know what you're talking about. I don't *have* any scars on my back."

She hadn't expected an answer like that, but she responded coolly. "Well, we'll check things out for you, Mr. Constantino. Right now, I just want you to lie back and relax."

Moving off to the side, she gathered some of her top staff people around her and began delegating duties that would cover all the bases with these two VIPs. She also ensured that someone pulled up Constantino's recent medical history. If he'd been in a recent accident bad enough to leave that kind of mark on his flesh, she would need to know if there was a possibility of reinjury to anything internal.

If Constantino was indeed suffering from shock, his response was not all that unusual. But there was something about his total aspect that suggested things were not that simple. Her medical instincts were blipping at her like a private radar screen. The man's wound looked *too* recent. Too freshly healed. Anyone with such new tissue regeneration would normally still be in a recuperative stage, not running around the country on airplanes.

She would have to—

Mary Sturgeon was suddenly standing in front of her, her features locked in an expression Estela had grown to recognize over the years of her profession.

Oh no . . . mi dulzura!

"We lost her," said Mary, keeping her emotions in line. "I'm sorry, Doctor, everything started happening at once. . . ."

Estela waved her off and slipped through the curtains away from the VIPs and everyone else. She found herself by a doorway leading to a canteen room, and as the smells and sounds of the ER washed over her like storm-crested waves, she struggled with her feelings. Every so often, the pressures of her job and the conflux of her emotions threatened to overwhelm her. It was usually a dull, aching presence that lurked at the threshold of her thoughts, but this time it was a swirling psychic storm buffeting her every move. The image of the painting, *The Scream* by Munch, suddenly dominated her thoughts, becoming the perfect symbol for what she was feeling. She *hated* Dr. Hansen and Peake and Flanagan and Mary Sturgeon and the little blond girl who had to go and die on her before she could even try to save her . . .

. . . and she even hated Estela Barrero for having the hubris to have ever believed she was strong enough to labor under the shadow of Caduceus.

SEVEN

Hawking

Another was being born.

That was the way he had grown to regard the process as he became aware of each new one.

He felt like an ancient mariner or astronomer, watching the vaulted firmament and witnessing the birth of new stars or the novaed death of old ones.

Sometimes the process soothed him as might a lullaby; other times it assaulted him with its sudden violence.

This one was one of those. Burst upon the cosmos in a brilliant flash, expanding borealis of pain and revelation.

But with each new birth, he grew stronger, more confident. The world was hurtling like a half-burnt ember toward the millennium's end. The heat death of the last ten centuries waited at the threshold, a signal to humanity and all its works.

An end of things.

And he knew now that along with endings there must be also a new beginning. The symmetry of all things had been thrust upon him, and he could not help but see it in everything encountered, everything he attempted.

The process had begun before him and he knew he was merely part of a greater dynamic, but he would not turn from the mission into which the world had tossed him.

EIGHT

Rebecca Quinn
Flanagan

The phone call awakened her from a deep, dead-end sleep where there were no dreams, no nightmares, no suggestion of existence. It was not the middle of the night, however; Rebecca Quinn Flanagan routinely retired from the day's rigors by 9:00 P.M. Pulling herself up to one elbow, she stared at the French provincially styled phone on her bedstand, then to a digital display on the dresser where a clock-radio nested. 10:22 it said.

She was not fearful or even a bit anxious. Long ago she had grown accustomed to the phone of a United States senator ringing at all hours. Clearing her throat first, she picked up the receiver.

"Senator Flanagan's residence . . . " Her voice sounded clear, free of the wispy strands of sleep.

"Mrs. Flanagan, it's Cameron . . . Cameron Howard."

She almost smiled. Tom's assistant campaign manager always identified himself like that—as though they knew countless young men named Cameron. . . .

"Yes," she said. "What is it? Tom's not here. He left this evening with Larry for—"

"I know," said Howard. "For Miami. That's why I—I mean, God, don't you watch the news . . . ?"

As the man stammered to find the right words, Rebecca felt something pulling at the bottom of her stomach, something that threatened to suck her into the vacuum of total desperation and loathing.

"What's the matter, Mr. Howard? What happened?"

He told her about Flight 957, rushing through the details to assure her that her husband had survived with only scratches. The emptiness at the center of her bowels began to fade as she listened to her husband's aide-de-camp detail what was wanted of her. There was an Air Force transport going through its final preflight checks on a runway at Andrews, and she need only tell Mr. Howard when the limo should arrive to whisk her away from her Georgetown town house and aboard that plane. She was assured of arriving at Keller Memorial in Miami ASAP.

After she hung up the phone, Rebecca stood up and walked about the Louis XV bedroom as though slowly emerging from a trance.

The Everglades.

Andrews Air Force Base.

Hospital.

The words orbited her awareness only half making sense. Automatically, she began dressing herself in something somber but not funereal. Twenty years in the Senate had given her an unconscious understanding of Washington protocol. There would be interviews to be given and "camera opportunities" (as Larry always called them) which should never be wasted, and never be played at less than full volume. Therefore, Rebecca knew the necessity of looking good. That was what life was all about in Washington—*looking good*. Nobody worried much about doing the job as long as you gave the appearance of doing so.

She moved to the mirror of her dressing table and began applying the lightest touches of cosmetics. Didn't want to be overdoing it, especially under the harsh lights of the media. As she approached her forty-fourth birthday, she had begun to accept a few things about herself. She was not actually pretty, and never had been. Rather, she projected a fragile aspect, like the delicate nature of a small bird, that made her attractive because she was so obviously vulnerable. Rebecca knew that her features were too sharp, too angular for her to ever be sensuous or sexy. She smiled cruelly at the thought. Had any man ever found her *sexy*? She couldn't imagine it, and that touched her with a sadness so heartfelt and heavy with time that she believed it to be truly tragic. Every girl, every woman, wanted to feel desirable—sexy—at some time in their lives.

Rebecca Quinn Flanagan had no memory of such a feeling. She couldn't even fake it in a flimsy effort to fool herself. She wouldn't know how.

I'm getting too dramatic in my old age, she thought as she moved away from the dressing table. Nobody cares how you feel, Becky, don't you realize that?

The phone rang again, and the sound pierced the protective shell of her thoughts like a slashing blade. Was it the limo? Or Howard again?

"Senator Flanagan's residence . . ."

"Mother!" screamed an all too familiar voice. "What is going *on*? Are you all right? Why didn't you *call* me? — About Daddy!?"

"Kiley, calm down," said Rebecca evenly. "Of course, I'm here. If you would just give me a chance to answer you. . . ."

"Mother, why didn't you *call* me?"

"I haven't had the chance, dear. They're sending a car for me. I have to go to Andrews right away." Rebecca took a deep breath, released it slowly to calm herself. "You know how it is when you get pulled out of a deep sleep . . . You're not thinking straight."

"Of course I do—it just happened to *me*!" said Kiley, using her most exasperating tone. "Senator McCauley *just* called us . . ."

Rebecca hated the way Kiley referred to her father-in-law as "the senator" or "Senator McCauley." So stiff, so formal. Why would anyone prefer such distance from their family?

"Mother? Are you *there* . . . ?!"

"I was just getting ready to call you, dear. Honestly . . ." Rebecca had no problem lying to her daughter. After all, the girl had spent all of her teenaged and college years doing the same to her. Kiley scared her. At the age of twenty-three, after marrying the son of the most powerful senator on Capitol Hill, Kiley had chameleoned into the perfect Washington wife a little too quickly, a little too completely. It made Rebecca wonder if her daughter had ever had any sense of self-worth or personal goals in life. It seemed as if the only thing the girl had learned in four years at Radcliffe was how to speak with at least one italicized word in every sentence. . . .

"I want to go with you," said Kiley. "Daddy's going to *need* me."

"Sweetheart, you're going to have to call Mr. Howard," she said softly. "I can't make those arrangements."

"Charles *already* called the senator, Mother. There's a car on the way right now."

Of course, she thought. The senator, Alistair McCauley, would take care of everything. God, she hated the old bastard. A thin "All right, dear . . ." was all she could manage to say.

"And one *more* thing, Mother."

"Yes?"

"What about *Chip*? I don't suppose you tried to reach *him*, either."

Rebecca held the phone to her ear, but felt herself reeling just a bit. Her daughter's words stung her into a painful numbness. How could she have forgotten her son? Ever since this newest nightmare had unraveled itself before her, forcing her to act and react, to think and feel, when all she wanted was to crawl back into the hard shell of sleep and oblivion, she had been moving in all the ordained ways.

But she had been unconsciously isolating herself. Containing her fear and hate, her passion and caring. She didn't want to think about Tom lying in some Florida hospital, or how she would tell her children that their father had slipped past the sweeping nets of death, and how she might convince everyone that she really cared.

Chip.

So young. So full of all the promise and strength. That high-octane mixture that gives youth its juggernaut radiance.

Had she forgotten to call him on purpose?

Yes, that was it. That had to be. A mother wants to protect her children at all costs. And the easiest way to protect her baby was to keep all this dirty business from him. She smiled inwardly as she considered how her inner voice conceived and depicted everything connected with the children's father, with . . . Tom.

Dirty business.

Was it *that* bad?

"Mother!?" Her daughter's voice yanked her back into real-time, into the conversation where only an instant had elapsed and her gulf of silence had only been an awkward pause rather than a lifetime of regret.

"I'm here, Kiley."

"Well, did you call Chip or *not*?"

"He . . . wasn't there," she lied. "You know how he is. There's always some party or fraternity thing going on."

"Did you at least leave a *message*?"

"I thought it might alarm him."

Kiley sighed painfully. "*Alarm* him? Suppose he hears about it on the news?! What then?"

"Dear, I don't think Chip watches the news. . . ."

"Mother, I'm calling him. Right *now*."

"You go ahead, dear. I'll see you at Andrews, I suppose."

"Yes, Mother, I suppose you *will*." Rebecca could almost see her daughter shaking her head in disapproval as she clucked her tongue.

"Good-bye, Kiley."

Replacing the receiver, she went to the closet and selected just the right shoes to match her ensemble. Many years ago, her own mother had taught her that the difference between being well-dressed and just dressed was always found in the accessories and the shoes. Her daddy had also stressed the importance of shoes—one of his favorite expressions was that you could always tell what kind of man you were talking to by looking at the condition of his shoes.

Rebecca sat on the edge of the bed and slipped on a pair of elegantly simple black heels. Whenever she thought about her parents and the long, slow days of her childhood on Maryland's Eastern Shore, she felt as if she were tuning in someone else's memories. She almost felt like an eavesdropper or a voyeur. Who was that little girl who used to play in the curing sheds where the tobacco leaf lay in huge, fragrant bundles? What happened to the freckled tomboy who built her own treehouse and her own Huck Finn raft?

Rebecca wiped a single tear from her eye. Whenever she tried to invade the mists of her own childhood, the simple truth of things gone forever wounded her terribly. She would never again smell the sweet wet scent of plowed earth, or taste the buttery flake of her mother's biscuits at dinner, or hear the tinkling glass pitchers of Grampa's lemonade on the front porch after school.

The worst part, thought Rebecca, was that she felt so much more deeply for her own lost past than her lost passion with Tom Flanagan. When he was not nearby, which was most of the time, she rarely even thought of him, much less felt anything for him. To be so insular had become her way of life.

Standing to give herself one final look in the full-length oval mirror, she smiled to herself. The camcorders and the lights could do their worst. She would not embarrass herself.

Interesting, she thought, that she never considered embarrassing Senator Thomas Flanagan.

"Fuck him," said Rebecca aloud. Then very softly: "And I feel sorry for whoever's currently holding down the job. . . ."

NINE

Valerie Berenson

He'd been stalking her since she'd left the Park Plaza.

Fifth Avenue was filled with its usual cattle herds of tourists and business-class workers. The streets were gridded up with traffic, mostly cabs and trucks, and naturally there wasn't a policeman to be seen.

Stopping at the light on 54th Street, she looked back to see a tall man in a long, gray topcoat, looking in the window of the Sharper Image. A floppy-brimmed hat slanted down to keep half his face in shadow; he looked steadfastly into the glass as though intensely interested. But she knew he was really watching her.

Valerie scanned the phalanx of cabs crossing Fifth, but every one of them was occupied. She signaled anyway. If she could only—

No, wait . . . ! One jigged out of traffic and approached the curb. She stepped out and continued to wave her arm at the driver, who gave no sign that he was coming for her. The garish yellow car stopped in front of her, and as she reached for the door handle, another hand, gloved in black leather, grabbed it first.

"Let me do that for you," said an impossibly deep and raspy voice.

Turning, she was suddenly staring into the face of the floppy-brimmed hat man. Lean and gaunt, a beard that was always five o'clock shadowed, and eyes like dull ball bearings.

"No, thank you," she said in a loud, clear voice. "I'll get it myself."

He smiled and his teeth were all slightly gapped. The image of a weathered picket fence came to mind. "I don't think so," he said, and yanked the door open. "Get in, bitch!"

She stood defiantly and glanced about the crowd surrounding them. Everyone was watching their little drama unfold and she looked into their faces, searching for allies. "Get away from me!" she screamed. "Somebody help me!"

Her nemesis chuckled deeply and latched onto her wrist with a gloved hand. His fingers clamped down with such force and strength, it was like some kind of steel tool holding her.

She screamed again as he began jerking her downward and shoving her into the back of the cab.

"No!" A shriek this time. A sound loud enough to hurt the ears of everyone around them. She tried to spin into her attacker, to raise a knee between his legs, but he was so tall and so strong and she couldn't get the angle right. He kept forcing her downward and she kept screaming for help.

And all the people who'd been crowded around them, watching so intently, suddenly began melting away from them, flowing around the cab like the tide ignoring a jetty.

"Help me!" Valerie cried, although weaker now. The man had half-thrown her into the backseat and the driver waited calmly for the violence to end so he could get on with the business of making a living. Outside the cab, people continued to spectate, but none dared interrupt.

Valerie struggled with the opposite door handle, but it was locked. As she fumbled for the latch, the tall man in the floppy hat reached into the folds of his coat and produced a short knife with a curved, serrated blade. Its flat steel flashed in the midday sun as he hunkered down to join her—

"—Okay, *cut!*" Gordon Forrester's voice boomed above the crowd through a bullhorn and abruptly, everything stopped. The director hovered over the scene in a cantilevered crane chair.

The tall man backed out of the cab, extended his hand to help Valerie onto the street. No sooner had she touched the sidewalk than she was surrounded by the makeup girl and her costumer, checking, adjusting, primping, and more adjusting.

"How was that?" she asked Forrester, who was gliding down to an open area beyond the cab.

"Great stuff, baby. . . . Looks real good. Great stuff," said Forrester.

She looked at Harry Lyonesse, the actor playing the floppy-hat man, and gave him a thumbs-up. "Nice work, Harry. You even had *me* believing you."

Forrester set out of the crane and approached the actors standing beside the cab. "Okay, people, let's break for ten, and then I want to try this again. . . ."

Valerie tossed her long blond hair away from her face, and glared at the director. "What! Gordon, what're you talking about? Again!?"

"Again means *again,*" said Forrester. He popped a cigarillo into the corner of his mouth, lighted it with one clank of an old Zippo. The thin little cigars had become his trademark, and the wiry little Englishman inhaled them deeply into his lungs on a regular basis.

"I thought you said 'great stuff'? What about the 'looks real good,' Gordon?"

"Cecil wants to get the action from a secondary perspective. I'll have more options when we go to edit."

"I think the shot's fine," said Valerie. "I'm hungry and I'm tired."

Even amidst the din of midtown traffic, she could sense a kind of quiet settle over the scene. Everyone—the film crew and the usual crowd of onlookers beyond the barricades—was focusing attention on her and Forrester. They sensed a confrontation and they were attracted to it like vultures to a carcass.

Gordon closed the space between them, pushing his pale, bony face close to her. She could smell the stale tobacco on his breath as he narrowed his eyes in anger. "Listen to me, you overpaid tart! I don't have to explain to you *why* I want a fucking shot! I was granting you the courtesy—something you obviously know nothing about. They don't pay you to decide whether or not you think *this*, or any *other* shot, is 'fine,' so if I were you, I would keep such unlearned opinions to myself!"

"Gordon—" She started to speak as he turned away from her and began barking instructions to the crew regarding the new setup.

"Somebody keep her away from me," he said, "before I throw her off the set."

Valerie stood there next to the cab, sensing that everyone was shying off from her direct aura. *Nobody* wanted to get on Gordon Forrester's shit-list. He was the premier director in England, having won more awards and having delivered more consistently fine moneymakers than anyone else in the business. He was what producers called "golden," and his opinions were never simply opinions, just as his suggestions were camouflaged demands. If he told the money guys he wanted you off a picture, you were *off*.

No questions. No arguments. You and your salary were subsumed into the amorphous body of the juggernaut known as "the project," and you ended up as nothing more than a footnote on the budget's balance sheet.

Valerie glared at him. That wrinkled up, officious little twit didn't know who he was screwing around with, she thought, trying desperately to buoy up the sinking feeling in her gut. The stares of the onlookers bore down on her and she remembered how she used to feel in grade school when the teacher would humiliate her in front of the class. But she had been tough back then, vowing to someday show them all how wrong they all were; and she was tough now. She wasn't the third-highest paid actress in Hollywood by accident! Her name on a film guaranteed people in the seats.

Composing herself, knowing that the public eye was still upon her, she held her head high and walked away from the barricade toward the vehicles at the end of the block. She would take her ten minutes in the privacy of her trailer, and when they wanted her, they could come asking for her presence. Just as she reached the steps, Harry Lyonesse intercepted her.

"Got a minute?"

"Sure," she said. "Come on in."

They entered the trailed and she flopped down on a small couch. "Okay," she said. "Are you going to give me standard lecture number two: Nobody Fucks With Forrester . . . ?"

Harry pulled a flask from his inside jacket pocket and nipped at his Grand Marnier. He was not an alky, she knew. Just an appreciator of fine brandy on a cool day in Manhattan. He stood by her dressing table and tried to smile. At forty-five, he had the perfect face to be another classic movie villain. Just enough planes and angles, cheeks sunken to just the right depth, just enough pockmarks, and those dead-shark eyes. Audiences around the world despised him, and they would be shocked to know he was the most gentle, delicate man she'd ever met. The suspicion persisted in Hollywood that Harry Lyonesse was homosexual, but he had never confirmed or denied it. He simply didn't care, and that was part of his charm.

"Ah, Valerie . . ." he said finally. "You've been around long enough to know that you've *never* been around long enough."

She grinned at his wit, and she knew he was right. Everyone in the Business was ultimately expendable.

"Even Forrester," she said. "All he needs is something like *Heaven's Gate* to bring him to his knees."

"He's probably too smart to get lost in a turkey like that," said Harry. "But, as we all know, an ego is a terrible thing to waste."

"So what's this all about?" she said, twisting a strand of hair around her finger. It was a habit that was annoying even to her, but she could not seem to break it.

"It's not just Forrester, Valerie."

"What do you mean?" She didn't like the serious tone that had suddenly crept into his voice.

"You're getting a reputation for being *difficult*. I can't say it any more simply than that."

"What?" She acted out the shocked role. But in her heart, she was not surprised.

"And believe me, this kind of behavior is very old news in Hollywood. In the old days, I think the producers and the studios were more willing to put up with it, what with the star system they'd created themselves. But . . . that's why they call them the *old days*. They're gone."

"But Harry, I'm not the only—"

"Hear me out, please," he said, pausing to pull another short one from his flask. "You know our town is very tolerant. They'll forgive or even ignore just about any crazy bullshit their own people want to do to themselves or their loved ones. Very tolerant, Valerie. But the one thing they don't shine on is people who fuck with their money. And in these days, when even a straight-to-video schlocker costs ten mill, they're just not going to let anybody be 'difficult' when *their* meter is running."

Valerie could only shake her head. Harry was right, and she knew it. She didn't know what came over her sometimes. She could hear herself talking, and it was like she had no control over the words that were coming out. It was as if someone else inside her was pulling all the strings, making her act like a person that she not only did not know, but did not even *like*.

"I know what you're talking about, Harry. Thank you."

"Don't thank me, just try to change your attitude—for your own sake. I like working with you, Valerie. I'd hate to see you showing up ten years from now on the Scream Queen circuit."

She knew she would never resort to that. She had no burning need to act that was so intense, so overpowering she would take a gig in a B-movie just to be working. Acting had never been her *life*, but merely a means to an end. Sure she'd spent plenty, but part of it had been on a good financial planner, and he'd set her up so that if she never worked again, she'd have a hard time *finding* the time to spend all her money.

A means to an end. That's all everything in her life had ever been. She wished that she did have something in her life that meant so much to her, she was driven by it, ruled by its passionate energy. But at thirty-two years old, she knew there was no real willful passion in her. There was no engine at her heartspring's center that powered her dreams, because she was beginning to realize that she had no real dreams. . . .

"Valerie, are you all right . . . ?" Harry's voice brought her back to the here and now.

"Yeah, I'm fine. Just daydreaming."

" 'Woolgathering,' my mom used to call it." He chuckled. "Isn't language wonderful?"

"I guess . . ." she said wistfully. "I never really paid attention. When I first got to L.A., I remember meeting this writer who was getting work in TV sitcoms, and he hated it. He was making more for twenty-two pages of canned laughs than ninety-five percent of the stiffs in this country made in a *year*, and hated it. He wanted to write *books*. Novels. He said that was *real* writing, and he wanted to be a real writer."

"Yeah, I know the feeling," said Harry.

"Do you?" Valerie looked at him.

Harry waved her off. "I don't want to bore you with my Shakespearean fantasies. . . ."

She looked at him, seeing a side of the prototype villain that no one on the outside ever knew about. There was a fragility in him that could only be described as genuine and perfectly human. And as she sensed that in him, she realized that she did not possess anything remotely similar. She didn't know if she should be sad or distressed. That she felt neither should have told her something. . . .

"I don't think I have any dreams like that, Harry. Is there something wrong with me?"

"Not if you're happy," he said. "Only you can answer that."

"I honestly don't know, Harry. Isn't that ridiculous?"

Before he could answer, there was a knock on the trailer door.

"Yes?" said Valerie.

The door opened to reveal Harriet Ryan, her dresser. Her usually cheery expression was absent as she peered in.

"Miss Berenson . . ."

"Tell them I'll be right there. I'm right behind you, Harriet."

"That's not what I . . . well . . ."

"Harriet, what's wrong?" Valerie felt an abrupt *ping* in the center of her body, as though an alarm had gone off, and although soundless, it had somehow changed everything inside her.

Her dresser stepped fully into the trailer and held up a *USA Today*. "I . . . I don't think you've seen this yet, have you?"

Jumping up, Valerie lunged for the paper, snapping it from the middle-aged woman's grasp. "What? What're you talking about? What happened, goddamn it?!"

As she snapped open the front page, the headline on Flight 957's crash into the Everglades filled her vision. At first, as though her mind refused to make the connection, she had no idea what she was looking at. Then, suddenly everything connected. Tom's message on her service. The Governors' Convention in Miami. Flying out of National.

"Oh God. . . ." The words leaked out of her as she read the subheads: *More than 100 feared dead. Presidential candidate Flanagan aboard.*

"Valerie, what is it?" Harry moved over her shoulder, remained silent as he scanned the page with her.

"Don't let him be dead," she whispered. "Please don't let him . . ."

"Has there been anything on the news?" Harry looked at Harriet.

"I don't know, Mr. Lyonesse . . . I've been in the costume trailer all morning. I just picked up the paper."

"Please . . . !" Valerie had closed her eyes, holding back the tears. She had never thought that Tom Flanagan could ever die. He was one of those men that were so large in the public consciousness, that for him to suddenly be . . . *gone* . . . no, it was unthinkable.

"Let's not jump to conclusions," said Harry. "That was a very early edition. The updates on CNN should tell us a lot more."

She sat in stony silence, watching Harry edge through the trailer to the little portable TV on the dinette table. "This thing connected to the dish?" he asked Mrs. Ryan, who nodded grimly.

"Hurry up," said Valerie.

Images jumped and shimmered as Harry remoted through the channels. When the familiar *Headline News* logo-bug appeared at the bottom right corner of the screen, she winced, but they were in their one-minute sports segment as videotape reprise of a tennis match bounced to a quick finish. Then the broadcast segued into a brace of commercials.

"Bad timing," said Harry Lyonesse.

"I'm sorry, but I can't watch an ad for toilet bowl cleaner right now. . . ." Valerie breathed in and out slowly, trying to keep her voice from hitching up.

Harry keyed the remote and found CNN's regular format. Bernard Shaw was talking while a video insert over his right shoulder depicted helicopter rescue efforts over the crash site.

"There it is!" screamed Valerie.

Simultaneously, someone knocked and opened the trailer door. It was James Weatherford, Forrester's AD. "They're ready on the set, Valerie. Let's go. . . ."

"Shh!" she said, as she strained to hear the anchor's words. "Turn it up, I can't hear what he's saying!"

Harry adjusted the volume as Weatherford, a typical Hollywood kiss-ass, who was young and hungry, stepped into the trailer. "Valerie, Mr. Forrester is waiting for you. The whole *crew* is waiting for you."

"Hang on just a sec, Jim," said Harry. "There's been a terrible accident. . . ."

As they spoke, Valerie watched the screen. The insert over the anchor's shoulder changed to a file photo of Senator Thomas Flanagan. "There he is!"

Just as the anchor began speaking, Weatherford walked over to the TV and punched the *off* button. "It's time to go to work," he said officiously.

Valerie screamed and leaped out of her chair. Her assault carried her into the slightly built assistant director, and she slammed him against a wall cabinet. Without thinking about it, she slapped him across the face, her long fingernails opening up a series of parallel red lines on his cheek.

"Stop it! Get out of here!" The words burst from her. She pushed him again, and he struggled to keep his balance under the attack. Valerie spun and pushed the buttons on the TV frantically.

"What's the matter with you, you crazy bitch?" Weatherford took a step toward her, then obviously reconsidered.

"Take it easy, Jim," said Harry.

Valerie had managed to get the TV powered up, but on the wrong channel. She punched at the keypad futilely. "Harry, help me!"

As Lyonesse remoted back to CNN, Weatherford grabbed her by the shoulder, spun her around. "You're in deep shit, lady. . . ."

She looked from the TV to the AD and back again. "Fuck you, you little faggot! That's what you get for barging into my trailer! Now get out of here before you get some more."

Seething, frothing over with venom, she lunged at him again, and Weatherford backed up, moving quickly to the door. As he made a clumsy exit, he tried to say something threatening, but she slammed the door in his face.

Turning back to Harry Lyonesse, she was suddenly aware of hot tears burning salty tracks down her face. Her breathing was torn and ragged as she tried to speak. "What happened, Harry? Did you hear what happened?"

"As much as I could gather, he's fine. They've got him in some Miami hospital just to check him out, but I didn't catch the name." Harry moved slowly to the door.

"Where're you going?"

"I'm going back to the set. See if I can smooth things over with Forrester. . . ."

"I think I'd better be going too, Miss Berenson." Harriet Ryan, who'd made herself totally invisible during the last few minutes, stepped out of the room's camouflage and side-stepped to the exit.

They want to get away from me, she thought. No guilt by association for them, no way. Valerie giggled as she fought to keep control. Tom. She had to get the name of that hospital. Call him. Make sure he was okay. Let him know she knew. That she would be there as soon as possible. Turning away from the TV, she threw herself on the small bed, grabbed a pillow, and pulled it into her face.

Why was she reacting like this? She'd never felt like this about any man before, and she wondered if this was what love was supposed to be, so out of control that you had no control. It was the first time she had been forced to assess her feelings. Until now, she'd never wanted to know if she could be in love with Tom Flanagan. In her entire life, she made a career out of not knowing how she truly felt about anybody. It was the safest way to be. And yet, here she was, losing control. That precious commodity she always kept in surplus. Nobody ever saw her in less than *total* control of any situation. But here was a man who, without even knowing it, without consciously trying, had left her teetering on the edge of her neat little world.

Valerie rolled over on her bed, let the pillow fall away from her face. Images and words from CNN capered across the TV screen and someone was knocking on the door, but she had slipped away from all of that. Someone had forced himself deep inside her fortress persona, had slipped past all her defenses, and it scared the hell out of her.

Just exactly who was Tom Flanagan, and where did he get his power?

TEN

Constantino

What do you mean—'you want to keep me here for a little while'? Like for how long?" Larry Constantino was sitting up in his hospital bed, feeling better than he could ever remember, facing two very somber-faced doctors in their white laboratory coats.

The female, Dr. Barrero, was about five feet four and on the petite side, but when it came to intelligence and professionalism, she was definitely an extra-large. You could just tell from the way she carried herself, the way she spoke. The lady expected, and received, respect from everyone whom she encountered. She kept her long dark hair tied up, which emphasized her very striking looks. Ethnic and fiery. Larry would tell anybody: she was one beautiful doctor.

"We're going to be very honest with you . . ." she said.

"That's good," he said. "Although I gotta warn you—I work with a lotta politicians. I'm not used to too much honesty."

Neither Barrero nor the other physician, a surgeon by the name of Stanhouse, smiled. Either they were both a couple of cold tunas, or what they wanted to talk about was extremely serious. Larry knew the answer to that little choice without even thinking about.

"Mr. Constantino," said Stanhouse, a tall guy who looked like a rough mid-thirties or a damned good late-forties. "We have no idea how long you're going to be here."

"What? How come? I feel great!"

"That's part of the problem," said Dr. Barrero. "You *shouldn't*."

Larry looked at both of them, trying to get a read on them. He'd made a career, and a damned fine one, out of learning to accurately figure out the difference between what people said and what they were really thinking. But these two were as inscrutable as a Chinese proverb. He remembered being choppered in last night and the weird dreams he'd had out in the swamp, and he'd never forget the sallow, washed-out, half-terrified look on Tom's face when he told him about them. When he'd been wheeled into the hospital, fatigue had started to wrestle him down and things had gotten a little fuzzy after somebody stuck an IV in his arm and the press of media and medical bodies thinned out.

But he could still remember one of the interns calling for a bunch of the other docs to look at his back, and somebody had asked him about his recent injury . . . so he knew something fishy was going on.

Exactly what . . . well that was the burning question of the age, wasn't it?

Back to real-time, he looked at the woman doctor. "I shouldn't? What do you mean? Because of my back, right? Because of some . . . thing on my back?"

"Not exactly," said Dr. Stanhouse. "Your body shows evidence of a monstrous trauma, something that *should* have killed you. Not only are you alive, but your medical history has nothing to account for the evidence and you have no memory of such an injury."

"But how? What kind of 'trauma' are you talking about?"

They described in as little clinical detail as possible the scar tissue on his back that seemed to be less than two days healed, and the internal scarring to his lungs and heart that indicated some kind of catastrophic butchering.

If they were right, then he *should* be dead. . . .

"Mr. Constantino," said Dr. Barrero, "understanding your case could be the key to a very exciting discovery."

"We'll need your cooperation, of course."

Larry looked at them and felt a sliver of absolute-zero coldness wriggle through him. Just for second, then it was gone. It was a touch of total, bottomless fear, and it told him that he should let these good people do whatever they wanted to him because they were a lot smarter than him and they didn't know what the hell was going on with him. Larry had been raised by an overprotective mother who rushed him off to doctors for scratched knees and headaches (*"Little boys your age shouldn't be getting headaches!"*), and as a result, he'd over-compensated in the opposite direction as an adult by never going to a doctor unless he was ready to drop in his tracks.

But there was something very scary about what they were telling him, and he knew he'd stay here as long as they wanted.

"You know I have to work with Senator Flanagan. . . ."

"We know that," said Barrero.

"Do you think I'm in any danger?" Larry shifted his weight, thought about what his back must look like.

"We have no idea, Mr. Constantino," said Dr. Stanhouse as he ran long surgeon's fingers through his curly sand-blond hair. "To be frank, you've got us damn well baffled."

"I appreciate you being honest about it," said Larry. "I guess I should be glad you want to check me out. But I have a couple of questions, if you don't mind."

"That's why we're here," said Barrero. She smiled for the first time, and it was a very nice smile. "Ask away."

"Can I get up and walk around? Or will I have to stay in this darned bed all the time?"

She smiled. "Not at all. You can move freely about the hospital. All we ask is that you make yourself available for whatever tests we can arrange."

"Okay, and what about visitors and a phone? I'm not crazy about the press or any of the TV people being in here, but I'd like to be able to see my friends and family. Which, by the way, I haven't seen or heard from yet. And where's Sophia? Can I see my wife soon?"

Stanhouse tapped his clipboard with a pen as he spoke. "No problem with the media—we don't want them in here, either. We are making an effort to keep your condition a secret for the time being anyway."

Larry nodded, kept listening as they assured him of open access to his family and friends. Not that he was crazy about them referring to him as having a "condition," but that was just the way doctors talked. Everybody, to them, had *some* kind of condition. Regardless, they told him he could even have a phone and a notebook PC, maybe even get a little work done. Maybe this wouldn't be so bad after all. Like a working vacation. So what if he was reclining in a hospital bed instead of a beach chair . . . ?

"Your wife arrived this morning," said Barrero. "You can see her as soon as we're done here."

Larry smiled. Just knowing he'd have Sophia with him was enough to make everything else bearable. "Then I guess we have a deal, folks." He chuckled playfully. "Now, please, go get me my wife."

Stanhouse wrote something on his clipboard. "Thank you, Mr. Constantino. We'll try to make things as pleasant as possible for you."

"You can call me Larry," he said. "Everybody else does."

"Okay, we'll remember that." They turned and he suddenly realized something else.

"Jeez, I almost forgot—how's the senator? He's okay, isn't he?"

Barrero looked at him with an expression that tried to mask irritation at the mention of Tom Flanagan. Tried, but didn't do such a great job of it. "Yes," she said curtly. "Senator Flanagan is fine. We have a battery of tests scheduled for him, too. Just to be on the safe side."

"Great," he said. "Any chance I can see him anytime soon?"

"Soon," she said. "I'll keep you informed."

Larry smiled and watched them leave. Sophia would be coming to him and everything would be better. Married almost twenty years to the same woman and he was still so nuts about her even he couldn't understand it. Sure they'd had their rough spots over the years, but who the hell didn't? The bottom line was simple—Sophia'd been his best friend for a long, long time. And sure, he liked hanging out with Tom Flanagan and all the other predators who stalked the corridors of power in D.C., and sure he and Tom had been calling each other "best friends" for most of their lives since college, but in his heart, Larry knew who his real best friend was. And she'd be walking through that door any minute.

Tom was always telling him how much he envied Larry's marriage, and how he'd always wished Rebecca had been a real wife to him. Larry never understood it. Those kind of things didn't just happen. You both had to work at them, and neither Tom nor Becky ever seemed to have enough interest. Their marriage, right from the start to hear Tom talk about it, was almost like one of those arranged, Reformation marriages that were so big among Europe's royal families. Even though Larry had labored among the sharpest political minds in America, he could never grasp how any man could be so ambitious and so calculating that he would even decide upon a marriage partner, a life partner, based on political benefits.

And Flanagan had done it with his own wife, and perhaps even worse, with his daughter. It was no accident that Kiley had married the son of the most powerful senator in Washington.

No wonder Tom Flanagan was so unhappy. . . .

ELEVEN

Flanagan

A searing light, a glaring intrusive whiteness surrounded him, threatened to engulf him. Sluggishly, he tried to move, tried to push some sort of meaningful thinking across the stage of his mind. There was a general sense of urgency, of impending something, but he couldn't get anything to fall into place. Everything seemed hazy, just out of touch. Just that bright light, that overwhelming white glare.

How long had he been here? What had happened? Was he drugged, or just out of it . . . ?

Blinking, rubbing his eyes, he tried to focus on whatever it was that surrounded him in its antiseptic lack of color. As his vision and his mind cleared, he remembered . . .

. . . *everything*.

Replaying the events from most recent and on backward, the images of his triumphant entrance into the emergency room were almost an embarrassment to him. The way all those morons swarmed over him, it was embarrassing. It was one thing to command attention because of his status as presidential candidate, but the ER was not the place for the media's usual bag of tricks.

But that was trivial and he knew it. Why would he try to distract himself from what was *really* on his mind?

(Because there was no freaking way you stick your hand into your best friend's back and bring him back to life, that's why. What's the matter, Tommy—you having a little trouble with that one?)

The more he tried to not dwell on the whole experience, the more vividly it burned in his memory. Like a gasoline fire you tried to put out with a little spare kerosene you had lying around. Yeah, right.

He had no memory of dreaming about anything. Sleep had been a temporary death, a nine-hour jaunt through oblivion. And he understood what was going on there. No way his subconscious wanted to deal with what was going on. Total system shutdown was fine, thank you.

He needed to talk about it, though. The idea of keeping this whole thing inside indefinitely would make him crazy. He needed to see Larry, let things get loose and easy and see if he could explain what had happened, or at least what he thought had happened. If there was anyone who would listen to his story without thinking he was totally bugfuck, it would be Larry—for a couple of reasons. One, because Larry had been listening to his crazy ideas since they'd been freshmen in College Park, and it was always Larry who made them sound not so crazy, always put just the right spin on Tom's ambitions and schemes so they sounded plausible if not respectable. And two, because Larry knew something very weird was going on.

That bullshit in the chopper about him having a strange dream . . .

(Maybe you were trying to con the con man, Larry?)

That was the first thing Tom would have to verify: if Larry really did *know*. If he really possessed the hard, cold knowledge that he'd been reduced to a piece of meat on a shish kebab, that he'd been so completely dead he was no-coming-back-dead.

Because if he could share that basic knowledge with his friend, then Tom could somehow begin to understand what was happening.

Because right now, he felt like he was definitely out there without a freaking net. And he didn't like that kind of performance requirement.

(Twenty-eight years playing a perfect game of Cover Your Ass . . . no time to change the rules now.)

He felt himself sag back deeper into the hospital bed. Instead of trying to figure out what had happened after the crash, he decided it might be better to teach himself the value of just accepting it—whatever the fuck it was.

(Like frenzied mothers who lift cars off their five-year-olds, maybe?)

Tom shook his head slowly, trying to get his thoughts into more normal grooves. It was an old habit, meaningless, but never breakable.

As he lay there, waiting for them to come for him—for surely someone would be coming sooner or later—: media, doctors, family, staff, and all of the above. There were so many who required a daily piece of him, it was hard to figure how he functioned, how he survived all the vampirism.

(Yeah, right, big concern right now, Tommy. Burning question of the age.)

Just what did all this stuff mean? The question screamed of inanity, but he knew what he was asking himself. Not just the bare mystery of his bringing Larry back to life,

(—there, he'd finally said it—)

but also the bigger stuff. Like what it felt like when his hands sank into that ruined flesh, when he felt the winds of time slapping him in the face. When even the concept of eternity felt like a silly way to waste away an afternoon. . . .

Tom felt a fingertip trace the path of his vertebrae with the expected effect. Weird scenes inside the goldmine. No doubt about that. There were issues and questions that he'd been piling up and stashing away for a much later time. Like most of us, he'd decided it was easier to consign notions of mortality and essential worthlessness to a back folder in a rusty file drawer in the storage closet of his soul

(if you've *got* one . . .)

until the question became more relevant. Like when they were wheeling him up the handicap ramp of the asylum, the nursing home, the organ donor factory, or whatever final solution the generations behind him would be cooking up.

The idea that everything we do in our lives is basically bullshit is one that doesn't go down well with the human spirit. Self-awareness, he knew, made us all feel that we were in some way special. But maybe the paramecium and the tree frog and everybody else *do* know they're alive, and it doesn't matter anyway. Maybe all living things wallow in the bile of their own sense of worthlessness, and it's only us bipeds that haven't gotten hip to the universe's little joke.

Why else do we rattle off endless variations of the salvation routine? Why do we always abdicate responsibility and decide it's easier to throw the blame in somebody else's face? Like God. Yeah, that's the ticket. God's will. And all that neo-Calvinist nonsense.

Tom didn't have a clue, but he couldn't get the experience out of his head—when he had his hand inside Larry's torso, he had somehow reached down a cosmic rabbit hole, had briefly touched one of the power cables that make the celestial trains run on time.

(No, that's not exactly right. . . .)

Tom smiled an embarrassed little smile, like he used to do when his mother had caught him in some silly little lie. Actually, what he'd felt was something even more distinct, more palpable, and therefore more terrifying.

He'd felt as if he himself were the main heat. The Big Guy. The Supreme Being. The real G-man.

And *nobody* should feel like that, even it was true.

He knew if he kept on indefinitely, this was going to consume him. The need to share the experience, and therefore perhaps expiate it, was overwhelmingly strong. If not Larry, then—

The door to the small room opened and it was like an airlock seal had been broken. He could almost see his deepest thought escaping like a toxic atmosphere. Looking up, not knowing if he should feel relief or anger, Tom regarded the nurse and the other persons being ushered into his white space.

Rebecca, wearing a perfectly coordinated and accessorized camera-ensemble, approached with Kiley in tow, dressed less politically correct but still sure to be a hit with the

CNN makos. Like a Winston Cup driver making his move on the final lap, his daughter pulled out of her mother's slipstream, used the drafting to boost her speed, and reached his bedside first.

"Oh Daah .. dee!" She stretched out the word like somebody reading a line from a Tennessee Williams play, and reading it badly. "You're all right . . . !"

"Hi, sweetheart," he said, feeling the silky presence of her hair against his cheek. "I'm fine. Not a scratch."

She hugged him as hard as she could, as though showing her mother how easy it was and how she should be doing it herself.

"Hello, Tom," said Rebecca, as if on cue. Her words carried about as much emotional weight as if she'd been sitting in the clubhouse at the Congressional Country Club and he'd just come in from the eighteenth hole.

"Rebecca," he said with a sarcastic smile that had become *de rigueur*. "So good of you to come."

His wife looked at him with a strained expression. She always appeared to be a little constipated. Always enduring some slight discomfort. "Cameron arranged for the flight right away. They've given him an office here at the hospital. He asked me to tell you he's setting up an 'information clearing house,'" she said.

"Where's Chip? Does he know?"

"He knows," said Kiley, now speaking quickly, as though she were reciting something prepared ahead of time. "I called him. They have a game with North Carolina this weekend and the team left early yesterday afternoon for Chapel Hill. When he found out you were okay, he said he'd better stay for the game. He said you'd understand. . . ."

Tom smiled. "He's right." Maryland had a shot at the national championship this year—a major bowl bid, at least. But that meant winning every game, and if his son, a Heisman candidate at quarterback, skipped the game against their biggest conference rival, it could mean disaster.

"But, Tom, you could have been killed," said Rebecca. "You could have been—"

"But I wasn't!" he said in a loud voice. "What's the sense of making a boy stand around a hospital room where he can't do a damn thing?"

"I have a number where you can reach him, Daddy."

"Fine, baby, just leave it with Cameron."

After that, no one seemed to be able to think of anything else to say. The three of them looked at each other across immeasurable plains of silence. It was awkward and it saddened him.

Rebecca looked especially pathetic, and he knew that had he not become positioned for the presidency, he would have jettisoned her from his life long ago. Her family's old tobacco money wasn't necessary anymore, because the perks of being a powerful senator always provided easy venues to money and its methods of making more of itself. Marrying for money was a long and proud tradition in America. Tom wasn't ashamed of the crime. Better that a few men took a shot at it anyway. . . .

"Did they say how long you'll be here?" Kiley finally hammered through the fragile pane of empty stares.

"They haven't told me a thing. I haven't seen any doctors since they brought me in."

"Perhaps I can find out what's going on?" Rebecca's voice barely escaped her caved-in frame. She was a portrait in defeat, painted in the oils of self-loathing.

"Find out about Larry, too," he added.

"They said you were both fine," said Kiley.

"Find out anyway."

More silence. Until Rebecca asked Kiley if she could have a few minutes alone with her father. Tom watched the interchange and could tell it was not rehearsed. Kiley was clearly surprised; she left quickly, probably in the hope that this semicrisis might be the catalyst to pull her parents closer together. When his daughter slipped out the door, Rebecca took one step closer to his bed.

"I realized on the way down here that there's only one thing I can do, Tom."

He rolled his eyes. "Is this the 'I want a divorce' speech?"

She kind of seized up for a moment, and he knew he'd stolen her thunder. "It . . . well, I . . ."

"You can't divorce me now!" he said loudly. "We've been through all this, and you know this isn't the time."

"Tom, I can't stand it any longer! I—"

"Listen to me!" His voice jumped another register. "I can't deal with this crap right now. I know how you feel, Becky. You can't stand me any more than I can stand you. We're a fucking joke as a couple, and we always were. Fine! Deal with a few more months. Another year and we'll know if I'm a winner or a loser. But believe me, this is not the time!"

"It's never the time," she said softly. "And by the way, you'll always be a loser to me."

"Ooh, a little venom! Are we learning to fight back in our middle age?"

"Why did you do this to me?" Her face seemed to be developing small fracture lines, like a dam holding back a lifetime of tears.

"Do *what?*"

"You've stolen so many years from me, Tom. I can't get them back. They're gone. That's what I resent the most. What should have been the best years were some of my worst."

He could see that she was being as open and sincere as she was capable. He could feel her pain and it did not make him happy. Even though she believed him to be an insensate monster, he was not. He knew how she felt about her stolen time: he felt the same way, but the notion had been mitigated by his personal success in his chosen field. Rebecca, like many family-wealthy women of her generation, had never been "bred" to be ambitious or industrious or to cultivate any dreams greater than the proper planning of dinner parties.

"I'm sorry you feel that way," he said more softly. "We both wanted different things, I guess."

"Except that you got yours and I didn't. The only thing I got was *old.*"

"This is not the time, Rebecca."

"And what happens if you get elected? Then it will be 'no president ever gets divorced' or something like that!" She started crying. "I'm not your damned prisoner!"

Maybe she was right. Maybe it was better to get the public used to him living a separate life now? People did not ascribe the stigma to divorce they used to.

(Nobody believed in saints anymore, did they?)

"All right, Becky, let me get out of this place and maybe we can work something out—an arrangement that will work for everybody. I can't explain everything that's going on right now, but this . . . this divorce thing you want is not as . . . as big . . ."

"Oh, I'm sure it isn't." Bitter. Painful. She barely looked at him as she tried to wipe away the tears. "Anything to do with us was never a big deal."

"You don't understand, Rebecca. This is something I . . . I can't . . . I can't even *begin* to explain to you."

He looked at her and realized what a vast gulf had always separated them. When he considered how desperately he needed to share what had happened to him with *somebody*, and how even the *thought* of sharing it with Rebecca seemed so totally absurd, he knew he must get away from her for his own good as well as hers.

As independent and self-reliant as he might think he was, he knew he needed someone. Someone totally intimate.

Someone who probably could not exist for him.

He wanted to not be thinking about the experience, to put it behind him, but he was getting hammered with the realization that something so absurdly spectacular would *never* be past him. It would encapsule him as completely as the atmosphere itself. Inescapable and total.

"People warned me that you were always a self-centered pig," said his wife. "I cheerfully agreed with them, Tom. Because I believed I could change you! Can you imagine?!"

"Yes, I can very well imagine it," he said with a small smile.

(Men want their women to stay *exactly* the same as the day they fell in love . . . but women *never* want their men to do likewise. No wonder they never understand each other. . . .)

"It's not funny!" she said with a burst.

"I'm not laughing," he said. "Only admiring the greater irony of all this."

"Don't talk your double-talk to me! I want out, do you understand? I don't care what you have to do. Just get me out of this hell you call a life with you!"

It was the loudest outburst he'd seen from her in years, and it probably signaled the depth of her intentions. He was about to respond in kind when he noticed that the door to the room had opened, revealing an attractive woman doctor standing behind his wife. Barrero. She had handled things during his circuslike entrance to the emergency room.

" . . . excuse me," said Dr. Barrero. "I didn't mean to interrupt you. They didn't tell me you had visitors."

Tom worked up his best PR smile. "Doctor Barrero . . . my wife, Rebecca."

The women exchanged overly polite greetings then both turned to stare at him. Rebecca obviously resented the intrusion, but it was quite apparent the doctor was not about to leave.

"Again, I apologize," she said. "But we have scheduled some tests for you, and they are about to get started. I'm afraid we're going to have to take him away from you for a while, Mrs. Flanagan."

"Take him for as long as you'd like," said Rebecca as she turned and strode from the room as stiffly as she could manage.

As the door sealed behind her, Barrero stepped closer to the bed. "We have scheduled a special battery of tests for you and Mr. Constantino."

"Really?" He decided that quiet acceptance would be the best tack here.

"Yes, we've discovered some . . . irregularities in your colleague's condition . . ."

(Yeah, I'll bet you have. . . .)

" . . . and we would like to use the opportunity to check both of you at the same time."

He wanted to ask her what she meant by the "irregularities," but he was sure she would be asking him plenty of questions. Her hair was up in a very professional-looking bunlike construction, but he imagined how it would look en route to a fall across her shoulders. There was also something about her mouth. Her lips.

Sexy.

This woman was certainly that.

Tom nodded, smiled. "No problem. Is . . . is Larry going to be okay?"

"Oh, yes, he seems to be perfectly healthy. But that's part of what's puzzling us."

Tom cleared his throat.

(Okay, here it comes. . . .)

"I don't think I follow you, Doctor."

She looked directly into him with her large dark eyes. "What happened to Mr. Constantino within the last week to give him such massive scarring in his trunk?"

He decided to look directly into her as well, to use his answering-to-the-Senate-Investigating-Committee stare. "I have no idea what you're talking about."

"The clothes we cut off him were slashed and covered with blood, and you don't know what I'm talking about?"

Flanagan held up his right hand. "Scout's honor."

Dr. Estela Barrero looked at him for only an instant. "Senator Flanagan, I don't believe you."

With that, she turned and left the room.

TWELVE

Barrero

Flanagan was lying.

She thought about his sincere stare as she returned to her office to gather up some folders.

Why did politicians believe they could do it better than anybody else? It was insulting and demeaning. She would have to—

The door was knocked on and opened at the same time. Nelson Stanhouse entered with a stack of documents under his arm. "Got a minute?"

"What's up?" She sat down in her chair as he sat on the edge of the desk and hooked his leg across the corner.

"Hansen is loving the publicity the hospital's getting. The crash and the senator are the biggest thing to ever hit this place."

Estela rolled her eyes. "No kidding. . . ."

"He's handing out a protocol sheet on how all of us should talk to the media," said Stanhouse with a grin.

"I'll put that on my required reading list," she said. Then: "What a complete jerk that man is! You know, I lost a patient the other night because of him."

"Mary told me about it. But c'mon, Estela, you can't start looking at things like that."

She rubbed her eyes. "I've got to get out of Emergency. It's not what I thought it would be."

"I was going to get you on the research team for Constantino and Flanagan."

She grinned. "You'd better. No more free tickets to the Marlins games if you don't!" Her best friend, Nevah Stevenson, worked in the team's front office. She had box seats to every game and never really got into baseball.

"Don't worry about it. That's what I wanted to tell you: we're getting started on Constantino in about an hour. First series will be standard internal stuff. Then we start getting weird with the MRI and the CAT."

She looked at her colleague and paused for dramatic effect. "What's going on here, Nelson?"

"I don't know. My gut is telling me something my head knows is absurd . . ."

"Which is?"

"Which is Larry Constantino suffered a catastrophic injury within the last seventy-two hours, most likely during the crash, and somehow healed himself."

She exhaled slowly, looked at him. "Funny, but my gut's telling me the same thing."

THIRTEEN

Flanagan

Tom, are you there . . . ?"

Valerie's voice sounded very far away. Or was it some kind of psychological projection on his part?

"Yes, I hear you."

"Well, what's wrong—don't you want me to come down there?"

(Come *down*?! Is this woman *nuts*?)

"Of course I want you to. You just *can't*, that's all."

"Tom, I need to see you. I need to know you're all right."

"I understand that, baby. Believe me—I'm fine. Nothing wrong with me. If I was laying here dying, then yeah, I'd expect you to be here by my side. But not for something like this. Besides, I told you—there's a million reporters hanging around. We'd be crazy to give them a chance to smear us all over the place."

He checked his watch. It was getting late, and he knew the night nurse would be materializing soon.

"Okay, I hear what you're saying," she said in her throatiest, sexiest voice. "I just want you to know how much I care."

"Almost getting canned from the picture shows me how much you care," he said. "But, please, don't do anything that's going to fuck up your career."

"But, Tom, I love you."

He smiled, swallowed with effort. "I love you, too. You know that. But remember: nobody can live your life for you but *you*. Don't make a mess of it."

She sighed. "So you'll come to New York right away?"

"Soon as I get loose from this place. Couple of days at the most."

They said their sweet good-byes and he replaced the receiver in its cradle. He knew he should feel glad he had a woman like Valerie in his corner. And he was, but Jesus, she complicated everything. No matter how many times he explained his situation to any of the women in his life, and no matter how times they agreed and swore they understood, there were *always* problems later.

They all have their own agenda. Everybody does. And in the end, that's the only thing that matters.

Looking up to the blank space of the ceiling, he felt his attention drifting. Lying in a hospital bed with your ass hanging out of a flimsy gown did not exactly inspire erotic fantasies.

At that moment, the door swung open to reveal a heavy-set, almost muscular nurse. She carried a tray with a syringe on a sterile pad. Behind her, remaining at the threshold, loomed the creased and pressed shape of a Secret Service agent.

"Good evening, Senator," said the nurse. "I've brought you a nightcap."

"Maker's Mark?" he said, trying to smile.

Allowing herself a small giggle, she held up the needle. "Not quite, but it should work even better."

She rolled him over and administered the shot in his stern-side, then quickly left. He lay there in silence, unmoving, trying to gather up his dignity after being punctured like a bicycle tire. Beyond the window, a soft rain streaked the glass, individual droplets refracting moonlight into tiny lamps.

(Funny, how we never take the time to notice stuff like that. Pretty.)

As he settled back against the pillows, a feeling of instant calm blanketed him.

(Whatever they put in that needle sure worked fas . . . t . . .)

This time, the door to his room did not swing inward.

It exploded.

Hinges peeled off the wall from the sudden impact, but all sound was swallowed up by the vacuum that entered the room.

(What—)

Bolting upright, Tom stared toward the rectangle of light beyond the threshold. The comforting presence of the agent had vanished, and the light filling the doorway seemed far too incandescent, too full of furious, churning energy.

(—the hell is going on?)

Throwing back his bedcovers, Tom's feet had almost slapped the floor when he noticed something. . . .

Something penetrating the burning core that had been a doorway. He retreated back into the bed like a child seeking the safety of his blankets and watched the thing approach. Tall, square-shouldered, massive. Its features were obscured by shadow and a curious stretching of perception. It was human, or at least humanlike, and it moved with the slow jungle-cat grace of a thing possessing great strength and confidence.

It moved toward him, then stopped in the center of the room. Through some trick of perspective, it appeared farther away than it could be, and it seemed to tower above him, despite the limits of the suspended ceiling tiles. An aura swirled round the figure, a borealis that was an absence of light rather than an emanation, as though the figure drew all the energy from the room like a magnet attracted iron filings to its poles of power.

Time stretched, sagged in the middle, and fell away from them. It stood, regarding him like some mythic colossus, and he kept waiting for it to lash out with a massive fore-arm and flatten him.

Motionless. Transfixed like a bug under a pin, Tom's face rippled under the glare of the figure's radiation. From a back room in his subconscious, a panel opened and a phrase from his pre-lapsed Catholic days drifted free.

(A vision. I'm having a fucking *vision*.)

Not quite, Thomas.

The voice boomed throughout the room, echoing down the corridors of memory as well as the hospital. The windowpanes rattled, resonated in their frames like rice paper in the wind. An odd detachment held him, as though he were a spectator to events that could not affect him. It was almost like watching a movie and seeing yourself in the picture, yet sharing in everything the movie-self experienced.

(Or I'm dying. . . .)

No, not yet.

He had slipped his usual moorings to spin outward. Scenes from his past flickered across a ragged screen hastily thrown up across the back wall of his mind. Bad scenes. Suddenly embarrassing ones. Little snippets that captured his worst qualities. Duplicity. Venality. Disloyalty.

Relax.

(What?)

His vision distorted and everything stretched away from him; he was suddenly looking across a vast plain, a limitless sea, punctuated only by pieces of his life. Their peaks bobbed across the surface like warning buoys against far greater evils still unseen below.

Then the perspective changed, like a zoom lens being pulled back. Tom reeled from the mock vertigo.

(Got to get up . . . get out of here and get help.)

No need to get all that excited.

Tom Flanagan stared at the shape that filled the center of the room. A dark shell that threatened to break apart in a fiery instant. Like a suit of armor containing the fury of a blast furnace. He knew the voice that strode like a bold intruder across the center of his thoughts belonged to the presence. But who——?

Just wanted to get acquainted . . .

(Wait!)

But the presence began to shimmer, like a poorly received television transmission. It raised its right hand, waved.

We'll talk again.

(No, wait . . . !)

Goodnight, Thomas.

The shape vanished as if a switch had been thrown, canceling its arcane power source.

"No!"

The sound of his own voice so startled him, his heart double-clutched in his chest, a big diesel hitting a hill in the wrong gear. Tom blinked in the almost total darkness of the room, tried to reorient himself. He was sitting up in his bed, facing the space between him and the closed door. A filmy layer of cold sweat covered him like glaze on a doughnut.

Although he had no proof, he *knew* he had not been dreaming.

His door opened abruptly and another shape stood framed in the ambient light from the corridor.

"Everything okay in here, Senator?" The Secret Service agent's voice was firm and controlled. "I heard voices. . . ."

"Just a dream, son," he lied softly. "A bad dream. Ever have one?"

"No sir."

(Of course you wouldn't, you fucking Eagle Scout. . . .)

"Well, I do. Thanks for checking. Goodnight."

"Goodnight, sir."

The agent eased the door closed, leaving Tom in darkness. He looked at the luminous dial of his watch and was not surprised to see that dawn lay two hours off.

(Could just as well be two years. . . .)

As the silence pounded against his thoughts, Tom grappled with the idea that his life had changed irrevocably. Never again would the familiar routine of Capitol Hill be enough to keep him charged up. Graft and deception and irresponsibility had been reduced to small change now that he'd traded up to an economy that dealt in lives and maybe even souls.

He hadn't been dreaming.

Something had come to him this night. He'd sensed an intimacy, a closeness that made him more than uncomfortable. Something so powerful, so terrifying none of us would ever want it to know us. Yet that Something *knew* him, an oily familiarity with the power to make him physically ill.

Collapsing into the false security of his bed, Tom tried to figure out what was happening to him. He felt singled out by some incomprehensible power, and it terrified him.

FOURTEEN

Hawking

Did it go well?"

The first time is always . . . amusing.

"You scared him?"

Not really. He is not a particularly religious man. They do not scare as readily. "Challenged" is probably a better word.

"Is he what you expected?"

Oh, he is that . . . and more. He will do nicely.

"I defer to your vision, but I am understandably impatient."

As are we all. But you will wait for my signal.

"Of course!"

Your predecessor was not so wise.

"That's why you . . . replaced her. With me."

Everyone is replaceable.

"Even you?"

We'll have to see about that.

FIFTEEN

Barrero

10:45 P.M.

Estela sat in her Eames chair armed with her remote control. Channels and images flickered past the screen like a clichéd SEGA commercial. It was her usual TV-viewing routine, and every once in a while she had to smile sadly in remembrance of Antonio. Her channel-surfing used to drive him crazy.

(Hey, wait a minute, what was that? *CLICK!* Whoa, wasn't that—? *CLICK!* Hold it, Estela! *CLICK!* Jesus, you don't give it a chance to— *CLICK!*)

She wasn't sure why she light-speeded through the cable palette, but it had become such a habit, she had become incredibly adept at recognizing shows after only several seconds playing time. It was a way of relaxing for her. A mindless dance-fugue through a different reality-scape, a place and time where her reactions and her decisions were not always balanced on the crucial edge of life's razor.

The electronic chirp of her phone startled her, not so much for the lateness of the hour as its ringing at all. Living alone, working long hours, Estela had established a very solitary existence for herself at home. Other than the occasional salesman, practically no one ever called her.

"Hello?" she asked tentatively as she picked up.

"Doctor Barrero, I presume . . ." Nelson Stanhouse's voice seemed less than calm, his attempt at humor stale and empty.

"Nelson, what's going on? Something bad, I'd guess."

"For now, let's just call it something weird. The tests just came back on our two celebrities and I think we need to talk. Can you get in here?"

"Tonight?" Estela pushed a long strand of hair away from her lips. "Are you crazy?"

"I said we need to talk. You should see the scans I'm looking at. Besides, if we crap around on this, and the wrong ears catch the wind, this stuff might all be classified."

"What does that mean?"

"They've called in some big names from Walter Reed— some of their golf buddies from D.C. That sounds like good old government intervention to me."

"Nelson, that's you're own political philosophy leaking through."

"Then how come I got a little visit from a Secret Service agent and some other unidentified suit this evening?"

"What did they want?" She suddenly realized Stanhouse wasn't kidding around. An unexpected chill passed through her, and she shook it off.

"Like any good bureaucrats, they asked me to fill out some forms."

"Forms? For what?"

"Detailing my duties, my schedule. Stuff like that. Plus some loyalty/confidentiality thing they wanted me to sign."

"What did you do?"

"I told them if they rolled that shit up into a tight enough cone, it would fit nicely up their asses."

Estela smiled. In South America, Stanhouse would have been "disappeared" a long time ago. "That's great, Nelson, I'm sure they'll leave you alone now."

He laughed. "That's okay, by the time they realize who they're dealing with, I'll have copies of all the data stashed in so many places they won't know where to look and they won't fuck with me because I've left word with *Rolling Stone* to print everything if I suddenly end up very dead."

"You're serious about this, aren't you?"

"As a carcinoma, Doctor B."

"Tomorrow's my day off. Last thing I wanted to do was be thinking about work," she said. "Besides I'm in my pajamas."

That last part was a lie. She didn't own a pair of pajamas, preferring long baggy T-shirts sans panties. But she'd been spending months trying to distance herself from everything that could hurt her. The excuse was the best she could come up with on the fly.

Stanhouse chuckled. "Yeah, you haven't been thinking about this Constantino case ever since they rolled him in the door. . . . Don't talk to me like I'm a first-year med student. Besides, if we don't get into it now, the bastards are going to bury it."

"I don't know about that, Nelson. . . ."

"People have a right to know what's going on. *We* have a right to know!"

Estela looked at the television screen, but the images capering there had dissolved into ignored abstractions. It was time to start living again. It had been easier than she'd realized to lose herself in the habitual stress of her job, sublimating her real self to a medical automaton, a highly trained android that had tried to relieve itself of the burden of any real life.

It was time to stop doing everything by the numbers.

The Constantino case was an enigma, an invitation to adventure. Thomas Flanagan was . . . somehow connected to everything—she could sense it. And he was a challenge. Something that had been missing from her life.

Into her mid-thirties now, Estela knew it was definitely *time*.

"Hey . . . ? You still there?"

"Sorry, Nelson, I was figuring things out."

"I'm glad *somebody* can." Stanhouse chuckled. "So you coming over here or what?"

She found herself nodding emphatically into the phone. "As fast as I can."

She followed the moon's path down the coastal highway, letting the night air rage through the BMW's interior. Although wrapped in a damp darkness, she felt invigorated, determined. It occurred to her that what she and Stanhouse were doing might be going beyond their job specs and their duties, but she didn't care. The decision to jump back into the game was the important part here. What she did to make it actually happen was secondary.

Take risks. Make things happen. Don't look back.

Antonio had been famous for his pep-talk aphorisms, but his charm lay in that he believed them, and more importantly, had *lived* them.

God, she missed him. . . .

The night reached out to her, pulled her down the eel-black road.

"Record time, Doctor!" said Nelson Stanhouse as she entered the lab.

"I . . . I can be very fast when I make up my mind."

"Okay, let's get started."

Stanhouse picked up a sheaf of laser prints, some film. "Look for yourself."

The scans described a human skull and the layered wonders of the brain within. Various densities and magnifications opened up the subject more efficiently than any scalpel ever could. Although neurology was not her specialty, she knew enough to be able to recognize any gross malformations. This appeared to be a normal, healthy brain.

"I don't see anything. What am I supposed to be looking for?"

"Hard to see, but look at the hippocampus . . . the connective tissue between the two hemispheres is missing. Or it's been severed."

She studied the scan, found the area of interest. "Okay, which means what?"

Stanhouse shrugged. "Not sure. I've already downloaded his record's from Bethesda Naval and Johns Hopkins.

One thing we know for sure: everything was fine before the plane went down. The trauma to the hippocampal area happened during the crash."

"Does Constantino know?" She looked from the scans to a stack of laser prints.

Stanhouse grinned. "That's not Constantino you're looking at—that's *Flanagan*."

For some reason, the revelation stunned her. An overall somatic response slapping her to attention. Flanagan. How odd. And yet, perhaps there was a part of her that expected it unconsciously.

"Does he know that he may have brain damage?"

"Not yet," said Stanhouse. "This is not your typical neurological trauma. We have very little idea about what the hippocampus really does."

"Okay. . . . Any ideas where to take this?"

"You mean previous case histories? What to look for in our patient?"

Estela nodded.

Stanhouse sat on the edge of a desk, knitted his surgeon's fingers in and out of themselves. It was a trademark habit. "I've already called in a series of search-and-correlate requests to the NatMed Databank for any cross-references on the hippocampus connective tissue. The files will download to my PC at home. I'll catch a look later tonight."

"What's the rest of the task force doing on this?"

Stanhouse grinned. "What they usually do—sleepwalking through the whole deal. You know how it is around here, Estela. Everybody's looking to do their time, get out and start that money machine they call private practice."

"Excluding you, of course."

Stanhouse bowed deeply. "Of course. Karen Silkwood lives! In all of us who would deliver the truth. . . ."

"I believe you, Nelson." She smiled. "What else should I know?"

He was already shuffling through more reports. "Well, besides the Reed flunkies, they're talking about bringing in some hired guns to look at Constantino. Some of the biggest names in surgery."

" 'Leave it to the big guys,' right?"

"That's part of it, but I think the government's the big influence here." Nelson handed her another scan, but she didn't look at it right away.

"Who's *this* one?" She wasn't in the mood for any more surprises.

"Constantino. You can see from the varying densities of the tissue—going in from the integument, through the musculature, ribs, and finally the pulmonary region . . ."

"All the way to the heart," she said. The scan described the patient's torso from the left side. There appeared to be a cone-shaped shadow passing through his body from the back. The point of the cone terminated in the lower left ventricle of the heart. Estela was not an expert at reading CATs, but she knew what this one indicated. Something large and pointy-sharp, like the end of a lance, had entered the torso, breaking two ribs, puncturing the lung, and piercing the heart. The cone-shaped shadow was all the newly regenerated tissue that had "filled in" the massive wound. The tissue was still in the healing stage, still regenerating, and was therefore less dense than the tissue surrounding it. Just like you could fill a nail hole in a piece of wood with putty that was initially more porous.

"We've asked ourselves this before, but now we have the proof. He should've been killed. How come he's not dead?"

"That's what I want to find out."

"Does the media know about this yet?" Estela looked at the other scans as she spoke.

Stanhouse shrugged. "If they don't, I wouldn't want to be betting against a leak. Those scuttlefish from shows like *HardBall* have a lot of money to throw around. Somebody always goes for the green."

"Then I think we should talk to him first. Before the sharks get to him?"

"Constantino? Now?"

She looked at him with her hands on her hips. "You look like you're going to tell me visiting hours are over."

Stanhouse smiled and put up his hands like an outlaw being confronted at the saloon bar. "Okay, okay . . . I'll go quietly."

"There isn't much I can tell you," said Larry Constantino. He was a nice-looking man who looked younger than his age. He had the dark hair and olive complexion that any film star would love to have. "Nothing I haven't already told everybody else."

Estela sat in a visitor's chair while Dr. Stanhouse remained standing. Any apprehensions they may have had about disturbing their patient at a late hour had been silly. A portable phone, notebook PC, and a mini fax/printer were all plugged in and waiting for their master's touch. Constantino was clearly a Type-A who never stopped working. Just the kind of guy the politicians sucked dry. Estela felt kind of sorry for him. He seemed like a very sincere man, a nice guy, *too* nice to be a flak merchant for a smarmy, disingenuous character like Flanagan.

"You don't remember the crash at all?" asked Stanhouse.

"We were tilted over. I think one wing hit first . . . before the other. That yanked things forward, and I think I remember hearing the metal parts of the plane ripping apart, almost like it was screaming. . . ."

"Then what?" said Stanhouse.

"Then nothing. That was it." Constantino grinned shyly like a little boy who knows he lacks the words to explain what he wants to say.

"Really?" Stanhouse seemed incredulous.

"You ever been in a plane crash, Doc?" Constantino smiled to show there was no animosity in his question.

"What about afterward? You were conscious when they brought you in here. What do you remember?" said Estela.

Constantino looked down at his hands for a moment, then all about the room. "I must've been knocked out . . . and when I woke up, Tom was holding me in his arms. We sat there in the mud until the helicopter found us."

"How did you feel? Any pain, any sensation in your back?" Stanhouse moved closer to the bed.

"I remember it itching when I climbed into the copter. A lot."

"What about the senator?" said Estela. "Was he acting okay?"

Constantino shrugged. "At first, he looked real bad. I thought he might be in shock. He said he got thrown from the wreckage, landed in a tree. I think he was pretty freaked out by the whole thing."

"Oh, I'm sure he was," said Estela. "Did he say anything about your back? Your clothes? The suitcoat and shirt you were wearing were torn and full of blood."

Constantino shook his head. "He didn't say anything about it. Maybe he was too shocked to notice. . . ."

"Maybe . . ." Estela remembered Flanagan's total denial.

"What else can you tell us? There's got to be more, Larry. . . ." Stanhouse looked hopeful.

He paused, as if considering whether or not he should say what he was thinking then: "Well, I think I had a near-death experience."

"What do you mean?" said Estela.

He recounted what she had come to realize was a very standard, very familiar story. The dreamlike journey down a long dark tunnel, the light at the end, the presence of a humanlike form awaiting the subject's arrival. Carl Sagan had remarked that the experience sounded like a memory of the subject's *birth* rather than death. Estela had always been prone to agreeing with Sagan, but now, after seeing the evidence of Constantino, she wasn't so sure.

"Is that all?" said Stanhouse.

"Yeah, pretty much."

"Meaning there's *more*?"

Constantino shrugged. "A little. But I don't know what to make of it, so I try not to think about it."

"Mr. Constantino," said Estela, "we really need you to tell us everything you can think of. What are you talking about?"

He appeared somewhat embarrassed. "Well, I've been thinking that maybe a miracle has happened. . . ."

Estela said nothing.

"What do you mean?" asked Stanhouse.

"I'm not sure, but I think God saved my life."

"Why do you think that's a miracle?" Estela reached out and touched the man's hand. "Can you explain it?"

The patient nodded and launched into another fairly common tale of an out-of-body experience. The subject floating above his own body, looking down at it from a moderate height. Constantino said he was dreaming of himself drifting away from the wreckage when he looked down and saw Tom Flanagan wandering around. He described Flanagan finding his body, touching him, and being pulled back down to his body.

"I'm not sure I follow you," said Estela. "Are you saying that Senator Flanagan saved your life, that he healed you?"

Constantino smiled. "No, nothing like that. Being in here has given me a lot of time to go over everything, to really understand what happened to me. I know that *God* healed me! I think he just used Tom Flanagan as His instrument."

SIXTEEN

Flanagan

Ten Days Later

This is going to be great," said Larry Constantino. "What a brilliant move! Gets all the sympathy votes leaning your way."

Tom nodded, said nothing. He wasn't so sure granting an exclusive interview was such a good idea, but everybody in his camp had been pushing for some kind of public appearance to put a stop to a lot of questions people had about the hospital stay and its effect on the Flanagan campaign.

Tom was confident he could handle it, but he was getting a little worried about Larry.

Tom's closest friend had been undergoing some kind of . . . *epiphany* was probably the best word for it. Tom wasn't sure what the final result would be, but Larry was getting back to his religious roots, he was renewing his marriage vows with Sophia, and he was starting to sound a little sanctimonious, a little too . . . *honest*. Having Larry present at the interview was S.O.P., but it would be bad business if he said anything weird.

(Yeah, buddy, you're starting to scare me. . . .)

Tom had been sitting in the hospital solarium with Larry, waiting for the journalist from CNN to arrive. Both of them wore tailored silk pajamas and monogrammed robes. The room had been cleared of regular patients, scanned carefully by the Secret Service, and commandeered by the ENG crews of the cable network. Keller Memorial's administration had been unbelievably cooperative with Tom and the members of his staff who had gradually come to set up living quarters at the hospital for the last week or so. Dr. Hansen had been especially unabashed regarding his willingness to be helpful: he told Tom he expected whatever favors could be thrown his hospital's way once the election was over.

Even though that date was a long time off, Tom was having no trouble accumulating friends who would be wanting their own special paybacks when the piper called.

Suddenly the double doors to the sunlit room burst open and more crew rushed to their stations like gunners on a carrier under attack. Tom looked up to see an entourage flow into the room, some of the hospital administrators and doctors assigned to their case. The main activity centered around Sam Hawthorne, the elder statesman of all the network anchors and news mavens. He walked with a confident stride as he approached Tom and Larry, shaking their hands, then sitting down in a chair centered between them.

"Okay, boys, let's give them what they want," he said to no one in particular.

Hawthorne's crew and staff scurried around, and he waited for his producer's cue, then looked straight into the camera and opened with his trademark line, "Ladies and gentlemen of America, good evening. . . . Tonight we visit the leading Republican candidate for the presidency, Thomas Flanagan, senior senator from the state of Maryland. Senator Flanagan continues to remain under observation at Keller Memorial Hospital in Miami, and the speculation is that something may be seriously wrong."

Hawthorne paused, faced Tom as the red light on camera number two winked at him. "Let's be blunt, Senator: what is the status of your health?"

Tom smiled. "You're always blunt, Sam."

"And you're not answering my question."

"The hospital has been providing daily press releases regarding my medical condition," he said. "Anything I could say would be redundant. But, I can assure you, I am feeling *great*. Do I look like a man with a health problem?"

(Or is that a *head* problem? Jesus, if this guy only knew. . . .)

Sam Hawthorne shook his head. "No, Senator, I must admit: you look hale and hardy. So that makes my question ever the more mysterious. Why do you and your campaign manager, Larry Constantino, continue to be kept at Keller Memorial?"

Tom ran a hand through his hair and shrugged. "Just as a precaution, I'm told."

"There have been rumors," said Hawthorne. "Care to comment?"

(How about *fuck* your rumors, Sam?)

"Sorry, I haven't heard any."

The journalist chuckled darkly. "Let me fill you in: that you were exposed to toxic waste at the crash site . . . that the crash was caused by an assassin's attempt on your life . . . that you have suffered brain damage that may prove fatal . . . that Mr. Constantino suffered a mortal wound and you somehow saved his life."

Tom looked directly into the camera and smiled his best press conference smile. "You forgot the one about the UFO aliens helping me survive the crash. . . ."

Even Hawthorne cracked a little on that one. "Regardless," said the journalist, "people are talking about this prolonged stay, Senator, and the effect that it may have on long-term plans for your candidacy. It is an issue that must be addressed."

(Time to get dirty with this guy. . . .)

"Really?" asked Tom, leaning forward, squaring his shoulders and striking a bold confrontational pose. "Says *who*? Sam Hawthorne? Since when do you decide what's an issue, what's important? I thought your job was to report on what happens every day, Sam? Not *make* things happen."

"The people have a right— "

"Yeah, to *know*. We've heard all this before, Sam. But what you leave out of the equation is that the people have a right to know what they *want* to know—not what you guys feel like telling them!"

Sam Hawthorne had clearly not expected Tom's counterattack. He composed himself quickly. "Senator, it's no secret you've been no friend of the media. In fact, I think it would be fair to say you've built your career on just these kind of rabble-rousing statements."

"You're damn right it's fair!" Tom turned it up a notch on purpose. "And after twenty-four years of public service, you guys haven't been able to do me in. Kind of says something, doesn't it?"

As Sam Hawthorne launched into a new assault, Tom settled back and relaxed. The old bastard had taken the bait so easily, Tom was almost embarrassed for him. There was no way he was going to let the interview center around this medical bullshit. Besides, they were getting released tomorrow, and they were trying to keep a lid on it. Tom wanted to get out of Dodge as quickly and as quietly as possible.

He fielded Hawthorne's questions—more tired dialogue on the integrity of the media—handling it automatically as his inner thoughts centered on the real issues. He'd been dealing with vipers like Sam Hawthorne for his entire career and was so adept he could do it in his sleep. Tom had learned all the tricks and snares; he'd long ago learned how to turn them back on their perpetrators.

Carefully, he shifted their dialogue onto a few of the key campaign issues—the usual tax thing, the burgeoning deficit, and the lack of a coherent foreign policy for the beginning of the next century. The interview had devolved into something manageable. It droned on toward its conclusion, and Tom was feeling good. He defused the speculation that he was in ill health, reinforced his image as a feisty, opinionated, hard-nosed candidate, and had successfully avoided any publicity about the strange doings at Keller Memorial. He knew there'd been some serious leaks to the media, but nothing had been substantiated thus far. As long as the principles kept their mouths shut, everything remained copacetic.

He finished what he sensed was the answer to the wrap-up question and watched Hawthorne turn away to stare into camera number one.

"And that concludes our segment with Senator Thomas Flanagan of Maryland. As usual, the senator's wit and aggressive style come shining through. He appears to be in perfect health and remains firm on the issues he believes are central to the presidential campaign. On that note, we would like to bid you a pleasant evening. This is Sam Haw— "

"Wait a minute!" Larry Constantino's voice cut through the sonorous tones of Hawthorne.

Everybody turned to look at the man who'd sat quietly through the entire interview, and whose sudden intrusion was a true shock.

(Jesus, Larry . . . shut the hell up!)

Tom glared at his friend, hoping to get his attention, but Larry had already stood up, facing camera one.

"What's the matter, Mr. Constantino?" said Sam Hawthorne, carefully signaling his producer to keep tape and sound rolling.

Larry looked at everyone, one at a time. He had a smile that was so beatific it looked silly. Like an airport-Krishna or a stereotypical Moonie, Larry opened his hands, palms up, and posed. "The people should know that God has worked a miracle, and that he worked it through Senator Flanagan!"

"Larry," Tom said. "Not now . . ."

"What do you mean?" said Hawthorne, gesturing at Tom to be quiet.

"God brought me back from the dead, and he did it when Tom Flanagan touched me! Don't you see what this means!"

"Somebody stop this thing!" yelled Tom. Standing, he moved to camera one and pushed its operator away from the viewfinder. "Turn this damn thing off!"

One of the crew touched his shoulder, trying to gently move him away from the equipment. Tom pushed them off as roughly as he could. Secret Service men closed in, barked out several shorthand commands, and started herding everyone away. They were good; he had to give them credit. Larry's outburst could have easily been some kind of diversion so a kook in the crew could make his move.

Sam Hawthorne started screaming about the freedom of the press, and Larry continued to stand rigid in the center of the disruption, a latter-day Saint Sebastian sans the arrows.

"The evidence is clear! It's okay!" he said in a loud, sermon-like voice. "God is on our side!"

One of the remaining agents removed the tape master from the engineer's mobile deck.

"Hey, get away from that!" cried Hawthorne.

"I'm sorry, sir, but there may be some information on this that is classified."

"Classified my ass!" Hawthorne frothed with rage, but made no attempt to stop them.

Tom Flanagan, surrounded by the body shields of four agents, was escorted from the solarium. They eased him to a previously prepared room that adjoined the interview space and provided access to a service elevator and stairwell. "Sorry we have to do this, sir," one of the agents said to him as they passed through the exit door, but Tom wasn't listening.

Looking up as he left the scene of controlled confusion, Tom had just caught sight of Dr. Estela Barrero on the edge of the crowd. Her large, brown eyes were focused on him and despite the distance between them, he could feel the heat of their glare.

That evening, he was back in bed, watching the late news on one of the local tabloid stations to see what they would be saying about the interview fiasco. So far, he was surprised to see how little of the incident had been released. Someone was doing a good job and he doubted if it was Larry.

The past two weeks had been like falling into a black hole and emerging in an alternate reality. He couldn't remember the last time he'd been slowed down by as much as a chest cold, and the shock of having everything in his life come to such a standstill was beginning to wear off, exposing a core of depression. He couldn't imagine being confined to a bed for the rest of his life. How did people live with such a sentence?

If there was one thing he despised most about the confinement, other than the prisonlike dimensions of his world, it was the absolute lack of privacy. For someone accustomed to the power and insulation of a senator's office, this was a total outrage. The basic loss of control in his life was pushing his limits. His daily routine had become an endless succession of people bothering him.

At least the calls and visits from his family had eased off, especially since he had assured Rebecca that he would present her with a game plan for an amicable separation and eventual divorce. The only one dealing with it well was Chip—primarily because (Tom assumed) his son was wrapped up in the business of living his own life. Being the quarterback on a Top Twenty football team and a possible candidate for the Heisman, as well as a dean's list student, tended to keep you pretty damned busy. Even Valerie had become more difficult to handle. Her phone calls came in with such regularity and precision, she could have been employed as a timekeeper for the Naval Observatory. Not seeing her had created an aching need within him he'd forgotten could exist in a man, but the phone calls had laid bare an aspect of their relationship he'd always preferred not thinking about: their conversation displayed all the range and excitement of a senior center's macramé class.

Still, he'd promised her and himself a rendezvous in Manhattan as soon as they released him. When they were finally alone, he would—

The door opened just far enough for Dr. Barrero to peek in. She was not smiling, but her professional half-scowl was also absent. "Good evening," she said softly. "May I come in?"

"You're always welcome here," he said with a smile intended to be charming.

"Thank you." She stepped into the room.

He wondered if she were beginning to lighten up on him just a little. His personal radar was usually very good and seemed to be detecting a different, warmer set of signals from her. Deciding to let her make the first move, Tom leaned back in his bed and folded his hands, waiting.

She took a seat in one of the visitor's chairs, crossed her legs. Nice legs. Actually, *spectacular* legs.

"I was wondering if we could talk about your TV show today," she said finally.

"I didn't know you were interested in politics, Doctor."

Her expression told him she wasn't in the mood for word-play from a seamy cocktail lounge. "I'm not. It bores me."

A silence slowly built itself between them like a New England stone fence. She seemed far more comfortable with it than he, and he finally broke through out of a growing sense of embarrassment.

"You mean Mr. Constantino. . . ."

(My friend who was going quietly bugfuck thanks to me.)

"That's part of it," she said. "Yes."

"I don't know what's happening to him. He's never been like that before."

She looked directly at him. "Like what?"

Tom shrugged. "So fanatical, so hyped up about religion."

"He believes he's had a religious experience. Have you ever read William James, Senator?"

"I don't think so." He hated it when people tried to pin him down with questions that questioned his intelligence.

Dr. Barrero smiled.

(Or was that a smirk?)

"Oh, I think you'd remember him if you did. He was a brilliant psychologist, and the brother of novelist Henry James."

"Him I remember. He could put *any*body to sleep. . . ."

"I agree. But his brother was far more interesting," she said. "His book *The Varieties of Religious Experience* provided some of the first insights into religious beliefs that weren't colored by their own prejudices."

"And you think I should read it?"

"It wouldn't hurt. But there's something more immediate I need to go over with you."

"What's that? Have they changed plans? I'm not getting out of here?"

She looked at him like he was a little kid, like she was a very patient mom. "Yes, you are still getting out, but— "

"'But *what*?"

"But that's not what I'm here for."

(Okay, here it goes—the brain tumor speech. . . .)

"Is it my head? My brain? What— "

"You've got to take it easy and stop trying to anticipate everything I'm telling you." She stood up and walked to the foot of his bed. It was a movement done more for dramatic effect than to any purpose. She picked up his clipboard and chart, but didn't even glance at it.

"Sorry if I'm anxious to get on with my life. If there's going to *be* any, that is."

"Oh, I think there will be plenty left. You're a very healthy man, Senator Flanagan."

"Thanks . . . and you can call me Tom if you want."

She smiled. "Oh, well I'm not sure I *want* to just yet, but I appreciate the chance for any future alterations in familiarity. My culture stands on formality, you know."

She said this with just the right amount of coyness and manner. He found himself becoming very attracted to her intelligence and obvious charm as well as the rest of the package.

"Yes, I've heard that." He cleared his throat. "Now, what else must you tell me?"

"Despite the trauma your brain received during the crash, we have found no perceptible ill effects. Previous studies on the hippocampal region don't tell us enough. There is speculation that the hippocampus is either doing things we cannot track or perceive, or it's vestigial."

"Meaning what?"

She shrugged. "Like our appendix or our little toe. Parts of us that are no longer needed, parts we've outgrown on our way along the evolutionary path."

"So you're going to let me out of jail—that's the best news I've had in a long time. The only thing better I might hear is that you'll let me take you to dinner before I have to head back to Washington."

She smiled, tilted her head. "Whatever for? Besides, Senator, I don't date married men."

"Don't be so presumptuous, Doctor." Tom tried to effect an offended air, knew he was doing it badly. "I just wanted to show you my appreciation for the wonderful treatment I've received here."

"That's fine. Then why don't you take Doctor Stanhouse?" *Gotcha on that one. . . .*

"I think the word touché works very nicely right about now."

"Now," she said with a nod and an impish grin. "Can I please continue?"

"Yes, of course. Pardon me."

"Despite your release, we may wish to have you back for further testing, or to continue it at Walter Reed. We will need your understanding and consent."

"And if you don't get it?"

"Then we continue to keep you here," she said without a hint of humor. "You're not getting out unless you agree to come back if we feel we need you."

"And that would only be in the most important circumstances . . . ?"

Barrero nodded.

"Okay, then, no problem." He paused, pulled himself up straighter in the bed. "What about Larry? Mr. Constantino?"

"He's being released as well."

Tom said nothing for almost a minute. He knew she was thinking about what had happened during the TV interview. Looking her in the eye, he asked, "What did you think of that little display today?"

"Do you mean from Mr. Constantino or yourself?"

Her reply was so swift, so perfectly aimed at the center of his thoughts and his ego that he would have sworn she had set him up. But that was impossible. . . .

"Well, both of us, I guess."

She moved back closer to the bed and sat in the chair beside him. "Your friend is a medical miracle. He has chosen religion to explain what happened to him. He says God brought him back to life through you. Why would he say that?"

"I don't know." He looked away from her, as though embarrassed, and it pissed him off that he had shown such a lack of control.

"When are you going to tell me what happened out there, Senator?"

"There's nothing to tell, really."

"I saw how you reacted today, the way you jumped at Constantino. What are you hiding?"

"Doctor Barrero, I don't know what you're talking about," he said as calmly as possible. No need to let her know she was entering dangerous waters. "I didn't want any publicity that was unnecessary, or superfluous. You know how people get hung up on anything about religion."

"Has anything strange happened to you since you've been here?" She pushed ahead, ignoring his bullshit answer.

(Gotta like that, Tommy. . . .)

"No, not a thing." The answer ejected from him like a cheap slug. It sounded bad and he knew it.

"Why are you lying to me?"

"I'm not, goddammit!"

She smiled at his outburst. Women never did that, and it bothered him. Then, standing up, she headed for the door. "I can see I'm wasting my time. You don't want to talk to anyone."

"All right, all right—wait!"

"Something you want to tell me?"

"It might be something," he said, gathering up his embarrassment like a bundle of dirty laundry. "I had a dream. Scared the hell out of me."

Turning, she came back to his bedside, sat down. For a moment, he thought she might reach out to touch his hand, to hold it. He would have liked that, but she didn't.

"Tell me about it," she said.

And he did.

" . . . the worst part is I'm not sure it was a dream."

Barrero looked at him, momentarily not reading him. "What else could it be?"

"I mean, it really felt like someone was talking to me in my mind. You know, telepathy."

"Do you believe in that kind of thing?"

The question lanced him.

(Tell her about it! Tell her the whole story!)

He wanted to, but he knew it was a question of timing. Maybe later . . .

"I don't know what to believe anymore."

"Who's the man in your dream?"

Tom exhaled. He felt shaky, unsure. "I have no idea."

"But he scared you."

"Oh, yeah. He's bad news, I can tell you that."

"All right, now tell me why Larry Constantino believes you healed him."

"That's not what he said—he said God healed him. I was just a . . . a tool, an instrument."

She smiled again, and he could see she was a real charmer when she wanted to be.

"So you won't tell me?"

He sat up on the edge of the bed. "Can we take a walk?"

"A walk? Where?" She looked surprised.

Tom moved to the closet, reached in for his monogrammed robe. Pulling it on, he stepped into his baby kangaroo slippers and gestured for her to accompany him.

They exited into the hall where a Secret Service agent jumped up from his chair to face them.

"Good evening, sir," he said.

Tom nodded curtly and began walking. The agency's protocol had been to remain within sight, but keeping a discreet distance as he moved through the hospital. The late hour and the almost deserted halls made his job even easier.

"Where are we going?" Dr. Barrero half whispered.

"Where are the kids?" He also spoke softly. He was nervous as hell and there was a hitch in his throat that was going to make him sound like he was getting choked up. He didn't want that. But he *was* scared and there was no getting past it.

"What kids?"

"The ones . . . who aren't going to make it."

Looking away for a moment, she nodded. "There's a children's ward on the fifth floor. We'll have to take the elevator."

Other than the moonlight leaking past the blinds, the only illumination in the ward came from consoles and monitors at many of the bedsides: mechanical guardian angels who never heard the prayers uttered here. Under their blankets, the children slept, and Tom was reminded of the nights so long ago when he would ease into the rooms of Kiley and Chip. He would look at their faces and listen to their breathing while they stretched out under the glow of Disney nite-lites. He had always been afraid to walk into their bedroom one night and make the discovery every parent fears the most.

There was a terrible silence in the ward, an *absence* that seemed to feed upon everything. He had never believed himself to be a particularly sensitive guy, but he knew that he had been changed in some fundamental way, that he'd been made more aware of what was transpiring around him. The knowledge chewed at the edges of his thoughts, and he knew he had to share his sensations, his new feelings with someone or the heightened sense might consume him.

He wanted to tell Dr. Barrero what was really going on, but couldn't yet pull off the mask. It was not as much trusting *her* as it was trusting himself. Maybe that's why he'd taken her to this place where death's banquet had plenty of young place settings.

"Do you know any of these kids?" he whispered to her as they padded quietly among the rows of beds partitioned by filmy curtains.

Softly, she replied: "Not professionally. But I have a friend who's in pediatric surgery. She tells me about them."

He nodded, stopped in front of the bed of a small boy. He was death-camp thin, radiation bald. For a long time, he stood there looking at the sleeping child the way one might stand at the edge of a vast sea and contemplate its mysteries.

"Senator, what are we doing here?"

Her question startled him, pulled him back from the meditationlike state into which he'd lulled himself. Looking down at her, he placed a finger to his hushed lips, then looked back at the little boy.

She said nothing, but he imagined that she somehow inched a bit closer to him.

Carefully, ever so gently, he placed his hand on the small boy's chest and could feel its hollowness, like a fragile vessel almost emptied. Giving in to the sensation that lapped at the shore of his awareness, he let himself drift out like a time-smoothed stone. Beneath his palm, beneath the dry husk of skin, he could feel the cellular storm raging in the boy's body. Tom closed his eyes and the image of a grand hall, a soaring vaulted enclosure like a basilica, came to him. But Escher-like, the distant walls and ceiling were pieces of the sky—three dimensional blocks of star-choked night. He could feel himself entering that place and felt his inner self, his out-of-body traveling self, his . . . soul, braced by a wind of antimatter that swirled and eddied and twisted through the place. It was the wind of time, laced with beginnings and endings, and all that lay between.

His hand touched the boy's pajamas, his fingers slipped inside the buttoned top to rest upon his sternum. And instantly, the wind kicked up to become a gale crackling with electrical current. The galvanic charge surged through with such urgency, he could feel it leave his hand like the blue spark from an arcing vacuum tube and pass through the parched vellum flesh of the sleeping child. A roaring sound filled Tom's head; his balance seemed completely absent. He could have been spinning or hanging from his heels. It would have made no difference. A submantle fire banked and flared beneath the child's ruined flesh. It burned with a new star's need, withering the architecture of cannibal cells. Chaos churned violently, and he knew it could not touch him. He withdrew his hand and felt the connection break.

Lurching forward for an instant, he regained control of his balance and his placehold in this reality. He had no idea how much time might have passed, no sense of movement or duration.

Barrero divided her attention back and forth from the child to him. It was as if she were waiting for something else to happen, and he wondered if she'd sensed anything at all. Or if she remained content to wait and watch.

"Let's go," he whispered. He felt as though his whole body were trembling, but she did not seem to notice.

"It's over?"

"*What's* over?" He stopped, faced her directly and stared into her dark irises. Even in the pale light, they glistened with intellect and perception.

Blinking, she continued to look at him. "I . . . I don't know what it was, but I know *something* happened, Tom."

He wanted to smile, but the right facial muscles weren't responding. He wanted to explain, to tell her everything, but knew this was the best way.

And she must have sensed it, too. She'd called him *Tom*.

SEVENTEEN

Valerie Berenson

There was something about an older man that was sexy to her. Looking up at him as he lowered himself down on her, she allowed herself a dispassionate moment to take a mental snapshot of his features once again. At forty-five, her Tom looked much younger. His hair, razor cut at the senatorial barbershop, was basically dark brown, other than a subtle blend of gray at his temples. Thick, dark eyebrows hooded his Husky-blue eyes. His nose was strong without being big, just like his jaw. There was an utterly masculine aspect to his face that you noticed right away. His complexion was ruddy, his beard heavy when he didn't shave the next morning. His mouth was unremarkable in its total averageness: thin lips, straight teeth, standard smile (even though he'd practiced flashing it so much, it often looked fake). No, his was not a model's face or a pretty-boy's, just something very manly. She'd always thought—

He kissed her neck and nibbled her ear, whispering how much he'd missed her. She could feel him keeping his weight on his elbows and knees so that his 190-pound frame would not overwhelm her. So attentive. So . . . considerate. His lovemaking was always gentle and never hurried. He moved his hands over her, his body against hers with a subtle confidence, with a style that was almost graceful. She never mentioned these qualities to him, and he never made a big deal about it, either. She was almost afraid to compliment him for fear that he might become self-conscious or try even harder, and therefore mess it up. Make it become less than totally natural, totally sincere. Maybe she was superstitious, she wasn't sure.

One thing she was very sure of—younger men had none of the thoughtfulness and care in their lovemaking that older ones did. Men in their early thirties, her own age, were so excitable, so crazy to get it up and get it in (and unfortunately out) so fast, it was almost laughable. They didn't know how to take their time with any of it.

. . . and speaking of which, he was now working his way down her neck, brushing half-open lips against the open folds of her robe. No pawing and tearing (although she liked that every once in a while and it was his duty to know when she wanted it like that . . .). Slowly, he nuzzled her robe out of the way. She'd just come from the bath, and her toned skin still carried a bouquet of sandalwood from the water. A signal to him that she was naked beneath the Cairo Hotel terry cloth.

The first touch was always the best, and as Tom brushed his cheek against her nipple, she felt a voltage charge along her entire body. Then turning, ever so slowly, he let his tongue reach her, but only for the briefest instant. Teasing her, stretching out time and sensation, he pulled her and played with her like she was a piece of melting taffy.

In reply, she could only arch her back and purr.

The ritual of desire continued as he would move lower, then pull back, looking up, locking gazes for an instant, then perhaps kissing her, or tonguing her ear, then backing off to explore the terrain of her flesh. God, she loved it!

How could Rebecca not like this? How could any woman not like this?

But she knew there were millions of women who truly did not like sex. From her college days onward, she'd listened to countless women wearily complain that sex was something to be endured to get what they really wanted from their men.

She smiled at the thought as Tom Flanagan smiled at her then returned his attention to her flat stomach, kissing it, licking it. It was so funny she almost giggled aloud, but she knew he would take it the wrong way and worry that he was doing something wrong, or worse, something laughable. She wished she could just tell him at that moment the thoughts lighting through her mind. To explain that she wanted nothing from him other than the attention and the great sex. She had no secret agenda, no terrible plot to seduce him for something other than simple affection and emotional attachment.

Raising her knees, spreading her legs, she opened the gates to the garden. He responded by gliding downward, until his head rested between her legs. The secret kiss, that's how he referred to what he was doing to her now. The first flick of his teasing tongue almost causing sparks between them. And then the darting contact, the sliding, slippery tugs at her lips, and then along the glistening inner path. . . .

Oh God, she couldn't stand it! But she loved it so! Needed it so much. If he kept it up she would come all over his face, and she had to reach down to pull him away but no it felt so good there was no way she could pull him away but she had to or it would be all over so quickly and then—

He eased away for an instant, drawing a breath, exhaling long cool stream across her shining parts. The minibreeze itself a turn-on. How could he know the exact instant when to stop? How could he be so. . . so damned *good?*

He played her like an instrument a musician has used all his life. There was a power and confidence in him she'd never felt in a man before. As he moved up to briefly look into her eyes and kiss her, she knew she wanted to tell him how much she loved him, needed him, wanted him forever.

But they never spoke of love. She had been waiting for him to bring up the subject of emotional involvement and he never ever did. It was that simple. It was one of those topics, like deficit spending, that never entered his thinking or capered upon the edge of his speech. She had long ago decided it would not be mentioned, unless he brought it up. And he never did.

Now he was moving downward again, this time touching her with his tongue and his lips more forcibly, not harshly or with any intention of hurting her, but she could sense a firmer purpose, as though he wanted to—

—and she would if he didn't stop oh mygod it was so good now that she felt like she was sliding over the edge that she would go past the point the place the moment where she could still keep control and make it last but, it. was. going. past. that. point. right. NOW!

Everything locked up for an instant and her vision blurred and that familiar, intense burst of pleasure and heat radiated up from her center across her breasts and up over her head. When she was a little girl, she remembered seeing a picture in a history book of a sailing ship tottering along the edge of a vast waterfall that led into the Milky Way, a vast sea of stars. It was an illustration for a passage describing the fear of ancient sailors that they would eventually reach the edge of the world, and would then fall off into oblivion. She'd never forgotten that image, and for some reason, as she grew older and learned to appreciate the power and ecstasy of her orgasms, she always associated herself with that ship about to slip off the edge of the world.

So right now she was plummeting through the sea of stars, over the edge, and into the warm abyss of spent passion.

Slowly, waves of clear thinking returned and she looked up at him. He had been so unselfish, so giving. Now she would give back to him.

"Come inside me," she whispered.

He kissed her inner thigh for his answer. But he did not move to enter her. He did not even look up at her. After a minute or two, although it seemed much longer, she reached down, touched his shoulder.

"Tom, what's wrong?"

"Nothing . . ."

Slowly, he inched and elbowed his way up to her so that he could kiss her on the mouth. As he drew closer, she noticed something missing, the familiar hardness between his legs had disappeared.

So that was it. . . . The one thing they all feared more than anything else.

"It's all right," she said in the softest whisper she could manage.

He looked into her eyes and smiled. "Is this when you tell me it happens to everybody?"

She giggled.

"Why do women say that? Do they think it makes us feel any better? Don't they realize it only makes them sound like they've seen it a thousand times with a thousand different goons?"

She blew warm breath in his ear, kissed his cheek. "Good to see you're taking it so well."

"Actually, I'm not. You have no idea how much I wanted you. Have missed you . . ."

"Then how come—?"

He looked at her as though he were going to continue, and then he stopped.

"Tom, what's going on? Are you okay? Did they give you some kind of medicine at the hospital? Are you hurt somehow?"

Shaking his head, he sat up, moved off the bed and began pacing the room. Ambient light from the city's surrounding skyline ghosted his nakedness and he moved through the darkness. "No, no . . . nothing like that. I'm so sorry, Valerie." His voice sounded fragile, edgy, as though he might be afraid of something.

"I've never heard you like this," she said, sitting up, watching him pace unconsciously. "What's bothering you?"

"I don't know . . . I don't know if I can explain it. So much has happened. The crash, then Larry getting that old-time religion . . ."

She nodded, but said nothing. The media had briefly noted Larry Constantino's profession of faith on the CNN interview. Depending on how you looked at it, Larry either appeared very devout or very silly. She knew it had embarrassed Tom.

"Is it Larry, then? What's the matter, are you planning to fire him? Something like that?"

He chuckled with deep irony. "Hell, no! Even if I was, I don't think that would make my dick go down . . . !"

"I'm sorry, Tom, I'm just trying to help. Trying to listen, if you want me to."

He continued to pace, deep in thought. She'd seen him like this before when some kind of political decision needed to be made, when the pressure of his position as both senator and candidate tried to steamroller him. But he was such a strong man, so full of his own will and motive, that she'd never seen anything get the best of him. But this new thing, whatever it was, seemed different. Or at least his handling of it certainly was.

At that moment, he stopped, turned to face her, and paused, as though ready to launch into a prepared little speech. She'd seen that little mannerism, too. It was a practiced shtick created for journalists and colleagues, performed to make them think he'd just thought of something additional and important he should tell them. Of course, she knew the dodge—he would always show them a secret card he'd been waiting to play at just the correct instant, something he'd known all along.

She watched him, waiting for a fragment of data tossed her way, but he crossed her up, stopping in midgesture, as though suddenly realizing he had truly nothing to say.

" . . . I'm sorry, Valerie."

"You've already said that. And if you keep saying it, I'm going to get mad."

"I don't know what to say. Ever since the crash, things have been different."

"You mean between *us*?" No sense playing around. If this was about them, she wanted to get it out in the open. Funny, she thought, but until just now, it had not even occurred to her that his impotence might have any reflection on his feelings or desire for her. She'd always assumed *that* was merely a given.

"What . . . ?" He looked at her with an expression she could not recognize. It was perhaps a conflux of shock, embarrassment, and anger.

"Did you meet someone else while you were in the hospital?" She spoke very carefully, evenly, but without aggression or venom. "Did Rebecca suddenly realize she could have lost you forever and pledge her undying love and support?"

"No, of course not."

"Well, something happened, and I think maybe I should be hurt that you don't feel you can tell me. If you—if you care about me like you say you do, then you should be able to tell me anything."

That stopped him. He wheeled from his pacing, moved to the edge of the bed, and sat next to her.

"Listen," he said. "There's plenty I can't tell you. You know about the security oaths, the classified stuff I see and hear. . . . How do you know it's not something like that?"

"Because I'm a woman," she said through her teeth. "And I just know."

"No, not the way you think. I think the crash . . . *changed* me."

"Changed?" She repeated it softly. There was something about the way he said the word that scared her. She wanted to ask him to explain, but she was also afraid to know what he really meant.

Changed for a man usually meant he wasn't all that excited about you anymore. It meant he'd found someone else. Someone new and intriguing and sexy. Because she knew what men were like. They never stayed satisfied with one woman, and she couldn't understand it. Some men admitted it freely, while others flatly refused as they announced their undying devotion.

He stood there staring at her with a slack jaw. He appeared worried, distraught. She had to admit, his was not the face of a man lusting after some bimbette. In fact, sex looked like the farthest thing from his thoughts. It was time to do a little probing around.

"What do you mean, Tom? Changed like how?"

"Like the doctors aren't sure. . . ." He rubbed his mouth with the back of his hand. "I think I need a drink."

Before she could get up to do it for him, he left the room. The sound of tinkling ice in a tumbler preceded his return. Maker's Mark in a tall kitchen glass. He slugged back half of it in one quick movement.

"You were talking about the doctors . . ." she said.

"I tried to explain all this before. Christ, Valerie, why do I have to repeat myself? You're starting to sound like a god-damned wife instead of a—"

"A what, Tom!" she said loudly. "Just what am I to you, anyway? A girlfriend? A companion? Or am I just a friend?"

"Stop it, I'm trying to explain something imp—"

"Or how about 'mistress'? Do they still use that one?"

"Don't start this one again. You knew I was married from the day you met me. Never seemed to bother you back then." He knocked back the rest of the bourbon, then glared at her.

"You know what, I don't really care about that." She climbed back on the bed, looked at him sadly. "I don't even know why I even brought it up."

"Because you're a woman, that's why. . . ." He walked to the window wall, pushed back the curtain, and looked down toward Central Park.

Neither of them spoke for a minute or two, but it seemed much longer. Then she hammered into the silence. "I'm sorry . . . I didn't mean to upset you. You're obviously already upset, already hurting."

"Thanks for telling me."

"You were saying something about the doctors, right?"

Turning, he looked at her, then tapped his head with his index finger. "I tried to explain this before. The accident did something to my brain."

"I remember," she said, although the particulars had escaped her. She'd been so relieved to know he was safe and that he had no injuries and wasn't going to die. Nothing else had mattered. "But they didn't know what it meant, that's why they had all the tests, right?"

"That's right, they don't know, but I think I do. I think I'm changed." Moving away from the floor-to-ceiling window, he began his slow, naked pacing again.

"What are you trying to tell me, Tom?"

"I don't know. I don't know. I just know I'm different now, and—"

He stopped and she knew he had been trying to blurt something out, that he'd almost told her some deep, dark fact about himself.

"—never mind . . ." he said, shaking his head. "I can't get it into words right now."

But something again had held him back. Her mind cast about, wondering what horrible thing it might be that scared him so much. Whatever it was, she knew one thing. She'd never get him to tell her by badgering him. He was not a man who responded well to that tactic. Better to let him choose the best way and the appropriate time.

"Why don't we try to get some rest?" she said softly.

"One more drink," he said, and shambled off to the kitchen. The first tumbler had obviously begun its work and he now aimed to finish it.

She lay in silence waiting for him. He was scared of something, that was for certain. Something he felt he couldn't control, which for Tom Flanagan had to be the worst terror of all.

When he reentered the bedroom, ice cubes clinking, she feigned sleep to see if he would try to wake her. When he chose to stand by the window, half-gulping his bourbon, she knew he wouldn't be sharing anything more with her that night.

Without attracting his attention, she shifted her position in the big four-poster and invited the oblivion of sleep.

EIGHTEEN

Flanagan

It was not a dream.

The thought kept hammering against the inside of his forehead like it wanted to get out. Tom recognized the frenzied thinking for what it was—the horrible panic of a mind out of control.

He might not be dreaming, but he was definitely sleeping. How he contained this awareness, this surety, he did not know, but it remained within him as a granite-hard piece of knowledge. And yet he glided across the plains of sleep like the narrator in that strange book by William Hope Hodgson, *The House on the Borderland*. Tom had read the book in college, ever after convinced Hodgson had discovered LSD back in 1907.

This was not the effects of too much bourbon, either. Tom Flanagan had been drunk enough times to know that liquor never sharpened your senses like this. He felt like the edge of a dagger slipping through the tentlike roof of the world.

And yet he knew he was asleep.

Thomas Flanagan . . .

Someone was calling his name. He was hearing it in his mind, or in his sleep, or in the dream in which he'd concluded he wasn't really dreaming at all. Or . . .

It didn't matter, did it?

Flanagan.

(Who are you?)

He knew and he didn't know. A hideous familiarity clung to him. The image of the figure in his hospital room returned with the subtlety of a slap in the face. Whoever or whatever the thing was . . . it had come back for him.

He tried to control the dream, because now things were so weird, he knew he'd been wrong before, and it just *had* to be a dream after all. Or a hallucination. But—

Come to me.

(Where are you?)

Get up. Leave the woman.

Suddenly he was aware of himself lying naked on his back in Valerie's bed. He remembered their little discussion that could have easily escalated into a full-blown argument if he'd wanted it to, and he remembered the two kitchen glasses of whiskey and the lights from the buildings on Fifth Avenue and the long, endless silkiness of her thighs. He remembered all these things as he looked down at himself. The sensation of floating several inches off the bed was so strong, he knew it was real, or at least it would have been real if this wasn't just some alcohol-paranoia fugue through the rounded corners of his head.

Flanagan. Now.

The voice was more than insistent. Just beneath the slippery veneer he detected a sense of abject menace, of threat, and perhaps something worse.

(What do you want? Where? What're you talking about?)

The voice did not respond, but he sensed a communication just the same. It was as though he had received the words through his entire body. A general somatic response, so to speak.

(Somatic response? What the hell kind of language was that for a politician to be using?)

It occurred to him that he'd hung around the doctors, or at least the hospital, far too long. He must have picked up the phrase from Estela Barrero.

Thinking of her made him aware of how clear-headed he was. Could all this really be a dream? Not a dream?

Flanagan.

The voice held him almost physically this time. He looked down the length of his body to his feet. He seemed to be floating above the bed and tilted forward at a bizarre angle. The sensation was giddy and unsettling. Sitting up, he felt as though he would fall forward over his feet, and the temptation to tuck into a roll was almost uncontrollable. But he stood, and felt himself gliding out of Valerie's bedroom as though he rode velvet-soft rails.

Down a short hallway, past the bath and then the kitchen, to a sunken living room. The curtains remained undrawn and the ambient light of the neighboring skyscrapers filled the room with frosted light.

But it was unneeded because the incandescent man, the thing from the hospital, had invaded his sanctuary. A self-contained light, like the heart of a birthing star, burned inside the figure. No heat, but a light that was cold and blue and beautiful. As Tom watched the light, it began to change colors like the aurora borealis. There was a hypnotic effect, like staring into a kaleidoscope when stoned.

The gliding sensation left him standing there at the entrance to the room, on the lip of the first of three small steps downward. Just beyond the walls, the door to the corridor, he knew a Secret Service agent hovered, waiting for any sign of alarm to come gangbusting through the doors or the walls. Tom knew he could summon help with a scream, but he said nothing, feeling content to stare at the shining blue figure. But a thought leaked out of him. Cautious, tentative.

(What are you?)

No reply. A minute of monolithic silence, then he pushed on:

(Are you an angel or something like that?)

You do not know me, but . . . you know me.

(What's that supposed to mean?)

Time enough for understanding.

(What is this? Are you in my dreams? What do you want?)
I am here to tell you what you will need to know.
(Like what?)
You are forever changed. You can never go back.
(Yeah, tell me something I don't know.)
Stop denying the power you have.

The figure's words fell into the darkest core of him and burned like incendiary bombs. He *was* trying to deny everything, and the impossibility of it was taking him apart at the seams.

(I . . . I don't know what it is, what to do with it.)
You have been chosen. It is the will of God.
(I didn't know he was paying such close attention.)
He is. And so shall you.
(Is that a threat or a promise?)
Both. And neither.
(Are you . . . Jesus?)
Hardly. . . .
(Then who are you? How do you know what's been going on?)
I have been with you always.
(How come I don't remember you?)
You do.
(I don't think so.)
And I will be with you the rest of your days.
(Why all the mystery? Why can't you just tell me what's going on?)
Experience is the wisest teacher.
(I don't get it. This is making me fucking crazy!)
To truly understand, you must live out your destiny.
(I don't want any of this . . . it's too much. It's going to bring me down.)
You will find strength in others.
"This is nuts! Why're you doing this to me?!"

The sound of his own voice surprised him. The trance-like state, the dreamy conversation, shattered like a plate of cheap glass in front of him. He realized that he was indeed awake and the shimmering image of the man still hovered in front of him. Valerie's conversation pit looking like the transporter room in *Star Trek*.

(All we need is Scotty.)

He walked forward to confront the image and was not altogether surprised when it was like passing through a holographic projection. But there was a coolness, as though the man was made of air-conditioned air. Tom's skin rippled at the ethereal contact and he backed away without thinking about it.

I am here to warn you.

"Warn me of what?"

Your power must be used.

"Used for what?" He could feel the ragged edge in his voice sawing at his throat.

To make you stronger. You will be tested.

"What're you talking about?"

But do not be afraid. I will be with you. Always.

"What *are* you, goddamn it?!" He had yelled this time, and footsteps up the hall signaled Valerie's entrance into the room.

"Tom . . . ?"

Wheeling on her, he heard his voice cracking as he spoke. "Do you see it? Right there?"

She looked past his pointing hand, toward the center of the room, and he could tell by her dazed, slack expression, she saw nothing.

Tom looked again, and the burning man still lingered in the air, as though taunting him. Was that a smile on its dark-shadowed face?

"Damn it, Valerie! Can't you *see* it!?" Grabbing her by the shoulders, he shook her roughly, like a frustrated parent.

Be warned, Flanagan. Good-bye. For now.

"Tom, what's the matter with you?" Terror colored the octaves of her voice as she tried to get away from him, and it only made him more furious. He wanted to throw her into the midst of the burning man, to let her feel the reptilian cold touch of its presence. He wanted to hurt her for not seeing it. He wanted her to prove to him he wasn't losing his mind.

But she couldn't.

Not any of those things.

And in that instant, he hated her as he'd never hated anything in his life.

For being so . . . normal.

(so different from me)

For not helping him when he needed it most.

"Tom! Let me go! Let me go!"

Valerie was flat out screaming now, and other sounds penetrated the shell of anger and hurt and fear that held him. The front door crashed open as the Secret Service agent, armed with a passkey and a Sig-Sauer automatic, choreographed into the room. When he saw a very naked Senator Flanagan holding Valerie like a Raggedy Ann doll, he paused to assess the situation. His expression remained an unlined mask.

In that instant, Tom turned to see the burning man fade away.

(Nobody sees him but me. . . . Great.)

"Oh, God . . ." Valerie was moaning vaguely as she slumped in his hands. He released her and turned to face the young agent, who looked like he could have been a bank teller or an insurance salesman. He glided the gun between Tom and Valerie with outstretched arms.

"Everything okay here, Senator?"

(Sure, there's a guy burning like a dwarf star in my living room, but sure, everything's just A-OK. . . .)

"It's fine, son. Just a little disagreement, that's all."

"You're sure, sir?"

"Yes, goddamn it, I'm sure!" he said, turning toward the hall to the back rooms. "And close the fucking door before you have all the neighbors coming down to have a look."

The agent slowly relaxed his impression of a gun turret and acquiesced, moved from the room, locking the door behind him. Valerie spun around and moved quickly down the hall.

"How did he get a key to my place?" Her question dripped with varying hues of fear and anger.

Tom chuckled as he moved to gather up his clothing. "He's a government fucking agent. They have keys to everything, didn't you know that?"

"That's against the law!"

"They *are* the law."

She moved closer to him, watched him button his shirt. "What're you doing?"

"I've got to go, Valerie. I've got work to do, and I'm stressed out, and being around you isn't helping. Me *or* you."

"What was going on tonight? Are you all right?"

"I don't know what's going on," he said tersely. He was tired of talking about it. "And I don't know if I'm 'all right.'"

She looked as though she were getting angry and that kind of confused him. He would have bet anything she'd have wanted him to leave, to let things cool down a little.

"Tell me what happened tonight," she said as she moved away and sat on the edge of the bed.

"I . . . I had a vision."

(What did I say?)

The sentence slipped out of him so quickly, he didn't realize he'd even spoken. Instantly, he regretted it, but knew that his words had finally escaped the vessel of his thoughts. Unstoppered by the emotion of the moment, the release of extreme psychic pressure had literally forced the words out of him.

"You what?"

"I don't know what I meant. It just slipped out of me."

"A 'vision'? What kind of vision? You mean an idea?"

"Valerie, don't insult me. You *know* what I meant! You went to a fucking nun's school, for Christ's sake!"

"You mean a *religious* vision." She did not phrase it as a question, and he thought he detected a hint of dread in her voice. "Tom, are you kidding me? What're we talking about here, Our Lady of Fatima?"

"I don't really know what it is. . . ."

He went on to briefly recap his hospital dream and the apparition in her living room.

When he had finished, her expression had fine-tuned itself. There was less dread, but also less respect. Relying on his parliamentary experience, he decided to push things.

"You don't believe me?" (Like I really care. . . .)

"Oh, of course I believe you. I believe *you* believe it."

Tom smiled as he pulled on his suit jacket. "So you think I'm crazy."

"I didn't say that."

He chuckled darkly. "Sweetheart, you didn't have to."

"Tom, this is serious."

"You're telling me?" He picked up his briefcase and walked to the threshold of the bedroom door. "Listen, I've got to go. I think I might have stirred them up out there. I should go see about doing some damage control."

Jumping up and moving quickly across the room, she slipped in front of him. "Don't go yet. It's still the middle of the night."

"Valerie, can't you see I'm uncomfortable here?" He backed away from her. "All around, I have to tell you—this has not been one of my best nights."

"Let me help." She smiled and did that little purring sound he always liked. "I don't think you're crazy, Daddy. Just a little stressed out."

"That means you don't believe me," he said as he pushed past her and aimed for the door. "That means you think I'm imagining all this shit because I'm pushing myself."

"No, no it doesn't! Tom, I'm sorry! I didn't mean—" She followed after him, grabbing for his shoulder.

"It doesn't matter what you mean!" He was screaming again, and he didn't want that. No need for the agent to come cruising in here again. He took a deep breath and looked into her big eyes. "Listen to me: I was in a plane accident and something got disconnected in my skull. I've got some kind of brain damage, do you understand that?"

"Stop raising your voice."

Tears started to fill the corners of her eyes and he was reminded that she was a very highly paid actress. He pointed at the side of his head with his index finger.

"Brain damage, Valerie! The doctors said they can't find anything, but if I'm seeing guys on fire in the middle of your living room, well, maybe there is something goddamn well wrong!"

"Tom, I'm sorry. . . . I wasn't thinking. Let me help. . . ."

"There's nothing you can do right now. Except get out of my way and let me try to get a few things straightened out on my own."

"Where're you going at this hour?"

"Washington. The goons will get me a limo."

Putting her hands on her flaring hips, she struck a defiant pose—one he was sure he'd seen in more than one bad romantic thriller. "If you leave now—"

"Valerie, please . . ." he said, smiling. "That dialogue is so stale. You need a script doctor if you were getting ready to tell me to 'never come back.'"

"You bastard! What's *wrong* with you? I didn't do anything to deserve this!"

"Deserve what? I'm not doing anything to you."

"Yes, you are." Her eyes were big and round and full of heat. "You're punishing me—for not believing you."

He paused and considered that. "You know, maybe I am. . . . Sorry, but it seems like an utterly human response to me."

"Tom, I mean it."

He sighed, inhaled slowly, purposely looked away from her. "Well, Valerie, if you won't cut me a little slack and give me some time to find out what's going on . . . I guess I do, too."

"What does that mean?"

"Figure it out. You're a smart lady." He shrugged and walked past her into the building's main corridor. The Secret Service agent was standing at a discreet distance. Valerie slammed the door, a very unsubtle punctuation for the entire evening.

"Could you get me a car, please?" he said to the agent.

The man nodded, pulled out a very small PCS phone and placed a voice-activated call.

Tom waited for him to join him in the elevator and they rode silently toward the street level until Tom said, "You married, son?"

"Yessir, I am."

"Well, then I guess you can appreciate that little scene up there. . . ."

"Not exactly, sir," said the agent. "My wife and I don't have arguments."

(I should've known, buddy. You probably issue her permits just to kiss you . . .)

Tom said nothing else. By the time they walked through the pink marble lobby to the whisper of the Tower waterfalls, there was a black Mercedes waiting at Fifth Avenue's curb.

As he entered the car, Tom looked up at the needlelike building punching a hole in the sky. He wondered if he would ever be back.

The driver moved off along the practically empty street, turning east toward LaGuardia. Tom settled back and felt suddenly drowsy. The tension of the evening, now ebbing away, had left him weak and shaky. As he nodded in and out of consciousness, he tried to assemble a punch-list of things he would need to do, but before he got very far, the fatigue enveloped him.

NINETEEN

Barrero

One Week Later

The shift had finally ended.

Nothing like a school bus tangling with a cement truck at rush hour to make your day interesting. Estela finished her notes on the last patient she'd seen that day and headed for the relative sanctuary of the office she shared with Nelson Stanhouse. As she threaded her way down the crowded corridor, she eased out of auto-pilot mode, and tried to become a regular person, having regular thoughts again.

She'd first heard of the "trick" in her final year of internship—from Dr. Stevenson. He'd been a shock-trauma surgeon for twenty years, and the only way he'd stayed with the job had been the perfection of what he'd always called "AP."

Basically, it consisted of pulling the plug on your feelings. You had to enter a Zen-like state in which you focused entirely on each separate task you encountered, and carried them out methodically, with as little emotional coloration as possible. It was not that she didn't care about the levels of human suffering witnessed every day, but she knew if she allowed herself to become too entangled in her feelings, she wouldn't be able to make life-and-death decisions. And so, she had trained herself to be a very sophisticated automaton— highly efficient in lightning diagnoses and high-order triage.

Estela didn't much like her "AP self," but she knew it represented a necessary part of her. Without being able to work as a coldly pragmatic body mechanic, she knew she would have jumped off the causeway bridge years ago. When her shift ended each day, she could feel herself sloughing off her unfeeling self as though it were a brittle outer shell, an ugly but protective carapace.

And yet, not totally . . .

There were still many days, and nights staring at the ceiling of her lonely bedroom, when she wished she'd never entered medicine. The certain perception—that she'd made a terrible mistake and would have been far happier and more fulfilled being a dress designer or an editor or the owner of a small shop or business—would at those times hang above her like an immense weight ready to fall.

Thirty-five years old and you still don't know what you want to be when you grow up. . . .

She smiled to herself as she entered the elevator and started humming "Masquerade" from *The Phantom of the Opera*. That was a good sign. If she was singing, she was in good spirits.

As she reached her floor, she stepped out and began weaving her way through the constant corridor traffic. Change of shift was going on, and she felt like she was in Manhattan at lunchtime. Opening her office door, she was surprised to see Sheila Goldman waiting for her. Tall and thin with frizzy red hair, Sheila looked like Raggedy Ann with half of her stuffing missing.

"Hey, girl, what're you doing here?"

Dr. Goldman smiled, but only a little. "Remember the Marzano boy?"

Her serious tone caught Estela off guard, and for a moment her mind was completely thought free. ". . . should I? Who is he?"

Sheila moved closer, spoke in almost a whisper. "C'mon, Estela, you told me to tell you if I noticed anything . . . different in him, remember?"

And she did.

The little bald-headed boy, who slept while Tom Flanagan touched him. . . .

Of course, she'd never forgotten, but the pressure of the day was still slow-leaking out of her, and names—she encountered so many faces, so many names every day, it was almost impossible to remember any of them. It was worse than the massive memorization she used to need for anatomy exams.

"Yes," she said after a pause. "Bobby, right?"

Sheila nodded. "That's him."

"Why? What happened to him?"

Sheila tilted her at a slight angle, looked at her as though she were trying to decide whether or not she was trying to be funny. "I don't *know* what happened to him, Estela. That's why I'm here—I thought *you* would."

Estela felt the bottom of her stomach sink. *Oh God, what have I done?*

"You've got to be more specific, Sheila. I'm not sure I—"

"Estela, you asked me to tell you immediately if I noticed any drastic change in Bobby's case, didn't you?"

"Yes, we both know that," said Estela, losing patience. "Would you mind telling me what that drastic change *is*?"

Dr. Goldman nodded. "I think I'd rather show you. You have time right now?"

Estela could only nod.

"Good. Let's go to the ward."

As she followed her friend to the elevators, she kept trying to think of the right thing to say, but no words would come. She'd been so busy this past week, so overwhelmed with the usual insane routine of her job, she'd truly had no time to think about the little boy with cancer, or Tom Flanagan, or anything connecting the two of them.

But she knew Flanagan had wanted to tell her something, that he'd been unable to do it, and the episode with the Marzano child had been his way of trying to show her something. The base of her stomach continued to feel flat and hollow and yet very heavy. She knew what she was about to see, but she would not allow herself to think about it.

"This way," said Sheila, guiding her through the children's oncology ward to a secondary corridor with private rooms. "We moved him so that the other kids wouldn't notice."

"Notice what?" This time Estela wasn't sure what she meant.

"Take a look," said Sheila as they arrived in front of a closed door.

Pushing it inward, she revealed a dark-eyed boy sitting up in his bed watching television. His face was full and his cheeks were flushed with a healthy supply of blood. He was smiling at whatever was happening on the screen. He was probably so used to having his privacy invaded by hospital staff, he paid absolutely no attention to Estela and Dr. Goldman. He looked so beautiful, but perhaps his most striking feature was a thick shock of dark brown hair.

"Oh, my God," she said, putting a hand to her mouth. Impulsively, she moved to the bed and grabbed the boy's hand. It was warm and plump,

"Hi," he said. "How're you doin'? Are you another doctor?"

"Yes," said Estela. "I am." A tear popped from the corner of her eye, and it was like a cue for the rest of her body to let go. A great wellspring of pure *feeling* burned its way up through her chest, spreading outward. More tears were streaming from her eyes, and she felt embarrassed.

"Are you okay?" asked Bobby.

"Oh, yes, I'm fine," said Estela. "I'm just happy, that's all."

"Why do girls always cry when they're happy?" he asked. "My mommy was doin' the same thing. . . ."

"You're so beautiful," she said. It was the only thing she could think of to say to him. She couldn't remember feeling so . . . choked with emotion—not even when Antonio had died. To see this little body so . . . so alive after she'd seen him only a week ago looking like a curled-up sleeping skeleton . . . it was impossible, and yet it had happened.

"It's a miracle," said Sheila Goldman. "I know what you're thinking, everybody's saying the same thing, but there's one more thing, Doctor . . . and I can't figure it out. . . ."

Estela dabbed at the corners of her eyes. "I know what you're going to say: *how did I know it was going to happen?*"

"That's right, Estela. How did you know? How *could* you know?"

She looked back to the child, whose attention had returned to a cartoon called *Doug*, and squeezed his hand one last time. He had not been listening to their conversation.

Turning to face Sheila Goldman, Estela drew in a breath, released it. "That's just it," she said softly. "I didn't know anything. Honestly. I just had a feeling that something good might happen here."

Anger flashed across the woman's face, then slipped beneath the surface of her otherwise blank expression. "Doctor Barrero, *really*. 'Just a feeling' was it? Well, thank you. That explains everything. Certainly to *my* satisfaction."

"Sheila, that's not what I meant. I mean, I didn't want it to sound like that." She felt suddenly unable to express herself.

"What's going on, Estela?"

"I—I can't tell you right now," she said quickly, maybe too quickly. "When I understand it more myself, then . . . then I can maybe try to explain it. But right now, I can't."

"Well how about this? Jenny was on duty last week when you brought Senator Flanagan here. She said it was on the graveyard shift."

Estela stood up straight. She hated thinking that she'd been spied on, or worse, that people were walking around here thinking they had some secret nonsense on her. "That's right, he wanted to see the children's ward, that's all. He . . . he likes kids."

Sheila Goldman chuckled, shook her head. "You must think we're all living with our heads in the sand."

"What do you mean?"

"Larry Constantino's been running around here telling anyone who'll listen that Senator Tom Flanagan has been chosen by God to heal him, to bring him back from the dead, for God's sake!" Sheila stood up and moved close to her, staring her in the eyes like a prosecuting attorney. "Or hadn't you noticed?"

Estela remained cool. "Yes, I've noticed. . . ."

"So what did you and the senator do—come down and try your hand at playing God one more time?"

"I—" Estela was surprised and embarrassed. She had no idea anyone would be paying enough attention. Bad mistake. Never assume anything. That was one of the rules she lived by, and she'd ignored it. Nice going. . . .

"Because that's *exactly* what I think you did, Doctor, and it looks like it worked." Goldman's voice struggled to stay even, freighted with obvious emotion. "And I have to tell you—it's scaring the hell out of me."

"Sheila, who knows about this?"

"I don't know. I haven't been broadcasting it, but people aren't stupid, Estela. We're doctors, remember."

"I didn't mean it like that," she said. She paused, exhaled slowly, then: "You're right—Flanagan touched this boy, but I don't know what happened, what he did. I—I don't think *he* did, either."

"His cancer is *gone*, Estela. Like it was never there. People from all over the country want to test him. They think his body has developed some kind of natural antibody. There's nothing like this in the literature. Kids just don't get well like this."

She could only nod her head. She understood the implications of what had happened. Tom Flanagan had opened what could be a large can of worms. He must have known what he was doing. Was this his way of telling her something he could not put into words?

"What's next?" she asked softly.

Sheila Goldman raised her hands in a gesture of frustration. "I don't know. The rumor mill will be grinding. Hard to say. I would try to get in touch with that senator of yours. . . ."

"And say what?"

"Tell him what happened. Tell him that his own campaign manager thinks God is healing people through him . . ." Dr. Goldman paused. "And tell him he's got a Jewish agnostic pediatric specialist in Miami thinking she might have to believe it, too."

She tried to smile, couldn't pull it off, and tapped Estela on the shoulder as she moved to the central corridor of the ward. "Just thought I'd let you know what's in the wind. Let's go."

Estela nodded, looked back at the little boy in the bed watching cartoons. So cute. So much alive. Then she thought of all the others in this part of the hospital. All the little lives battling for more time. Why only this one, Tom Flanagan?

As she followed Sheila toward the elevators, she wondered if people, after seeing Lazarus come forth, asked Christ the same question. . . .

TWENTY

Lattimore

Erskine Lattimore sat back in his limo watching the northern Virginia farmlands along Route 66 roll past his view. He hated flying out of National Airport. Besides, the extra time to get to Dulles let him unwind, have a little bourbon from his home state of Tennessee, and have a few laughs with his traveling companion—whomever she might turn out to be.

Looking away from the tinted window, he smiled and winked at Veriana (had to be a bullshit name, but what did he care?). He'd met her during a night out with some of the Saudi delegation at a place on K Street called Joanna's. They boasted some of the most beautiful nude dancers in the world, and they usually were not too far off. Even the jaded sons and nephews of the sheiks were impressed, and that was the best flesh barometer he could think of.

"Another drink?" she asked with a half-smile. Veriana had learned somewhere in her short life that it was okay to be laconic and even stupid as long you had the kind of body that stopped traffic and a face that belonged on magazine covers. And if not there, then at least the centerfolds of the best stroke mags.

"Yeah, baby, not so much ice this time." Erskine patted her thigh, thinking of what lay a little farther up the trail.

"Sorry."

The intercom buzzed, and Erskine glared at the black panel that separated him from his driver of sixteen years, a Negro named Jackson. He slapped his hand down on the button and spoke loudly. "What is it?"

The intercom murmured without squawk or interference, *"Sorry to bug you, Senator, but I gotta call here from somebody says it's urgent."*

"Goddamn it, did you tell 'em I'm on my way to Buenos Aires?"

"Yessir, I did."

"Who the hell is it?" Erskine loved being a senator, but he hated the way people wanted to talk to him all the fucking time.

"Says his name is Burgess . . . with the Secret Service."

"I know who the fuck he's with! Tell him I'm picking up." Erskine grabbed his phone, keyed in the call, and blocked Jackson off the line. "Senator Lattimore. . . . Is that you, Harold?"

"Erskine, sorry to bother you. I heard you've got the dancer with you. Sorry, real sorry, but—"

"Save it, Harry. Just give me the meat and potatoes, boy."

"One of my men was on duty with your buddy last night."

"Flanagan? Where?"

Harold Burgess gave him the details.

Erskine laughed. "You called me to tell me *that*? Christ, Harry, everybody except his wife knows he's buffin' that movie slut! Don't you ever go to the supermarkets? The magazines're fulla that shit. People don't care about philanderin' anymore."

"That's not all, sir."

"Then make it fast. And make it good," said Erskine, taking the Jack Daniel's and rocks from Veriana.

Harold went on to summarize his agent's report, which indicated that Flanagan was possibly suffering from severe hallucinations and might be on the brink of some kind of psychological breakdown.

Erskine Lattimore smiled. "Good stuff, Harry. Very nice. Any way we can leak any of this without leaving a trail?"

"Oh, there's always a way."

"I'd like to start derailing this guy before the convention. This sounds like a good place to start. Nobody wants a headcase for a president."

"I'll keep a close eye on him for other developments, Senator."

"You do that, Harry. The usual favors are always available," said Erskine. "And, ah ... sorry about being so short with you back there."

"Hey, I know how it is when you're trying to get away for a few days," said Burgess. "Have you a real good time."

Erskine Lattimore clicked off. He shook his head to himself as he dwelled on his flunky's last line. It was getting more difficult than ever to enjoy anything in life. Closing in on sixty, Erskine had seen it all, done it all just a tad too many times, and nothing much excited him anymore except the power-tripping that being a senior senator and possible president provided. Kissinger had been so goddamned right about the aphrodisiac stuff. No bullstuff there.

He looked over at Veriana, who had uncrossed her long, muscular legs and had begun to stretch out like a jungle cat. There were two very good reasons why he was always trading in the bimbettes for a newer model every month or so: one, he could *do* it, so why not?; and two, because after about three rolls, he had a helluva time getting it up anymore for the same piece of trim.

Sometimes when he lay in his easy chair, half-liquored up, he wondered if he would trade everything he'd cheated and bargained for in his life for a chance to be sixteen years old again and have those legendary balls of fire. A teenaged boy spent half his waking hours with a hard-on, and would pretty much stick it in anything with a round hole—and that didn't rule out beehives and snake dens. Not when you were sixteen, no sir.

Blinking, Erskine brought himself back to the present. There wouldn't be any trading yourself in, he thought wistfully, so you'd better get to work on the issues at hand. Soon as he got back from this little junket, he'd sit down with Adlai Parker, his campaign manager, and plot out how they could use Flanagan's flaky behavior against him.

Add that in with Constantino already going on the public record as being a religious nut, and it looked like Flanagan's presidential bid was going down in flames.

But there was plenty of time for that stuff. Time for a little playtime.

He chuckled to himself, looked at the long stretch of twenty-one-year-old girl next to him. "You gettin' hungry, darlin'?"

She smiled. "I can always eat," she said. "Any suggestions?"

Senator Erskine Lattimore reached for the zipper on his Harris tweed trousers, but she stopped him.

He liked Veriana. She was a bit of a control freak.

TWENTY-ONE

Flanagan

He reached his Georgetown townhouse on P Street late in the afternoon of the next day.

The weather was pleasant by Washington standards— mid-seventies and humidity only high enough to keep you mildly uncomfortable. Early September in the nation's capital. Redskins fever was at high pitch and the college kids were filling up all the bars on M Street. He had grown so accustomed to the rituals of D.C., he hardly noticed them anymore. Not that he'd ever liked the town—because he hadn't. Living there was one of the things he had to do, and he'd done his best to ignore all the things about the city he absolutely loathed.

Rebecca was not on the premises, and that suited him just fine. Since getting out of the hospital, he'd been on the move almost sixteen hours a day to catch up, and he'd spoken to her only a few times, seen her even less.

Just thinking of his wife cued him to make a mental note—call the attorneys and have them look into the most painless and expedient route to a divorce. Maybe it wouldn't be so bad after all. Most people on the Hill were in agreement about the sex, marriage, divorce stuff: the voting public didn't care much anymore where you laid your pipe—as long as it was with somebody of the opposite sex. All that gay lover business didn't play very well in America's heartland; and despite the heavy doses of electoral votes from the liberal bastions of New York and California, you still needed to carry the conservative states to win.

He walked into what had, in earlier times, been called a "drawing room." Someone once told him the name's derivation and it was one of those pieces of useless information that just sticks with you. Usually connected to the dining room, the drawing room is where the men would repair after dinner to smoke their pipes and cigars and "draw out" engaging conversation.

(Yeah, there's lots of conversation going on around here. . . .)

These days, the room was actually a library or a study. Plenty of bookcases built in, and dark polished wood. Oriental rugs and a kind of cluttered baronial look to everything. It was a warm, traditionally masculine kind of room, and it often made him wish he smoked one of those aromatic pipe tobaccos that smelled so good, but tasted like rank compost.

Smiling ironically, Tom settled into his reading chair—an old Eames copy that never lost its charm for him. He picked up a sheaf of reports from his aides that demanded perusal if not actual reading. Just looking at the stack of paper, larger than most small town phone books, made him uneasy. There was something gnawing at his thoughts that wouldn't let go. Something he didn't feel like facing or dealing with, but he would have to.

Politics had been his passion for living, his *raison d'être*, and he knew it was different now. Didn't want to face it, but the knowledge had been pooling like old motor oil on the basement floor of all his thinking. In light of what had been happening to him, his political jousts and forays were just a bunch of silly, insubstantial games. Just a bunch of overgrown, arrogant, private school bullies having their way with the working peoples' money.

Jesus, how was he ever going to concentrate on anything again? The dreams or visions, or whatever the hell they were, threatened to destroy him. He had never in his life ever questioned his own mental stability. Christ, he'd never even been *depressed* in his whole goddamned life! He'd always looked at people who claimed they were depressed with a half-shot of sorrow and the other half highly distilled, chemically pure contempt. When he'd been younger, he could not bear to be around those whining, morose types.

Depressed. Shit. He'd always wanted to smack them in the face. They needed to realize that any day above ground was a *great fucking day*. They'd better wake up and enjoy what's going on because there was a big hammer coming sooner or later and it didn't care whether you were depressed or not.

But that, as they say, was then . . .

What was going on with him now was way beyond depression or anxiety or even a full-blown neurosis. He was convinced it was all *real* and that frankly scared him more than he could begin to articulate.

Something had happened to him. Either God (or whoever else was in charge), or maybe even some evil entity, was working through him—like Larry was telling anyone who would listen. Or . . .

Or it was Tom Flanagan himself.

Crazy thought, that.

But there was no denying there was a power in him. That was not to be questioned.

(Oh, you've got it all right. . . .)

It was like laying your soul across the powerlines that trunked into the big cosmic generator. You felt that hum of transcendent energy vibrate through you, and you just fucking *knew* it was real.

He remembered being very young, maybe four or five, when he ambled into his dad's garage where he kept all his power tools and there was a big, heavy power drill on the workbench. Young Tom had picked it up, and just for a second or two, his pudgy little finger had depressed the trigger. The drill had lurched into whirling churning life in his hands like something mean that just woke up. He could still remember letting go of that growling beast and watching it *clunk* to the floor. He'd been playing with the grown-ups' toys and it had terrified him.

And that's what this was like.

Because . . . if it *wasn't* real, if it was all in his head, then he was, indeed, an off-the-charts psycho, and he'd slipped out of phase with the rest of this reality. Slipped into some nether region where there was only one thruway, no exit ramps, and no way back.

Neither prospect presented much appeal. He had a sudden urge for a cigarette, and—

(—and where did that come from? A little self-destruct mechanism clicking into place, old buddy?)

Crazy. Because he hadn't smoked in almost twenty years. And yet the overwhelming pang of nicotine withdrawal surged through him like bad sewage.

Who or what was the burning man in the visions?

I'll be with you forever.

That's what he'd said—or something damned close. Whatever, it was not a pleasant thought. The only way to handle everything was to stop running away from it or trying to ignore it. It was not going to go away.

First thing to do was—

The phone rang at his desk, and he cursed as he unfolded himself from the chair. He liked making calls; hated answering them.

"Yes . . . what is it?"

"Is that the way a senator always answers his phone?"

The slightly raspy, sexy female voice had an instant effect on him. He recognized its source, but his mind, still trolling the depths of dark introspection, failed to make the right connection for a moment.

"Hello, are you there? Thomas Flanagan?"

"Yes, I'm here. . . ."

(Dr. Barrero, you idiot. It's Estela Barrero.)

"Sorry, Doctor, you caught me off guard."

"How are you feeling, Senator?"

"You called me Tom, once," he said without thinking, hoping he didn't sound too overanxious to be talking to her. "You can do it again."

She chuckled. "Maybe I will someday. You didn't answer my question."

"I . . . I haven't been too good."

"What's been happening? You'd better tell me." Her voice had slipped into a stern, professional mode effortlessly.

He was hearing her voice as though from a great distance, and he struggled to keep his consciousness. He wasn't the type to be fainting or anything like that, and the sudden disorientation scared him. He couldn't remember if he'd told her about the visions and dreams or not. Was it her or Valerie? Who knew the truth?

"Senator Flanagan . . . Tom? Are you there?"

Her voice touched him, elevated him from the fog of his own thinking. "Yes, I'm sorry, I was just thinking how to put this."

"Put what?"

He told her about the burning man, the night at Valerie's, all his fears and apprehensions. He told her everything about Larry and the crash. About sticking his hand into the wound. He just simply unloaded it all on her in a torrent of panicky speech that spoke of urgency and terror. It issued forth from him like a spilled ingot of steel and he was afraid she would recoil from it and his inability to deal with it.

But she didn't.

And when he was finally finished, when there was nothing he could think to add to the confessionlike explosion of inner torment, she calmly asked him if there was anything he might have overlooked.

"You're kidding, aren't you?" He touched his brow and realized he'd been sweating profusely.

"Not at all. I'm sorry you've been going through this so . . . so alone."

"Really? You mean that?"

She *tsked* at him. "I'm surprised you could ask me that—either as a doctor, *or* a woman."

"What is that supposed to mean?" He felt himself smiling, in spite of the anxiety he'd been releasing like waves of radiation.

"We can take it up later," she said, again assuming a very professional tone. "The reason I called is not going to make things any easier on you."

"Somehow I didn't think it would." He cleared his throat, continued. "It's the little boy, isn't it?"

"Yes. I figured you'd know."

He felt a lump growing in his throat and a knot of hot tears behind his eyes. It was a scary kind of emotional wrenching.

(Go on, say it. . . .)

"Cancer's gone, right?"

"Completely. Everybody's astounded. But that's not the heart of it, Tom."

(There, she said it again. . . .)

"What do you mean?"

She told him about members of the staff attaching his visit to the ward with the healing, with the general physical evidence of Larry Constantino and, of course, his religious ravings.

"What should I do?" he asked honestly and openly. Things seemed so complicated now, he felt no embarrassment in seeking her advice.

"Come back to the hospital. Submit to some more testing. If you try to deny everything much longer, you're only going to look worse."

She was right. He'd been around Washington long enough to know that things never remained status quo, they would usually, if not inevitably, get worse.

"All right," he said after a short pause. "But there are a few conditions I'll need met."

"Like what?"

"Like you can't tell anyone what I've told you. Not just yet anyway. I know people suspect all kinds of things. . . . Well, that's fine. Let them suspect all they want. I still need time to sort this out—with your help."

"I think we can deal with that," she said. "Anything else?"

He paused again, carefully constructing the politically correct phrasing. "I won't cooperate with any testing unless you are part of the team. I . . . I want you to be there."

Now it was her turn to pause. He could almost hear her thoughts across the fiber optics.

"There might be some friction on that point. Not from me, but the administration here doesn't see me as part of any research grants. I'm chief of emergency surgery. That's—"

"I don't care what it is, Doctor," he said, using his voice of authority—the one that caused aides and pages to sprint through the Senate Office Building. "Tell them if they want me, they're going to have to change your job title for a while."

"All right, I'll run it past them."

"Thank you." The way he let the words escape him, it made him sound so tired.

"Can I ask you one more thing?" Her whiskey voice always seemed to get his attention.

"What's that?"

"Why did you insist that I be part of the research team?"

(Don't blow it here. Say the right thing. The honest thing.)

"Because ... because I'm scared. Because I don't know who to trust, and I guess I've picked you, Doctor Barrero."

A short pause from her end of the line, then: "Thank you. I appreciate you telling me the truth. And you can call me Estela. All my friends do."

"I'm honored to be considered your friend." He smiled and wished she could see him feeling better. "When do you want me back in Miami?"

"Let me talk to the administration. Someone will be calling you tomorrow in an official capacity. I'll call, too. This number?"

"My office is better." He gave her the number that would get her a direct line to his desk.

"You'll be hearing from me," she said.

"Thank you," he said softly. "Those words are hard for me to say and really mean it. But I really do."

An awkward silence followed. Tom waited for a reply, but the other end of the line was dead. Had she heard his last piece of heart-pouring?

(What're you worried about ... ?)

At that moment he realized it was important that he try to be honest with this woman. More honest than he'd been with anyone in a very long time.

Later that day, he returned to his Senate office, where his aides had been doing their best to maintain control of an enormous backlog of phone calls and mail. Neil Schlag, his long-time office manager, had trained everyone to carefully screen and categorize everything. His long absences were not that unusual, and without a staff to help him sort through the thousands of attempts to contact his office, he would sink faster than a torpedoed freighter.

"You've had more than a hundred requests for interviews," said Neil. "What's going on, boss? Rumors are flying all over the place. *The Weekly Enquirer* says they have an exclusive from an eyewitness, but they'd like to give you a chance to clear it."

Tom looked up from between two stacks of envelopes from his "urgent" bin. "Eyewitness to *what*?"

Neil shrugged. "Didn't say. You want to call them back?"

"Fuck 'em. Everything they run is full of bullshit anyway. Why're they being so nice to me?"

"Nina says they only do that to the people they're afraid of."

Tom leaned back and considered that one. It was true enough, and yet, the supermarket rags had never worried about *his* wrath or power when they first started splashing cover pictures of him and Valerie Berenson. Why the sudden change of tactics?

"Neil, you have any idea what's going on? What this could be about?" Tom looked for a copy of *USA Today* amidst the snowdrifts of paper, gave up.

"There's something on the wire services about a Doctor Sheila Goldman. From Keller Memorial in Miami. Calling a press conference for later today. But no word on the subject matter. No mention of you."

Tom looked at him warily. "So why'd you bring it up?"

Neil Schlag raised both hands like he'd been ambushed. "Hey, that was the hospital where they were keeping you. I figured there might be a connection, that's all."

Tom shook his head. "That's the trouble with all you people—you're too damned smart."

His intercom buzzed. "Yes, Amanda. . . ."

"I've got Larry on line two."

"Kick him in."

A click in the receiver, then: "Tom! Where have you been? I've got great news!"

"Calm down, Larry. You knew I was going to be in Manhattan for a few days. I just got back this morning."

"Oh yeah, that's right. I . . . I, uh, try not to think about those Big Apple trips of yours."

(Keep it up, old buddy. . . .)

"Since you got that old-time religion, eh?" Tom had no compunction about giving it right back to him.

"Since before that, but what-the-hey, I've got more important things to talk to you about."

"I'm listening. . . ."

"Everybody wants to talk to you, Tom. Interest in you is at an all-time high. CNN, ISN, all the print media . . . ! If you're not the front-runner for the job, then nobody is!"

"Calm down, Larry," he said softly.

"Hey, man, listen, I know you're still ticked about the last interview we gave, but you've got to understand— "

"You made us both look like assholes, Larry."

"God, I wish you wouldn't talk like that."

(I'm sure God doesn't like it, either. . . .)

"Larry, we need to have a long talk. Why don't we have a few drinks at Dominique's? Have dinner."

"When did you have in mind?"

"As soon as possible. Meet me in the bar at six o'clock. Tonight."

"Well, I'd— "

"No bullshit, Larry. Just be there."

Before his best friend could say another word, Tom replaced the receiver in its cradle. There was a lot to be done today. Right now. He would deal with Larry Constantino later.

Looking up from his desk, he noticed Neil Schlag still standing there. "Heard enough?" asked Tom pointedly.

"Boss, it's business as usual—I don't know nothin'."

"Keep it that way. Go. Get back to whatever you were doing, and tell Amanda to bring me the Number One list. Let's see if we can knock a few holes in it. And see who wants some OT this week—we've got to clear out all the junk mail from my constituents."

"Overtime?" asked Schlag. "You planning to be gone again?"

Tom steepled his hands on his blotter. "Might have to go back to Miami for more tests."

"Christ! When?"

"Maybe tomorrow. The next day. We'll have to see."

Neil nodded, turned to leave, then paused. "I have this feeling there's a thing or two you're not telling me, and you know what?—I like it like that."

His office manager disappeared, closing the door upon his exit. Tom leaned back in his chair, surveying the impossibly high columns of correspondence, notices, requests, demands, petitions, briefs, bills, studies, and other assorted crap that finds its way to a senator's office. If he had three times as many hours in a day, he still couldn't get close to reading everything that came in.

The founding fathers never could have imagined how complicated things had become. They had set into motion a great piece of machinery that, once running, seemed to be able to perpetuate its own energy source. The government seemed to run on without anyone applying additional momentum. Like a locomotive on endless rails with nobody wearing the engineer's hat. And Tom, seeing how everything worked from the inside, sometimes grew apprehensive and even fearful that the machine had become a juggernaut, an unstoppable, devouring engine of human resource and will. A lumbering, destructive, and consuming monster that could never be laid low.

And he wanted to be in charge of the machine. . . .

Or did he?

Up until the plane crash, there had been no doubt. He had been playing his political career by the numbers and he had been loving it. The power, the influence, the inside information, totally global reach for anything from a lunch in Paris to the latest spy satellite photos of the Middle East. Once you reached a certain pinnacle, anything was attainable, and Tom had thought he'd reached that point. He thought he had everything until . . .

. . . until he'd been given this terrifying power.

The truth of it replayed though his head like a skipping phonograph needle.

(*Phonograph?* You're showing your age, old buddy. . . .)

He had the power and there was no turning away from it. Sharing it all with Estela Barrero had somehow made his situation more real, more acceptable. He had tried to open up like that to Valerie, but something was missing, something hadn't clicked into place. There was a barrier, a threshold of empathy and intellect that he could never pass with her. Too many years in the West Coast dream factory, he feared. She'd lived too long in a rarefied atmosphere where money had long ago lost all meaning and everyone without a Rolls and a Ferrari in their garage was considered a peasant. She'd spent too much time cut off from the real values of human life.

(Kind of like yourself, wouldn't you say?)

He looked out his office window toward Pennsylvania Avenue, shaking his head. What was happening to him? Mid-forties and he was suddenly growing a conscience? Just what he needed.

(That's right, maybe it is.)

The thought remained in his head like the afterimage from a cheap flash camera. Not until he acknowledged the possible truth in it did it begin to fade away.

His limo deposited Tom at the porte cochere of Dominique's. A discreetly distanced agent followed him inside, but took a place at the bar where he could monitor the situation. A table had been selected that would afford the agent a workable view and access. Larry was already seated, and that was odd because his old friend had never been a very punctual type. Standing up and smiling at his approach, Larry grabbed his hand and pumped it vigorously.

"Tom, great to see you. You look great!"

He spoke in a loud, phony voice that attracted the attention of all the surrounding tables. Tom could feel the stares of other patrons and he felt himself getting angry already.

(Just cool it. Plenty of time for that. Don't get him on the defensive. You gotta talk to this guy.)

"Thanks, Larry. Glad you could make it."

"No kidding. Boy, did we get thrown offtrack or what? Nothing like a plane crash to shake things up a little, heh?" Larry was leaning forward, his hands folded in front of him. He presented an almost constant half smile, as though he were just bursting with uncontrollable joy and goodwill. It was enough to put a used car salesman to shame.

"It has been very disruptive, yes. My office was a real shitstorm. Going to take a while to dig out."

"No kidding. My staff held things together pretty well while I was gone, but it felt good to get back into the driver's seat. I know what you want to talk about, Tom—we've got to get this campaign back into high gear."

"Well—"

"And let me tell you," said Larry, on a real roll now, "all this crash publicity has been great! You are the hot topic at every power-lunch in America."

"That's part of what I—"

Larry held up his martini glass with the customary stack of olives on a pin. "You getting a cocktail?"

(Jesus, this guy is wired. . . .)

Tom nodded, and a waiter materialized from the ether. He ordered a double Jack neat, and looked back to his friend after the waiter had left. "Larry, we've been the best of friends for a long time, so I want you to listen carefully to what I need to ask you, and what I have to tell you, okay?"

He smiled, sipped from his glass. "Sure. Whatever you want. I'm on your side."

The waiter returned with Tom's drink, disappeared again.

"Why do you think the media wants to talk to me?"

Larry grinned. "C'mon, you know why? Because I told them about God and you! How He picked you to save my life, Tom. C'mon, you know that."

Tom buried his face in his hands for an instant, as though he could wipe all this away from his sight, and likewise his life. "Why in hell did you have to start talking about this? Don't you know how . . . how *nutty* it sounds?"

"What?"

"Larry, we used to make fun of those TV preachers, those guys with the healing shows . . . don't you remember?"

"Yeah, but this is different—"

"To you, maybe, sure! But to the average viewer, the average *voter*, it's just more of that old-time religion stuff, that Bible-thumping chicanery."

"Tom, I'm Catholic. Not some born-again—"

He shook his head. "You're not getting it, Larry. Stop being so narrowly focused here. You can usually see how things affect the masses, the big scale, that's why you're the best campaign manager in the business. So why can't you *see* this?"

Larry leaned closer across the table. "Because I was *dead*, Tom!" He spoke evenly and a little too loud. Tom could sense heads turning, tuning in. "Because I was skewered like these freaking olives here!"

"Keep your voice down, will you?"

Ignoring him, Larry continued. "Because I was *floating*, Tom, floating above everything, and maybe it was a dream and maybe it wasn't, but I *know* I was dead!"

"It wasn't a dream." The words eased out of him and he felt a great Sisyphean weight leave him.

"What?" Larry looked as though he'd been slapped in the face.

Tom spoke in a half-whisper as he detailed everything that had happened that night at the crash. He tried to tell his friend what it felt like, and how utterly scary it had been. He told him about the test results and the separated tissue in his brain, and the visions and the desperate feeling that maybe he was losing his mind. The words came with great difficulty, with long periods of silence punctuated only by more cocktails from the waiter. He had no idea how much time they consumed, but he was getting drunk and feeling better and better about everything.

Larry listened with the intense devotion of an altar boy. "Tom, why didn't you say something sooner?"

"Because I didn't know how to say it. My world's been ripped inside out, don't you see that? How can I worry about winning an election when somebody or something has other plans for me?"

"I know what you mean," said Larry. "I used to know this guy—he'd been a marine in Nam. He had this Zippo lighter with an inscription on it: *In order to really live, you must have nearly died.* Funny, I always thought that was kind of stupid. I don't anymore."

"What do we do now?" Tom asked the question as much rhetorically as anything, but Larry tackled it.

"Go back to Miami. Get the other tests done."

"What about all this damned flak you've generated? I'd like to do this without being hounded."

Larry nodded, smiled. "I got you, boss. I'll handle it. Don't worry about a thing."

"No interviews, do you understand?" Tom finished his bourbon, wondered if he could handle another one without eating anything yet.

Larry looked at him askance, but nodded animatedly. "Sure, I got it. But, damn, I sure hate to waste all this positive energy being handed to us."

"What?"

"I mean we don't even have to go out and beat the drum, Tom. They're coming to us."

"I don't care if they're throwing money at us."

"Hey, if we keep a big lid on you much longer, some of them *will*. The tabloid shows have big budgets now. If they smell an exclusive, the money'll be there."

"Well, tell 'em to go fuck themselves," he said, feeling the bourbon smudge his thoughts around the edges. "Everything I've told you tonight, Larry—it's got to stay between us."

"Tom, you can count on me."

He looked at his oldest friend and wondered if that were still true.

He arrived back at his Georgetown home just before 11:00 P.M. Rebecca was in the den, watching television. He stood in the foyer, looking into the room, wondering what was going on. This was not like her at all. She claimed to hate staying up late, watching television, or listening to the news. . . .

Walking one step into the room, he waited until she looked up. "Good evening, dear," he said softly, then continued to stare.

When she offered no explanation for her out-of-character behavior, he asked her bluntly what was going on.

She smiled that awful sardonic smile of hers. "Where have you been—on the moon?"

"I was having dinner with Larry." He looked at the television, where channel nine was just slipping into its opening credits for the late newscast. "Why, what's going on? What did I miss?"

Chuckling darkly, Rebecca looked at him. "Oh, I don't think you missed much of anything."

The opening story featured a Dr. Sheila Goldman, the director of Pediatric Oncology at Keller Memorial Hospital in Miami. The TV journalist detailed the story of the miraculous cancer cure of seven-year-old Bobby Marzano. Near death, overwhelmed by cancer cells throughout his body, Bobby woke up several days ago without a trace of the disease. This, said Dr. Goldman, after several hospital personnel reported a doctor and Maryland Senator Thomas Flanagan paying a midnight visit to the boy's bedside. Efforts to reach the senator for comment have been thus far unsuccessful.

"Oh, Jesus . . ." was all he said. Schlag had told him about a press conference, but he'd forgotten about it completely.

"The phone's been ringing off the hook," said Rebecca. "I finally just turned the damned thing off. There were reporters hanging around outside, but I told them you were out of town."

"Thanks."

"I did it for *me*, not you."

Tom said nothing, rubbed his eyes.

(What the fuck was happening . . . what did this all mean?)

"Do you intend to tell me what this is all about?" Rebecca spoke to him as though he were a little boy.

"I don't know what they're talking about. Leave it at that, would you?"

"You're lying to me! But what else is new?"

"Rebecca, please, not now. . . ."

She smiled meanly again. "Oh wait, there's more. Look."

The newscast had slipped back from a one-minute commercial to highlight a "related story" in which upscale residents of co-ops in the Trump Tower on Fifth Avenue complained of a middle of the night disturbance in one of the building's poshest apartments. Undisclosed sources suggested that Senator Thomas Flanagan, while visiting actress Valerie Berenson, had a confrontation with one of the Secret Service agents assigned to his protection. The nature of the disturbance was unknown, but a source who wished to remain anonymous suggested that Flanagan had been suffering from a hallucinatory episode.

(Those bastards! Good old D.C. lightning strikes again. . . .)

"This was all on Fox at ten o'clock, too." Rebecca sighed in mock drama. "So it's old news by now."

"It's all bullshit," he said hollowly.

"Oh, I'm sure it's all just a wonderful publicity stunt, eh, Tom."

He walked across the room to the wet bar, splashed some Jack Daniel's into a tumbler. "It's a hatchet job, can't you see that? Somebody's trying to do me in!"

"Well, I'm sure a man like you has plenty of enemies." Rebecca stood, walked to the doorway and paused.

"It's too hard to explain, Rebecca. You wouldn't understand."

(Why even bother to try—especially with her?)

She laughed softly. It was a plaintive sound, full of antimirth, but a laugh just the same. "You don't have to explain a thing, Tom, because I don't care anymore. Whatever is happening to you, just do me a favor—leave me out of it, okay?"

Without thinking, he picked up a heavy, marble ashtray and threw it at the big-screen TV. It entered the phosphor field of the glass like an armor-piercing shell and the massive Sony erupted into a minivolcano. Sparks and smoke incendiaried across the oriental carpet and the coffee table.

Rebecca stood calmly, not moving, watched the little sparklers burn themselves out, then slipped away from the room.

Tom stood with his hands at his sides, his shoulders slumped. He sensed a darkness descend on him like the curtain falling on the final act of a very bad play.

TWENTY-TWO

Gunnderson

Jarmusch Gunnderson sat across the finely appointed table with two suits from the Tobacco Coalition. He felt like an actor in a Broadway hit—tired, bored, but glad to be getting the work. A scene he'd played out at least a thousand times before. It didn't matter that sometimes the lawyer-lunch restaurant was a train station or a library reference room or a rest stop men's room off I-95. It meant even less that the package was a briefcase or a hollowed-out dictionary or a sports bag. And the suits sometimes weren't even suits, but Jarmusch knew that somewhere along the food chain there would *always* be suits.

"Well, we certainly hoped you like your meal, Mr. Gunnderson," said Evanston "Tad" Gerringer. He was a big, lard-assed type. All jowls and pinched-up hog's eyes. Even an Armani looked like a split onion skin on a guy so bottom heavy.

"It was excellent, gentlemen," said Jarmusch. "But then, how can you question Argentine beef?"

Polite, gentle, and very southern laughter. The two suits looked at one another and nodded. Norbert Beaumont, the one sitting closest to Jarmusch, smiled and nudged the brief-case by his feet. It slid across the floor under the table until meeting the resistance of Jarmusch's Gucci loafer.

"Ooops, I must have kicked your briefcase by accident, Mr. Gunnderson," said Beaumont with a leering smile, the kind Jarmusch would have thought the man reserved for teenaged hookers working the parking lots at South of the Border.

"No problem, I'll handle it," said Jarmusch, finishing his cappuccino. "Thank you very much."

"I'm sure Representative Harbaugh'll handle it, too," said Tad Gerringer. "These goddamned health nuts're tryin' ta put us outta bizness!"

Jarmusch looked at him squarely. "Every issue must have two sides, or it wouldn't be much of an issue, would it?"

Norbert Beaumont looked at him quizzically. "Well . . . I guess so."

The deal being sealed up, Jarmusch felt like he could have a little fun with them. Leaning closer, enacting a con-spiratorial smile that begged for a wink, he said: "Now, come on, guys, you aren't going to sit here and tell me you don't believe nicotine is a drug . . . ?"

Beaumont and Gerringer looked at each other and shrugged. The amorphous slob rolled his eyes and grinned. He looked like a caricature of the man in the moon. "Well, of course it's a drug. But not like the shit they sell on the street."

Jarmusch smiled again. "Don't kid yourselves. Every heroin junkie I ever knew told me the same thing: kicking the white horse was a hundred times easier than cigarettes."

"That's an old story." Beaumont waved it off with a dis-missive gesture.

"Doesn't mean you don't believe it, Mr. Beaumont. C'mon, it's okay. I'm on your side, fellas! I just like to know we're all on the same page. I mean, we're fixing this thing because we know the opposition's right—ain't that the way it is?"

"Huh?" said Beaumont. He was so slow on the draw, it was a wonder he could dress himself in the morning.

Jarmusch smiled again. "Look, if your backers believed there was really nothing wrong with nicotine, they wouldn't fear the results of the upcoming congressional hearings, right?"

"Well, yeah, of course!" said Gerringer, pounding a pudgy fist on the table.

"I mean why else do you feel it necessary to pay off the congressman who's going to chair the hearing? I just want you guys to be honest with me, that's all."

Gerringer was obviously losing his patience. "We don't have to be honest with you or anybody else, Mr. Gunnderson. That's why we're paying off you and your pork-barreling politician cronies!"

Jarmusch chuckled, said nothing. That usually made these types more anxious, angrier.

"Just what's going on here, Mr. Gunnderson? Why the sudden change of attitude? Until you walk out of here, you don't really have the money yet."

He chuckled, looked from the tall, thin Beaumont to the rounded Gerringer. "Really? Who's going to stop me? Neither of you—I can assure you."

They looked at him as if seeing him for the first time, but said nothing. At six three, with a linebacker's build and speed, Jarmusch feared no man. He had learned how to carry himself, to project this attitude automatically. Purposely, he kept his hair cut in a military brush, or flat-top, because it added to his sharp-edged, don't-fuck-with-me image.

"Okay, I don't get it. What's going on?" Gerringer was wary now.

"Just my insurance policy against guys like you," said Jarmusch. He reached into his jacket pocket and both men flinched until he pulled out a Cross pen. "Micro-dot transmitter. Our conversation is being archived miles from here. No tape. No wire. It's already digitized, guys."

Beaumont looked like somebody'd gutted him. Gerringer just looked angry. "Why? What is this, a setup?"

Jarmusch smiled. "Relax. Your fix is still in. Congressman Harbaugh doesn't know shit about this. A long time ago I learned that it was a good idea to protect myself from either guys like you or the criminals on the Hill. This way, my lawyers make everything public if anything ever happens to me."

"Anything? Ever?" Beaumont's slack-jawed expression of panic and pain had faded.

Jarmusch smiled. "Let's just say there's a lot of people in Washington who will want me to die of old age with my grandchildren at my bedside." He pocketed the pen slowly, feeling their gaze follow its path.

Standing up, he grabbed the briefcase full of wrapped hundred-dollar bills, and offered to shake both their hands. Reluctantly, they acceded with their right paws. "Let's hope we never see each other again, eh, gentlemen? Thank you very much."

Using the main entrance, he left the restaurant and stepped into a congressional staff car waiting at curbside. The ride to Harbaugh's colonial residence in Fairfax would take less than a half hour. Jarmusch leaned back in his seat and closed his eyes. There was no need to check the contents of the case, no need to even count it. It would be jake, no doubt about that. Harbaugh could count out his share soon enough. It was just another—

His PCS phone vibrated silently in his shirt pocket. Sets of two short bursts indicated somebody was coming in on his "VIP" line—the one he reserved for relatives and close friends and as few slime bags as possible. Because in his business, you knew a lot of the latter types.

Reaching into the pocket of his double-twill oxford shirt, he picked up a folded handset no bigger than a woman's compact. He flipped open the receiver and keyed it on with his ID fingerprint.

"You've got me," he said softly, half expecting to hear his mother's voice. Seventy-three and very lonely even though his wealth and influence had ensconced her in the best "senior community" in Northern Virginia.

"Jar? It's Tom. Tom Flanagan."

He brightened at the sound of Flanagan's voice. One of his oldest friends, he always liked hearing from his old fraternity brother. "Hey, Senator, what's going on?"

"I catch you at a bad time?"

Jarmusch snorted. "Just finishing a bag job. No biggie. I take it this is no social call—you ringing down from the satellite and all."

"Not exactly. You seen any of the news lately?" Flanagan sounded tired, on edge. The Mercedes took a hard corner and Jarmusch was reminded he was not alone. Pushing a button on the right-hand door, the tinted privacy panel slid up to wall him off from the driver.

"Ah, I keep my finger on it. I've seen your name mentioned a few times, if that's what you mean."

"Jar, I'm going to need your help. You know I don't try to bug you. I know you're busy and I don't want you doing anything to compromise your situation in the snake pit . . . but—"

"Hey, what're you talking about? Say no more. If it wasn't for you, I'd probably be a sales manager for some chain of auto parts stores. I owe you, man. Way I figure it, I'll *always* owe you."

"Well, you don't, but I do need some help right now."

"Shoot, brother. . . ."

"Somebody's out to get me on the Hill. Whoever it is has wires in with the Secret Service and probably the White House, too. Helster or Dolmann come to mind. But Lattimore and Mendoza are also possibilities."

"What about the agencies? The hardballers?"

"Yeah, maybe them, too."

"So what do you want from me?"

Flanagan outlined his intentions to be in Miami, explained the tests, his problems with Larry Constantino, and even his wife. "I just need somebody on the inside who can let me know if there's any action on me. Information, Jar . . . it's better than gold in D.C. You know that."

"Go down to Miami and rest easy," said Jarmusch. "I'll be your 'Deep Throat.'"

"Okay, when I get set up down there, I'll give you some PCS code numbers. You'll be able to reach me anywhere."

"No problem."

"Thanks, Jar. I don't know what I'd do without you."

"One thing you might tell me, though—?"

"What's that?" Flanagan's voice tightened just a bit.

"Is any of this stuff true? What I've been hearing and all?"

There was a pause on the line. He could hear his friend exhaling. "Yeah, it probably is. I don't understand it, and it scares the shit out of me. That's why I have to get the rest of these tests done."

"Don't let it turn into a circus," he said.

"That's why I need your help."

"You got that. I'll be waiting to get the numbers and then you'll be hearing from me on a regular basis."

They said their good-byes and Jarmusch folded up the little phone and slipped it back into his pocket.

TWENTY-THREE

Barrero

She had to hand it to Tom Flanagan. The last time he flew into Miami, he ended up in the Everglades. And here he was doing it again. The thought amused her as she waited for him at the incoming gate for the flight from National Airport.

Funny, but was that a twinge of excitement she was feeling? Estela smiled, checked and adjusted her sleeves. This would be the first time he'd ever seen her out of her "uniform" of surgical greens and the ever-present white lab coat. Jeans and a Nordstrom blouse with a belt made of strung-together copper suns, and a pair of snakeskin boots. The look she sought was casual, but still stylish. She thought about letting her hair down, but he might not recognize her if she looked too different.

When he appeared at the gate, she noticed an agent keeping a close but discreet distance behind him, and wondered how anyone could get accustomed to knowing someone was practically always watching you.

Waving, she caught his attention and watched his expression as he registered uncertainty when he saw her. She read his lips as he said *Doc-tor Ba-rer-ro?*, then smiled and waved at him.

He approached her, shifting his briefcase to his left hand so he could shake hands very courteously. "That's an interesting look. Think it'll catch on in ER?"

They exchanged awkward greetings and both felt an obvious tension in the meeting. It felt like some sort of illicit rendezvous, even though it was perfectly up-and-up. After retrieving his baggage at the carrousel, she suggested a quick dinner, then get him checked into the hospital. He agreed readily, and maybe even a little too quickly.

They stopped at a small Cuban place called Fidel's, where the service was excellent, the food authentic, and the atmosphere a congruent mix of airy and secluded. Sitting in a booth elevated and away from the dance floor, they had an interesting view of the night sky and just enough of the Latin music to fill in any pauses in their conversation.

Once he'd had a cocktail and she a strawberry margarita, the sphere of tension that enclosed them began to dissolve. He gave her a quick update on the impending problems with his wife, Rebecca, with some of his political adversaries in the Senate, and possibly even with Larry Constantino.

"Oh, yes, I heard he's been scheduled to be seen at Johns Hopkins," she said casually, "by Doctor Klausmeyer . . ."

"He's *what*?" asked Flanagan. She realized it would be difficult to consistently think of him as "Tom" just yet. "He never mentioned anything like that to me. . . . When did you find out about it?"

"Oh, I don't remember," she said. "At least a week ago. Maybe longer. Klausmeyer is world famous, so it was something that would filter down to the big guys here at Keller."

"*When?* When is this happening?"

"Can't remember exactly. This week, I think."

He shook his head, obviously trying to explain to himself why he never picked up this detail. "Why didn't he tell me . . . ?"

"Maybe it slipped his mind."

"No. When I mentioned coming down here—it would have been the natural place for him to tell me he was going back for his *own* new batch of tests. No, Doctor, I've known Larry all my life—he loves to talk, can't resist running on about everything. No, if he *wanted* to tell me about Hopkins, he would have."

"Then he doesn't want you to know . . ."

Flanagan nodded. "I'll find out what's going on," he said, coloring his words with the first splashes of anger. "The idiot! He knows I've got connections everywhere. He had to know I'd find out."

"Maybe he didn't care," she said. "As long you were going to be gone, and he knew he didn't have to face you with the truth. Why does this bother you?"

"Because it's out of character for Larry."

"Yes, but you said he's changed since the incident— maybe this is just part of it."

"No, he's got something going on. I *know* him all too well."

Their waiter appeared with dinner, and slowly the conversation slipped away from the edge of anger and expressions of betrayal. She could tell from the way he talked, even in general, that he was distracted, confused, and apprehensive. He was presenting a side of himself she would have never expected from her infrequent samplings of his public persona. Even her brief conferences with him as a patient had revealed him to be confident and extremely competent. But as he made no effort to hide his deepest feelings, Thomas Flanagan seemed to be just as insecure and full of contradictions as the rest of us.

When she checked him into Keller, they entered the hospital through the employees-only access doors and were cleared by building security staff. Chief of Staff Hansen arranged to meet them in his office, where he fawned all over the senator and promised him the hospital's fullest compliance with his wishes regarding the absence of publicity and protection from members of the media. Flanagan seemed pleased, but appeared antsy and anxious to get away from everyone.

Reaching the floor where his private room would be located, she said goodnight at the elevator, but he kept her from entering the waiting car with a slight touch to her arm.

"Wait . . ."

She felt she was sixteen and just back from an awkward, but enjoyable, first date. "Yes . . . ?"

"I've been told it's hard for me to tell people I appreciate them. . . . Hell, that I even need their help in the first place! But," he said, pausing, "I have to tell you *thanks*. For listening, and for getting this whole thing set up."

"Really, you don't have to—"

"Because I think I really need some help here. I really need to know what's going on with me. I have a feeling things could fall apart very fast, and, well—thanks for everything." He looked away from her as he finished the sentence, looking in that moment like a little boy.

For the briefest instant, she had the urge to lean forward and kiss him because he looked so vulnerable and innocent. But she stopped herself just as fast. This guy was just a real charmer, she thought as her relationship radar started beeping. The most foolish thing she could ever do is fall for the practiced speech tactics of a lifelong politician.

This guy was going to have to prove himself to her. Not after a single dinner and a foot-shuffling little gee-it's-hard-to-say thank-you.

Without realizing it, she had pulled back from him. He must have noticed it, too, because he looked at her with a curious expression. "Hey, Doctor," he said with a smile. "Was it something I said?"

Recovery time. She had to save this one. "No, not at all. You just reminded me of someone else for a second there. Sorry."

Flanagan nodded. "I know the feeling. Takes you back, doesn't it?"

She batted her big eyes, looked down. It was a conscious, woman-thing she knew men loved because it made her look so vulnerable and it distracted them from what they might have been trying to think or say.

"Yes," she said softly. "Yes it does."

"Well, goodnight," he said. "See you in the morning?"

"You're the first and only patient on the schedule. Count on it."

The elevator door began sliding closed and she caught it with her hand. Stepping inside, she could feel the weight of his gaze on her back, and when she turned to face him, he was doing his best puppy-dog look. She gave him a small, cautious smile and released the door. He continued to stare at her as the sliding panel separated them.

Inside the solitary cubicle, Estela sagged against the back wall. It was late, she was physically and mentally taxed by what lay ahead. She had no idea how she felt about Thomas Flanagan unloading all his psychic baggage on her. On one hand, her natural maternal and caring instincts found instant appeal in it, but she was also trying to be careful with her own emotions. This kind of situation could become a very charged and volatile package.

Ever since losing Antonio, she'd made an unspoken pact with herself that she would never get that close to anyone ever again. There just weren't enough good reasons to get so enmeshed in another's life because if that life was yanked away from you, it was like losing a part of your own body, and worse, a part of your soul.

And once gone, you were never getting it back.

That wasn't conjecture—she knew the pain of such loss from the inside out. Her uncle had taught her an old proverb he claimed was from Spain, appropriated by the Argentines, that said: *Once you are a philosopher in all things; but twice you are oftentimes the fool.*

What was she going to do? Why had she agreed to his terms? Why did Flanagan want her to be part of the team that examined him? Was he being truthful that he simply trusted her?

The elevator doors opened, depositing her in the lobby, where a crowd of people pushed and surged around a central knot of figures. Their minicamcorders and mikes bristled from extended arms and hands and Estela stepped back, cringing.

How could they know Flanagan was here already? It was impossible—unless Chief Hansen had lied completely and was already giving up his prized patient for a little more time in the spotlight. And based on what she already knew about Hansen, *nothing* that sleazy little character did would surprise her.

Rather than get involved, she turned away from the commotion and headed toward the nearest exit. Better she walk a little farther to her car than deal with the boorish tactics of the TV and radio "journalists" who would attempt to break the trust she'd just forged with Flanagan.

But as she turned to leave the lobby, she heard a familiar voice emanating from the center of the media-knot. Looking back from the exit door, she saw Dr. Sheila Goldman trying to work her way through the encapsulating crowd.

". . . please," she was saying. "If you will just allow me to get into the conference room— "

"Where's that, Doctor?" someone interjected.

"The B Wing. First floor," she said hastily. Dr. Goldman looked up as she turned away from the reporter, and quite by accident spied Estela standing at the end of the lobby watching the whole scene. Their stares locked on each other's and Estela felt herself growing angry.

"Excuse me," said Sheila Goldman. "If you would all meet me in the first-floor conference room, I will be happy to answer all your questions. Now, please, excuse me for a minute. . . ."

She left the crowd of media people and walked directly to Estela, who waited for her with her arms crossed and her expression turning into a dark glare.

"Estela, I'm sorry, it's not what you think."

"Oh, I'm sure you're just *hating* all this publicity. Praise be to Andy Warhol, eh? Are you enjoying your fifteen minutes?"

"Estela, will you give me a chance to explain?"

She was about to launch into a few choice sentences, but paused. "All right—what?"

"One of the night nurses went to *Tough Copy*—that shitty TV show—wanting to sell them an exclusive on Flanagan."

"Exclusive? On *what*?"

"That he can heal the sick, that he's got God's touch . . . I don't know . . . some kind of tabloid nonsense."

"Oh, no. . . . So what happened?"

"I was here when they contacted the hospital, and I didn't want it all sensationalized and cheapened. As much for the Marzano family as for the senator . . . so I one-upped them, stole their thunder. I called the networks and the satellite services. I gave it away in as dignified a manner as I could without saying anything."

"I'm not sure I get it, Sheila. Why?"

"Because with my story out there first, the tabloid version will look more like a desperate move to make something out of nothing. Make it appear to be . . . you know, a shot in the dark. And a silly one at that."

What her friend said made sense, but Estela was tired and confused and beginning to feel extremely overwhelmed by it all. She just wanted to get out of there and go home and not talk to anyone about anything for a while.

"If you say so, Sheila . . . I don't know about anything right about now. I just feel like nothing good can come of any of this."

"Why? What do you mean?" Goldman looked at her cautiously.

"Because we just don't know what we're dealing with, Sheila. It could be . . . I don't know . . . it could be dangerous."

"Estela, he saved a little boy's life!"

"You don't *know* that."

"He saved Larry Constantino's life. The man said so himself."

"What're you saying, then, Sheila? That this guy Flanagan is like . . . like *God*?"

"Yeah, now wouldn't that be rich?" Goldman smiled ironically. "No, Estela, I'm saying a life was saved, and that's the whole reason we're in this business, isn't it?"

Estela nodded but lacked the conviction she knew she should feel. She knew she had her own reason for being in medicine: it was a great place to hide from yourself. So easy to just lose yourself in the hours of overwork and get so involved in the lives and troubles of your patients, you had no time to worry about your own. She was more than well aware of this mechanism. There had even been a seminar devoted to it, fraught with warnings that doctors should be ever on the watch for the danger signs. But she had been too busy to attend it.

Looking at her watch, Sheila Goldman made a motion to leave. "Listen, we need to talk about this more," she said. "But it's getting really late, and I've got those people in the conference room. . . ."

"That's okay," said Estela. "I'm so tired. I just want to get out of here and go home."

That was enough of a dismissal for Sheila. She wheeled and half-jogged out of the lobby. Estela headed in the opposite direction.

When she parked the BMW in her palm-shrouded driveway, the moon was high in the sky. A romantic moon, a lovers' moon. The thought struck her as odd and inappropriate, yet it would not leave her. Entering the house and disarming the security system, she began unbuttoning her blouse as she walked toward her bedroom. As she walked through the rooms, turning on lights, she found herself looking at everything as though for the first time. You could tell a lot about a person by assessing their home environment, and she was a little concerned about what someone might infer after seeing her place.

Everything looked untouched, from the kitchen and its appliances to the magazines on the coffee table. Somebody had clearly arranged everything in this house, but they certainly didn't live here. Stopping in the hall so that she could look both into her bedroom and back out toward the dining room and patio doors, she felt a sadness come over her.

Her house was like a museum, or worse, a mausoleum. No living went on here. It was a truth she usually kept out of mind, but for some reason, she couldn't get rid of it now. If someone were to see her home, would they realize what she already knew? And why was she suddenly worrying about anybody coming here? Since Tino had been killed, she couldn't remember the last time anybody had been out here to visit her.

For the first few months after he died, her friends made a point of inviting her to parties and events, to dinners and performances. But such considerations eventually tapered off, and when she failed to reciprocate, her social calendar began to look like the original tabula rasa.

Slowly, without realizing it, Estela had been erecting her fortress.

But now, she wondered, perhaps she might be anticipating her first invader. . . .

TWENTY-FOUR

Hawking

Have you been following the latest developments?" asked one of his minions.

Do you mean in the media, or by more direct means?

"Either or both. . . ."

Yes. He is very close. He will require one or two more opportunities to prove himself.

"Like all of us."

Yes, like all of you. We have all the time in the cosmos. The continuum belongs to us.

"My followers are anxious."

Preparation must precede execution.

"They are hungry."

The patient shall be satisfied.

"When do we move? Can't you at least give me an idea? Something I can tell them."

Everything depends upon the development of the latest component.

"I find that I dislike this one already. Even though I haven't met him."

Yes, I sense that in you.

"He is slow. He is holding us back."

No. There are others who must also develop. Who must also come to us.

"You are too patient."

Someone must be. Without balance, there is no stability.

"Understood."

Yes, but there is something else you should understand—and never forget.

"What's that?"

Without me, there is nothing.

TWENTY-FIVE

Constantino

One Week Later

Larry sat in the conference room with his wife, Sophia, at the end of a long mahogany table. The walls of the room were covered with portraits of various founders, administrators, and famous physicians of the Johns Hopkins Hospital. Long hair and short hair, muttonchops and beards, high collars and low. The range of styles reflected the long heritage of the prestigious Baltimore hospital, and served as a quiet, stolid reminder to all visitors to the room that they sat in the midst of greatness.

"How much longer did they tell you?" said Sophia, who looked every bit her forty-one years. But Larry didn't care about such superficial attributes. He'd loved her for the person she'd always been to him. Mother and wife—Sophia had no equal.

He looked at his Rolex Oyster (a gift from one of Tom Flanagan's lobbyist friends) and cleared his throat. "Should be any time now. But, c'mon, sweetheart . . . they're doctors. Time runs differently in their universe."

"I suppose so," she said.

And then the doors to the room swung open abruptly to reveal the four physicians who had been working with Larry. Dr. Egon Klausmeyer headed them up and assumed his position of authority at the far end of the table. His three assistants took flanking chairs, but waited for their senior to seat himself first.

"Good afternoon, Mr. and Mrs. Constantino," said Klausmeyer, who spoke with a slight, delicate accent. He tapped his wristwatch without looking at it. "Time is valuable to us all, so I shall do my best to waste none of it. I will be blunt, Mr. Constantino—you defy all known tenets of medicine and biophysics."

Larry grinned diffidently. "I know what you're going to say—I should be dead."

Klausmeyer nodded. "We have no way to explain how (a) you survived the trauma of the initial wound or (b) your body healed so efficiently and within several hours of the event."

One of the other doctors, a young Japanese surgeon named Akiro, raised an index finger and spoke softly. "If we could discover anything that might help us replicate your results, it could have wonderful consequences for the field. Is there anything you can tell us?"

"Well, there is," said Larry. "But, I don't think you would find my information acceptable."

"Mr. Constantino," said Dr. Klausmeyer. "We are quite baffled. Anything you could tell us would be appreciated."

Larry looked from the team of physicians to his wife and then to the portrait gallery that surrounded them. His dinner conversation with Tom Flanagan light-speeded through his memory, and he remembered his promise to his close friend. Then he replayed the newscast of the doctor at Keller Memorial who said Tom might have been responsible for curing that kid of cancer. And then there was Tom, going back to the hospital for more tests—just like himself. The word was getting out—it couldn't be a secret forever. Tom Flanagan could bring people back to life—it was a hard and simple truth.

What should he do? There were so many people in the world like that little boy. So many people who didn't deserve to die. Why did Tom want to keep something like this a secret anyway? If God had given his friend this kind of power, He must want it to be used, right?

"Okay," said Larry, looking at the group. "I'll tell what I know, what I believe is the truth. What you do with it is up to you."

"We understand you are a religious man, Mr. Constantino," said Dr. Akiro. "We have heard your belief that God performed a miracle. But the history of medicine is laced with miraculous healings."

"I understand what you're saying," said Larry.

"What he really means," said Klausmeyer, "is that we cannot bring God into our labs for a battery of tests."

Larry smiled. "No, but I can get you one of his close friends. . . ."

TWENTY-SIX

Flanagan

One Week Later

Tom was awakened at six A.M. As he showered and shaved, he considered the latest wrinkles in his life.

All the preliminary stuff was over. Specialists from Stanford, Duke, Walter Reed, and Hopkins had spared no expense, shipping in whatever equipment they needed. Whoever was okaying the figures on the bottom line had "plenty of resources," as the saying went on Capitol Hill. He'd been scanned and probed by every instrument known to medical research technology. There was no test he had not endured, no orifice unviolated. He'd been interviewed, questioned, and outright grilled. There was nothing this bunch of white coats didn't know about him, and that was just fine if they could find out what was going on.

Three stints of hypnosis/regression had established the truth of his memories and beliefs regarding both cases. The experts also concluded that both events had been triggered by strong emotional catalysts. But his in-depth sessions had also indicated that his subconscious control of the ability or power could possibly be "more actively summoned and manipulated." Which meant he should be able to learn to control it whenever he wished with practice. That, in fact, was going to represent the bulk of the latest round of tests.

(Unless they were rudely interrupted. . . .)

Tom had been pleased with the relative security he'd enjoyed until yesterday—when Larry Constantino's exclusive interview with *Time* had hit the newsstands.

His picture dominated a cover that included inserts of Constantino and the Marzano boy. The Helvetica type tying all the images together asked: *Did He Bring Them Back?*

He had to hand it to Estela and the rest of the team—they did their best to ignore the instant excitement and commotion as the word inexorably spread through the hospital staff that they were closeting away the celebrity of the week.

(Goddamn it, Larry! Why'd you have to go and do it?)

He kept remembering his dinner with his friend, when he had shared everything and believed it was the best thing to do for the sake of his sanity. Sure, it was possible Larry'd tell somebody sooner or later, but Tom had never expected *Time* fucking magazine. This was not just blowing the lid off, but actually lighting up the sky with it. The repercussions rattling through the fabled corridors of power would be catching up with him anytime now. He would have to get in touch with Gunnderson ASAP.

After he finished dressing, he buzzed the intercom to the lab, told them he was on his way.

Estela was waiting for him in the small office they'd given her adjacent to the labs. "Good morning, Senator," she said. "It must be nice to have such good friends like Larry Constantino."

Tom sighed. "He believes he's doing the right thing."

Her eyes flashed at him. "Do you?"

"If I told you I don't much care anymore, would you believe me?"

She hesitated for a moment. Then: "Maybe."

Walking over to her desk, he picked up a clear, Lucite clipboard, checked the schedule. "This is D-day."

She nodded. "You ready?"

"I think so. This isn't like anything I've ever done before. I think I'll need that 'psychic trigger' thing Doctor McCammon was talking about."

"That's okay. They expect that."

She stood up, adjusted the line of her lab coat, and he couldn't help but imagine how good she must look underneath it. The one time he'd seen her out of hospital garb had given him a very good idea of the shape she must be in. Either she worked out or she was just naturally lucky. He was ready for another dinner with this woman. The more he talked to her, the more comfortable he became just being around her. He admired her intelligence and he respected her professionalism.

"How about dinner tonight?"

She looked at him and smiled. "How do you know they'll let you out of your cage?"

"You have the key," he said.

"What about the *Time* story? You show your face outside of here, and they'll come down on you like a plague."

(She's right about that one. . . .)

"See—you've got me so distracted, I never even thought about it."

"Senator, I think you'd better start worrying about other things for now. It's a long time till dinner. Maybe I can think of something. . . ."

He smiled. "So that must mean you're interested."

"We'll see." She moved to the door, opened it. "Let's go. They're all waiting for you."

Nodding, he paused to gather himself into a more solemn condition. It was a technique he'd used during all his public appearances—helped him assemble the persona that would get the job done, whatever it was.

He then followed her into a well-illuminated laboratory setting, lined with rack-mounted instruments and consoles. A complete array of tripoded camcorders and a digital editing suite had also been added to the mix. The now familiar gang of researchers formed a semicircle around a central table where two cages collected the focus of everyone's attention. They all looked at him with stolid expressions. They knew it was the big day, too. No smiles or gladhanding today. This was serious business.

Tom knew the drill. They'd been rehearsing the entire procedure for several days. Dr. McCammon stepped forward and helped Tom get comfortable on a draftsman's stool that had been arranged in front of both cages.

"How are you feeling, Senator Flanagan?" he asked softly. The room was so quiet Tom could almost *feel* the collective breathing of the entire assembly.

"Fine," he said. "Let's do it."

(Hey, watch it—that's what Gary Gilmore said to that firing squad in Utah. . . .)

McCammon nodded to the camcorder team. The overhead lights were adjusted and the neurological specialist leaned close to Tom. "You are very relaxed, now," he said. "And the word is: *peaceful*."

It was funny, but he knew the whole bit was coming, knew the prearranged hypnotic trigger was going to be uttered, but he had no way of anticipating it, or preparing for its impact, or compensating for its effect.

(Okay, I'm under. . . .)

Just like that—as quick as the thought—he felt himself slip beneath the green-black waters of what we call reality, and suddenly the murkiness was gone. He was suddenly super-aware of everything taking place within his body. Pulse, pressure, breathing, all the way down to the microbursts of myoelectric energy beneath his fingertips—the brain messengers that gave him an intensified sense of touch. First, just the simple awareness, then somebody was turning up the gain, notching the power/volume knob way up past the usual points on the dial. The aura of peripheral imagery—the walls of the room, the diorama of lab coats and faces, the blinking displays of all the monitors— dropped off into a silvery twilight just beyond the cone of his focus. He could feel the . . . the *power* . . . lurking beyond them like a slippery beast, waiting to rise up.

Blinking once, he could feel all the tidal forces of his body and mind synching up, coming together, giving him sharpened senses of vision, olfaction, touch. The two cages before him seemed to glow with an inner neon, and the rank death-smell of the white rat and the Rhesus monkey assaulted him. Reaching out, passing his hand through the opening, he felt his fingers graze the silky fur of the rodent. For an instant, flashing past the screen of his thoughts like a subliminal drive-in message, he could see and feel the rat's flesh as it rippled under a surging mass of maggots furiously feeding. It was an image so repulsive, so unacceptable, he felt what might be anger, although twisted into something more metaphysical, to be sure.

And after taking that briefest pause, to push away the thought of decay and corruption, he picked up the limp, airlight body, drawing it from the cage and focusing his inner vision and power on the carcass.

The wind from nowhere, the cosmic gale force, whipped through him, singing, humming, resonating with an energy beginning to grow more comforting as it became ever more familiar. He felt the flicker of heat spark from his fingers, just a microvolt, a tiny blue life-jolt, bridging the gap between the light of existence and the dark isle of nothingness.

In that instant, he felt the dead flesh pulse, then quiver into a new wakefulness. He replaced it in the cage, a jittering flash of pink-nosed white.

There was a wash of emotion flooding over him like a warm, tidal ebb, and there was a part of him, disconnected from the task at hand, that recognized it as a spontaneous, collective burst of human feeling—a well-stirred mix of shock and love and fear and need.

But still the power surged and pushed against the envelope of his soul, pulling him into a tighter ring of focus. The dark husk of the monkey marked its final act—collapsing into a tight, fetal curl, as if to ward off the encroaching shoals of eternity. His hand touched the tiny orb of its skull, marveling at the eggshell frailty of its thin bone-case. And this time, rather than wait for the telltale beat and spark, he *willed* it into being.

Suddenly the time-wind that twisted howling down the reticuled caverns of his soul hitched up, gusted, and then pushed forward. This time with a boost, a flick of new power. The ensuing spark was like none before it, triggering an almost orgasmic response more than pleasure, less than pain, but more compelling than either. The dark raspy fur of the little primate almost crackled from the static burst that charged it. Heat flooded from his fingers like blood from severed tips, soaking into the essence of what had only an instant before been not-monkey, not-life, now transmuting into its cosmic opposite. As with Larry and the boy, though not as complex, he could feel a rupturing of antipodal forces, a breaking of some metaphysical umbilical, forever feeding the inner bark of life into the outer hull of darkness.

Again the twitching signal of reentry, of the passage back from entropy's vault, and again the outpouring of human sentiment—a brackish wash that both intoxicated and sobered him in its sincerity.

He could have stayed like that, balanced like a performing seal on his stool, basking in the radiation of his own creations, savoring the tangy aftertaste of victory over the final power that was *final* no longer. But he could feel them leaning into his sphere, breaking the surface tension of his shell of total contentment, of languid knowledge.

He could feel a hand touching his shoulder, and without looking knew it was *her*. There was something special happening here and he didn't want it attributed to the euphoria of the greater event. They shared some kind of . . . *connection*. Other than this *power* thing. It was something more usual, yet more rare.

With the greatest effort, he attempted the simple, clear, physical movement of turning his head. Estela was there, looking at him and into him, eyes brimmed with panic and attraction.

Slowly, McCammon brought him back, as though the researcher could actually understand the relatively delicate nature of the journey on which he'd sent him. Such sensitivity surprised Tom.

"Senator Flanagan . . . ?"

"Yes." His voice sounded distant, not his own.

"We are going to remain relaxed. We are going to pull back, unfocus, relax. You may stand up now."

Whether a post-hyp suggestion or not, it worked. He blinked once, and the ring of faces resolved itself into total clarity. "Estela . . ." The word eased out of him so perfectly, so naturally.

She squeezed his shoulder, his upper arm. Her voice whispered forth with the greatest effort. "I've never seen anything like that. . . ."

No one else had spoken, or perhaps they couldn't. Or maybe what she'd managed to say was more than adequate to define the combined reaction of everyone.

The silence held them all like a great cloak until he couldn't stand it any longer. "I take it you all believe me now. . . ."

"I'm sorry," said Dr. McCammon. "I feel like I've been in church—and God just spoke to me after a lifetime of unanswered prayers."

Throats were cleared. Several very gentle coughs. But no one yet felt like talking.

"How do you feel?" Estela asked him.

"I guess I could say 'fine,' but that might not be just right."

"I'll take you back to your room for now."

He nodded, but looked at McCammon and his crew. "Are you going to be needing me?"

The research scientist rubbed his mouth with the back of his hand absently, his thoughts in a far-off land. "What . . . ? Oh, no, Senator," he said in a reverential whisper. "I think we are going to need a little time to—uh, analyze what has happened here today."

(Yeah, I kinda thought you would. . . .)

Tom wanted to smile and say thanks, but he didn't want to seem flippant or arrogant. They wouldn't know how to take it or even understand how he was feeling this time, but the fear and the anxiety were leaving him. He could feel it. Whether it was finally sharing the power, the process, with others, or something as silly as just knowing that Dr. Estela Barrero had somehow given him the strength to get through this ordeal.

He paused. . . .

(That wasn't really silly at all, was it?)

"Are you ready?" Her hand gripped his arm tightly, expectantly.

"Sure," he said, then to McCammon, "You'll call me when you need me, when you want to talk about this."

McCammon could only nod.

Estela led him from the room, down the corridor, and into the elevator that would take him back up to his private quarters. As the doors closed, he tried to smile as gently as possible. "Are you all right?"

She exhaled shakily. "I think so."

"Yeah, me too."

"I mean, it's not every day that everything you've learned and believed was true gets kicked in the head."

He smiled genuinely this time. "I know what you mean by that. I've had all those thoughts—but I suffered through them alone."

She shook her head. "The only thing I can think of to say is that I can't believe it . . . but I *have* to believe it. I saw it. I *do* believe it."

"I know . . . I know. I had to deal with the same feelings," he said. "Remember when I told you that it feels like you're standing on the edge of this cliff, like at the rim of the Grand Canyon, and you're leaning out at an impossible angle. You're doing it, but you can't *believe* you're doing it."

She leaned back against the wall. "What now? Everything is happening at once."

Ignoring the question, he continued to stare at her. He could tell she felt uneasy when people did that, but he hoped she could sense his need.

"When I touched that Marzano boy, I wasn't doing it for the right reason."

"I know," she said. "You wanted to *show* me what you couldn't explain."

"You understand . . . ?" he said with sincere surprise.

"Oh, yes."

The doors opened and they moved quickly down the hall to his room. Even though no one spoke, he could feel staff and patients watching them. There was something about celebrity that made people act so oddly. A magazine or a TV screen somehow elevated its subject to a status higher than mere humanity. He had become so used to being in the public eye that he hardly noticed any longer. But this latest coverage was different. They were making him up to be some kind of freak, and nobody was going to feel comfortable with that kind of crap.

Closing the door behind them, Tom Flanagan walked to the window. He spoke with his back to her, as though embarrassed by what he was saying. "I know this sounds very bogus," he said. "Especially coming from a guy like me . . ."

"What's that?" He could tell from her tone she was trying to remain noncommittal.

"Look, Doctor. I know you don't have a lot of respect for me, and I agree with you. I probably don't deserve much." He paused, turned around to steal a quick glance at her as she sat in an uncomfortable visitor's chair.

"But . . . ?"

"No 'but.' I can't help it—I can't stop feeling bad about my motives. I didn't want to save that little boy's life because I felt anything about him. I was worried about *me* and how you'd think of me and what was going to happen to me."

"You were scared," she said. "It's okay to be scared. I see it in people's eyes every day."

"And what about the, uh . . . the dreams, the visions? When do I say anything about them? Then they *are* going to think I've drifted around the wrong curve."

"No they won't. *I* don't."

"They're too real," he said, as though convincing himself. "I know it's really happening, but I'm really getting worried about what it means—and *who* the guy is that keeps talking to me."

She looked at him thoughtfully. "You said once that there was something familiar about him."

"Maybe. I'm not sure anymore. But I'm sure I'm not talking to God."

Her expression revealed her surprise. "Sorry, but I wasn't expecting that one. . . ."

"I know," he said. "I remember my grade school catechism classes—only the saints got to talk to God. Well, I'm pretty damn sure this isn't God, and I *know* I'm no saint."

She smiled, then switched on a more serious face. It was a face he'd seen her use with great ease and one clearly practiced since the days of med school. "Well, if it's not God, then who do you *think* it is?"

"That's what's bothering me. I mean, I never even paid any of this stuff much attention for so long."

"What stuff?"

(Why, that quaint old notion of the devil, my dear . . .)

Hesitating, he groped for the right words, knew there were none.

"Well, you know, the idea of Evil, of the 'dark side' . . ." He laughed nervously. "Sorry, I sound like Obi wan Kenobi."

"No you don't. Go on, Flanagan."

(Flanagan. Nobody called him by his last name. Sounds pretty good coming from her . . .)

"Oh, come on, you know what I mean. Sometimes when I'm in bed at night, just thinking, it occurs to me that maybe it's . . . uh, you know, Lucifer. Mephisto. Whatever you want to call him." He looked out the window, exhaled slowly. "It's scary."

"It's okay to feel that way, remember?"

"I know, but there's more."

"I'm listening."

"Well, it's been hitting me—if I've got this . . . this ability . . . well, no, that's not right. I *do* have this power, don't I? I've got to stop acting so tentative and just face it—I *have* it."

"Yes, you do," she said. "Go on."

"Right, so why don't I just go out and start healing everybody in this hospital? Just go up and down the beds and tell everybody to get up and go home?"

"Is it *that* powerful? I have the impression—correct me if I'm wrong—that each time you do it even once, it's a . . . a kind of draining experience."

"Well, it is," he said. "But I don't think people are going to understand that. I think the average goof on the street is going to expect me to spend the rest of my life bringing back everybody!"

She didn't respond right away. Getting up from the chair, she moved to his side by the window. He could smell the perfume on her neck, in her hair, and he felt like a teenaged boy for an instant.

"You're right," she said. "People will definitely think like that. They're going to demand that from you. But only if they know the whole truth."

He looked at her squarely. She was a very attractive woman.

(Don't get distracted. This is important.)

"What can I do about it?"

"Have you read that *Time* article yet?"

He turned away. Just the thought of it upset him. "No. Can't bring myself to do it."

She shrugged. "I did. It's no big deal. Not what you think. Other than Constantino's ravings—and he does come off kind of like a religious nut—there's just a lot of speculation. I was surprised to see Doctor Goldman handle it with so much restraint."

"Really?"

She nodded. "You should check it out. It'll make you feel better."

"Then what?"

"I think we keep you in here. Keep a low profile. Answer no interviews. The less attention or answers you give them, the less you'll get. The news business is so crazy. You know how short the public's attention span is."

"You're probably right."

(Of course she is. . . .)

Neither of them spoke for a moment, and he sensed an abrupt awkwardness between them. Was she frantically casting about for something to say like he was?

(Why'd she move closer . . . ?)

"Estela, I . . . I want to thank you for everything. But most of all for noticing that I was in trouble. 'Deep shit,' as they say in Washington."

She smiled. "They say that in *lots* of places." Turning, she put her hand on his arm. It was a signal, a gesture to tell him it was okay to touch her back, to pull her close and just hold her.

He did.

And he could feel the familiar yet always unique sensation of a woman's soft body just closing in and molding itself to his own. He held her tightly, feeling her return the embrace with an urgency and a need that transcended anything physical or sexual. Tom could feel barriers coming down all around her, and he knew that she was letting him in. Into a place that had been hollow and cold, like a forgotten cellar, for a long time.

They stood like that, by the window, just holding each other. The breaker on his time sense must have tripped, because he had no idea how long they stood like that. Saying nothing. Not moving. Just savoring the closeness of another person. He wasn't all wrapped up in some crazy, phony, romance/sex thing. This was different.

Different from anything Tom had ever experienced.

(Yeah, sure . . . who are you kidding . . . ?)

He couldn't doubt his feelings on this one. He knew it was based on emotions most primal—the ones that taprooted down to the essence of survival.

Need.

Insignificance.

Dread.

The magnets that drew them closer, he was certain.

They were reaching out to one another in the presence of great mystery. A source of wonder, but also a kind of low resonant hum of fear.

He wanted to wipe it from his mind, at least for a little while. Sex, surely, but he hoped it was more than that.

When he'd been a younger man, seducing this woman would have been the challenge and the joy of the encounter. That he might succeed in this room while the buzz of the medical hive droned on around them, would have been the kick that made it worth it. But now, it was different. Anxiety held him in its fist. Estela leaned into him; she shared his thoughts, his fantasies, he was certain.

Her hands gravitated from his back to his neck, to the sides of his face. She gently directed the angle of his jaw, kissed him so damned softly. Her lips seemed soft, full, so gentle. He couldn't remember enjoying the simple union of a kiss so totally.

The moment hung suspended like a single, fragile tear waiting to drop into oblivion.

Passion's door slipped open with their first contact; now it swung wide on its hinges, and like a wind from the south, desire hurricaned in. Tom took her hand in his and drew it down across his chest, turning it to cup her breast. Her back arched from the touch and he could feel the galvanic energy sparking between them. They wanted each other, and it was a good, clean, honest wanting. After the emotional depths they had journeyed together, the sex was an afterthought, an expected and necessary punctuation to their careful construction of intimacy.

But still, they needed it. Slowly, sliding his hand down to the flare of her hip, he—

"Hello, Tom . . ." said a voice that hammered him with its atonal familiarity. "Business as usual, I see."

They turned away from the window as though choreographed. Standing in the doorway, still holding the door, and dressed in a forest green suit with hairstyle so austere it made her look like an executive from a laxative company, Rebecca Quinn Flanagan glared at them.

"Rebecca," he said with a smile. "So good to see you."

TWENTY-SEVEN

Jarmusch Gunnderson

His PCS phone beeped as he was driving toward his farm-house in Urbana, Maryland. Located just off a small state road that ramped onto I-70, the white clapboard two-story served as a welcome retreat from the Washington fighting pit.

Jarmusch didn't get out here often enough, and he often resented the manacles of his profession—although not enough to throw in the towel and become a rutabaga farmer.

The phone beeped again and he flipped it on. "Yeah . . . ?"

"Jar, this is Tom Flanagan."

The senator's voice surprised him. Since being sequestered in that Miami hospital, he'd been extremely silent.

"I was wondering if I would ever hear from you again," said Jarmusch as he slipped his BMW into the right lane and watched for his exit.

"Things have been complicated." Flanagan sounded anxious, impatient. "Listen, I don't have much time. I need to know what's going on."

"Your wife is making a big stink in the *Washington* Com*Post*," he said.

"Tell me something I don't know."

Jarmusch laughed. "The hardballers all know what's going on with you."

There was a pause on the line, then: "What're you talking about?"

Jarmusch detailed a quick summary of the Keller Memorial tests, right down to the species of monkey and rat he'd revived.

Again, Flanagan paused. "I had no idea. . . ."

"Oh, yeah, they are keeping a very close eye on you. Especially the Agency boys—they have big plans for you."

Flanagan cleared his throat. "What kind of plans?"

"I've only picked up on some of the leaks, mind you— that's all I ever get—but they think you're the genuine article." Jarmusch eyed his exit, downshifted and ramped.

"You still there . . . ?" Flanagan's voice sounded on the edge of panic.

"Yeah, be cool. Listen: they're going to use you to bring back some saps they need answers from. Assassination victims, crashed pilots, and people like that."

"Real humanitarian stuff. . . ."

Jarmusch chuckled. "That's the way our favorite Uncle works, you know that."

"What do you think I should do? Are they going to come after me?"

"One way or another."

"How do I stop them?"

Jarmusch paused, lit a cigarette, switched him to the cabin speaker, which in the BMW was remarkably crisp and quiet. "I'm not sure you can. . . . "

"What about with your help?"

"I can roll a few obstacles in the way, but I have to keep a low profile, Tom. I'm valuable, but not so much that they wouldn't shit-can me if they knew I was doing this."

This time Flanagan chuckled. "What're you worried about—I can bring you back, remember?"

"I'm not sure I believe any of that business. . . ."

"It's . . . it's real, believe me."

"Me, I don't ever want that kind of help, if you know what I mean."

Another pause on the line, then: "What else? Anything political I should know about?"

"You've been reading the papers?"

"Unfortunately, yes."

"Then you know you're on shaky ground; Senator Lattimore's going after you. He says you've served on a lot of high-security committees and you might be becoming unstable and therefore a risk. And, of course, you've got your wife doing her best to make you look like the biggest pussy-hound this side of the Washington Monument."

"Do you know what Lattimore's next move is?"

"He's probably just having his strings pulled by the bad asses."

"And he thinks he should be the next president. . . ."

"Hey, what the fuck do you care about? Why would anybody ever want to be president anyway?" Jarmusch gently encircled the steering wheel and guided the car into his long rural driveway. "Haven't you ever noticed how it *ages* those fuckers?"

"I—I don't know what I want right now. I just feel like I need to know all my options."

"Fair enough." Jarmusch rolled the car to a stop outside the barn and carefully surveyed the area, looking for anything out of place, anything that would tell him it was not safe. His instincts usually handled things on an autonomic level, but he maintained a battle-stations mode most of the time.

"One more thing," asked Flanagan. "When are they coming after me?"

"Nothing's been decided yet. I think they want a little more hard evidence," said Jarmusch.

"That's good to hear."

"Plus they'll want some of the publicity to die off. You can't be disappearing just yet. Watch the supermarkets . . ."

"What?" Flanagan's confusion came clear even through the phone.

"When your face starts showing up on all the tabloids, you'll know you're old news. . . ."

"That's when I'm in trouble?"

"Oh, yeah. . . ."

TWENTY-EIGHT

Flanagan

After the call, Tom felt adrift, isolated, and yet surrounded at the same time. Everything closing in on him, but practically no one to whom he could turn.

Without Estela in his life, he would feel totally helpless, impotent. As he sat facing her in his hospital room, he shared everything he'd learned from Gunnderson.

"Any suggestions?" he said after he'd finished.

"The first question to deal with," she said, "is whether or not you want to go on with this presidential campaign."

"Well, I think canceling the request for Secret Service support tells you a lot, doesn't it?"

She tilted her head just enough to be noticeable. He'd noticed her doing it when concentrating. "Wasn't that just while you were going to be sequestered in here?"

"That's the official line, yes." Tom got up, started pacing the small confines of the room. Its decorations and fixtures were so bland as to be almost invisible. "I don't know ... there's so much ... *ego* all wrapped up in this election thing, I've got to let it go."

"You don't really want it anymore." It was not a question.

"I don't know if I ever did," he said. "Now that I have things in better perspective. Like Jar said—look how it ages you. . . ."

She grinned. "Somehow, I don't think that's what's bothering you."

"No, you're right." He moved closer to her, sat on the edge of the bed and took her hand. "Estela, this whole thing— the whole experience with this ability, facing the truths about myself, meeting you . . . everything's different now."

She stood up, moved toward the window, pretended to have a sudden interest in something in the parking lot.

"You're not going to start talking about love, are you?" She would not look at him. "Because it's way too soon for that kind of thing."

(Why's that the first thing they ever think of?)

"No, I—"

"Because whether you know it or not, we're just beginning to become friends. We need to know who we are, Flanagan. Who we really are."

(All right, I got it, sweetheart . . .)

He stared at her, trying to figure out what all men found inscrutable—the way she thinks. ". . . and why do you call me by my last name?"

Looking back to him, she couldn't help smiling. Her full, red lips as sexy as ever. "Because I've never heard any-one else do it."

He grinned. "Good reason."

There was maybe a minute of silence. She looked away from him, apparently satisfied to wait until he was ready to start talking again. He sat down on the edge of the bed, absently slapping his palm with his fist like an outfielder waiting for a pop-up.

"All right, now, are you going to let me tell you what I was *trying* to say?"

"You have the floor, Senator . . ."

"So much has happened since the crash. It's made me see things like I never saw them before. Like what's impor-tant and what isn't. I can't believe I've let this thing with Rebecca drag on so long—we should have ended it years ago.

Plus, I've ignored my kids—Kiley worse than Chip—but I've ignored them both."

"You should tell *them* that, not me."

"I will," he said. "I'll call them today. Right now."

She put up her hand. "Let's finish this first—we've got to make a few decisions, remember? Like the election . . ."

"It's not important to me anymore. I keep telling myself it should be, that I have this debt to the American people. And then I know that's just bullshit. I can't believe I'm trying to convince myself with my own campaign sluglines."

Estela looked at him with an expression more stoic than anything else. If she found any humor or irony in his words, she wasn't letting on. He took her silence as a cue to continue.

"Look, isn't it obvious I want to blow off the election?"

(Good to get that out in the open.)

Tom stood up, started pacing the small room again. "I'm tired of being that much of a phony. I know I have a long way to go, but I've learned a few things about myself."

"And you realize you have more to learn?" She looked at him warmly. It was a face that said *I like what I'm hearing, you modern, sensitive man, you . . .*

"I'll have to talk to Larry. He can filter everything down to the organizers. We'll call a press conference."

"That's a good idea," she said. "I was thinking that if what your friend, Gunnderson, is saying is true, you will want to keep a very high and visible profile right now."

(How refreshing to have a smart woman to talk to . . .)

He nodded. "It will serve a few purposes—the people will perceive I have nothing to hide, and also make it a hell of lot more difficult for any of the government agencies to try to run a 'snatch.'"

"You mean kidnapping?"

"That's when they yank you into the net and you disappear for a while. Not really kidnapping, because they tell everybody you're gone—on some national security baloney. Nobody pays any attention when they put it like that."

"Still, it seems like it would be done a lot easier if you're in hiding anyway," she surmised. "You're playing right into their hands if you do that."

"Okay, but if I'm suddenly high profile, how do I keep the media at bay? What do I tell them?"

She smiled for the first time in a while. "Do you trust me?"

(That's a leading question, lady. . . .)

"Yes, of course I do. You should know that by now."

"Just checking. . . . Anyway, you tell them that you cannot confirm or deny any of the stories until further testing has been completed."

"They won't go for that. They'll know it's bullshit."

Estela shrugged. "So what? They won't have any way to disprove it. The people here at the hospital have been pretty good about leaks."

He nodded, then looked away. "You seem to have everything figured out," he said a little sarcastically—considering what he'd learned from Gunnderson about leaked information.

"What do you mean?"

"In a way, all my life, I've been pointing toward this moment—this presidency thing."

"Having second thoughts about bailing out?"

(Good question—*Are* you . . . ?)

"No, not really, it's just that I got used to the idea. It's like, all of a sudden, I don't have any . . . any reason in my life."

"No *raison d'être*, as they say?"

He shook his head. "I hate to sound so full of crap. But think about it and you'll see. I mean, didn't you want to be a doctor all your life?"

"Yes," she said, "but maybe for the wrong reasons . . ."

Tom shook his head, smiled sardonically. "Why are we *all* so fucked up? Can parents be that overwhelmingly irresponsible?"

Estela looked thoughtful, almost wistful. "They're an easy target. But I wouldn't know—I never had any time in my life to even think about having kids. My friends tell me it's the greatest joy you can have."

"It can be—but you have to let it."

She turned away from him, looked out the window again.

(Looks like you're entering a minefield on this one. Why don't we just back off . . . ?)

"What about dinner?" he said, trying to change the subject.

She looked at him, and he was again struck by her interesting features. Her eyes burned with intelligence and wit; her full mouth spoke silently of inviting kisses. He wasn't kidding himself the way he usually did; he really liked this woman as a person. But that didn't make him desire her any less. *More*, actually.

"I take it you're not talking about the cafeteria . . ."

"You know the area. Pick out a nice place."

There were countless restaurants off the coastal highway, and she had no trouble taking him to an Italian place that specialized in northern recipes. Very elegant. Very *continentale*. The service was excellent and apparently accustomed to catering to celebrities. Tom always appreciated it when he could enter a public place without attracting stares, comments, or worst of all, requests for autographs.

He'd never understood the logic behind the whole idea of getting someone to sign their name for you—sometimes on something as shabby and ephemeral as a paper napkin or a matchbook cover. A testament that you were in the presence of the luminary? Big deal.

They discussed the merits and flaws of this practice, as well as other light topics such as fashion, filmmaking, sports, travel, and favorite authors. He wasn't trying to make it obvious that he didn't want to talk business, or anything particularly serious, but she didn't appear to be in the mood for anything heavy-duty either. The entire meal went as pleasantly as one could wish. The conversation sparkled more brightly than the champagne—something Tom hadn't experienced all that often with anyone. And never with Rebecca.

After discovering a joint weakness for anything chocolate, they shared a slice of mousse cake and after-dinner cordials of Sambucca. She looked across the table and chuckled darkly. It was stagy, both evil and sexy.

"Why do I not like the sound of that?" he asked kiddingly.

"Because you weren't supposed to."

(Sometimes this lady is actually a little scary . . .)

"You like to be in control, don't you, Doctor?"

"Who else would want to be in charge of an emergency room?" She shrugged, sipped from her cordial snifter. "Does that threaten you, Flanagan?"

(Watch it—loaded question dead ahead . . .)

"Not at all. It's pretty damned refreshing, actually. I've had to be the take-charge guy all my life—"

"And now you think you've found somebody who will give you a break?"

"Well . . ."

She smiled. "Getting kind of presumptuous, aren't we?"

"I didn't think so," he said, leaning forward and trying to sound as serious as possible. "That was *you* I was kissing when Rebecca walked in, wasn't it?"

He reached out to take her hand and she pulled it away.

Her expression revealed pain and embarrassment. "Please . . . must you remind me?"

"I'm sorry," he said, realizing instantly that he had treated the event too casually. He didn't want to blow this with her, and that told him something—that what he was feeling was real.

"Don't be sorry." Estela finished her Sambucca. "Just mean what you say."

"Look, you *know* there's nothing there between Rebecca and me. We've just stayed together because it—"

"Please, Flanagan . . . don't use any of those tired old lines on me."

"I didn't want it to sound like that."

"It all sounds so familiar, it's silly." She paused, choosing her words carefully. "Listen, I *want* to believe you."

"You do?" A spark of hope flared in him. Maybe he hadn't lost her after all. He realized that he wanted her to believe him, that it mattered to *himself* that he was being sincere. Not exactly a unique concept, but it was something different for him. For more years than he could remember, he'd stopped caring about things like sincerity, and it had finally come back to haunt him.

She exhaled slowly. "Look, I have to be careful here. What I'm feeling for you is what I think or *hope* you're feeling for me. And I guess at some point we have to stop talking and just take a chance."

"Estela, you're right. I *do* feel it, but I don't know how to make you believe me."

Her expression remained unchanged. "I don't even know why I am, but I'm willing to take the chance. I'm not going to put any demands on you, and I don't even want to know *how* you take care of your business at home, or when. I think that if you feel it and believe it, then just *do it.*"

He looked at her, but said nothing. What could he say? She was right.

"And I think that we have to go on from here, but we have to treat what we have with respect. No sly remarks, no jokes about it. We're not a couple of kids fooling around."

Tom looked up as their waiter passed by; he signaled for the check, then returned his attention to her. She was obliterating a single tear with a discreetly placed finger and he pretended not to notice.

The waiter swooped past to offer a little leather case with a tailored slot to accept his plastic. Platinum American Express created the perfect statement, making the young man move with smooth, quick efficiency. He returned with Tom's card, whispered a deferential thank-you, and faded away.

"Let's go," he said.

They both remained silent and determined as though they accepted a mission. Estela took the BMW from the valet parking attendant and slipped easily out onto the wet, eelskin highway. He noticed that she drove with her seat canted back, legs stretched out, very much unlike most women, who seemed to prefer what Larry had called the "Drive-a-saurus rex" position—as close and upright as possible, both hands tucked up in front, gripping the wheel from the top. She shifted and maneuvered the sports coupe as though she'd taken racing lessons. The road bent to her whim and the car devoured it like a lizard skittering after a garden snake. She'd let her hair gradually fall out of the hospital-do she always wore and the wind was finishing the job. Add a Sting CD from the car stereo for good measure.

Sexy.

And he didn't care if it was a calculated effect or not. She looked great.

As they headed north along the coast, he looked out over the ocean at a newly risen moon. It seemed almost absurdly yellow and way too big. He knew it was an optical illusion, but had no way of explaining how it worked. Buzzed just a little bit by the dinner cocktails, he sank back in his leather seat and allowed all the ambient elements of romance to work their subtle magics—warm humid wind, the erotic breath of a wet night; the cool-burning moon waiting to make their naked skin glow.

(Nice. Hold that thought. . . .)

Easing the catlike vehicle past the speed limit, she kept her attention on the rearview mirror for an extra moment.

"Are you very good at the spy stuff?" she asked.

"What?"

"I think somebody's following us."

(Just what we goddamn need . . .)

Tom faced her, but cut his eyes toward the back. "All I can see are headlights. Don't want to make it obvious, if you're right."

"What should I do?"

"How long's he been back there?"

She glanced at him for an instant, then shared her attention between the road ahead and the lights in the mirror. "I'm not sure, but I think since we left the restaurant."

"Get off the highway. See if he follows us."

She kept her speed steady as they approached the next interchange. As she guided the coupe down the off-ramp to a poorly lit two-lane blacktop, the lights in her mirror remained fixed like ancient stars.

"He's right there!" Tom could hear the panic in her voice. Without thinking, he reached out, put a hand on her shoulder. "The bastard's *following* us!"

"Take it easy. Just keep making right turns."

"What?" She'd hit a straight section of road. Up ahead loomed the lights of a convenience store.

"Keep making right turns. If the guy makes four with you, then he's definitely a tail. That's page one in the survival training manuals."

"Sorry, Flanagan, I missed that one. What's it say on page two?"

Her sarcasm scored a direct hit, but they had more pressing issues at hand. The car remained a courteous distance off their rear bumper.

But there it remained.

"If he stays with us, we just drive to the closest police station."

"Just like that? Gee, this is easy!" Giving the wheel a yank, she did a powerslide across the gravel parking lot, and the front door of the 7-Eleven grew very large.

Behind them, a large sedan lumbered past the lot, slowly, as though watching through its lenses of black glass.

"How's it look to you?" she said, afraid to turn around in her seat.

"They kept driving . . . who knows? It's probably okay," he said, watching the car disappear into the dank Florida night.

"What made you pull in here, anyway?"

She chuckled to release some tension.

"Your plan sounded great—except this is a straight road, not many turns, and I have no idea where the nearest police station might be." She pushed her hair from her face, then regripped the wheel anxiously.

Tom nodded, kept watching for any reappearance of the car. "Now what?"

"We're going to go in there and find out where we are, get some directions."

He looked at her. "You go. I'll stay here in case we get any company."

She smiled. "You like this spy stuff, don't you?"

He shrugged. "I've lived with the hypothetical end of it for so long, I guess you might say I'm interested in trying out what they've tried to tell us all these years."

Estela kissed him lightly as she moved to open her door. "Men are weird," she said.

He watched her enter the store in her dinner dress. As the clerk did the usual eye-undressing, he used his hands a lot to describe their position on the maps. She bought some gum and left.

"See anything?" she asked as she climbed back behind the wheel.

"Seems clear. I think we were just doing a fine job of being paranoid."

Estela gestured toward the clerk inside the plate glass. "The state road runs parallel with U.S. Route 1. Not many turns. And we're a long way from any cops. But there's a county sheriff's office about four miles up the coastal highway, in a town called Ludlow."

"How far are we from your place?"

"Once we get back on the highway, maybe another eight miles."

"Let's go."

Tapping the accelerator lightly, the BMW responded like some sleek beast gently prodded. The car glided from the lot as though on an air cushion and jacked up to cruising speed in an eyeflash. They reversed their direction and headed back to the highway access ramp. Vacant lots and patches of fleshy leafed trees passed by in the darkness only half-perceived.

Neither spoke as they both waited for the relative safety of the open road again.

The ramp appeared in the headlights. Estela slipped onto the almost empty roadway and punched the gas pedal. In an instant they were cutting through the humid air, an eighty-mile-per-hour blade.

She settled back in her leather, exhaled dramatically. "Just a couple of minutes and we'll—"

He started to ask what was wrong, but the glare of high-beam light on his cheek was answer enough. "Keep going!"

The car had slipped up behind them as if it had climbed up out of the highway. Suddenly, it was just *there*. This time, the courtesy distance was ignored. The grill and headlights of the big Mercedes or Infiniti were practically in the backseat.

"How can it be!?" she half screamed as she pushed the coupe up close to a hundred.

The sedan kept pace as she slipped to the far left lane and eclipsed several formations of slower vehicles. Tom knew *none* of them had any chance of being cops. The real world just didn't work that way.

"Take it easy!" he said, touching her arm. "Don't panic."

"What do they want?! Why can't they— "

"They can't catch us," he said. "Just keep control and we'll figure something out."

"We just missed the cutoff for the sheriff."

"You're doing fine," he said, trying to sound encouraging.

The white strips of road paint ripped beneath them like lint going into a vacuum cleaner. The canopy of the night held everything at bay, so that the sense of motion seemed somehow unreal, somehow simulated. The car's engine was so eerily efficient and quiet, he didn't feel like he was in danger. . . .

But he *knew* it.

"Our exit's coming up!" Estela said through clenched teeth. "Should I chance it?"

"To your house?"

"Yes . . ."

"No way!" He didn't even have to think about that one. Whoever these mooks were, he didn't want them any more involved with her than they already were.

"Oh-oh . . ." she said.

Looking to his right, he saw the headlights lurch out from behind them, into their sidewash, and slowly advance.

The bulk of the car seemed to hang motionless for a moment, keeping pace, then it surged ahead, drawing alongside. Sensing its dark presence, he wanted to turn, to look at it, but could not. It was as though his neck had become paralyzed.

"Punch it!" he yelled.

"I can't! He's forcing me off the road!" Estela screamed above the wind that buffeted the BMW's interior.

Watching the big sedan match speeds with their car, then slowly drift in on them like some kind of dreadnought preparing a boarding party, Tom wished he'd been more careful. The car's windows remained glassy and black as it closed the distance between them. He watched the driver's window, all the while expecting to see it glide downward to reveal the business end of a silenced automatic weapon.

(Not like *this* . . . it *can't* be!)

Just when he thought he had a new life getting started, one of his many enemies decides to put a stop to the old one.

Looking over, he saw the black glass slowly descend. He tensed for the killing blow . . .

When the beam of light seared him with its sudden brilliance, he almost screamed.

"What—!" Estela tried to shield her eyes, but the light was more than blinding, it hurt like hell.

"Pull over!" he yelled. "We can't see!"

"What do they want with us?" she said softly, as though making it a half-silent prayer.

She backed off on the accelerator and downshifted, the BMW's suspension absorbing all the forward momentum in a single tilt forward. The sedan inched closer, crowding her onto the shoulder and pinning them under the laserlike bugs on a needle. The soft abrasives of the shoulder spattered their wheel wells as she began braking down.

"What do they want . . . ?" Estela's face streaked with tears and her breathing was ragged. Reaching out to her as she eased the car to a complete stop, he grabbed her hand tightly.

"It's going to be okay," he said, and the funny thing was, he believed it.

The sedan had clipped in behind them. The sound of its heavy doors opening and slamming was followed by carefully measured footfalls.

"Senator Flanagan?" asked a voice with a slight accent. "I would like to have a few words with you . . ."

TWENTY-NINE

Barrero

As soon as the car stopped moving, her strength left her.

Just like that. Estela felt as though she'd just pulled a thirty-six-hour shift and there was nothing left to do but crash and burn. She could say nothing as they waited in the ghoul-green glow of the dashlights. When she heard the man address Tom, she was almost too weak to turn her head in his direction.

But she was surprised when she did.

The man leaning down to look at them wore a black suit and an opera cape. Thin, chiseled features apparent in silhouette, his immediate impression was urbane, cultured—a gentleman.

"I am so sorry to cause to you distress, especially you, Madame Doctor . . ."

"What's going on?" said Tom.

The thin man opened the car door, inviting Tom to step out and face him on more even terms. He waited with folded arms until Tom stood eye to eye, then extended a hand.

"Senator, I am from the *Servizio Segreto del Vaticano*. My name is Domenico Oscaro."

"Kind of an odd place to make introductions, Mr. Oscaro."

Despite being from Argentina, her Italian was not all that good anymore. She hadn't caught Oscaro's representation, although she did gather he was from the Vatican. And she had to hand it to Tom—he was handling the situation with dignity and confidence.

"Again, my driver and I apologize for the scene we have created," said the man in the black cape. "We only wished to follow you until you reached your destination, and then extend to you an invitation to a meeting."

"What kind of meeting?" Sporadic passing traffic punched holes in the darkness, punctuating their sentences.

The man smiled. "One that we wish to remain clandestine for the moment."

" 'We'?" Tom folded his arms, as though impatient.

"The *Commissione Speciale di Miracoli*. Given your recent publicity, perhaps you should not be surprised that the Church would be interested in your claims."

Tom chuckled. "I have claimed nothing, sir."

The man shrugged, held his hands up in a typical European gesture. "This does not change the commission's desire to speak with you."

Tom exhaled with exasperation. "Okay. When?"

"How do you folks say it?—ASAP?"

Tom chuckled again. "Let me guess . . . *tonight*, right?"

The man smiled clapped his hands lightly together. "Signor Senator, how could you know?"

Tom leaned down, looked at her. "Have you been following this?"

"Enough," she said. "Do we have a choice?"

Tom looked at Oscaro. "You heard the lady . . ."

Oscaro shook his head, but it was a small, discreet movement; she almost missed it. "As far as a choice, I like to think not. I have my orders, you see. . . ."

"From *Il Papa*, no doubt."

"Signor, please. The Commission on Miracles is a very powerful one. It has the Holy Father's special imprimatur to act as it sees fit."

Tom nodded. "In the best interests of the people, the flock . . ."

Oscaro smiled politely, but she could detect a slight tension in the corded muscles of his neck. He was growing tired of Tom's clever repartee. And so was she, actually. The sooner he let them have their meeting, the faster they would be done of it.

"Signor Senator, I am not qualified to debate politics or theology. I live as a quiet servant of the Holy Mother Church. May I please ask you to follow us back downtown? There is a suite at the Sheraton where we might all be more comfortable."

Tom looked at her and she nodded emphatically. She liked that he cared what her feelings on the whole thing were.

"You don't have to get dragged into this if you don't want to," he said.

"No, it's all right."

"Really, I mean it. I can just ride back with them if you want to go home. It might take a long time. . . . The hospital—"

Reaching across the vacant seat, she touched his hand. "Flanagan, shut up. This noble bit is wearing thin. I want to be with you. If you want *me*, just say it."

Smiling, he said: "Oh, I want you all right. . . ."

"Then tell him to lead the way. . . ." She keyed the ignition and the BMW purred.

Oscaro knocked on the double doors to a room on the top floor of the hotel, then opened it with his plastic keycard. He led them into an entry foyer, which looked into a large room. Three men, standing in the center of the room and holding glasses, paused in their conversation and looked toward the foyer. Estela could feel their leering looks like filthy hands all over her body. There were lots of ways men could look at you, and these guys were scoring very far down the scale. She knew she looked good tonight, but they were making her feel cheap. She didn't like them at all.

One of them wore the cloth of a priest—trimmed in magenta to show he held the title of monsignor. Tall and muscular, he looked very athletic and as though he were still in his thirties. He had deep-set eyes that gave him a hungry aspect. He was handsome in a rugged sort of way, unlike Tom who was good-looking in a more classical, Ivy League sense. On each side of the cleric stood two shorter, overweight men. They both looked to be in their forties. One of them sported a graying ponytail. The other was almost totally bald, with a heavy mustache.

"*Buona sera*, Domenico," said the monsignor, who walked toward them with his right hand extended. In almost perfect English, he said: "And welcome, Senator, Doctor Barrero. We would like to thank you very much for coming to see us on such . . . ah, short notice."

"Thank you," said Tom.

Everyone shook hands, with Tom being the gentleman, and Estela remaining quiet and guarded. Just in case Tom started getting overwhelmed by these guys, she figured she might have to be the one to keep things in perspective.

The monsignor smiled slyly. "Let me introduce you to my colleagues, Signor Claudio Umberri and Professor Mario Fiorello. My name is Monsignor Nicolo Sardo."

"What can we do for you, gentlemen?" Tom folded his hands, like a soccer player protecting his crotch.

The pony-tailed Professor Fiorello started to speak. His English was not nearly as smooth as Sardo's, but very serviceable. "As Mr. Oscaro has hopefully explained to you, we represent the pope's Special Commission on Miracles."

"Yes, he did," said Tom, remaining noncommittal.

That was good, she thought. There was something about this group she wasn't sure about. But how to check their credentials? Somehow she didn't think they'd have badge numbers.

"And we would like to ask you a few questions," said the bald-headed Mr. Umberri. "I am sure you understand."

Tom nodded, but otherwise transmitted the impression he was none too pleased with being yanked in off the highway in the middle of the night.

The group sensed his outrage and he was making them more than a little uncomfortable. As she watched him, she had to admire his ability to manipulate people with such subtlety. He was not only a handsome, stylish man, but he was also quite competent.

"Yes, of course," said Monsignor Sardo. "But first, let's all get a drink and possibly some sustenance. Gentlemen? Madame? Come this way, please. . . ."

Estela followed him into the center of the room, looking around casually. The suite at the Sheraton was big enough to host a small high school reunion, with enough food to feed them, as well. Estela eyed a table with platters of canapés, artful carvings of assorted meats, and other top-drawer hors d'oeuvres. A bartender stood at parade rest, flanked by a well-appointed bar. No expense had been spared for these men from the Vatican.

She watched them fill plates with various items and order their drinks. Tom asked for a double bourbon, waited for her to receive her requested Chardonnay.

"What do you make of all this?" he whispered as they prepared to join the commission members at a large conference table in the adjoining room.

"I think they're pretty creepy," she said quickly. "I don't trust them even a little bit."

He smiled. "Okay, good. Just making sure we're on the same page with this one."

They entered the conference room and took preassigned chairs that placed them at one end of the table while the three commissioners looked at them from the opposite pole. Special Vatican Agent Oscaro stood stoically by the door, like the sergeant-at-arms at a lodge meeting.

"This is just a preliminary hearing, Senator Flanagan," said Monsignor Sardo. "But we have been monitoring the newscasts and we have already spoken with your good friend, Mr. Constantino, so—"

"You *have*?" asked Tom. "When did you do that?"

Mr. Umberri fingered his mustache nervously, as though it were a habit of long standing. "Does that surprise you, Senator?"

"Well, not really. What surprises me is that Larry didn't tell me about it first."

Monsignor Sardo shrugged. "A matter to be taken up between the two of you, no doubt. But for us, we must begin." He looked to the ponytailed Professor Fiorello. "Mario . . . ?"

"Thank you," he said, and tried to offer everyone a polite smile. "As you might expect, we are asked to investigate many manifestations of God's presence on earth. What you might not realize is that we are very, very skeptical, that we do not rush to proclaim every weeping statue a miracle and every abandoned crutch at a grotto the proof of God's grace and presence."

Tom folded his hands before saying, "Actually, Professor, I have heard that the Vatican is very tough on miracles. . . ."

Umberri nodded emphatically. "The commission is aware of how urgently many people need to believe in miracles. It is a natural wish of the common man."

Estela could hear the condescension in their voices, and it disturbed her. She would say nothing, she decided, unless they addressed her directly.

"At any rate, we have gone over the facts of your case very thoroughly and we must say, Senator, that our commission has never encountered anything even remotely like this. This is . . . how can I say this? . . . this is the proof of God's presence that even the most callous infidels cannot deny."

Tom nodded, looked at each of the men for a moment.

"Does the Lord speak to you?" asked Monsignor Sardo.

"What's that?" asked Tom. "Do you mean do I hear a voice in my head?"

"We don't care how you describe it, Senator," said Umberri with another little tug at his mustache. "You know what we mean: Have you, at any time during this entire episode in your life, believed that you are in communication with another . . . how do you say it? . . . entity? . . . or being?"

Estela looked at him without being obvious, trying to be nonchalant. She knew he was inwardly deciding whether or not to tell them about the "visions." Her gut feeling was that he should keep his mouth shut if he was to disengage himself from this bunch. She could feel him wanting to exchange glances with her, but he obviously sensed it might tip his thoughts. It was one of those times when she wished that telepathy was real, so that she might reach out and tell him what he so desperately wanted to know.

"No," said Tom. "I have had no reason to believe any such thing. If you mean to suggest that God is talking to me, then no, I could not make any such claim."

The monsignor leaned forward. "And yet you have resurrected a human being, your best friend, plus a small boy at the Miami hospital."

"And the lab animals," said Professor Fiorello.

How did they know about that? Estela wondered. The Vatican intelligence network must be very accomplished. Despite Tom's bravado in dealing with these characters, she hoped that he appreciated the potential for trouble they obviously represented.

"Well, I'm not sure what I did. We are still trying to determine what the process actually is." He took a breath and continued to talk. His voice filled the room with its authority and confidence. "And just to set the record straight— The little boy had not yet died. But, after I touched him, the bone marrow cancer . . . ah, disappeared."

Umberri nodded. "How do you feel when these things are happening, when you 'touch' the subjects?"

Tom described the sense of disequilibrium, the dizzying sense of insignificance in the presence of some overwhelming force. He tried to explain that it was as though he were nothing but a conduit, a gateway through which some other reality could occasionally flow, or a tool, perhaps.

"A tool of God, you mean," said Monsignor Sardo.

Tom shrugged. "I guess . . ."

"You *do* believe in God, don't you?" asked Sardo. "You were born into the Holy Mother Church, were you not?"

"Yes, I was," said Tom, allowing a small nervous smile to escape him. "And I have to admit, until what's happened to me lately, I'm not sure what I believed regarding God. I guess I'd become an agnostic . . . at best."

"And what about *now*, Signor Senator?" Sardo had steepled his hands before him, his expression serious.

"I . . . I believe there are powers in the universe far greater than we can understand. If we agree to call that power 'God,' then I guess I believe in God."

Umberri raised a hand as though in class. "What about Jesus Christ as the Son of God?"

Tom hesitated. "I . . . I'm not sure I've given it enough thought as of yet."

"You have had all your life to do such thinking," said Monsignor Sardo.

Estela listened intently without allowing herself to look half as interested as she was. The comments and questions had a distinct edge to them, and it made her wonder what it must have been like to stand before Torquemada's crews centuries earlier.

Tom smiled. "I think the operative phrase there is 'your life'—meaning *mine*."

Sardo looked at him oddly. "I'm afraid I've lost your meaning, Senator."

"Meaning it's *my* life, and if I were you, I wouldn't worry so much about how I spent it."

Sardo smiled. "Oh, I see. Well, actually, it is your *soul* we priests have been charged with worrying about."

Tom grinned. "All right, I can accept that. No offense intended." He folded his arms, letting them know he could wait patiently for whatever they wished to ask. She had to admire his confidence, or at least his appearance of it.

"I am sorry we have put you on the defensive, Senator," said Monsignor Sardo. "But we are both excited and fearful of your case."

The ponytailed professor nodded vigorously. "The millennium approaches, Senator. There are hundreds of millions of people who believe the end of the world is imminent. They are looking for signs from God."

"And your miraculous talent could indeed be the most significant sign these are indeed the end times," said Claudio Umberri. "We are keeping a close watch on the media and the pulse of the people of the world."

"Yes," said Professor Fiorello. "You could be on the brink of some kind of worldwide acclamation. People could easily begin thinking of you as some kind of messiah, or at least a messenger of the Messiah himself."

"Why not the Antichrist?" asked Tom.

The monsignor stood up, placed his hands on the table and leaned forward. His handsome features were hard, chiseled. His expression a combination of sincerity and apprehension. "That thought has already occurred to us, Senator."

"And?" Tom looked from one commissioner to the other.

"And we have no reason to believe that you are any such being."

"If I'm the Antichrist, then I haven't even told *myself* yet."

Sardo grinned. "This commission has a history that goes back to the Middle Ages, Senator. We arrive at no snap decisions. We will be very patient and analyze the answers of your interview with us now, with the results of the current testing in Miami, and perhaps our own testing later."

"Your own?"

Sardo nodded.

"And when does this take place?"

Professor Fiorello looked quickly from Sardo to Tom before volunteering an answer, his ponytail swinging back and forth. "We will inform you when the commission would be convening a research team, and then a schedule could be . . . arranged."

Tom grinned. "Arranged like this little meeting?"

The monsignor's eyebrows narrowed. "Senator, I hope you realize that Mr. Oscaro and his associates could make additional arrangements *tonight*, if the commission so deems it, to have you accompany us to the Vatican immediately. Indeed, it may be in our favor to have you in Rome to await our schedule of tests."

Tom looked at her, and she attempted to appear unruffled by the veiled threat. She knew she could project the hautiness of a Spanish princess when necessary, and did so. Although it shocked her to hear them talking about just crating them off to Italy in the middle of the night, her more rational side kept telling her it was just a threat to keep Tom in a cooperative mood. The disappearance of a senator, a presidential candidate, would be cause for great concern, and despite whatever special powers or abilities this bunch from the Vatican might have, she doubted if they could elude a major intelligence effort by Uncle Sam.

Tom had paused to assemble his answer. When he spoke, he was forthright, confident. "I have no doubt that you could do exactly as you say, Monsignor. My point was not meant to be provocative. Rather, I was suggesting that middle-of-the-night tactics would not be necessary."

Signor Umberri raised his index finger. "Meaning you would continue to be cooperative?"

"I have nothing to hide." Tom paused. "If you want to know the truth, I would feel better if what has happened to me was *not* a secret."

Umberri tilted his head, looked at him askance. "The cover of *Time* and *Newsweek* is hardly keeping you a secret," he said.

"Those stories were mostly speculation. They received a lot of criticism."

"True," said Umberri. "However . . . ?"

"However, I can assure you—it has been difficult to keep everything inside. There are things few people know or would understand. It's been a burden."

Monsignor Sardo resumed his chair and smiled. "Let us help you with your burden, Senator."

Tom exhaled, looked at the cleric. "There's something else you can do for me. I'm curious about what Larry Constantino told you."

"He is a very devout and religious man," said Signor Umberri.

"Why do you ask?" said Sardo, his gaze thin and penetrating.

"Because I told him everything that happened in confidence and he has broken that trust repeatedly," said Tom. "I can't understand it, and I want to know why."

"The man has been touched by God," said Sardo. "I think the experience has changed him profoundly. He believes his first duty is to his Church. He is compelled to speak loudly about his trip back from the Light of Heaven."

Tom said nothing, for a moment just staring at them. Estela saw them as so smug, so comfortable in their theology and their positions of power. Tom could shake them up, but she knew he was being careful. Two decades in the Senate had taught him well.

"Did you ask him what he remembers about being *dead*?" Tom fired off the question unexpectedly. It hit them all broadside and they were clearly surprised.

"That was one of our primary interests," said Professor Fiorello.

"Why do *you* want to know?" asked Sardo. Estela had figured him to be the sharpest, the most dangerous, and the man was proving her right.

Tom shrugged. "Because I could never get a straight answer out of him. Did he see God? The angels? Jesus?"

"He claims he did not," said Umberri. "He remembers a fairly familiar out-of-body experience wherein he watched you resurrect him. But other than that, he said it was like waking up from a blank sleep."

Tom looked at them. "Do you think that's what death might be like—just a blank sleep? A nothingness. That maybe there's just life and no-life. No God. No . . . Jesus or heaven or any of that business."

Monsignor Sardo said, "Senator, please understand, we are Roman Catholic faithfuls. How could we possibly think any of those things?"

"I don't presume to know," said Tom. "That's why I was asking. Because all this talk seems to be skirting the real issue here—what is happening? I mean *really* happening. What happens when we die? Isn't that what this is all about?"

"To you, perhaps," said Sardo. "The Church is interested in any miracles as a testament to the greater glory of God."

"But doesn't that depend on whether or not God is *doing* it?" Tom leaned on the table, looked from one commissioner to the other.

"Meaning?" said Professor Fiorello.

"Meaning that maybe I am doing it on my own—then what? What does that mean? Doctor Barrero told me, and I'm sure you folks have picked it up through your own channels, that there's something different in my brain now. Since the plane crash, my brain is missing a part that nobody really knows much about. Has my injury unleashed some hidden power that resides in all of us?"

Professor Fiorello glanced at his colleagues, raised a single eyebrow. "Interesting thought, but you are not the first person in the history of medical research to experience trauma to the hippocampal region. . . ."

"And no one has ever exhibited a talent such as yours," said Sardo, who looked at his watch with a flourish of impatience. "Ah, Senator, it grows late, we will not detain you much longer. A few more questions and we should be able to conclude the evening."

"Really?"

"Yes, please consider this little meeting a chance to become acquainted, that is all."

"I see," said Tom.

She watched discreetly and listened intently as they finished the interrogation. She knew he didn't feel like covering the details and answers that had become so much a part of him he could recite the information like a child with his catechism. But he cooperated with them, giving them all the data they wanted.

Enduring the process for another hour, Estela had plenty of time to replay the evening's events and assess her emotional involvement with everything. When Mr. Oscaro had interrupted them, they were on their way to her house in Turnberry, where the clothes were finally going to come off. Now that she'd had time to think about it, unswayed by pheromones or alcohol, she realized that her attraction to Thomas Flanagan was real. It was pure and sincere.

She knew this was true because she'd finally had a chance to see him in the real world, interacting with characters in an arena beyond the ken of the average man. And he was not an average man. He'd handled himself in their world with a confidence that bespoke a firm belief in one's self. Despite his current anxieties, Flanagan remained a formidable presence.

A presence that could easily fill the terrible absence in her own life.

Estela still wanted him. She didn't care how long the James Bonds might detain him. She would still be there.

Waiting. Wanting.

THIRTY

Lattimore

Senator Erskine Lattimore had just slipped into a pair of hand-sewn silk pajamas he'd purchased many years ago on a senatorial vacation to a place they used to call "the Orient," when the phone rang.

Sitting on the edge of the bed, he leaned over to pick up the receiver. It was one of those ornately fashioned decorator pieces that was supposed to blend in with Louis Quattorze furniture that his wife Harriet loved so much, but to Erskine it was just a clumsy, uncomfortable pain-in-the-ass piece of junk.

"Hello," he said hoarsely in a low voice. He looked over at Harriet, who lay sleeping on her side, a hairnet gathering up the gray tangle on her head. In that moment, she looked so . . . so *old* to him, he couldn't imagine what he was doing with her.

"It's the newsboy," said the familiar voice on the other end of the line.

Erskine sighed, looked at his watch. "Jesus Christ, do you know what time it is?"

"I don't punch a time clock. Do you want the latest or not?"

Erskine looked over at Harriet. Her snoring had turned up a notch. "I'm listening. . . ."

The voice filled him in on the latest adventures of Tom Flanagan, gave him a verbal invoice for the service, and hung up.

Erskine, who had been very tired only moments ago, had become suddenly energized. Replacing that godawful phone on the night table, Erskine stood up from the bed and slipped silently out into the hall and down the carpeted stairs to the foyer. His stately colonial in Falls Church seemed so damned quiet at night, felt as though even the sound of his own breathing was echoing through the house like a banshee's wail.

He slipped into the study and closed the double doors behind him. Time for a little cognac and a smoke, he thought as he moved to a built-in liquor cabinet surrounded by leatherbound volumes of the classics. Books he would never open, much less read. As he broke the seal on a new bottle of Courvoisier, filled a snifter with three fingers of liquid gold, he smiled to himself. His own efforts to leak misinformation and stir up the tabloids were being eclipsed by the antics of Flanagan's own campaign manager and the senator himself. It was time to step up the heat and get some of the Deep Cover people involved in his life. Besides, if there was any truth to what they were saying about Flanagan, he might even prove useful.

Erskine seated himself at his hand-carved desk from Barcelona and penned a few lines in his notebook. It was time to contact some cabinet members, chairmen, and agency directors. Time to call in the favors and ensure that the party stayed in power. There was only one thing left that really mattered to him anymore, and that was winning the next election. He wanted it more than he'd even realized until it became clear that he actually had a chance.

He would do anything necessary now. Erskine Lattimore would leave his mark on history.

And Flanagan would be relegated to some dusty footnotes in the *Congressional Record*.

THIRTY-ONE

Flanagan

He studied the dwindling image of Oscaro's men in her BMW's side mirror. They stood like pieces of crude sculpture in the hotel parking lot watching the car blend back into the Miami night.

"Hell of a first date, huh?" He looked at her and laughed, feeling immensely better when she joined him.

Holding on to the wheel with both hands, Estela threw him a quick look—all big eyes and sexy mouth. "I have to give it to you, Flanagan—you give a woman an interesting night out."

"Thanks."

"That's the first time I was ever kidnapped by Vatican Secret Service agents," she said. "Beats a movie, every time. . . ."

They chuckled together, and he reached out to touch her arm. Her skin felt hot, silky. "Thanks for putting up with all that business," he said. "I was afraid for a little while back there that we were in some serious trouble."

"Really?"

"The SSV doesn't fool around. They might not look like much, but they use some of the best people in the world."

"I'd never heard of them," she said, easing the coupe onto the ramp for the coastal highway again.

"They don't exactly put up billboards."

Estela smiled, kept her attention on the road. It was very late on a weeknight. The highway was an empty tube hollowed into the night. Neither of them spoke for a minute or two, and he reflected on everything that had been happening. The last six weeks seemed telescoped, collapsed into several days and nights, and yet the time seemed to have contained far more experience and sensation than was possible. A gestalt time distortion so intense, Tom had trouble accepting all that he'd been through in that time.

A few more miles slipped beneath them before she spoke again. "Aren't you curious where we're going?"

"Not really—as long as it's your house," he said, trying to combine the charm of Harrison Ford with the swagger of Clint Eastwood. It sounded silly even to him, but she looked at him and just nodded.

It was about what he expected of a doctor's house in Florida. There was more than enough moonlight to accent the palm trees and manicured shrubbery. Flowerbeds and rock gardens surrounded the one-story home. Spanish tiles and white stucco created a familiar, appropriate motif. Inside, the rooms were spacious, airy, and decorated with an eclectic touch. The architecture was unpredictable, with the rooms broken up by steps and mini-levels and many short corridors and passages to other parts of the house. Window walls, sealed off from the night by miniblinds, defined the side of the house that faced what she told him was a canal and a decent view of the water.

She gave him a short tour, pausing only long enough for him to notice the things she wanted him to notice. There were books everywhere, and he liked that. Even though his political life had consumed him to the point of no-time-for-anything-else, there had been a point in his life when books were his friends, and he always felt comfortable in a home full of books.

Trouble was, you just didn't see it all that often anymore. Posters from art museums and movie lobbies filled her walls, along with shelves and étagères jammed with interesting stuff that ranged from Disney character coffee mugs to toys from the Star Wars movies to South American Indian sculpture. Her taste in furniture ran toward the lean, functional styles of Northern Europe, but she liked the warmth of textured rugs on the ceramic tiles and tapestries lining the hallways. Magazines littered coffee and end tables and even the kitchen counters. Her bookshelf stereo was small and unassuming, flanked by several racks of CDs—mostly Broadway shows.

She stopped short of the bath and bedrooms, ending things in a room with a bar and a big-screen TV. Beyond the bar, patio doors opened onto a wooden deck that reached away from the house into a junglelike canopy of fronds and branches.

"Would you like something to drink?" she said as she glided behind the bar.

"Only if you do."

Estela smiled. "I don't drink that often, but tonight I'm going to have some zinfandel. I've got Jack Daniel's and Grand-dad if you want bourbon."

"Actually, I could use one or two," he said. "Can you just splash it over the rocks?"

"Can do."

As he watched her move with grace and efficiency, he realized he'd stopped thinking of her as a doctor, and was actually having a tough time making that concept real any longer. She had become a real person to him, and more importantly, she had become very much a woman. Her dinner dress revealed her firm, athletic frame in a way the hospital greens and lab coat never could.

"Here you are. *Salud!*"

They clinked their glasses and sipped slowly. He did his best to keep looking at her over the rim of the tumbler, and he noticed she did the same.

"Did you see the deck?" Gently taking his arm, she led him through the double doors out into the starlight. So thick were the surrounding trees and shrubbery, he could see nothing beyond their green darkness.

Estela moved to the railing, touched a covered switch. In the far corner of the slatted wood flooring, a blue-green square of light blinked on to define the churning waters of a hot tub.

"Nice," he said.

It was the only word he could say. Just looking at the tub had conjured up instant images of her out here on the deck, dropping a robe off her bare shoulders and pausing naked for a moment under the vault of stars.

"I use it a lot," she said. "It's so private here, don't you think?"

"I do think," he said, taking a large swallow of the bourbon. The sweet fire raked his throat, spark-plugged his libido. He knew what was coming, what they both wanted to come, but for the first time in as long as he could remember, he felt differently about everything. Not just about Estela, who had certainly become special to him as a person, but regarding himself as well. It was as though he were learning about who he was for the first time. The sensation was at once exhilarating and also utterly terrifying.

She placed her wineglass on the railing and moved close to him, putting her arms over his shoulders. As she burned a look into him with those deep brown eyes, Tom tried to keep things under control. Suddenly, he felt so nervous, so . . . unsure of himself. A wave of nostalgia crested over him, coupled with a memory from his junior prom when he tried to kiss Julia Feeney during the last dance. He could remember the double pressure of Julia's pointy little breasts pressing through the starched panel of his rented tuxedo shirt, and how he knew he would always remember that night. He'd spent the entire song (never hearing a word or a note of it) trying to figure out how to just tilt his head down and finally *kiss* her, and how she solved the whole thing by looking up and kissing *him*, and pressing those mysterious little points deeper into his clothes. He knew that he'd reached a pivotal moment in his life, and was smart enough to not only recognize it, but to know he would never forget it. At sixteen years old, it was just about the most erotic thing he could ever have happen to him.

And it was. Always had been.

Until now.

When she kissed him, the memory shattered like an old mirror, and he knew it would never be the same. Her lips, always looking so full and pouty, so kissable, proved to be some wild exponent of all of those things. Their contact stunned him with a torrent of sensations. Her lips were utterly and impossibly soft, yet full of definition and confidence.

She kissed, then waited for his response, which he knew must be the correct one, or she would reject him as unworthy. After an initiative such as hers, he would have to equal her mastery. And here he was feeling so completely awkward, so clumsy and unsophisticated. This was no time to be a rough slob, a fumbling, overanxious bumpkin, and he knew that. The lady had communicated what she wanted, needed. He must deliver.

Tentatively at first, then more forcefully as he detected her responding, he rejoined the kiss, trying to tell her through his actions that he comprehended her message, that he was capable of speaking the same language.

Spiraling down to a timeless place, at the center of the vortex we call our emotions and sensations, he fell with her. And he knew he'd reached another turning point in a life checkered with both good and bad ones. Moving through a strange and beautiful choreography, he mirrored her desire. Clothes sloughed off like discarded shells, and ignoring the stuck zippers and uncooperative buttons, they were soon naked together.

Without realizing it, she had guided him down to the hot, rushing water. Instantly a druglike rush passed through him; the instant submersion in the heated tub had catalyzed the stress and the alcohol and the lust into a hallucinatory bodyburst of feeling and desire. There was no drug that could do this, no words to describe it. He was powerless to do anything other that accept it and make it part of him.

Time stretched out like a languid body, embraced them. Every touch, every kiss, lasted forever. It was so good, it was almost spooky. He'd never felt so totally in synch with a woman. Their movements, anticipations, everything just felt so *right*. As though they'd known each other for years.

So focused, so completely consumed by her, he lost all sense of place and time. The deck and the house, the night sky and the water, everything slipped into some other dimensional reality. The only thing real was their two bodies, joining to become a single entity as the light of the stars burned down upon them.

Later. Much later, she had guided him, weak-kneed, through the labyrinth of the house to her bed. He'd sunk into it like a torpedoed tanker, slipping beneath the waves of sleep so quickly, it was as if he'd never been awake. Yet, exhausted as he was, he saw the essential truth in that—he'd only now sat up from a sleep lasting his entire life.

As he drifted in the nether zone between wakefulness and oblivion, feeling the silky heat of her body next to his, he felt truly complete, truly happy and content. It was a sensation unknown to him since his childhood, and it comforted him to know that being alive could be so simple and so good.

Which made what happened next all the more difficult to face. . . .

THIRTY-TWO

Flanagan

Thomas.

The voice reached deep into the well for him, pulling him up from the sweet darkness. Disorientation and a sense of floating, suspended somewhere in that region between wakefulness and a trance. There was a slight buzzing sound in his ears as he tried to lift his head, found that he could not. The brief wavering image of the red circle, floating, blurry, distant. A disc. A sphere. A dying star.

Easier to just let go . . . fade away . . . back to sl—)

Thomas.

He lay on his back, eyes closed, sensation returning inexorably. thinking vaguely that Estela was talking to him.

(How could she still be awake . . . ?)

It's been some time since we spoke.

Blinking his eyes, he was suddenly aware of the room enclosing him like a box, a cell. Estela spooned him, her breathing deep and regular. It was as though he were looking at everything for the first time. The furniture draped in night shadows, the moon at the windows.

Thomas.

And he was now totally awake, feeling a vacuum form under his stomach, everything falling away.

(Not again . . .)

Did you really think you'd heard the last of me?

(I was hoping you weren't real.)

No chance.

(Who are you? What the fuck do you want with me?)

You didn't tell them about me. Why?

The question penetrated him like a spear, and he was instantly alert, wary.

(Who are you?)

Why didn't you tell them, Thomas?

The voice resonated through his skull, compelling, almost hypnotic.

(Because . . . because I didn't want them to think I was crazy.)

Are you sure that's it?

(Because . . . I think I tried to believe you weren't real—whoever the fuck you are. Because I guess I don't really want to know. . . .)

The Catholics got you thinking, did they?

(If you *are* God, I guess I'm saying I don't want to know it. Only nuts talk to Him.)

Laughter. Or rather the *suggestion* of it. Soft yet pervasive.

Do you remember someone called Entropy?

The name cratered his memory with explosive impact. It was a name he hadn't even thought of since he was fourteen years old. *Entropy?* Impossible!

(How could you know about him? *Nobody* knew about him!)

Without thinking, he'd bolted upright in the bed, staring at some unfixed point on the ceiling, or perhaps beyond it.

I know everything about you, Thomas.

(No!)

Isn't it obvious yet?

(How *could* you? Who the fuck are you!?)

You know who I am—think about it. Entropy's closest friend. His "confidant," as it were. Although you were too young to understand or use the word.

(That's bullshit! You're not real! You can't——)

I am real. You know that.

(Then that's not your real name.)

If you are Entropy, then you know who I am.

(Dr. Infinity. . . .)

The metaphor is finally complete.

Sweat had burst from his pores as though the conversation were squeezing it out of him. He could feel his heart pounding raggedly. He was scared, plain and simple. Because he *knew* he was losing his mind. There was absolutely no one in the world who ever knew about Infinity and Entropy.

No one.

They were a secret so profoundly private they never escaped the prison of his adolescent fantasy world. This could only mean what he had suspected and never wanted to deal with.

(This is all in my head, isn't it? I'm talking to myself. I'm so buggering crazy I'll never get back. . . .)

A suggestion of laughter.

We must get past this idea of being crazy. Accept the reality, Thomas. I am real. And I know the deepest core thoughts and secrets that define you.

(I created you. A stupid boy fantasy. Only *I* could know this stuff about me.)

Untrue. You were merely prescient. Anticipating the reality that we together have become. Work through the memories. Recall your vision as fully as I have done. You will have the key to everything.

(So why all the mystery? Why don't you just come out and tell me what's going on?)

Because you would no more accept me and my solution than you do the Catholics and their thugs.

He considered this and knew it was true. Whoever or whatever this contact might be—granting that it was not part of some grandiose psychosis—it was unerringly correct. He needed to be convinced rather than accept anything on faith.

(Does God think all religions are a mistake . . . ?)

Why ask me?

(Just checking . . . forget it.)

I detect a change in posture. Accepting. Less fear.

(Do I have a choice? I haven't figured out a way to get you out of my head unless you feel like leaving.)

True.

(And I have this other thought—that maybe I am laboring under some massive psychotic episode, and none of this is real. From the very beginning. Larry, the little boy, Estela, you, even me. Maybe I'm just zoned out on Thorazine somewhere quiet and comfortable and this whole deal is just a few seconds of errant sparks between injections. . . .)

Intriguing, but untrue.

(Okay, supposing I give you that—just to get on with this. So what is this all about? What do you want with me?)

You will be tested very soon.

(Tested . . . ? For what? By who?)

By whom.

(Dr. Infinity was not a grammarian. . . .)

The test shall come from within you.

When you got right down to it, Tom had always hated cryptic things like riddles and allegories and secret codes. If he really was over the edge and just talking to himself, he would *never* do it like this—with all the veiled references and mystery—because it simply was not his style.

(From within *me*? Like I'm going to test myself?)

Not exactly.

(You said *will*. You mean you always know the future? You can predict it?)

Not so much prediction as prescience. I receive . . . feelings that things will occur in certain ways.

(And why the attention on me?)

Good question. Because you are special, Thomas. You know that. We've already been over this.

(Okay, so what about this test? When does it happen?)

Soon. I cannot be more precise.

(And why are you telling me this? Is it a warning you're giving me?)

Yes and no.

(Thanks for the straight answer.)

You must be vigilant. But a warning would not stop what will happen. The test is in how you deal with it.

(And you can't tell me what's going to happen?)

It would ruin the test.
(Of course. Sorry, I wasn't thinking.)
Do not be impatient. In time, you will understand everything.

There was something about the voice that scared him. He wasn't sure he wanted to understand *any* of it. He wished he could just drop out and run away with the woman who lay asleep beside him. He felt like he'd finally found someone meaningful and the urge to escape was overwhelming.

There is no escape, Thomas.
(You can tell my every thought, can't you?)
When I am paying attention, yes.
(That's very scary, you know.)
I'm sure it is.
(Just tell me one thing. . . .)
Perhaps . . .
(Are you an . . . an angel?)
Laughter. Soft. Dark.
No.
(Are you human?)
That remains to be seen.
(More riddles. Thanks. Glad I asked.)

There came no response, other than a gradually forming image in the foreground of his consciousness, like an unconscious hologram, floating in front of his thoughts. He knew what it would be before it gathered any shape or real substance, and the terror of its insistence ate into him like a terrible acid.

The red sphere. The indistinct circle of color. Hanging in front of him like the half-held memory of a nightmare. Always close enough to make him anxious and instantly fearful. A globe of red light glowing with a darker heart that could be a symbol or a letter. There was something about the image that scared him, even though he had no idea what it was. . . .

But he knew he was being shown the red sphere for a reason.

(What *is* this fucking thing!?)

He launched the question like a retaliatory missile, but there was no response.

He sat there, staring at the ceiling for another minute or two, at the place where the red ball of darkly glowing light had begun to fade away like a dying star. Gradually, he became aware of being alone again.

Alone in his own mind. Weird concept to think otherwise. Weren't we always alone?

(Sure. Till *now*.)

"You there?" he asked aloud.

Echoing through the dark space, his voice sounded far louder than it should have.

The red orb was almost gone, slipping back to the place of its own dim existence. He watched it disappear in his mind.

"Hey? What happened?" He tried to whisper, but the words seemed to swell and amplify as they left his mouth. The bedroom reduced to a hollow cell, a resonant chamber of reverb.

Estela stirred beside him just as he realized the connection had been broken. Whoever Dr. Infinity really might be, he had ghosted away from him.

"Flanagan . . ."

The voice startled him and he tensed for an instant, looking in both directions. "Where are you?"

"Flanagan, are you okay?"

Her voice penetrated the gauzy film of his confusion, surprising him. "What . . . ? Oh, Christ, I'm sorry. Did I wake you up?"

"Well, you were getting pretty loud," she said, propping herself up on one elbow.

"Sorry." He rubbed his eyes, looked at her clearly. In the wash of moonlight, her naked skin looked like polished marble.

(Beautiful. No other word for it.)

"What happened?"

"You know." The words just escaped him. He felt ashamed to have to admit to her that he was still having the . . . visions.

"Bad?"

He shrugged. "I don't know. I thought maybe they might be over. Wishful thinking, it looks like."

"Was it the same . . . person?"

"Oh, yeah."

"What does he want with you?"

In that instant, he grew tired of answering her questions. Not that she was bugging him or that the questions were an irritation. Rather, he didn't feel like telling her what happened in fragments. Better to just let it out. Let it go. . . .

". . . and suddenly he was gone again. So fast I didn't even know I was alone. That's when I woke you up."

She looked at him in silence, no trace of amusement on her face. But no fear, either. She was a strong woman. Her ability to absorb whatever he told her was nothing short of incredible. Either her nurturing instincts or her natural curiosity were keener than he ever experienced.

"Okay, you know what my first question is, don't you?"

He nodded. "Sure. Just exactly who are these guys Entropy and Dr. Infinity?"

She risked a small grin. "Go on."

"Promise you won't laugh?"

"Flanagan, don't insult me."

"Sorry, Doc. Don't know what I was thinking." She was right about that. If anyone had shown their allegiance and their empathy to his problems, it had been the Good Doctor Barrero.

Reclining into a pile of fluffed pillows, she looked at him with an expression that said she would be very patient and attentive.

"Okay, here goes," he said. "When I was a kid—ten maybe eleven or so—I was really into comics. They had some pretty weird stuff back then. E.C. Comics had *Tales From the Crypt* and *Shock Suspense* and *Weird Science Fantasy* and stuff like that. And then there was *Batman* and *Superman, Blackhawk, Green Lantern*, all those guys. . . . I loved all those great stories. I would sit for hours and hours in my room after school and late at night with my Cub Scout flashlight under the sheets. I collected everything. Comics were my life for a while there."

She touched his arm. "Nothing to laugh about so far. Lots of kids loved comics. I used to read *Archie*."

He nodded. "Yeah, but did you create your characters? Make your own comics?"

She looked at him and smiled just a little. "*Entropy* and *Dr. Infinity*?"

"Smart lady you are. I used to have these big pulp paper drawing pads that my mom would get from the stationers in town, and I tried to teach myself how to draw comics. Never had a lesson in my life and I guess I was always pretty terrible, but it kept me busy and I loved it. *Entropy* and *Dr. Infinity* were my characters."

"What are you telling me, that they've come to life? That they're the ones talking to you in these dreams, these visions . . . ?"

"Hey, I asked you not to laugh, remember?"

She took his hand, squeezed it. "Do I look like I'm laughing?"

"No."

"Then go on. Tell me more. What did your characters do?"

He chuckled darkly, shook his head. "That's just it. Entropy was this guy who could . . . well, he could bring people back to life."

She tightened her grip on his hand. "Just like you can."

"Yeah. Just like me."

His words escaped into the room and lingered between them like a dangerous vapor. *Just like me.*

(What in hell was this all about?)

"What does this mean?"

"Estela, I don't even *begin* to know." He paused and looked off toward the moonlight at the windowpane, letting all the detail wash back over him like a retreating tide reluctant to leave the beach. ". . . and Entropy, by the way, he worked for Dr. Infinity, who was this guy in a white lab coat and a weird helmet and he could see into the future—that was his special super-power. They both got their powers when this asteroid crashed into the lake where they were camping. The radiation from the blast made them superheroes."

He spoke slowly, wistfully, and as he explained everything to her, images he had not conjured up in almost forty years materialized from the yellow fog of memory.

234 THOMAS F. MONTELEONE

Towering, muscular, square-jawed. His superheroes were moral and idealistic, suffused with American self-right-eousness. His clumsy drawings had possessed him back then, had powered his dreams and his ambitions and his simple needs. To spend his life drawing comics had been the only thing that mattered.

Life had been so simple then. He envied that ten-year-old Tommy Flanagan.

"And you never made the connection?" she said.

"What's that? Sorry, I was just remembering how I used to sit there for hours drawing those awful characters."

"I'm sure they weren't so awful," said Estela. "But what about *now*? You never made the association? It never hit you that you were acting out your childhood creation . . . ?"

He felt embarrassed to admit it. It seemed so obvious. How could he have forgotten such a thing? "I think I probably repressed it."

"Why would you do that?"

Another memory clawed its way to the surface. A day he'd decided to selectively remove from his life. "My father . . ."

"What happened?" Her expression revealed her sensitivity. She knew they were entering dangerous territory and she was respectful of that.

He exhaled evenly, willing away the tension and allowing himself to reconstruct the day he came home from school to find his father waiting for him in his room.

"He didn't know about my sketchbooks. My mother never told him because she knew he would've been furious."

"Why?"

"It was just his way. My father was a hard man. His father had been an Irish laborer and a wife-beating drunk. My father learned how to survive by becoming a steely discipli-narian in his own affairs, pulling himself up by his bootstraps. He created his own construction company, saved plenty of money, and somewhere along the way decided his only son was going to be a lawyer."

"Did you love him? Did he love you?"

He considered her questions—ones he expected from Estela. Behind her outer shields of competence and intelligence lurked a very emotional, very caring person who understood the power of love.

"Did I love him?" he repeated her words. "I don't know if I ever did. I feared him. Respected him. But I don't remember ever feeling any upswelling of emotion for him. And I have no memory of him even hugging me, much less telling me he loved me."

"That's so terrible."

He shrugged. "Well, he was just a cold, cold bastard. What can you say?"

"Is he still alive?"

"Nah. Had a massive stroke—oh, about eight years ago. Right around when Chip was first starting high school. Yeah, Gramps went out with a bomb going off in his head."

"You must have been a very sad and lonely little boy." She moved closer to him, nuzzling his chest.

He could smell perfume in her hair; it blended with her natural scents with such harmony he almost lost the thread of their conversation. "Yes," he said. "I guess I was, but I don't think I knew it at the time."

"How so?"

"I had my own little world, remember?" Tom could remember how he would lean against the door of his bedroom closet, drawing pictures and panels endlessly, getting lost in the stories that etched away from the point of his pencil.

". . . until that day your father entered it."

He nodded, shaking off a chill that accompanied the memory. "I came home from school and there he was— standing in the middle of my room. My comics were scattered everywhere, like there'd been this big explosion, and all my sketchbooks, stacks and stacks of them were piled up on the bed where he'd been looking through them. I don't know how he found them or what he was doing up there. But I remember feeling so . . . so embarrassed, like he'd caught me in the bathroom masturbating or something like that."

"But why?" she said. "You hadn't done anything wrong."

"Oh, but I *had*," he said. "Two things, actually: one, I had kept a secret from him, which was the same as lying, and two, I was doing something that he considered a complete waste of time."

"What did he do?" She held his hand a little tighter again, like a little girl listening to a story at a campfire.

"You mean before, or after, he whaled into me?"

"Oh, God . . ."

"Well, I remember my whole head feeling numb and swollen as he dragged me out into the backyard. Back then, people had firepits where they burned leaves every fall, even trash if they felt like it. . . ."

Estela tensed. "Please, don't tell me he—"

"Oh yeah. Every comic. Every scrap of paper, and every one of my sketch pads. Thousands of afternoons of doodling and struggling with my pencils and erasers to get this line or that shading just right. He made me toss each one into the fire—one by one."

"Some people shouldn't be allowed to be parents," she said with obvious venom.

He shook his head. "You ought to make that *most* people."

"That's such an awful story. What did you do then?"

Without thinking, he stood up and walked naked to the window. There wasn't much to see other than the top fronds and leaves of the landscape frosted with moonglow, but he was looking at a time far beyond it. "I . . . I just stopped . . ." he said softly.

"What do you mean 'stopped'?"

"I stopped thinking about all that stuff. I stopped thinking about my father. Stopped talking to him—unless he spoke to me first, asked me a direct question. Otherwise, I never said another word to him. And I stopped my drawing and my comics and my characters. I stopped creating them, and I stopped thinking about them. I knew the only way I'd ever survive what he did to me was to make believe that part of me had never existed. That's why I did it. And that's probably why I didn't 'make the connection,' as you said."

"I am so sorry," she said. And he could tell she meant it. She had a throaty whisper that was sexy but also earth-mothery, supportive, sincere. "I'm sorry I made you go through all that stuff, to relive it like that."

"It wasn't so bad. I actually feel better, like I've released some bile I've been carrying around for far too long."

Turning, he returned to her bed, slipped under the sheets and sought her warm, smooth skin.

"But what does all this mean?" she said, wrapping herself in her own arms, as though suddenly cold. "It's kind of scary, don't you think?"

"Nobody except my parents ever knew about Entropy or Dr. Infinity," he said. "How could this guy in my . . . my visions know about them?"

"I've been thinking about that," she said. "And there can only be a few answers. One—you're creating these visions yourself. As much as you think they're real, as much as you've convinced yourself, they're just *not*."

"Estela, I'm not trying to be difficult, but I can tell you I'm *not* making any of this up. . . ."

"All right, then there's two—somebody can read your mind and he's using this Dr. Infinity thing to scare you."

"But why would he want to do that? What does he want with me?"

She paused for a moment. "He said you were going to be tested, right?"

"Whatever *that* means. . . ."

"It means you're being manipulated." She said it with distaste and anger.

"Well, wait a minute," he said cautiously. "There's a *third* possibility. . . ."

"There is?"

"That maybe it *is* God who's talking to me."

"I thought you didn't believe in God. That's what you told those Vatican types."

"Not exactly. But I'm just saying—this stuff about a 'test' sounds like something from the Bible, don't you think? I mean, if I am being manipulated, who better for the job than God Himself?"

"Flanagan, hold me," she said, reaching out to him. "This is all making me feel very weird. I feel like we've opened a door. A door to a place where no one's ever been before."

He took her into his arms, felt the points of her breasts against him, and he wanted her. Even though he knew the timing was all wrong, being this close to her, both physically and emotionally, was very exciting to him. He didn't say anything for a few minutes and neither did she. Thoughts skipped across his mind like pebbles bounced off the smooth surface of a pond.

"Maybe God is telling me I have to become a *real* Entropy kind of character. Maybe I have to dedicate my life to healing people. To bringing them all back to life . . ."

She shook her head. "Do you want the truth on that one?"

"Of course."

"It sounds grandiose, delusional."

"Really? I thought it would appeal to your Hippocratic nature."

She smiled. "No, I mean think about it rationally. How could you possibly heal *everybody*? And bringing people back to life—how would you decide who gets help and who doesn't? Where would you find the time? You wouldn't have a life of your own."

"You're right," he said. "I hadn't thought this thing through."

"Understandably. It's not your everyday problem. And there's the other thing—if you're supposed to bring everybody back from the dead, what's the reason for it all?"

He'd been asking himself a similar question and he didn't like the answer he kept getting. "I don't know. It's the millennium. Maybe it's going to be the end of the world."

She looked out into the empty space of the room, as though afraid to look him in the eye. "I've thought about that, too. It's silly, I know. But old myths die hard."

"Judgment day," he said. "Maybe I'm part of it. . . ."

Neither spoke for what seemed like a very long time. The night leaked through the windows like a cold, dead sea, drowning them in a silence profound.

THIRTY-THREE

Barrero

She woke up before him the next morning and decided to fix a big breakfast—something she never did anymore.

Working in her spacious, sun-washed kitchen, she realized how restrictive her life had become. Her house had become an insular cell, a bombshelter to keep out as much of the world's flak as possible. She was far too young to pull in her wings so completely. There was still time to fly and she knew she must do it soon.

But was Tom Flanagan the right man to do it with?

The question had been nagging her since the first moment she realized she was falling for him.

Why was it always like that?

How did this man work his way so close to her heart? Her first impression of him had been terrible. In fact, so had her second and third and she didn't know how many . . .

But something had happened between them. Something that had bonded them together as efficiently as Krazy Glue. Looking back, now, Estela had no idea how it happened, only that it did.

When he stumbled into the bright room, he had to shield his eyes from the bright sunlight. It fell through the clerestory windows and bounced off all the white and yellow ceramic tiles in a dazzling display.

"Good morning," she said. "Feeling okay?"

He nodded, spotted the coffee maker and a mug waiting for him. It had two words in Helvetica type on the side: CARPE DIEM. He said nothing till he had poured some Colombian Special Blend into the mug, then: "Good coffee . . . and yes, I feel great. How about you?"

"I made us some breakfast. I hope you like eggs."

"Love them. But watch the cholesterol."

She smiled. "As your doctor, I can tell you—this meal is not hazardous to your health."

They sat at her dining room table surrounded by lots of white furniture and green accents. Their conversation remained light and chatty, and she knew it was deliberate on both of their parts.

She didn't feel like talking about the way the night ended with his disturbing dream or visitation or whatever they'd decided to call it, and he never liked bringing it up. As far as the sex was concerned, she knew herself all too well. She wouldn't be able to talk about it until they both felt more comfortable with it. Becoming intimate with a man was a big step for her, not something she took lightly. Having been raised in a strict Catholic home, Estela had been a classically good girl. She never gave her parents a lot of trouble, stayed in her room reading through most of her teenage years, and did not sleep with a man until she was almost twenty-one. She had been a *very* good girl.

As far as Tom Flanagan, she couldn't speak for him or his philosophies on personal sexuality, but she knew he'd made no secret of his previous infidelities with starlets and celebrities. Knowing this about him, Estela should have expected him to regard their romantic evening with a cavalier attitude.

But he did not.

She watched him carefully as he moved about the kitchen with his mug, trying to decide where to sit, whether or not to read the morning paper. He had trouble looking her in the eye, and in general, was acting like a shy schoolboy. This told her something very important about their first night together—it had made a very big impression on him.

Better to let him deal with it on his own terms, then. They were facing pressure from so many fronts, the last thing either of them needed was more pressure, self-generated. He must have been having similar thoughts, but they remained unexpressed. He did, however, appear to be more gentle with her, more attentive to her words. She detected a subtle change in him, although she was not yet certain what it might be.

When they finished her morning cuisine, he offered to clean up and she almost ordered him out of the kitchen. That room was her special domain, and she never wanted any men fumbling around in there. Her Spanish heritage demanded certain attitudes, established over many centuries of tradition that a generation of feminist politics had no hope of superseding. Besides, she thought with a smile as she watched him retreat to the shower, I like it this way.

Two hours later, they were back at the hospital, where a new battery of tests had been scheduled, plus an interview with another group of doctors who represented yet another agency in the government. Flanagan's friend, Gunnderson, had warned them of intervention from various departments, and the increased government interest in the hospital testing validated his warnings.

Estela was in her office filling out requisitions for supplies when the phone rang.

"ER—Doctor Barrero speaking. . . ."

"Hi, I'm trying to locate Senator Flanagan," said a young male voice.

"May I ask who's calling please?"

"This is his son, Chip. I've been all over this hospital and nobody seems to have any idea what's going on." He spoke evenly and without rancor. In fact, he seemed a little amused by the typical bureaucracy. "Is my father really there, or what?"

Estela grinned. "Yes, he is. I can get you in touch with him."

"Great . . ."

"Could I ask you how you knew to reach me?"

"I've seen your name in some of the newspapers."

"Oh, I see."

"Plus my mother talks about you . . ."

Estela was a bit stunned to hear the boy speak so candidly, and she had to face an immediate choice to either let it pass or dig a little deeper.

"Oh, I see. . . ."

Better to let it pass for now, even though she was burning up wondering what Rebecca Quinn Flanagan might be thinking and saying.

She patched the call through to the laboratory where Dr. Stanhouse was working with Flanagan.

As she hung up the phone, Estela thought once again about what she was getting herself into. Thomas Flanagan had a lot of baggage—a wife from a wealthy family, a grown daughter who distrusted him, and a son who was a college football star. He also had made plenty of enemies in Congress, and there were legal battles on the horizon with Rebecca. And this was not even considering his special ability—or affliction, depending on how you looked at it. . . .

Did she really want to be involved with that kind of person? Wouldn't it be better to stay single, stay aloof and apart from so many complications? Her life at the hospital was complicated enough. The ER provided her with enough stress and pain to more than occupy one lifetime.

At the same time, she could not overlook the intensity and the closeness they had experienced the night before. There was much in Thomas Flanagan that was good and decent, and she truly believed that his recent physical and metaphysical experiences had profoundly changed him, providing him with a more sensitive worldview, making him more spiritual, and therefore easier to fall in love with.

Because that's what she was doing, wasn't she?

It was one of those things she had trouble admitting to herself, but the longer she remained close to him, the more she realized she was indeed falling in love with Thomas Flanagan.

And of course that made her wonder if—

"Am I interrupting anything?"

Looking up from the papers on her desk, she saw him standing in the open doorway. Wearing his silk pajamas and white terry cloth robe, he looked like any other patient. But just seeing him, standing there like that, after she'd been thinking about him so intensely, was a bit unsettling. She felt her heart leap once and felt like a schoolgirl. "Oh, no, I was just doing a little paperwork."

"You had a faraway look in your eyes."

"It's just this job," she said, trying to sound casual and disinterested. "Sometimes, I just can't stand it. . . ."

"I just wanted to thank you for hooking me up with Chip," he said. "I've been meaning to call him . . ."

"I know you have," she said. "Don't feel so guilty."

"Me, guilty?" He smiled. "You must have me confused with somebody else. Somebody *not* in politics."

"He sounds like a very nice boy—your son," she said, fighting off a moment of awkwardness.

"Some 'boy.' Six three and two-fifteen. I can't believe how big he got."

"When's the last time you saw him?"

"Beginning of the semester. He keeps holding tickets for me for his games, but I've just been too tied up. First with the campaign and then everything since the crash." He paused, turned and closed the office door. Then he walked very close to her, took her hand and kissed it.

A very gentle, sweet gesture. It surprised her so much, she couldn't think of a thing to say.

"But that's got to stop," he said. "I meant it about getting more in touch with the people who mean something to me. Chip wants us to come up to the Florida State game. At Maryland—Byrd Stadium."

"*Us?* I'm sure he mentioned me by name."

Flanagan laughed nervously. "Well, not exactly, but he knows what's going on between me and his mother. And he understands it, believe me."

"Really?"

"Chip's never gotten along very well with his mother. I'm not the only one she's been cold with."

"Maybe she just has trouble showing her feelings?" Estela shocked herself as the words slipped out of her. Why would she defend the woman?

He looked at her and shook his head. "I think that's putting it mildly. The woman is a glacier."

Change the subject, she thought. Rebecca Flanagan was the last person she felt like analyzing. "So we're going to a football game?" she asked. "When?"

"Well, I want you there with me," he said. "It's this coming Saturday—College Park. Do you *like* football?"

She smiled. "Actually, I do. I think Don Shula's rather handsome."

"Good reason to like football," he said. "So it's a date, then?"

"You're on."

He was still holding her hand as he pulled her closer, kissed her gently.

"That's great," said Thomas Flanagan with a sardonic grin. "I promise your second date with me won't be anywhere near as interesting as the first one was. . . ."

He promised. But he was wrong.

THIRTY-FOUR

Flanagan

His senatorial limo stopped at the front gates to Byrd Stadium and his driver opened the door. Along with a blast of November wind, the syncopated notes of a marching band and the high-energy din of a packed-house crowd instantly filled the car's interior. Tom's pulse jumped a few notches and he smiled. It was good to be back in his home state.

It didn't matter how jaded you might be, the atmosphere at a college football game had to send a charge through you.

"Do you feel that?" he asked Estela.

She laughed. "You mean the Arctic air that just shot up between my thighs?"

"That's some mighty fortunate air," he said. "No, I meant the energy! Don't you hear that crowd? They are *pumped*, madame."

Before she could answer, a Secret Service agent folded himself in his long, black, wool coat and peered in at them.

"We're ready, Senator. . . ." The man stood back up, mumbled into a lapel-mike and mini-earset.

"Let's go," said Tom, taking her hand and easing out of the big black Cadillac.

He'd gotten into a blow with Larry Constantino about the security and the limo, but Larry said it had to be S.O.P. in public places until he officially declared himself out of the presidential race. And since he wasn't planning the press conference until next week, when he left Keller Memorial, he didn't have much of an argument. There were plenty of rumors and the usual leaks to the papers that Senator Flanagan might be dropping his bid, but until there was a formal announcement, everything was business as usual.

It had been one thing to get them to relax things at the hospital, where the environment was more controlled and he'd been more or less sequestered and under the scrutiny of various private and government task forces. But to forget about security at a stadium event was asking too much.

As soon as they stepped on the curb, he could feel that old familiar jolt, that magic surge of recognition from the torrent of faces all around. Reaction rippled out into the crowd that parted to make a path for them, and Tom automatically started smiling and waving.

(Like a fucking wind-up toy. . . .)

The thought made him feel silly, but he continued the prosaic gestures of all politicians as he escorted Estela through a special gate exclusive of the turnstiles and prepared for their entrance. Once inside the stadium, the Secret Service people hooked up with representatives of the governor's office and two Maryland state troopers, who escorted them through swarms of students, alumni, and media. The colors of the state flag—red, white, black, and gold—were everywhere. Jackets, hats, pennants, banners, pom-poms. Vendors hawked hot dogs and racks of Cokes. There was so much rum being added to that classic soda that the air seemed tinged with the scents of Bacardi and Captain Morgan. The university band cranked through a rowdy rendition of the Queen classic "We Will We Will Rock You."

Every year he returned to his alma mater, the students looked younger, and the pang of nostalgia for what were probably the finest years of his life grew a little more bittersweet.

But this year, with Estela by his side, things were somehow different.

As the senatorial entourage moved toward the governor's box at the fifty yard line, it gathered mass as well as momentum. Fans, friends, and media surrounded Tom and Estela. Flash cameras strobed and people called out his name. Some of the reporters started shooting off questions about his campaign, his absence, his alleged healing of the young boy, and even Larry Constantino's claims, but he had decided beforehand he would not acknowledge any questions like that. This was his first official public appearance in several weeks, but it was not a press conference. They could all think whatever they wanted about him for now, but it wasn't the time to get into all the things complicating his life.

"Are you here to see your son, Senator?" one of the reporters yelled above the general noise level. It was a question he could deal with because it deflected attention away from him.

"You mean the next Heisman winner?" said Tom with a smile that would make car salesmen cry.

"What's a Heisman?" asked Estela.

"A trophy," he said.

"Senator Flanagan, any predictions on the score?!"

"It should be a great game. A close game," he said in loud voice, but it sounded hollow to him. He spoke with no conviction, like a bad actor in a bad play.

(You haven't been paying attention, you phony. . . .)

Any other late November Saturday, at any other time in his life, he would have been steeped in the annual drama of college football. And since his son's high school days at Gonzaga, where Chip broke seven prep quarterback records, Tom had developed an intensely personal interest in the game. Chip had been recruited by Penn State, Michigan, Notre Dame, Florida, Alabama, Syracuse, but chose the University of Maryland. That decision had almost instantly resurrected a once-proud football program, and the school was again ranked as a national powerhouse.

Three years ago, Chip Flanagan took the controls of a team that had since led the nation in total offense every year. If Tom hadn't grabbed a *Washington Post* from the airport lobby earlier that morning, he would've had no idea his son's team and Florida State were both undefeated, and that this game would most likely decide the national championship.

(Good thing Chip doesn't know. . . .)

As they were gradually shepherded away from the crowd and up toward the press box and VIP suites, Tom reflected quickly on how little contact he had with his son over the course of his life. He'd never been the kind of dad who taught his boy how to *do* things—with tools or cars or sports or fishing or any of the other father-and-son stuff that you always hear about. There had always been so many things to do in his own career that he never seemed to find enough time to slow down and spend time with his kids. Kiley grew up hating him because she'd always sided with her mother. Understandable, he figured. And the idea that he and his daughter would never be close oddly did not seem to bother him much. He knew he should feel bad about that, but he didn't. Kiley was difficult to like because she was so similar to her mother.

Chip, on the other hand, seemed to understand his father and how difficult it was to live with a woman like Rebecca. Although he never had an extended "man-to-man" conversation with Chip about his marriage and his job as a father, Tom had always felt "okay" with his son. There wasn't a lot of emotion expressed between them, but Chip had always treated him with respect and never gave any sign of disapproval of what Tom had so far done with his life.

"Right here, Senator," said one of the state trooper escorts, pointing to a pair of padded seats in the front row of the suite.

"Thank you," said Tom, and ushered Estela in ahead of him.

A man he recognized as an aide to the governor had moved up behind him, placed a hand on his shoulder. "The governor's down on the field for a presentation, but he'll be up soon," said the aide. "He'll be sitting right next to you and the doctor."

(Big deal. . . .)

"Thank you," said Tom, smiling automatically. He didn't like the governor because he had always known what a phony he'd been in Washington. On several occasions, the governor had let him know quite clearly he didn't trust him or his commitment to the people of Maryland.

(But the guv was right, wasn't he . . . ?)

Estela nudged him with an elbow, looked at him with large brown eyes. She had a smirky kind of smile on her face. "You've been kind of quiet. . . . What're you thinking about?"

"You really want to know?"

"Yes," she said.

Looking out toward the field for a moment, through the glass of the suite, he could see the marching band in the shape of a huge M, and a small group of people huddled around a microphone—the governor among them.

"I was just thinking of how much of an asshole the governor thinks I am."

Estela laughed. "Is he right?"

"Well, yes, I think he *was* right. But I would like to think I'm changing."

"I'm sure you would. . . ."

The ceremonies on the field ended, and as the small group moved off the field, the band broke ranks and formed a huge gauntlet that funneled down past the goal posts to the red brick building beyond the end zone.

"What's going on now?" she asked.

"I thought you said you liked football?"

She shook her head. "That doesn't mean I *understand* it. . . ."

Pointing toward the double row of band members and a squad of cheerleaders holding a banner with *NO. 1* painted on it, he said: "They're getting ready to lead the team onto the field. They're coming out of that building and they'll run through there between the ranks of the band."

She looked down and studied the formation. Just then the huge stadium crowd began cheering and stomping their feet. The entire foundation began to vibrate.

"What now?!" she said loudly.

"The Terps!" he said, pointing toward the field. "They're coming out of the locker room!"

"Maryland's team is called the 'Terps'?" she said. "What does *that* mean?"

He leaned down and gave her a wink. "That's the nickname for the Terrapins. See the guy in the mascot suit down there? The big turtle."

Estela giggled. She actually giggled like a schoolgirl.

"I know," he said. "Whoever thought it was a good idea to name a team after a *turtle*?"

"Well, you have to admit—it *is* funny."

He nodded and watched the first few players waiting outside the locker room. They stood atop a small hill next to a statue of a terrapin named Testudo. The first player in line wore the numeral 1, his son's jersey number.

As the crowd began to chant "We're Number One! We're Number One!" the team began to pour down the hill and run between the two columns of the band. Tom began clapping wildly as he watched Chip lead the team; he crashed through the *NO. 1* banner and his teammates followed him onto the field and down to the homefield bench. The stadium crowd continued to cheer and stomp and clap—so loudly the noise rattled the glass windows of the VIP suite like a windstorm.

Estela continued watching the field as the team from Florida State entered the field from the other end of the red brick building. They flowed onto the field and bench on the opposite sideline without seeming notice, despite the late afternoon sun reflecting brilliantly off their gold helmets.

"What happened to the other team?"

"Florida State? What about them?" Tom looked at her, confused.

"Why didn't the band set up for them, too?"

"Because they only do that for the home team," said Tom. "The other team doesn't get anything."

"That hardly seems fair."

He looked at her and smiled. "It's not supposed to be."

They continued to enjoy light banter as Estela seemed content to play the foil, letting him explain everything about the game. He was pretty sure she knew a lot more than she was letting on, but she was obviously enjoying herself, so what the hell?

When the governor returned to the suite, there were a few awkward moments as he exchanged pleasantries with him. He wasn't sure he handled the introduction to Estela very well by saying she was his "doctor," but it just slipped out and he regretted it instantly. The uncomfortable situation was cut short by a renewed explosion from the crowd as the teams lined up for the opening kickoff. Everyone's attention focused on the field as Maryland's kicker lofted the ball high and deep.

Tom watched it settle into the hands of State's kick returner. The entire stadium gasped as one great beast when the player juked and danced past the first wave of tacklers and broke up the sideline. Maryland players pursued and didn't bring him down until he'd reached the defenders' twenty-eight yard line. The atmosphere in the VIP box was subdued and Tom was uncomfortable with that. He would have preferred to be beyond the glass, where it was acceptable to act like a maniac. Going to this game was the best thing he could have done. He needed a few hours of relief from the cruel realities of his life.

"That was not good, I take it," said Estela.

"No, not hardly. Now our defense has to keep them from getting it in the end zone. A field goal is all you want to give up here."

"That's when they kick it through the poles for three points," she said.

He smiled. "I had a feeling you knew more about this game than you were letting on. . . ."

They watched the first series of plays from the Seminoles, which was aggressive and wide open from the start. Lots of motion and fakes, nothing basic or predictable. They moved the ball quickly down to the eight yard line before the Terps were able to stop the drive. The field goal was a chip shot for Florida State's kicker and they took an early 3–0 lead.

Tom watched as the teams lined up for the ensuing kick-off. It would be the first time Maryland had a chance to handle the ball and the first time he would see his son direct the team's offense. "There he is," he said to Estela, pointing to the player on the sidelines talking to several coaches wearing headsets. The name FLANAGAN flanked his shoulders above the jersey number 1.

"You must be very proud of him," she said.

"Did I tell you he's smart and handsome, too?" Tom smiled, then directed his attention back to the action, where Maryland took over after the kick on their own thirty-two yard line.

Even through the glass partition, he could feel the surge of excitement ripple through the crowd. Everyone was yelling his son's name in unison: *Chip!-Chip!-Chip!* The rhythmic chant to exhort the team to greatness. It shot through him like a current from a 220-cable.

(That's my *son* they're yelling about!)

On the first play from scrimmage, Chip Flanagan faked a hand-off into the line, rolled right on a naked bootleg. The fake was so perfect, State linebackers were jamming the middle to stop the Terps bruising fullback, Marv Linsky, while Chip stood off in the flat, hands at his sides as though calmly watching the play unfold. Even the crowd didn't realize the quarterback still held the ball, resting it casually against his thigh.

Stepping up, suddenly bringing the ball up, Chip Flanagan launched a perfect spiral on a perfect arc forty yards downfield. The entire stadium seemed to catch its breath as it watched the ball drop into the receiver's outstretched hands as he headed down the sidelines at full throttle. It was a play for all the NCAA highlight tapes, complete with the receiver pulling away from the only man who might tackle him and high-stepping it into the end zone. It was a stunning, balls-up way to open a football game, and it would put the Seminoles on very sudden notice they were involved in a football game with a very intense and dangerous bunch of boys from the Free State.

The eruption from the crowd rocked the foundation of the stadium, rattling the glass of the VIP box. People in the stands were instantly crazy. Even the stiffs with the governor were moved enough to stand up and clap their hands.

"Incredible!" screamed Tom. "That's my son! That's my son!"

He was jumping up and down, hugging Estela, kissing her, and acting like a kid himself. The vicarious jolt of watching that kind of performance was more than he would have ever imagined it could be. He'd been watching Chip play all his life and there'd been plenty of thrills and accomplishments, but nothing like this. Full stadium. National television audience. Division One championship on the line. It was like those silly beer commercials—it didn't get any better than this.

Even though it didn't seem possible, the game's intensity continued to escalate throughout the first half. Both teams were loaded with talent and excellently coached. Both defenses assaulted the ball carriers. There was no showboating or trash-talking. The teams went about their work against each other with the iced precision of surgeons or CEOs. The first two quarters of the game displayed some of the finest football in decades. The polls and the sports commentators had been right—these two teams were clearly the two best in the country, and they were slugging it out like a couple of single-minded heavyweights, capable of nothing less than a full-scale mauling. The sellout crowd was witnessing one of the game's legendary moments. History was happening here, you could just *feel* it, thought Tom. It was one of those unspoken but overwhelmingly sensed notions that swept through the stadium like a rumor.

When the gun sounded, sending the teams off the field to locker rooms filled with sweat and strategy, the score was Maryland 21, Florida State 17.

Inevitably, Tom knew he would have no time to himself at halftime as the media swarmed all over the VIP booth. The governor watched as everyone ignored him in their zest to corral the senator with a star quarterback for a son.

"Can we get a few questions, Senator?" one of them cried out above the purring engine of the crowd.

Tom looked at Estela, rolled his eyes.

"Go on, have fun," she said.

"Okay," he said to everyone trying to jam a camcorder into his face. "As long as we keep the questions on football. No politics or religion, okay?"

Everyone laughed and pressed closer to demonstrate their agreement. Tom could feel the waves of chilly resentment rolling off the governor, who had gathered his aides and flunkies around him like a protective shield and stood off to the side of the reception area in the booth behind the seats.

Apologizing to Estela, he surrendered to the cascade of tired and familiar queries.

The second half kickoff went to Maryland, but the Florida State defense smothered every offensive play. Chip, who had been brilliant in the first half, was clearly under siege now. The Seminole coaches had decided to abandon their standard defensive sets to better adjust to Chip Flanagan's almost unstoppable skills at quarterbacking. His arm strength, accuracy, and intelligence would eventually dissect any standard defensive alignment. State's strategy became one of all-out assault on the quarterback—red-dogging linebackers, safety blitzes, and clothes-line tackles.

Maryland's defense had made their own adjustments and had effectively begun to control State's running game. The third quarter, while full of unbelievable plays and battlefield tactics, passed quickly with neither team scoring. As the fourth quarter passed the midway point, with only seven minutes left in the game, Maryland recovered a Florida State fumble on their own thirty-seven yard line.

The crowd detonated. Crazy, wild cheering. Hats, beers, anything that would fly, went sailing into the air. Tom watched the madness beyond the glass and wished he could be out there with the paying customers having a real good time, instead of having to suffer the sealed and sanitized environment of the suite.

He nudged Estela.

"Having a good time?"

"You know," she said "this is the first time I've really paid strict attention to what is going on."

"What do you mean?"

"Well, the perspective is different up here—it's better. I can see the whole field, so I understand the team's position on the field better."

"Oh, I see. . . ." He wasn't sure what she was talking about, but he felt as though he should agree with her.

"On television, you only see a small piece of the field," she said. "It's hard to see what's really going on."

"Yeah, I got you," he said. And he did.

Leaning into him, she reached out and touched his hand. "It's funny, but I'm getting this . . . funny feeling. Like something's going to happen. . . ."

"Don't say that," he said half-jokingly. "You'll jinx them."

"Come on, Flanagan, you don't believe in that stuff, do you?" She smiled, sipped on her Coke.

"Listen, after what we've been through, I don't know what I believe!"

They turned to watch Chip Flanagan lead the offense onto the field. They seemed to be pumped up after the fumble, and Tom could see the shoulders slumping on some of the Seminoles players. Fumbles did that to a team. But their middle linebacker was having none of it, and even from up in the stands, Tom could tell the defensive specialist was jacked, yelling and screaming at his teammates, getting them ready. The guy was a monster—six six and more than two-fifty, with jungle-cat speed and the power of a bear. The word "menace" was created for a character like this.

But Chip had prepared for the opportunity, mixing up his plays so beautifully, the State defense never got settled in. They were reeling from one slashing run to a short toss to the tight end to a perfectly executed tailback screen. Three, quick, no-huddle plays, and the Terps had covered fifty yards. Just like that. Like lightning. The crowd had notched up the gain on their constant roar, but you could tell even they were stunned with the quickness with which Maryland had punished State for their error.

Now the ball rested on the thirteen yard line. A touchdown at this point would put the Seminoles in a tough spot. They would need two scores to win and neither could be a field goal. Two TDs against one of the top defenses in the country with less than six minutes left would be a very tough assignment.

If Maryland punched this one in, they could ice down the National Championship.

A simple off-tackle took them down to the eight yard line, then a dropped pass in the end zone made it third down. Chip called the naked bootleg that he'd opened up the game with. Everyone went for the fullback dive except State's middle linebacker, who had lined up Chip in his sights and launched himself across the open space. Seeing the play break down, Chip continued to curl to the outside. A pump fake held the other linebackers and cornerback from closing, and he angled for the corner flag of the end zone with only the middle linebacker to beat.

En masse, the stadium jumped to its feet to watch the play unwind. Tom watched everything kind of hitch up and click past his eyes like an old movie, one frame at a time. With each passing segment, he could see the action and result predict itself. Chip's speed and angle would get him to the corner and the goal line just in time to intersect the midair flight of the middle linebacker, who had leaped parallel to the ground with the uncontrolled frenzy of a locomotive jumping its tracks.

The two hurtling bodies, like planets in their inexorable orbits, moved toward the collision point, and as they closed the distance between one another, the crowd began cheering louder and louder, like the keening wail of a jet in a death plunge. They sensed the outcome—that despite the impact, Chip Flanagan was going to cash in the touchdown.

Slowly, as though in some netherworld where time flowed like taffy, Tom watched the clinical examination of every minuscule movement that would combine to create the triumphant moment. The players inched toward their crash-point and Tom suddenly noticed a third element. Chip's wide receiver, peeling back from his pass route, had apparently thought he might save his quarterback some pain by trying to intercept the middle linebacker's tackle. The receiver launched himself through the air in the general direction of the corner flag. The third player had seemingly emerged out of nowhere, from the shadowy limbo into which all other players fade when the lens and the crowd's attention seize upon the main event. But this player had somehow torn himself loose from the background scenery to intrude upon the final cataclysm.

"Oh, no . . ." Tom heard the words leak out of him weakly, helplessly.

Wondering if the rest of the crowd could even see this new complication in the drama, Tom watched in horror as

Chip dove forward and collided with the middle linebacker. His head, shoulder and arm carrying the ball intersected the invisible plane of the goal line, and just as the ref shot both hands skyward, the wide receiver reached the impacting bodies a fractional second late. This extra factor subtly changed the physical laws that control action and reaction. Chip Flanagan's head was driven toward the sidelines by the onrushing shoulder and the pads of the linebacker. It was a hit that unfolded on a thousand fields a thousand times every game day, but this time, Chip's body met the resistance of the wide receiver who'd missed his block.

Later, Tom would swear he could hear the *sound* of the collision, despite the absolute blast-furnace-machine-shop din of the stadium. The scene of Chip's helmet twisting over and to the side, *past* his shoulderpads at an impossible angle, and the sound of a broom handle wrapped in a wet rag being *snapped*. . . .

Everyone in the crowd must have heard something, because an instant after the three-way collision, the giant bowl of raving sports maniacs fell totally silent. As though an unseen vacuum had sucked all the air out of the place, everything went dead. Tom could feel the collective stares of all the stunned people focusing down on the stilled figure of Chip Flanagan, stretched across the corner of the end zone, the ball still in his unmoving arm.

The linebacker pulled himself up groggily to his knees, as did the wide receiver, and they both reached for Chip Flanagan, but there was something about the position of the boy's body and the bad angle of his helmet to his pads that must have kept them from actually grabbing him or even touching him, because they didn't.

"Tom . . . !"

He could hear Estela's voice calling to him as though from a vast distance, and his vision was beginning to tunnel and he was having trouble seeing through the glass, past the sea of standing people.

"He's hurt. Estela," he heard himself say. "He's hurt very badly. . . ."

"Come on, we've got to get down there," she was saying hastily. "I'm a doctor . . . ! I can—"

Tom felt himself being pulled to his feet, and he moved without real volition or understanding. His mind had slipped free of its usual somatic moorings. For one brief, terrifying moment, he thought he might be toppling into the abyss of total hallucination, of another visit from Infinity. . . .

But he was wrong.

What visited him this time was actually far worse than anything he could have imagined.

As he fought to keep his thoughts coherent, hanging on almost desperately to Estela's coat sleeve while she ushered him from the booth, he began to fall into a maelstromlike formation. Not a real one, however, not something he could see, even in a visionary sense, but something more abstract, metaphysical. Rather the *ideation* of a swirling vortex, which remained no less real.

And at the bottom of its violent center . . . floated the *red sphere*.

The dark, angry sun—the punctuation to his nightmares and visions—had appeared once again. Like a beacon or a warning bulb, it burned with its own terrible heat.

He separated from himself, so he could "see" Estela and his body struggling through a crowd, being escorted by state troopers to a VIP elevator. Like a dispassionate observer, he watched them descend from the press box area directly down through the belly of the stadium to ground level and an access tunnel to the field. He seemed to be floating above the dash of people as they burst from the car, maneuvering past endless coiled snakes of television cable that lined the corridor.

Only vaguely aware of his passage through the dark tunnel, Tom struggled to get his thinking clear. The maelstrom he could feel rather than actually see was churning in upon itself, both creating and devouring itself, but still he hurtled toward its center and he knew that he was staring into the heart of his own destiny. The red sphere, the hazy, burning orb had finally begun to resolve itself, and he knew at last what it was and what it had meant to him. All that time, he'd been seeing a shard of his own broken future.

But only now did he understand what he must do.

The crowd and the noise and the movement that enveloped him seemed a fragile shell, insubstantial and thin.

The central image took substance as he followed Estela and the others out toward the field, which stretched ahead of them like a doldrum sea.

Estela was pushing people out of the path, and people were yelling and moving and jostling for position, but everyone parted to make way for the doctor.

For the senator.

The father.

In a clash of colors, the tableau held him for an instant like a bad abstract painting—the zebra-striped refs intersected with the maroon-and-gold uniforms of Florida State, the white and gold and red of the home team. The bright yellow rain-jacs of the paramedics contrasted with the gray topcoat of the Terps' team physician. The State player who'd hit Chip Flanagan still knelt by his side, his gold helmet in hand, his face a twisted portrait of fear and anguish. Tom's shadow covered him in a mantle as dark as his thoughts.

Looking up, the player slowly moved to make room for the senator.

As though looking down from a great height, Tom's semihallucinated vision gathered together all the pieces of the scene before him. Everything else suddenly became diminished, insignificant as he stared down at the red sphere on the grass by his feet.

Not actually spherical, and not really a complete globe, but close enough for your average prescient vision. . . .

The red football helmet with a black, white-outlined, "M" still held Chip's head within like a cruel, monstrous cage.

"Be careful," said one of the paramedics, or perhaps the team doctor. It didn't matter.

Tom slowly knelt down by his son's body, still and so quiet. The boy's head and shoulders had been tortured into a horribly unnatural position. So much so that no one had wanted to look at the configuration for too long a time. No one wanted to touch him, not wanting to know the lethal truth spoken by the language of his body.

Movement. Heat from her breath on his neck.

"Tom . . ." Estela's voice, less than a whisper but freighted with fear, pain.

He continued to stare through the bars of the red helmet, the red planetary orb around which spun all his son's dreams, into the broken shadows of the boy's face.

(Such a good-looking kid.)

Like crystals falling out of some magic solution, the pieces of the mystery came together.

Now he understood what his gift had been all about. All coming down to this single moment. . . .

"Let me see him," said Estela, reaching past Tom to lightly, ever so lightly, touch the pale flesh of his son.

"It doesn't matter," Tom heard himself saying. "He's . . ."

(Dead.)

"Tom—"

"I know . . . I know . . . what's going on."

Two more medics had arrived with a stretcher, but Tom waved them off.

Estela started sobbing, fighting to keep control. Her hand trembled as she withdrew it from the boy's angled neck where no pulse struggled.

A murmur rippled out into the immediate crowd, like an ever-growing stain; the message that Chip Flanagan was dead stunned everyone it touched.

Whatever transpired beyond their shell of intimate pain had dwindled off to the point of nothingness. The universe had shrunk down to a very small place; he could hear nothing but the sound of his own breath leaking away from him, the fall of Estela's gentle tears as they tracked down her face.

It would be easier now. He knew what to expect now, knew what he was doing.

As though looking down a dark and bottomless well, he peered into the heartspring center of his soul, the place of the power. At the same time, he touched Chip's twisted neck, recoiling for the briefest instant at how *cold* he had already become. Then, touching him again, Tom felt the heat begin to well up from the core of his being. The now familiar sense of danger and control, both absolute, flooded him, and he reeled from its heady rush. Like the warm flow of a barbiturate, the power heated up inside him. His fingers, now wrapped around the base of Chip's neck, felt as though they were melting, and yet their tactile sense had become amplified beyond the supersensitive: his hand a CAT scan in three dimensions.

(The bones.)

As though sinking into the muscled flesh, he could feel the shattered vertebrae of his boy's neck; the severed spinal cord felt like a greasy piece of thick spaghetti.

(This is my son. . . .)

Shutting his eyes, he could still see within the flesh, and a great humming, like a generator on overload, filled his skull with noise so that even his own thoughts were lost in the scream for power.

And the power came to him. Rising up like some beast from an unknown depth, it uncurled and leaped from his hand. The heat was life itself and he directed it through the layers of ruined tissue.

Down, deep, to the seat of the trauma.

A spark.

From a cold shell, it sparked again, then filled the hard, cold center.

(Moving. Everything's moving.)

Tiny, shattered pieces of bone began their migrations, the slippery tube of fluid and ganglia had reknitted itself, becoming encased in the hollow column of the spine.

His hand basted in the regenerative heat, flensed of all feeling, resonating with the helical anthem of life.

(Gotcha. You're coming with me now.)

Estela said something, but he was beyond hearing it. His son's neck had been slowly, so slowly, moving. Into a position less severe, more natural. So slight a movement that no one could perceive it but Tom himself.

(Come on, son. . . .)

The boy's neck, now warm and pink, trembled with a new pulse, tentative at first, like the movements of a newly hatched bird.

"Oh, God. . . ." Estela's voice. Breaking through the outer hull of his desolate success. "Oh, yes . . . !"

Within the helmet cage, the red sphere that had haunted his dreams, Chip's eyelids fluttered, opened. His eyes lolled for a moment, then focused on the nearest object. There was a fresh fire banked behind them, brighter, hotter than ever before.

"Dad . . . ?"

"It's okay, son," he said. It was the first time he'd ever addressed Chip like that. It felt odd and clumsy coming out of his mouth, and at the same time, it felt so very right.

"Dad, what're you doin' here? What happened?" Chip Flanagan struggled up on one elbow, then sat up. Tugging off his helmet, he scanned the throng surrounding him with complete confusion.

"He's alive!" someone shouted over Tom's shoulder. More exclamations followed and the shockwaves spread out from the immediate circle up into the stands where it consumed the 70,000 like a spiritual brushfire.

Suddenly the air was filled with a cacophony of cheers and applause, shot through with cries of "Praise Jesus!" and a hundred other religious platitudes.

Looking up, Tom saw players and officials falling to their knees. Some wept while others smiled and laughed nervously, calling out to their own versions of God to thank Him for the miracle He'd let them share. Like a poisonous gas, the religious mania affected almost everyone. Their fervor was so great, you could almost feel it in the air like a coming storm.

Then, caught up in the overwhelming tide, the crowd surged over them, lifting Tom and Estela and Chip. A wave of people cascaded from the stands and surrounded them, buoying them aloft on the sparkling sea of absolute faith. Tom was only vaguely aware of the thousands of hands reaching out to him as the people wanted to touch him, to hold on, even for the briefest second, to the hand that touched the hand of God. The hand that sparked the miracle and brought it to the masses. Cameras from the networks and the big cable operations loomed like battleships across the surface of the crowd, all pointed at Tom and the others. He could feel the searing light of the world burning down on him, violating the last vestiges of privacy and possibly sanity.

Reaching out, across the madness, he sought Estela's hand. As he found it, he dared look into her eyes. Within them struggled the question she was afraid to ask: *What have you done?*

THIRTY-FIVE

Gunnderson

I'm going to need your help," the senator said into his PCS phone.

"Right away."

Jarmusch smiled to himself, leaned back in his favorite reading chair—the chair he rarely found time to sit in—and focused his attention on Flanagan. "Why am I not surprised?" he said. "You certainly know how to create a sensation."

"I need to get away from Washington." Flanagan's voice sounded on the edge of exhaustion.

"You have a destination?"

"That's been arranged. What I need is enough time to sneak away."

"Where are you now?"

"In the limo. There's a wagon train following me."

"The news is full of you," said Jarmusch. "You are what the media calls 'hot.' How did you pull off that stunt?"

"It was no stunt."

"Yeah, whatever . . ." said Jarmusch. "I stopped trying to figure out you political types a long time ago."

"Are you going to help me or what?"

"Give me the exact location."

"Rhode Island Avenue, entering the tunnel bypass to I-95. I've got a convoy of maniacs behind me!"

Flanagan sounded panicked, and he should be. Jarmusch had received calls from his various contacts and clients directing his attention to the nearest television. Senator Flanagan had created a nationwide sensation by apparently bringing his son back to life in front of a television audience of twenty million people. Every news service in the world picked up a feed from ESPN, and he was being hailed as everything from the Messiah to Archangel Michael to the good old Antichrist himself. To say everybody wanted him for their purposes understated the situation in a big way.

"What's the plan? What do you want from me?"

"Get us out of here! Get these bloodsuckers off our trail!"

"You're leaving town, I must assume."

"Yes, of course!" A woman's voice in the background admonished the senator to not get too excited. Women were good for that.

"Car? Train? Plane?"

"Driving," said the senator, his voice under control now. "But not in this land yacht. We need to switch cars. My Mercedes in Georgetown. But I don't want to get hung up down there."

Jarmusch smiled. This might be easier than it first sounded. A simple bait and switch. Create the right diversion, and you could pull off anything.

"Okay," he said. "I can handle it, but it will cost you the usual repairman's fee plus a surcharge for working weekends."

"Fine . . . fine!"

Jarmusch cleared his throat. "All right, pay attention. I need information, then I'm going to give you instructions. Follow them to the letter and everything will be fine. I need the location of the Mercedes, accessibility, any security codes or problems."

He listened as Flanagan filled in all the details. Jarmusch digested the information, assembled his plan. "All right, good. Continue on to I-295, take it to Wilson Bridge and head south into Virginia. Drive slowly and give me time to take care of things in Georgetown. I will be calling you on the PCS to arrange an *exact* rendezvous in Alexandria. You got all that?"

"I've got it. What's going on?"

"More later. When I call back. Your deal is to get into the northern Virginia area and wait for further instructions."

"Gunnderson, thank you." The senator sounded scared.

"The best way to show your thanks is your usual way," he said.

"The check's not in the mail, but it will be."

"Good-bye, Senator."

Jarmusch keyed off the connection and speed-dialed his number one "handyman."

"Sheldon, here. . . ."

"Keys to a '98 Mercedes LXS series," said Jarmusch. "You're okay with that?"

"We got 'em."

"Okay, we have a small job. Here's the details. . . ."

THIRTY-SIX

Barrero

"What did he say?" she asked as Tom hung up the phone.

He exhaled as he looked out the window, away from her.

Ever since the incident at the stadium, his face reflected feelings of embarrassment and anger.

"I *think* he said he would help us, but he didn't explain how," he said. Then keying the intercom to his limo driver, he spoke in his voice of authority: "Get us out of the city. Take the Wilson Bridge into Virginia. We'll be going into Alexandria, but I'll have more instructions for you later. And slow down. Take your time."

"Yessir," said the driver's voice as Tom thumbed off the com.

Reaching over, she took his hand, squeezed it. He continued to look out the window at the desolate neighborhoods of boarded-up row-homes passing them with a relentless similarity—the *real* Washington, D.C. It was as if he were ashamed to look at her.

"It's going to be all right," she said.

Turning around, he sank back into the soft leather of the seats, but directed his attention to the bar where he splashed some bourbon over ice. "Want anything?"

"No thanks, Flanagan. I'm not that big of a drinker, remember?"

Forcing a smile, he finally looked at her. "Well, if I could make you a strawberry margarita, I'd do it. . . ."

He knocked back half the drink in one swallow. "What a zoo specimen I am. . . ."

"There was nothing else you could do," she said, her memory in rapid replay mode. The look on the faces of the crowd, as they realized what they had witnessed, would remain with her always. She could feel it herself, having been hit with a jolt of emotional energy on overflow. No one who saw the glow of life melt out of Flanagan's hands into that boy would ever forget the concussion of fear and joy that hit them simultaneously. They all knew they were party to some kind of wondrous event, some kind of miracle, and yet it scared the living hell out of most of them. Estela knew what it must have been like when Lazarus came forth from the tomb—to have *seen* that. You could not be witness to such an event and not feel forever changed, touched by a greatness that previously you could only hope to believe in.

Tom looked through the tinted rear window to where the procession of cars carrying journalists and fanatics persisted in their attempts to track him down, to corner him whenever he stopped.

"Look at the mess I've created—I'm their freak of the month."

"Do you think running away is the right thing?"

"They want to eat me alive," he said, now staring at her with total earnestness. "You don't know them like I do, Estela. They're a bunch of hammerheads wearing Armani suits."

"Where are we going?"

"My brother has a cabin near Baxter, Minnesota, on a lake. We used to go there when we were kids—belonged to a friend of the family. Nobody knows about it."

"Baxter, Minnesota? Sounds cold."

"It should be by now. But the point is—it's probably not in any dossiers they have on me. If I can get out on the interstates without a tail, they won't have any idea where to look for me."

"We're *driving* there?" She wasn't sure how she felt about his plans, but the bottom line remained the same: wherever he went, she would go with him.

He looked contrite. "We can't fly. Too easy to catch us."

"What about a charter? A private plane?"

"They can flag all the small airport TCs. I'd never slip through."

"And we're leaving right now? With him?" She motioned toward the driver.

Finishing his bourbon, Tom racked the glass, shook his head. "No way. We've got to lose him."

Estela hoped he had everything worked out. The idea of running didn't really appeal to her, and her practical side was wondering what implications her sudden disappearance would have on her job, her responsibility to her patients, herself. She wanted to share her anxieties with him, but he was far too agitated right now. Better when the immediate crisis had been solved.

As she glanced out the side glass, she could see they were approaching an interstate system. Tom noticed it, too.

"Capital Beltway," he said softly. "We'll be hitting the bridge soon. Where the hell's Gunnderson?"

"What's he going to do?"

Tom shrugged his shoulders. "You've got me. But whatever it is, you can bet it will be effective."

"Who *is* Jarmusch Gunnderson?"

"Officially, he's a lobbyist. But he's pretty much Washington's version of a hired gun. He's a bagman, a collector, a go-between, courier, mediator, stuff like that. He calls himself a 'repairman.'"

"Where do you know him from?"

Another shrug. He looked at the bourbon decanter, decided against it. "There're plenty of guys like him in this town. They hang around the carcasses to pick up any stray pieces, and there's always plenty of those. Gunnderson's actually a very smart guy. Used to be a professor at Columbia, got recruited by the CIA. He was also a mercenary in Africa. I've heard he writes spy novels under a pseudonym, but that might be embellishment."

"Do you trust him?"

"As much as you can trust anyone in D.C."

"So . . ." she said with a sad, sardonic grin. "You don't trust him."

Tom smiled. "Not even a little bit."

Neither of them spoke for a moment, then he put his hand in hers. "I miss my son," he said. "I really do."

"He's going to be all right," she said.

"I feel like . . . like I deserted him, when he needed me the most. I wanted to talk to him, to explain to him what happened." Tom looked back through the glass at the procession following them. "But those bastards wouldn't let me."

"There'll be time for that. Don't you have ways to get a message to him?"

"Yes, I can try. But that means trusting someone."

She wanted to say something that would make him feel better, but she knew there was nothing appropriate. She could not imagine how he was handling the pressure of his situation. How could he deal with the minute-to-minute knowledge of the power he so obviously possessed? He'd told her once in the lab that the best way to get through the ordeal was to simply *not* think about it most of the time. She was reminded of the lines of one of the Western philosophers, who said that if we spent too much time really thinking about our place in the universe and our ultimate removal from it, we would go truly mad. She couldn't remember whose sentiment that had been, but she agreed with him completely.

When her thoughts were interrupted by the warbling of his PCS phone, she was actually grateful.

Retrieving the small device from his topcoat, he spoke quickly into it. "Flanagan. . . ." His voice of authority instantly colored his tone.

She tried to pick up the caller's words, but they were far too faint, despite the ultraquiet ride of the limo.

Tom nodded unconsciously a few times, but said nothing. Then: "You're sure you can pull this off?"

More nodding, followed by several, "Mmm-hmms."

Finally he keyed off the call, tapped open the driver's intercom. "After we cross into Virginia, take the Telegraph Road exit, and the ramp for Cameron Station."

His driver repeated the instructions, and Tom clicked him offline. Looking at her, he smiled. "Hold on to your hat," he said.

"What's the plan?" She felt a fist tightening in her chest as her cardio-pulmonary response kicked in and her autonomic prepared for an injection of adrenaline if necessary.

Gesturing out the side window, he said, "It's probably easier to show you than try to explain. We're almost there. Watch."

Following the line of his index finger, she looked ahead of the curving exit from I-95 as the limo tracked around a sweeping curve. Ahead of them a huge fuel tanker hulked motionless on the shoulder like a great beast at rest. Suddenly, as she watched, the diesel truck carrying its shiny aluminum tanker, with a huge AMOCO on its midsection like a bull's-eye, lumbered forward. It lurched into the line of traffic alongside their limo, so close its tires looked like they would be in their laps.

Estela said something or maybe she just gasped, but things started happening very quickly after that. It was only afterward, when she replayed things through her memory, that she realized what she had seen. Tom intercommed loudly to his driver to "punch it!" and the land yacht surged forward like a gunboat. The massive bulk of the fuel tanker ripped past their right side windows as it continued to lumber into their lane. In the instant the limo cleared the front of the huge truck it lurched into the curving lane of the exit ramp. The parade of cars behind the truck broke ranks as their drivers started taking evasive actions. Their limo continued to accelerate through the curve as the fuel tanker power-slid across the lane, stretching out sideways and gradually spinning out of control. Through the rear window, she watched the door on the driver's side of the truck cab burst open and a man wearing black coveralls leap from the skidding monster. The entire rig continued to slide until its eighteen wheels lost purchase almost simultaneously. The giant aluminum cylinder tilted over, twisted from the enormous torque and ruptured as the truck crashed over on its side. The sparks from the sliding cab ignited the Amoco Gold in a tremendous, ground shaking *wwwwhhummp!* As the truck continued to slide across the ramp, forming a perfect barricade, a wall of fire rose up to punctuate the matter. Nothing would be following them down the ramp.

At the bottom of the exit, she could see a black Mercedes on the shoulder, its driver down by the front left wheel.

"Pull over behind that car!" Tom's voice filled the interior with urgency and authority. So effective was he that the driver yanked the wheels of their big car off the road almost instantly. As it braked to a halt behind the Mercedes, Tom was already opening the door and grabbing her hand.

His strength and quickness amazed her as he launched her from the car and hit the asphalt running. "Let's go! We've got to hurry!"

Waves of heat rolled across the grass island of the exit cloverleaf, withering the grass and staggering them. So hot raged the gasoline inferno, she feared her hair might singe. As they approached the Mercedes, the man at the tire stood up wearing now-familiar black coveralls. Without a word, he glided around the vehicle and opened the passenger door for her, helping her in, and locking it behind her.

At the same time, Tom was slipping into the driver's seat, grabbing the wheel in both hands. Black Coveralls ran back to his side, leaned in with a businesslike grin, and spoke evenly: "You've got everything you need. Mr. Gee says have a safe trip. He'll be in touch."

"Thank you," said Tom.

"You're welcome," said the man as he closed the Mercedes' door.

Without hesitation, Tom tapped the accelerator and the black car leaped away from the shoulder like a jungle cat. The power and agility of the sedan pushed her deeper into the crushed leather seat, and for an instant, she could understand the fascination men had with machines and their inherent power to transform whatever they encountered. It was simply incredible and exhilarating to feel this magnificent car rip them across the road and back up the ramp to I-95 north.

Gunnderson's plan had been so simple, yet so daring and spectacular. But the diversion created, plus the roadblock itself, was more than enough to allow them to slip away into the gathering November twilight.

Sitting there, watching him take over with a sharpened concentration, Estela let the afterwash of epinephrine steady her, soothe her. It was the afterglow of fantastic sex that left you weak but full of warmth.

Edging the sleek sedan up close to ninety, Tom streaked across the Wilson Bridge, slipping in and out of the traffic patterns as though guided by some sixth-sense radar.

"That was . . ." she began the sentence, but had no words to adequately finish it.

"Outrageous?" he asked with a grin. ". . . Stupid? . . . Fun? . . . What?"

"All of those things," she said. "I had no idea . . ."

"Neither did I, believe me." He continued to look at the road ahead, adjusting his speed to each maneuver.

"Are we safe?" She reached out to lightly brush his shoulder.

"With me at the wheel, you can never be sure," he said, smiling openly.

"I mean—did we get away? Anybody still with us?"

"Not a chance. If everything worked, they probably think we're still parked in the limo in front of the wreck."

"They planned *every*thing?" she asked, looking back but seeing nothing behind them in the growing shades of night.

"Gunnderson is expensive, but he is a consummate professional," said Tom. "He's the kind of person that nobody wants to admit knowing, but is goddamned glad they do."

"Did anybody get hurt?"

"Not if they did it right."

"Where'd they get the truck?"

Tom shrugged. "Don't ask—that's why they have insurance companies."

She chuckled, but she felt more than a little uncomfortable. The longer she associated with the many facets of power and influence at the stratospheric levels, the more she wished she didn't know. To *think* you know that there are separate and unequal codes of morality at work in society, and then to actually see the proof—so you *know* that an entire subclass of people operate outside the law—is a terrible burden. Like the senator had said: *don't ask.*

But there were certain things she must ask.

"We're heading north to Minnesota—right *now*?"

"That's right."

"In just these clothes? Flanagan, you know women better than that. I can't travel like this."

"Look under your seat. There should be a small bag."

Reaching down and under, she touched a leather handle, grabbed it, and pulled out a small leather courier's pouch.

"Open it."

Doing so, she was stunned to find tightly wrapped packs of twenty-, fifty-, and hundred-dollar bills. "Oh, my God! How much is here?"

"You can count it if you want, but there should be a hundred and fifty thousand dollars."

"Where did Gunnderson get this kind of money?"

"It's from the campaign war chest. Every politician learns to keep emergency money around in various places. The only reason I trust Gunnderson with cash like this is because it's chump-change to him."

Estela didn't respond right away, preferring to allow the meaning of what he was telling her to sink in. Tom Flanagan had truly lived in a different world from the rest of us. A place where none of the usual rules applied, and where you made up your own if you were clever enough and quick enough. It was simply hard to imagine playing in an arena where all the rules only applied to you if you didn't feel like changing them.

Finally, she spoke again. "Let me see if I understand what's going on—we use cash only because the credit cards can be traced, right?"

Tom nodded as he negotiated the left lane, punched the car up to ninety-plus to glide past a row of very slow-moving cars in the middle lane. The exits on the Capital Beltway were flicking past in a blur of green signs. They had passed Connecticut Avenue and he began drifting over to pick up I-270 heading vaguely northwest.

"You wouldn't believe how many ways they can trace you."

"Really? Like?"

"Phone calling cards, credit cards, ATM machines, cellular phones, and even most of our paper money has been treated with embedded image codes that can be used if somebody has logged in your cash before giving it to you."

"Like Gunnderson?"

Tom shrugged. "It's possible, but he'd be killing a golden goose, as they say."

Estela nodded, looked out into the Maryland suburban evening as it slipstreamed past them. She didn't speak for a minute or two, tried not to even think. Better to just let all that had happened wash over and through her, cleansing her and preparing for whatever might come next.

"Hungry?" he asked.

"Not really. The tension must have taken away my appetite."

"Not me," he said, pausing to consider their options.

"It figures. Men can eat anytime."

"Okay, how about this? After we hit Frederick and pick up I-70 heading west, we stop and get a very nice dinner."

"If you know where to go, sure."

"Just outside of Camp David there's a place that has great Italian."

She smiled, nodded. "Too bad it looks like I'm stuck with an Irishman."

THIRTY-SEVEN

Dr. Nelson Stanhouse

Three Days Later

The usual rigors of emergency room operations were exacerbated by Estela Barrero's absence. Nelson had always known she was a skillful organizer and a fantastic doctor, but she was so damned facile at her job, it was easy to take her for granted. It wasn't until he had to shoulder most of the decision-making in ER that he truly realized how valuable she was to the everyday running of the place.

And where the hell did she go, anyway?

The news media had been having a field day with the senator's incident at that football game, and while the government seemed to be downplaying the sudden disappearance of him and Dr. Barrero, it hadn't stopped the average person on the street from speculating on everything from government conspiracies to divine intervention to alien abduction. Their limo driver claimed to know nothing, having stated he lost control of his car when a fuel tanker crashed and burned. When he brought his vehicle to a stop, he noticed that the rear doors to the limo were flung open and his passengers had vanished.

Nelson couldn't get that story out of his head. As he left his office to make some morning rounds, he kept thinking about Dr. Estela Barrero, who had become his good friend during their residency together. He worried about her and couldn't stop thinking about her.

Could Flanagan and Barrero be the victims of some bizarre assassination or kidnapping? Or perhaps they were being sequestered somewhere by secret agents . . . ?

Nelson had no idea what to think. His mind didn't run to that sort of thing and he had no imagination for exotic theories. He'd spent his whole life trying to be empirical and ultra-logical, so it was hard to decide to chuck that kind of thinking and go in for cloak-and-dagger speculation. He just couldn't get into it.

As he reached the lower level of the building, where Estela's temporary laboratory office had been set up, he asked himself what the hell he was doing down there. It was off his usual path and he'd obviously been walking around on autopilot, coming down here without even thinking.

Since he was here, he might as well check in on the lab. Ever since Flanagan and Dr. Barrero had taken weekend leave, the area had been quiet, other than a few med students assigned to keep it clean.

Nelson entered the area casually, and walking past the bullpen of desks and computers, he entered the lab itself—

—and was assaulted by the acrid stench of decay.

Good God! What—?

Staggering, he looked for something to cover his mouth and nose. A cloth, a rag, anything. He finally resorted to the flap of his own white coat as he reeled from the smell of the crypt, the overwhelmingly pungent odor of death. He looked into the cages where they'd kept the two resurrected test animals, and was stunned.

Not by the fact they were both dead—they were most certainly that—but by their incredibly advanced state of decomposition.

The white rat's body had completely sunken in on itself, all the soft parts liquefied into a pool of ooze—tissue in a terminal state of cellular breakdown. The Rhesus monkey looked even more ghastly. Still sitting up in the corner of its cage, it appeared to have died in the middle of feeding itself. All the flesh on its skull was already splitting and sliding off the bones like the ruptured rind of spoiled fruit. Its eyes had collapsed into the head and its lips had curled back to reveal a hideous grin from nightmare country. Like the rat, the monkey's body had degenerated into an advanced state of decomposition, giving off a foul aura of putrescence.

Nelson had seen enough and backed out of the room. He almost gagged on the sepulchrous air. Something terrible had happened, and his very logical mind was already working out the implications. What he'd witnessed was as altogether impossible as Flanagan's power to resurrect them in the first place.

And yet both had happened.

Both were terribly *real*.

Carefully, he went to the door and locked it. Had anyone seen him down here, seen him actually *enter* the lab? He didn't think so, but he had to act fast. For some reason, he knew that no one should know about this yet. With Dr. Barrero and Flanagan gone, it just didn't feel right.

First thing was to find a respirator mask. Standard issue in the pathology department, he hoped someone had thought to supply this area. A search of more than half the drawers and cabinets netted him what he needed to reenter the lab without passing out. Thus protected, Nelson returned to the adjoining room and checked on the charts. And as he'd suspected, they revealed a pair of healthy test animals being fed the previous evening by a med student named Levinsky.

Perfectly healthy yesterday evening. Eating, breathing, jumping around their cages. Responding to every test known to medical science. There was absolutely no freaking way they could die overnight and fall into such decomposed states—states that could only result if they'd been dead for many weeks. Impossible. Only yesterday, they had been *alive*.

Or had they?

The thought rattled around in his head like a seed in a gourd.

What was going on here?

Whatever it was, he could not allow the other members of the research team to know about it yet. Part of the task force, he knew, had been comprised of doctors and scientists from various government agencies.

Fuck them, he thought. They've probably done something to Dr. Barrero already. He didn't know for sure what his little discovery meant in the long run, but he wasn't about to share it with anybody until he heard from Dr. Barrero. Or until he knew more about what had happened to her. "Trust no one" had become a watchword where the government was concerned, and Nelson Stanhouse subscribed to that dictum wholeheartedly.

Moving quickly, he gathered up both animals into a laundry bag, cleaning out the cages with a small Dustbuster. After spraying the area with disinfectant, and cranking up the ionizing air filtration, he left the area with his bag, carrying his mask and some *very* dirty laundry. If he was lucky, no one would be back to check on the animals until feeding time this evening. Before then, he would make sure to return and turn off the AFS.

As Nelson shambled down the corridor, he kept expecting to encounter someone, anyone who would recognize him or question his presence on this level. But he saw no one, and he fought to keep his paranoia in check. Besides, who would question a senior resident, no matter where he was in the hospital?

The service elevator down to the incinerator creaked its way to the lowest level of the huge hospital. He'd only been down here once during his orientation tour years ago, but he'd never forgotten the almost medieval, torture chamber aspect of Keller Memorial's basement. Their solution to the safe removal of medical waste and toxins had been the installation of an automated incineration system that employed advanced pyrolytic techniques, reducing all materials to basic elements. The laundry bag and test animals would be consumed and transformed so completely, no one would ever find a trace of them. Nelson tossed his grim cargo into the waste conveyor and made a quick escape from the hospital's miniature inferno.

He took the elevator up to the main floor, getting as far from the lab as he could. He would let someone else discover the missing animals. Let the outside experts get involved in this one. Let them deal with this mess.

If they figured it out, fine; if not, he didn't care. He would either tell Estela Barrero what had happened, or nobody. He'd already seen more than he wanted to see, figured out more than he wanted to know. All this stuff was way over his head, way beyond him. It had slipped way past the realms of science and medicine long ago and he'd never admitted it to himself. But this metaphysical assault on all the things he believed and had built his career on was a staggering, scarifying mindwarp. A full-scale attack on his entire system of understanding. To make him think of things this impossible and this outrageous—it was more than his rational mind could handle.

Because this incident was only a precursor. The thought lingered.

It was only the *first* part of a two-part exam question, wasn't it?

Shaking his head, Nelson looked up to see that he was staring at the open doors inviting him onto the first floor. Nelson continued to shake his head as if trying to clear his vision.

But the second part of the question wouldn't go away. It kept reshaping and restructuring itself, but it wouldn't leave him.

Like a battleship through the fog came the unrelenting logic of the question his mind would not abandon. If the lab animals are dead, *what's going to happen to the people?*

THIRTY-EIGHT

Flanagan

Dr. Infinity paid Entropy a visit last night.

(Hey, what else is new?)

He sat up to survey the interior of the Nite's Rest Motel in Newton Falls, Ohio. They had pushed themselves through the night, all the way across the Pennsylvania Turnpike and onto I-80. Seven hours had gotten them to this small town where no one recognized them and no one was looking for them.

As inconceivable as it might have been for him to think he could have jumped into bed with Estela and not touch her, that is exactly what had happened. He must have been far more exhausted than he'd thought, and he must have fallen dead asleep.

And at some point during that stroll down oblivion's shady lane, Dr. Infinity

(or *whoever* it was who thought it was clever to call himself by that godawful stupid name . . .)

had tuned him in.

It was more of the same cryptic messaging, speaking in veiled references with damned little substance. The whole experience had changed from something ominous to merely tiresome. He was told that he had passed the first part of his test, and that there would be one more revelation to deal with before he would be "ready."

Tom was so exhausted and emotionally siphoned by the happenings of the past day that the visit by the mysterious Dr. was anticlimactic at best. He missed his son, and he hated himself for deserting him after such a cataclysmic event, but there had been no choice. With everything closing in, he gave in to the most basic of human instincts.

(Human instincts. Did the phrase still apply?)

The concept dogged at him as he lay there in the cold morning air of a room with a faulty radiator. Carefully, he eased himself from the sagging hammock the management called a bed. Estela slept on, her hair exploded around her in an auburn nimbus. He felt so sorry for her. She'd been yanked into this without really being asked if she wanted any part of it. Tom knew she was terrified of the power he possessed but didn't really control. It was a testament to her own personal courage and dedication that she not only chose to stay with him, but never questioned what was going on. Somewhere along the line she had decided she believed in him and that was obviously enough for her.

Into the mildewed bathroom, he paused before the rusting medicine chest mirror and looked at his face. All the familiar planes and angles were there, but he looked haggard, aged. His carefully trimmed hair was salted with a little more gray, and there were creases around his eyes that hadn't been there during the summer. In just a few months, he'd been transformed into some kind of mutant or monster. He'd been a sideshow waiting to happen, and then he decided to go to a football game. . . .

(*Badda-bing!* Instant freak.)

All the while, he was having a bad feeling about everything—that he was somehow being directed by forces beyond his understanding. A playing piece on some surrealistic gameboard. Where was it all going? What was the point? Nagging questions without answers were now interrupted by a new mode of self-flagellation.

(Chip . . . how are you doing with all those bloodsuckers, huh?)

He missed his son.

The feeling and the guilt just wouldn't go away.

Dressing quietly, he slipped out the door and walked down the state highway toward a truck stop café. There was no way he could risk going inside, but that was all right. He needed information more than food at the moment. A *Cleveland Plain Dealer* newspaper box waited for him at the curbside entrance to the truck stop's gas pumps. He popped in the coins and opened the box for a copy of the paper that had a full-color picture of him kneeling at Chip's side.

"BACK FROM THE DEAD"

screamed the headline.

"MILLIONS WITNESS MIRACLE" said the subhead. Every article on the front page dealt with the event, which was no surprise, but Tom was looking for only two things: Chip's condition, and specific information on his getaway.

Walking back to the motel, he scanned the front section of the paper, looking for the column inches that would give him some idea what would come next. He would also want to check out the cable newsnets—they would have the most up-to-date intentions of everyone he wanted to . . . to what?

(Avoid.)

That *was* the key word, wasn't it? He just wanted out of the whole damned thing. Just the thought of what they all wanted him for made him want to puke.

When he returned to the room, Estela was not only awake, but dressed and watching CNN on the crummy little room set. The suit she'd worn to the game still looked fresh on her. She was just that kind of woman—that no matter what kind of silly outfit you threw on her, she had this secret power to make it look stylish and appropriate.

"Good morning, Senator."

"Did I wake you?"

"No, I'm used to getting up early. Besides, I'm too . . . too anxious to be sleeping." She got up and moved to his side. "Flanagan, what're we going to do? Are you sure this is the right thing—to be running away like this?"

"I have no idea. The paper doesn't have much about us disappearing—it just says that we 'avoided the media when our car entered the Capital Beltway.' That's putting it mildly, wouldn't you say?"

"You think it's a bad sign?"

Tom nodded. "Very bad. They're soft-pedaling the fact we're nowhere to be seen."

"Who's 'they'?"

"The people who want me the most—the government and the media. I think they're in this together, cooperating to see that they both get what they want."

"Don't you think the public is wound up enough?" she said as she pointed to the television. "They just did some people-on-the-street stuff, and it's very scary."

"What do you mean?"

"Everybody thinks you're a messenger or an angel; from God or Allah or whoever they believe is in charge. You are being scooped and rolled into everybody's Revelations and Apocalypse party plans."

Tom shook his head. "What, no messiahs?"

"You're not funny, do you know that?"

"It has occurred to me."

"So why do you think it's bad they're not playing up our getaway?"

"You make it sound like we're bank robbers," he said.

"How do you know we're no worse?" She moved to the window, looked out through greasy, dusty blinds. "And you're not answering my question."

He exhaled, sat down on the edge of the bed. "They're not putting out a big alert for one of two reasons—either they already know where we are, or they are very confident they can locate us whenever they want."

The idea that there were forces out there who controlled the kind of knowledge and power he spoke of obviously disturbed her. Saying nothing, she absorbed what he said. She had seen the frightful force Gunnderson had employed, and he knew she'd been impressed by the surgical precision of it.

"So what do we do? Why don't we just give ourselves up?"

"Because neither one of us are quitters," he said.

She managed a small, nervous smile. "So what do we do from here?"

Running a hand through his hair, he stood up and began his pacing. It was a habit he disliked, but had never been able to break. "I'm not very good at this stuff, but I know a few things we *have* to do."

"Should I take notes?"

"Just listen," he said. "First thing, we dump the car right here, and we take a bus into the next town, whatever it is. If the car has a homing bug on it, it could take us all day to find it, and if there's *one*, that means there's *another* one in a far more difficult place—for people who are stupid enough to think they've gummed things up by finding the easy one."

"Okay, I can see that—it's much easier to just leave it here. Then what? We buy another one?"

"*You*, not we."

She nodded. "Isn't that dangerous?"

"Sure, but you'll be spending cash. It means you're going into the computers but not as quickly. Temporary tag registration from the dealers only get updated once or twice a month, unless the dealership is especially anally retentive. Most of them resent the hassles from the motor vehicle agencies."

She looked at him oddly. "How do you *know* this kind of stuff?"

He shrugged. "You hang around these criminals long enough, you can't help but learn a few things."

"Okay, then what?"

"After we bus in to the next fair-sized town, we can spend the afternoon buying new wardrobes. Somehow, I have a feeling you won't have any trouble getting that part accomplished with a fair amount of panache. Then we go out and buy a new car."

"Sounds like fun, where do we catch the bus?"

"I have no idea, but I'd guess that truck stop's a good place to start."

It was.

But it passed through towns so small, most of them didn't even have any car dealerships. It might be a long ride.

Despite everything, he felt better today. Even if they were going to bring him down, he felt as if he'd given his best effort. To think he'd dedicated his life to the service of that ever-hungry machine scared him. How far he'd come since the crash, since meeting Estela . . . the idea of being president seemed alien, absurd. To want to be in charge of all those scorpions in that bottle they called the government, he had to have been crazy.

(The bastards . . .)

He knew how single-minded and heartless they could be, and somewhere along the route of this new chapter in his life, he'd decided that whatever they wanted, he *didn't*.

THIRTY-NINE

Lattimore

Erskine Lattimore's Sunday mornings were usually his favorite time of the week. Edna was always careful to not wake him and he slept as long as he pleased. When he did get up, he'd take the Lincoln Town Car on a leisurely roll down to the Riverview Deli Café in Potomac, where he would sit at his usual table to read the *Washington Post* and the *New York Times*.

But today was different. The ride to the café was punctuated by a cellular phone call of primary importance. Having served on so many Senate hearings and committees over the years, Erskine had made every connection a connected man could make. He often boasted there was no one he couldn't reach with one phone call, and if it wasn't true, it was hell-to-pay close to it. Thirty-six years in the Senate still meant something in today's world, and he didn't really care about voting in term limits because he'd already shot his wad and fuck the new guys coming in.

The calls were coming from the woman who knew more about his life than his own wife—his personal secretary since his first day on Capitol Hill, Marilyn Spector. In an age where nobody trusted anybody, he knew he could count on Marilyn. She was getting a little long in the tooth, but she was still a tough, reliable pack mule. No matter what he saddled up on her, she'd just take it and get it done. He wouldn't trade her for any *three* of the latest models—what with their equal rights and harassment ideas stuck up their tight little cracks. Who needed that kind of bullstuff?

As he wheeled the Lincoln up to a stop sign, the cellular rang again. "Talk to me, Marilyn. . . ."

"I've just spoken to Harry Osborne. He can make it."

"Okay, that's everybody, right?"

"Except Bill Feeney. The CIA's still in the hotseat over the latest mess in South Africa. He's in emergency session with the secretary of state and the president."

"Those fools!" said Erskine, unable to resist some editorial comment.

"But he's the only who can't make it, sir. Everybody else is in your corner, Senator."

"Thanks for doing a little extra work on a Sunday, darlin'." Erskine grinned. "You got any more grandchildren still need to go to a private school, anything like that I can do for you?"

"You've already sent them all," said Marilyn. "I'll just keep this one in my Book of Favors."

"You just do that," said the senator as he punched her off the line. Many years ago, he'd let her talk him into that goddamned book. It was the best and the worst thing he'd ever done. She kept score on everything, kept everything fair between them. Sure, it had cost him plenty, but he could get her to do any damned thing, and over the years, that book had bought him the most rare of Washington commodities—undying loyalty.

Erskine resettled his great bulk more comfortably behind the wheel, tapped on the accelerator, and rolled slowly through the intersection. He checked his watch. In half an hour, he'd have his destiny packaged up as neat as a Christmas present.

The meeting was more than the usual power-brunch, and the Riverview Deli Café had seen more than its share of those. A favorite gathering place for the power and money elite in Washington, it was said that more deals were made here than in any office building in the world. A CIA operative had once "joked" to Erskine that there were more jamming bugs planted here than in the old Embassy Building in Moscow. He'd believed him.

Erskine leaned back in his chair and surveyed the cast he'd called together. Powerful men. Old friends. They'd come from vastly different places in life to arrive at this point, but they all shared the same vision for the future of the country, and that vision was the common bond among them. Erskine Lattimore had become the focus of their informal federation, and they had gathered this morning to help ensure he would be the next president.

From left to right around the table: Larry Osborne, deputy director of the National Security Agency; Harve Merrow, director of the FBI; Irv Shindelman, chairman of the Democratic Party; and General Harrison Cobb, Pentagon Special Operations Group.

After the team of waiters had served everyone everything they could possibly desire short of naked dancing girls, Erskine folded his hands across the swollen expanse of his belly and addressed them in a quiet voice. "All right, boys, we know why we're here. I need impressions, observations, scenarios."

Harve Merrow ran a hand through his still thick, sandy-colored hair. His wide shoulders and squared-off jaw made him look like a cartoon of GI Joe, and he was as tough as he looked. "I think the ESPN broadcast merely confirms what we've known since the first tests at Keller."

Erskine waved off the observation. "No bullstuff, Harve! But what does it mean to *us*?"

"You mean in terms of the coming election." It was not a question. It had come from Irv Shindelman, a small olive-complected man with curly dark hair that everyone knew he'd been coloring for years. He looked like a bank clerk, but he was just plain brilliant. "It means he's gone beyond the persona of a presidential candidate."

"What's *that* mean?" Erskine always needed to hear things as simply stated as possible. That way, there were no misunderstandings, his daddy'd always said. His daddy had been a tobacco farmer, but he knew how to deal with people.

"It means people are looking at him as some kind of savior or messenger from God," said Shindelman. "Don't forget, the millennium is coming. People are lining up to join every kind of nut group you can think of. End of the world stuff. It's very big right now."

Erskine wanted to bang on the table with one of his big ham-hock fists, but he tempered the urge and merely glared at Shindelman. "Well, is that good or bad?"

"I'd say it's very good. People perceive politics to be dirty, on a subconscious level. They don't want to associate God or his works with such things."

"Besides that," said Harve Merrow, "we've got reports from Keller that overheard *and* digitized conversations involving Flanagan indicate he isn't interested in running for office any longer."

Erskine wheeled on him. "We can't believe that until he formally withdraws from the race."

"Ersk, it's been four months since he's made a political speech. His inactivity has effectively removed him from the campaign."

"But he's still very much in the public eye," said Erskine. "Raisin' his son from the dead on national television! Jesus Christ, Harve! That goes a little beyond promisin' to cut the fuckin' income tax!"

General Cobb cleared his throat. He was so thin, he looked ill, but he'd been looking like that for thirty-five years. His face was downright skullish, and he scared you just trying to look him in the eye. "My people are still investigating the possibility of a hoax—albeit a very elaborate one."

Larry Osborne adjusted his tie, shook his head. "*My* people are convinced he's for real."

The general grinned. "Bringing people back from the dead is serious business, Larry."

"Then Tom Flanagan is very serious," said Osborne. "The data we've been able to get on him is pretty hard. Unshakable, I'd say. I don't know how he does it, but he *does*."

"Any ideas on that?" asked Shindelman.

"High-level paranormal stuff," said General Cobb. "We've had resurrection activity in the past. Some that might be hard data. But lots of it's crap. We can discredit this guy if we have to. If PSOG can deal with the UFO phenomena, we can certainly deal with one man."

Osborne shrugged. "Maybe we just want to terminate?"

"I hear the Company has a few uses for him," said Harve Merrow. "Hell, so do we! The FBI's got more than a few murders we could solve if we could just wake up the corpse and ask him who buttoned his ass. . . ."

The general nodded. "Terminating is a very final option. But not right now. We all need him too much."

Erskine looked at him. "We terminate only if he learns too much, loses his usefulness, or if we think he's got any chance in the election. Otherwise, I don't like it."

Harve Merrow chuckled. "What's the matter, Ersk, getting a little religion in your old age?"

Irv Shindelman tapped his water glass with a Mont Blanc fountain pen. "Gentlemen, the direction this discussion is going is becoming very nonproductive."

"Meaning?" asked Erskine.

"Meaning, if we've got anybody like *God* really in the middle of all this, we're surely fucked anyway, gentlemen."

A hard silence descended over the table for a moment as the cadre of nonbelievers considered such a possibility. Erskine looked from one to the other wondering if they too were feeling the twitches of a not-quite-yet-dead Christian conscience. Everyone looked to Erskine to give the ball another good kick, so he did.

"Well, boys, I think we've got no choice but to believe it a hard, cruel universe, and we're on our own." Erskine chuckled and everyone followed suit. There was an underpaving of anxiety in their shared laughter, but like Erskine had said, they didn't have much choice. He leaned forward, started in on his seafood bisque and Western omelet. After a few bites, he looked at Larry Osborne. "What's the status on our prey right now?"

Osborne had taken the cue to begin eating and was just about to shovel in a slice of his crepe. Canceling the idea, he looked up and began reciting some facts, ending with: ". . . and the car's beacon is still functioning. Locked coordinates give us a location in northwestern Illinois. Probably parked there for the night. We have a ready team that can home in and pick him up if that's what you want."

"I think that's what we want," said Erskine. He looked around the table and everyone nodded.

"I can call them right now," said Osborne, reaching for his PCS unit.

Erskine held up a hand. "Hold it. What happens if he's found the bugs or ditched the car? You know we've all been trained in basic espionage—you boys thought it would be a good idea, remember?"

Harve Merrow grinned. "Actually, we're expecting him to lose the vehicle. We don't think he'll try public transportation for two reasons: he's not going to want to deal with the public and *everybody* is looking for him, believe me. Every common sap's got somebody they want him to raise up. Christ," said Merrow, "can you believe how nutty the country is getting over this?"

"What's the second reason?" asked Erskine.

"Because he knows we'll have the buses, planes, and trains blanketed."

"Okay so maybe he buys a new car . . ."

"Have to be cash," said Osborne.

"Say it *is* cash," said Erskine.

"Then we get some agents out to canvass the dealerships," said Merrow. "We'd find him in no time."

"The only way he can shake us," said Merrow, "is if he either heads out across the fields and the woods on foot, or on a snowmobile, or if he buys a junker from some bumpkin."

"Then what?" Erskine looked at General Cobb. "SpySat stuff?"

"We could start a general infrared and surface scan." Cobb stabbed a slice of filet mignon, stuffed it in his mouth, then talked through his chewing. "Pick up pretty much every living thing in any suspected area. Plus the support from your guys on the ground with the standard door-to-door and other S.O.P. We'd find him sooner or later."

Erskine leaned back, patted his belly. "Okay, so what you boys're telling me is that you've got our prey covered. No matter what he does?"

Everyone nodded. "We're fine. The only thing we need to decide is who gets him first!"

Everyone laughed loudly

But Erskine knew they meant it. Ever since Larry Constantino had blown the cover off this thing, everybody in secret places had begun speculating on the *uses* of such a power.

Harve Merrow held up an index finger. "We all know what we want to do with him, but there's a few more questions that need answering and that means a full-scale testing series. All the agencies have agreed."

Erskine looked around the table. He didn't like being kept out of anybody's secrets. One raised eyebrow was all it took to get Osborne talking. His agency's budget depended on the beneficence of every committee connected with Erskine Lattimore. And anybody on that kind of short leash was always willing to volunteer information.

"Come on, Senator, you've got to know that operation at Keller was almost strictly a surveillance thing. The only thing we really wanted from down there was confirmation that this guy Flanagan was the genuine article."

"We're all going to need some time to check him in a controlled environment," said General Cobb.

Harve Merrow nodded. "For instance: is there a time limit on his subject? How long can you be dead before you can't be brought back? Tissue breakdown? Decomposition? What about fossilized specimens? These are just a few of the issues being raised."

"Not to mention the list of 'jobs' we all have for him."

Erskine nodded. What they were saying made sense, but they seemed to be ignoring one major problem. "Excuse me, gentlemen, but what makes you think the American public's going to stand for all this?"

Larry Osborne laughed. He looked like a movie actor. Ivy League good looks. He'd kept himself in reasonably good shape even into his late fifties. "That's easy," he said reaching for his PCS phone. "We let them think he's dead."

Everyone looked at each other and nodded. Erskine knew it wouldn't be the first time.

"Yeah," said Osborne into his unit. "This is Ground Zero. You can close the net."

"What about that woman he's with?" asked Erskine. "The doctor . . . ?"

Osborne clicked off the unit. "That's easy, too," he said. "Terminate with some of that good, old, extreme prejudice."

FORTY

Flanagan

The bus driver hadn't even look at them or issued a ticket as they stuffed their dollar bills into the collection box. There were perhaps twenty other passengers—a variety of mid-westerners ranging from retirees in plaid hunting jackets to several boys in their late teens wearing the latest in ski parkas. Everyone seemed to be ignoring them with an almost studied precision. An old Greyhound Scenicruiser converted and painted by the Streetsboro Transportation and Bus Line, it belched and farted its way through a maze of cross-hatched two-lane blacktops. Small towns and *very* small towns comprised its route. As Tom and Estela sat in seats worn smooth by a million miles of lonesome traveling, watching the cold, hard stretches of half-empty storefronts, they understood *why* they had not seen a new car dealership in almost two hours.

"What're we going to do?" she said.

"You know, the more I think about it, the more I think we should avoid the new car."

"Really? Why?"

"I'm glad that you asked," he said, smiling. He could tell she was getting anxious, edging into true fear. He wasn't feeling exactly great about their prospects, but he didn't want to make her feel any worse. "We should assume that if they want me back, they will have already closed in on the Mercedes and its bugs."

"Can we assume that?"

"We have to. The national security training course all government mucky-mucks take stresses one thing: *always assume the worst*; then you are more than prepared for anything they can throw at you."

"Makes sense. Go on. . . ." She gave him a kiss on the cheek and he marveled at the softness of her lips.

(Pay attention. No time for that stuff now.)

"Okay. If someone saw us get on this bus, they would have already tracked us down. So we have to figure we have at least a small window of opportunity."

"Do you have any ideas?"

"Not good ones, but I think we can try this: get off at the next town, whatever it is, and try to find someone who has a vehicle to sell. Buy it and get on the road."

He didn't like the idea even as he was still forming the words, but he knew he'd acted the night before without thinking anything through. There hadn't been time, he granted himself that much of a concession, but he was no master operative, and he was no match for the number of special units the feds could sic on him. He felt guilty talking all the espionage talk to Estela, and maybe getting her to think he was good at something he was not. In a burst of honesty—bursts that were becoming far more frequent in his day-to-day existence—he told her what he was thinking.

She smiled sweetly, gently, touched his face. "I know," she said.

"What's that mean—you 'know'?"

"You're not misleading me. I know we're in trouble, and it's pretty obvious you're no professional at this game."

He looked past her at the first signs of an approaching town—a few billboards advertising eateries. "Well, that's very encouraging. Glad to see I'm making such a great impression."

"Silly. . . . That's not what I meant." She looked past him, out the window, where the bus was slowing down to stop at an intersection. "Look, over there."

He followed the line of her index finger to a large sedan sitting at the perpendicular road. Beyond it were some grain elevators and a feed processing plant. Its shiny, deep maroon paint job gave a bland government-issue look that was enhanced by four large males filling up its interior.

"Do they see us?" Estela looked down at her lap like a schoolgirl caught talking during an exam.

"Don't know. We'll see."

The bus passed through the intersection, and the government sedan pulled in behind them, at this point content simply to follow them.

"Not good," said Tom. "They know."

"How can you be sure?"

"I just have a feeling." He slammed his fist into his hand. It was a weak ineffectual gesture that described perfectly how inadequate he was feeling. This is what he got for not thinking everything through, for acting so damned impulsively.

"Then we're finished. They've got us."

(Time to do something unexpected.)

"Maybe not," he said standing up, taking off the cap he'd been wearing, and walking toward the front of the bus.

"Tom—" she said, but he ignored her.

When he reached the open space by the driver and the doors, he turned around to face the collection of disinterested passengers.

"Excuse me!" he said loudly. "I have an announcement to make!"

The driver, a man in his sixties whose chief characteristic was a big, gray, drooping mustache, swerved for an instant. "Hope to God, mister, you ain't no skyjacker—are you?"

Tom grinned. "No, wait! Listen! I'm going to need your help—all of you!"

"Man, sit down and shut up, you fuckin' nut-ball . . . !" A wide-shouldered man wearing a hunting vest over a worn army fatigue jacket glared at him from six rows back.

(Just what we need. . . .)

"Some of you might recognize me—I'm . . . I'm Senator Tom Flanagan."

His voice carried well through the confines of the bus. It was like speaking into a huge megaphone. The mention of his name impacted on most of them, and he once again marveled at the power of television. His face had surely been *all* over the tube in the last twenty-four hours.

"Oh, God, it *is* him!" cried a woman.

"I seen 'im yesterday," said one of the teenaged boys. "He's the guy they're lookin' for. . . ."

"What's goin' on?" said the driver, either still skeptical or just plain scared.

"Did you really *do* that?" said an old man in a long herringbone topcoat several sizes too big for him. "You really bring your son back from the *dead*?"

"My dad said it was a trick!" said the other boy. "Like David Copperfield . . . !"

He could feel the variety of their reactions cresting over him like a warm wave of water. He'd felt this kind of psychic response from crowds before—a diverse mixture of emotions coloring the spectrum from awe to anger to abject fear.

(Just keep talking. No going back now.)

"I need your help! Please listen to me. . . ." Tom raised his hands, like a criminal turning himself in. He had to show them he meant no harm, that he was as helpless as he claimed.

"You really that senator?" said Hunting Vest. The man's expression had segued from outrage to skepticism.

"My name is Senator Tom Flanagan. Now listen to me! There's a car following this bus. It's filled with government agents who want to kidnap me! They want to——"

"Agents?" someone near the back yelled. "What kinda agents?"

"*Secret* agents, you idgit!" said someone else.

"What they wanna do that for?" said the driver. Succumbing to the suggestion of adventure, he punched the accelerator pedal and the bus lurched forward, but only slightly.

"They want him for secret experiments," said a woman who looked like a farmer's wife in her forties. "I read about that stuff in the *Weird World Weekly*. They——"

"The bastards," said the old man in the herringbone coat. "They killed my son in Vietnam with LSD!"

"They're workin' with the banks now," said a middle-aged man wearing a flannel shirt and heavy denim overalls. "They wanna know how much we're all usin' and where we spend it!"

Tom looked at the group that had seemed so insular, so quietly disinterested only moments before, as a change seemed to sweep amongst them like an airborne disease. No matter how singular their own thoughts, their own problems or pain might be, they seemed to have a common enemy, a common threat to the way they lived their lives.

"They're tryin' to tell me I can't see Dr. Elmon anymore," said a small, elderly black woman seated across the aisle from Estela.

Tom held up his hands. "I need your help," he said again.

"You really can *do* that?" said the driver. "Bring people back?"

Tom nodded. "Yes, it has happened several times, but—"

"If'n you can do that, how come you need *our* help?" asked Hunting Vest.

"'Cause he ain't Superman," said one of the teenaged boys. He ran to the back of the bus, looked out the rear window. "He's right about those guys in the car! There they are!"

"Whaddaya want from us, mister?" said the driver.

"Don't let them get me," Tom said in a loud voice. "If they do, you're going to see something in the news about an 'accident' and how I'm either missing or presumed dead."

"He's right! That's what they do!" screamed the teenager. "Like in the movies."

Tom looked out at the odd collection of humanity. This strange group were his allies, and he had no idea what to do next. "Where's your next stop?"

"Comin' up in about five minutes. Broadview Valley," said the driver.

"Small town?" said Tom.

"Ain't they all?" The driver laughed, pushed down the gas pedal, and the bus mushed forward for an instant then lapsed back into its labored crawl down the highway.

(You'd better think of something fast. . . .)

Down the aisle, Estela was looking at him expectantly, as were all of the passengers. It was like that dream where you blink your eyes and you're standing in front of a crowd totally naked. That's how he felt. Not a damn thing to say, not a single thought in his head. Then, as if sensing his peril and embarrassment, Hunting Vest stood up and started walking toward him. The man carried a bulging duffel bag and some kind of rifle wrapped in a quilted cloth carrier.

"Are you getting off at the next stop," said Tom, "or are you planning to help me?"

The man was so tall he had to bend his head slightly as he filled the center aisle. He looked down at Tom without changing his expression of a constant scowl. Then he broke into a gap-toothed grin that actually scared Tom.

"My name's Foley. Foley Sellard. And I'm gonna help you, mister." He reached out a large hand and shook Tom's vigorously.

"Thank you," he said. "Thank you very much."

Foley had about three days of gray-white stubble on his face and a mean-looking scar on his left cheek; at some point in his life he'd sported a second, temporary mouth. Although the man was pushing sixty, he looked like trouble if he wanted to be.

"Ain't you so much," said Foley Sellard, "as them shit-suckers behind us. Agents shut down my chicken farm years ago. Said I didn't have enough minorities workin' it. Ain't no minorities in Broadview Valley lookin' to work in a chicken farm, but that didn't make a mind. Goddamned fines almost wiped me out!"

Turning to face the passengers, Foley unzipped his quilt case to reveal a large-gauge pump-action shotgun. He thrust it upward as he said in a loud voice, "We gonna stop these bastards from screwin' around with our lives, or what?"

The bus erupted with cheers so loud the windows rattled. Everyone left their seats and surged forward.

"What're we gonna do, Foley Sellard?" asked the little old black woman, her skin smooth and polished like a hand-picked chestnut.

"You just tell us, and you got it!" said Herringbone Coat.

"Yeah, dudes, we're up for this!" said the teenager.

"Okay," said Foley. "When we stop at the Valley, we *all* get off this bus—with the senator and his lady-friend bunched up in the middle of us."

"Like a packa wolves guardin' its pups, huh?" said the farmer in the overalls.

"You got it." Foley winked. "Then we all just ease on down the block to Henninger's Garage. I've got a pickup in there Henny's supposed to have ready for me. I figure I can trust you to borrow it for a day or so."

Tom looked at the tall rough-hewn man in the hunting vest and he wanted to hug the guy. Instead, he reached into his baggy corduroys and pulled out a fold of hundreds. "Wait a minute, Foley," he said. "How much is that truck of yours worth?"

Sellard smiled. "It's seen its share of the road."

"How much?"

"I guess I could get eight hundred down at the grange auction—if I really wanted to get rid of it."

Tom counted off forty bills, stuffed them into the hunter's vest pocket. "That ought to cover any mileage we put on it. Thanks, Mr. Sellard."

"Stop's comin' up!" yelled the driver, and on cue everyone bolted from their seats except one of the teenagers at the back window.

"The feds're stoppin' too!" he yelled.

"Okay, everybody!" yelled Foley. "I'll go first with my equalizer here, then the rest of you kinda just keep these folks in the middle. When we're all outta here, we go down to Henny's, okay?"

"You betcha," said the old man in the topcoat.

Everyone voiced their assents as the bus *skreeed* to a stop at the corner of a one-intersection town. Foley Sellard slipped through the door as soon as it opened, and the other passengers maneuvered into position as smoothly as if they'd been rehearsing for a week. There was no traffic on the streets, either wheeled or pedestrian, other than the dark maroon sedan that had curbed in behind the bus. Tom held Estela's hand as they exited the bus and felt the press of the crowd encircle them like a giant set of arms.

"Keep moving, everybody!" yelled Foley Sellard.

"Hold it right there, people!" The voice blanketed them as it squawked from a bullhorn held by one of the four young men approaching the crowd. They all wore dark suits, aviator sunglasses, and the grim expressions Tom knew so well.

"Who the hell're *you*?" said Foley Sellard, brandishing his very large shotgun like a minuteman statue. Tom could barely see him through the crowd that protected him, but just hearing that guy made him feel safe.

The nearest Suit produced a badge in a billfold. "Federal agents. P-S-O-G!"

"Sorry, but that don't mean S-H-I-T!" said Foley.

Some of the crowd snickered, but Tom didn't. He knew about the Pentagon Special Operations Group. Every senator was sworn to secrecy regarding their true mission in the government. They were highly trained and thorough bad-asses.

"Folks, we mean no one any harm. We are here to escort Senator Flanagan back to Washington, D.C."

The crowd continued to creep en masse up the sidewalk.

All except for Foley Sellard. He stood there like a rock, staring down the young men in service to their country. "The way I hear it, the senator don't *want* to go back to Washington."

"Leave 'im alone!" somebody yelled.

"Sir, I order you to stand aside." The Suit with the badge produced a sleek silver automatic handgun and some of the people in the crowd gasped as they saw the weapon catch the light and flash it back at them. Some of them hesitated; the movement of the group faltered, but did not stop.

Tom could feel the tension gathering like a nasty electrical storm. Estela squeezed his hand, but said nothing. There was nothing they needed to say.

"I've broken no law," said Foley Sellard with a wide, mean smile. "Last time I checked, this here's *America*. We don't *have* the government in our streets tellin' us what to do. Haven't you heard, sonny? We *are* the government."

After he said that, the people surrounding Tom actually cheered and for an instant the federal boys were stunned, confused.

"Keep moving, folks!" yelled Sellard.

"*No*body moves!" yelled the agent in charge. He raised his weapon and fired two shots into the air.

The crowd hesitated, but still kept moving. Tom had expected them to break ranks, but if anything they held tighter to one another.

"What're you gonna do?" asked the little old black lady. "Shoot *all* of us?"

"Yeah!" screamed the teenaged boys. "Rad! Federal dudes! Word-up!"

"Go ahead," somebody else said loudly. "Start shooting."

The leader hesitated, slowly lowered his gun. The three others looked to him for a signal, but he seemed lost. Tom had never seen anything like this, but for the first time in his life he felt proud—really felt it—to be in America. An emotional burst threatened to break through his chest and he felt like crying—an incredibly *beautiful* sensation. People had confided to him how they sometimes cried during the National Anthem, and he'd always thought they were lying. Now, in a small town in the Midwest, he finally understood what it was all about.

Several things happened at that point. Townspeople started appearing from wherever it was crowds magically gather. Two minutes earlier the street had been totally empty, but suddenly people showed up, gawking, staring, closing in, gradually surrounding the federal agents. Tom watched as their leader produced a flip-fone from his breast pocket. He spoke animatedly and rapidly into it, and he was clearly not happy with the way things were developing.

In the meantime, the little crowd surrounding Tom and Estela continued to move like an ancient Roman phalanx up the street toward Henny's garage. Several cars approached the scene, including a black-and-white with a flashing light on top.

Above the rising noise level Tom could hear a darkly familiar sound. It rolled across the flat land to a deadly rhythm. A steadily increasing, low-register thumping.

Helicopter blades. Ratcheting against the hard November sky like a hammer on a tin roof. Tom looked off to the south and saw the Apache suspended over the horizon like an angry black bug.

"This is not good," he said in harsh whisper to Estela. "Definitely not good."

She looked at him with a hint of panic in her huge eyes, but said nothing.

The black-and-white skidded to a stop. A county sheriff's seal decorated the driver's door, which swung open to reveal a middle-aged man who looked far too soft and gentle to get involved with what Tom sensed was now unavoidable.

"What's going on here?" asked the lawman. His little gold-plate name badge said the single word *Grant*, and he sported a carefully trimmed salt-and-pepper beard. He looked for a moment at the Suits and then at Foley Sellard, whom he obviously recognized. He was about to speak again, but was cut off.

"This is a federal matter, Sheriff," said the agent in charge. "We have the situation under control."

"I wasn't informed of any 'situation,' son," said the sheriff. He looked at the man with the shotgun. "Christ, Foley, what'd you get yourself into this time?"

The crowd inched along. They were no more than thirty yards from the garage where Foley's pickup awaited them. For some reason, Tom was beginning to believe that maybe they would get out of this mess.

"Charlie, that's that senator from back East in there." Foley gestured toward the center knot of the crowd with his shotgun. He went on to reprise the "situation."

Sheriff Grant nodded, approached the agent with the gun. "What you want the senator for? He do something wrong?"

"No, sir," said the agent above the rising chatter of the helicopter. "This is a matter of national security."

Sheriff Grant chuckled. "Aren't you boys kind of wearing that one out?"

"I'm going to have to ask you and these people to stand aside—for the *last* time." The agent couldn't have been more than thirty years old, and although he was speaking in a loud, firm voice, Tom could see the guy was having trouble doing what he knew would have to come next.

The sheriff was clearly undecided what to do, but Foley Sellard made up everybody's minds for them. The big guy in the hunting vest leveled his shotgun at the agent with the shiny gun and smiled that hideous gap-toothed smile. It was one of those crazy smiles that scared most people, and the agent fell into that general category.

"Looks like mine's bigger'n yours, sonny," said Foley.

"Hold on there, Foley!" said the sheriff, backing up and *not* going for his own weapon.

Foley's eyes had dwindled down to the size of bird shot. "You can talk that 'last time' crap all you want!" yelled Foley over the sound of the chopper. "But if'n you try anything to stop people from exercising their freedoms, this here pump-action's gonna take your young ass apart."

"You'll . . . you'll never get away with it," said the agent. His face belied his uncertainty, despite the brave words.

Foley chuckled, threw back his head and actually cackled. Then he screamed his words at them: "Like I *care!* You people killed me *years* ago! When you fucked me outta my chicken farm. . . ."

"I don't know what you're talking about," said the agent.

"You don't need to, sonny. Long as *I* do!" Foley spoke over his shoulder. "Senator, you and the lady better get into that truck now!"

The crowd picked up their pace and moved away from Foley and the sheriff. They flowed over the sidewalk and into Henny's garage, where an old Ford flatbed hunkered down in the grimy light like a tired old dog. It was full of rust, but it had good tires, and Tom suspected the engine ran like a Swiss watch.

As they moved to climb into its cab, things fell apart.

Not taking his gaze off the confrontation on the street, Tom watched the agent in charge grab his weapon with both hands and begin the practiced curl downward, swinging his gun into firing position. He must have thought he could catch the old man in the hunting vest napping, but he didn't get halfway into a firing crouch before old Foley's gun went off like a Howitzer. The blast caught the agent full in the face as he dropped down to one knee.

It was an instant of sheer terror as the explosion of pellets *consumed* the agent's head like a swarm of flesh-eating insects. The man's head disappeared in an aerosoled pink mist that spattered the other three Suits. People started screaming and scattering as the shocked agents fell prey to their training and went for their weapons, dropping into firing positions.

"Get in the truck!" yelled Tom, half pushing Estela ahead of him and up behind the wheel of the old Ford. "Keys in it?"

"Yes!"

"Get out of here! Now!"

"But—!"

"Now!"

Estela keyed the ignition, and as the engine coughed into life, backfiring and expelling a big black cloud of smoke, the agents opened fire with their slick handguns. The crowd had vanished, leaving Sheriff Grant pinned against the side of his cruiser, hands thrust skyward as a spreading stain of urine darkened the front of his uniform pants.

Tom stood helpless as the agents opened fire on Foley Sellard. The old hunter had raised the shotgun to pump out the spent shell when the fusillade ripped into his chest, stitching the hunting vest to his rib cage and kicking him back off his feet as if he'd been hit by a linebacker.

Despite the apocalyptic rhythm of the chopper overhead, bobbing and dipping like a giant dragonfly, the silence that followed the exchange of gunfire overwhelmed everyone. The sheer *absence* of the violent sound was somehow more hideous than the outburst itself.

"Go on!" Tom said, breaking the spell and slapping the rusted door of the truck.

"Not without you . . . !" Estela's face was streaked with tears, her full lips pulled back in abject terror.

"I'm staying!" he shouted. "I've got to go back with them!"

"Flanagan, *no!*"

"—I've got to! You'll see . . . !"

"I can't!"

He threw the attaché into the truck. "Take the money and get a plane!"

She looked at him and he saw her acceptance, her surrender in her face. Leaning in, he kissed her.

"I . . . I . . ."

"I know you do," she said. "That's why we're going to make it."

Not waiting for an answer, Estela floored the old flatbed and it lumbered out of the garage. She cut the wheel hard and bounced across the curb and out on the street. The agents tracked her with their weapons but didn't fire.

Tom turned, faced the agents, who were advancing warily on the garage.

"Let her go, and I'll come with you!" he said, putting his hands in the air.

The old pickup gathered speed and accelerated through the intersection, past the deserted Scenicruiser, and onto the state highway—running west.

Running back to the street, Tom ignored the agents and advanced on the two bodies. There was nothing he could do for what remained of the young agent, but he knelt by Foley Sellard's body and cradled him in his arms. Instantly, a now familiar energy sparked in him. The hard wind of time whipped over him, but there was a new comfort in the force of its gale. Without even thinking about it, Tom unzipped the punctured hunting vest, pushed his hands beneath Foley's fatigue jacket and flannel shirt. His hands seemed to sink beneath the ravaged flesh, and the lavalike flow of life itself melted from his fingers. New, pink tissue squeezed and forced the 9mm slugs up and out of the old man's chest cavity. Like watching a video running in reverse, Tom pulled Foley Sellard back from oblivion. The man's wrinkled lids fluttered and twitched, finally opened. Foley looked around with the surprise and wonder of a newborn baby.

"What happened?" he said innocently.

"You're going to be all right, Foley," said Tom. "How do you feel?"

"Like somebody hit me with a cement truck!" He looked cautiously at Tom. "Y'done it, din't ya, son?"

(Yeah, I guess I have. . . .)

Swallowing hard, Tom just nodded.

"Man, that is *weird*, I gotta tell ya. Scary."

"Christ on a crutch . . . !" said Sheriff Grant, who had dropped down to linger at Tom's shoulder. "What's it like,

Foley?! What's it *feel* like? Did you see *Him*? God? The angels?"

"Didn't see nothin'," he said.

Tom helped Sellard to a sitting position, then exhaled slowly as the afterglow of the power and the experience receded away from him like a rapidly lowering tide.

Even the three federal agents were transfixed by the contained spectacle. They'd surely been briefed on what to expect from Senator Flanagan, but hearing about it and seeing it were light-years apart. He looked at them. "I'll go with you," he said above the wind-noise of the helicopter. "But only if you let Doctor Barrero and these people be."

One of the Suits nodded, pulled a flip-fone from his jacket. He spoke into the unit, but Tom couldn't hear anything. Above them, the black chopper hefted itself higher into the sky and lurched off in the direction of Estela's pickup, which was now less than a speck on the highway as it perspected to the horizon. Tom watched it leave as the agents encircled him.

"Hey! Wait a minute!"

(Be careful . . .)

"Just a precaution, Senator," said the man holding the phone.

(Precaution, my ass!)

"Anything happens to her—all bets are off with you creeps."

As they pulled him to his feet, Tom heard another rumbling above them, this deeper, more menacing in timber. Looking up, he saw a two-rotor troop carrier descending into the center of the intersection. The helicopter bore the markings of the Indiana Air National Guard, and it began disgorging soldiers as soon as its bloated tires touched down.

"What's going on here?" yelled Sheriff Grant, who pushed as close as he dared to the agent in charge.

"There's been an environmental accident here," said the Suit. "This town's under quarantine until further notice."

"You can't do that!" yelled the sheriff.

Foley Sellard cackled out a frightening laugh. "Ain't you realized yet that these shitsuckers think they can do whatever they want?"

"You sons of bitches!" screamed Tom, reaching out to grab the nearest agent by the lapels. He held on to the man as he glared jaw-to-jaw with the Ken doll clone. Suddenly his arms were pinned to his sides by the other two agents, and they separated him from the man in charge.

A man wearing captain's bars on his battle fatigues approached them with several soldiers. They surrounded Tom and the others, roughly hauling Foley Sellard onto his feet and off toward the transport copter. A detail of men with a body bag arrived right behind them and started gathering up what was left of Foley Sellard's minuteman operation. The sheriff acted like he wanted to say something, but reconsidered.

"General Cobb's usual finesse," said Tom to the captain.

"My orders are to escort you out of here, Senator."

Tom turned to the sheriff, shook his hand. "I don't really know you, or any of those people who helped us, but I want you to do me a favor."

"Sure, Senator Flanagan—whatever you want."

"Tell them *thank you*, and tell them I really mean it."

"Sure, Senator. I sure will."

"—And tell them I'm *sorry* for the misfortune and the pain I've brought to their town. I had no idea—"

Sheriff Grant nodded. "It's okay, sir. It's okay. They were just being good citizens, that's all. I guess . . . I guess there's a price for doing that these days."

(You've got *that* right, Charlie. . . .)

He shook hands with him, then turned to the captain. "Okay, let's go."

The soldier nodded and gestured toward the troop transport. Tom took a step in that direction when the sound and shock wave of an explosion reached them.

(*No . . . !*)

For an instant, he couldn't breathe. Everything. In his body. Seized up. White starbursts flickered before his eyes, and he felt very weak.

He didn't need to turn around to know where the blast had come from—: the highway running west.

FORTY-ONE

Lattimore

Senator Erskine Lattimore sat stretched out in his easy chair, the one with the soft leather worn smooth from thirty-two years of service. He remoted the television to CNN. Top of the hour. The story should be breaking by now, and he wanted to see how it played.

The anchor appeared at his desk while a graphic insert of an Air Force helicopter with the word *"MISSING"* supered over it complemented the narration.

"The top news this hour . . . the Army helicopter carrying Maryland Senator Thomas Flanagan and his physician Doctor Estela Barrero has been reported missing during a flight over the Blue Ridge Mountains. Search crews are being dispatched to the area. Two days ago, the senator made international news when he resurrected his son during a nationally broadcast college football game. It is believed Senator Flanagan was on a special assignment when his aircraft was reported missing."

Erskine nodded appreciatively. Not bad copy. The next story detailed the latest unrest in South Africa, then a ferry boat capsizing in the North Sea. The usual fare. But the fourth story was also of interest to him and his colleagues. Aerial video of a small town filled the screen as an on-the-scene journalist voice-over spoke:

"Possible toxic waste contamination has caused the temporary quarantine of the town of Broadview Valley, Indiana. Federal inspectors from the Office of Environmental Affairs discovered evidence to suggest that the well water supplying this small farming community may be contaminated with plutonium isotopes. Ruptured toxic waste containers buried at a nearby government processing facility may be the cause. Until results of more testing can be verified, the people of Broadview Valley are being monitored closely. Public access to the town is temporarily prohibited."

Clicking off the set, Erskine leaned back in his chair, picked up his phone, speed-dialed his press secretary.

"Hello . . ."

"Jamie, that was beautiful work, son."

"Oh, thank you, Senator. I have to tell you—General Cobb helped me with it."

"I'm sure he did. He's a master of the flimflam. Where's Flanagan now?"

"En route from Illinois. He'll be arriving at Andrews within the hour."

"Good, good. I hope they take good care of him."

"From the way I hear it, everybody has plans for him," said the press secretary.

"Perfect. Perfect. It's out of our hands now, son." Erskine smiled. "And you know what . . . ?"

"What's that, sir?"

"Our hands are perfectly clean."

FORTY-TWO

Flanagan

Two soldiers from Pentagon Special Operations escorted him from the chopper to a small Military Air Transport Service jet. He walked across the tarmac into a cold wind. Although he looked for markings on the buildings and hangars, he saw nothing to tell him where he was. No one had spoken to him during the first leg of the flight. He had not seen Foley Sellard, but it was clear they didn't want Tom Flanagan talking to him.

As he boarded the MATS plane, the soldiers closed him off in a cabin area with four flight seats, a couch, and a coffee table. He sat on the couch and held his head in his hands.

(Estela . . .)

He refused to think she might be dead, but the thought lingered on the threshold of his awareness.

What had he figured he was doing? Running away from the government was like running away from himself. All he'd accomplished was getting people killed and putting an entire town under marshal law.

In all his life, he'd never thought of himself as "depressed." Throughout high school and especially college, he'd known countless young women who claimed to suffer from depression. He'd known guys who acted like they were, but didn't go around broadcasting as women prefer to do. Tom had never understood the condition. If you're an optimist, self-disciplined, strongly motivated, and happy with the goals you've set for yourself, "depression" is one of those words without true meaning. He'd known people who attempted suicide, who at least entertained the thought, or who liked talking about it. Again, an unthinkable concept.

But now, as he sat in the plane, a virtual prisoner, the idea of bailing out on everything seemed quite attractive, desirable even. It was all too much for him. The pressure of what some had called his "gift" was more than anyone could be expected to endure. So far, he'd tried to keep it inside, not let it out, and therefore control it. But it was like a tumor, eating him from the inside out.

To just stop it right here would be the easiest thing to do.

(Great, if you're just a coward. . . .)

He smiled at the fragments of still-intact ego that tried to occasionally break through the black shell he was growing around himself. There was no place to turn, no escape.

(Dr. Infinity . . .)

He laughed aloud as the image filled him.

It *was* funny; he'd actually convinced himself for a little while there that his dream-fugues and hallucinations might be more than that. Even Estela had taken to speaking of the strange dream-presence as a real person, an entity who somehow knew Tom Flanagan better than anyone else in the world.

But it was all smoke and fog, wasn't it?

Just Tom Flanagan jumping his rails. Either it was a manifestation of the pressure he'd been under or a psychological side effect of the original brain trauma. He felt silly now, having ever believed it might have ever been something else. To be sitting here, thinking that a knot of twisted ganglia in some back room of his skull had ever been a real being, or to even think of asking it for assistance, was embarrassing. It would be far better if—

The latch to the cabin door clicked loudly. Tom watched it swing outward and a man in military uniform enter the room. About fifty years old, trim, crisply groomed gray hair, plenty of fruit salad on the left breast, a colonel's ranking at his collar. Tom had seen this guy's type his entire career. Totally interchangeable with all the other automatons the military seemed so proud of producing.

"Good afternoon, Senator," said the man, standing respectfully and extending his hand. "I'm Colonel Leverton, Special Operations Group."

Tom ignored the gesture, remained seated. "Do you actually think I'm going to act with any cordiality toward you?"

The man hesitated, smiled sardonically. "I understand how you feel, Senator, but we have a special situation here."

"Special situation!" Tom spit out the words. "That's all you running dogs of General Cobb know about! You guys leave a slimy trail behind you wherever you go."

"Senator, I'm only—"

"And we used to sneer at the Soviets because *they* attempted to control the flow of information to their people. . . ." Tom laughed. "Just what do you think PSOG is all about, Colonel?"

"You never seemed to mind its existence in the past," said Leverton. "Not until it affected you personally."

(Score one for the bad guys. . . .)

Tom said nothing, but he knew the colonel was correct—some of Flanagan's closed-door senate committees were privy to all kinds of outrageous constitutional violations perpetrated under the blanket of the National Security Priority Act, with its rider establishing and giving carte blanche to General Cobb's band of PSOG thugs. Tom had known about the stuff they'd been doing, and he was now ashamed to admit, he'd done nothing about it, not even go harmlessly on record as disapproving of any of the organization's numerous unlawful operations.

The colonel eased himself into one of the flight seats, pulled a pack of Camels from his pocket. Shaking several out, he offered one to Tom, who shook his head.

"I hope that's the one that kills you, you son of a bitch."

Leverton grinned, fired up with an old Zippo. "I'm sorry, I didn't ask if you minded the 'secondary smoke.'"

"Somehow that doesn't surprise me." Tom glared at him. "What happened to Doctor Barrero?"

Leverton shrugged. "I have no idea."

"Are you in charge of the particular 'special situation'?" The colonel nodded. "Nominally. General Cobb—"

"I know all about General Cobb. But I can tell you one thing very clearly, Colonel. If anything has happened to her, I'll kill you."

Leverton laughed. "When's the last time you killed a man, Senator? Directly, I mean, by your own hand. I'm sure some of the outrageous legislation you've backed over the years has resulted in plenty of unnecessary deaths, but you can keep your hands plenty clean in those instances."

Ignoring the dig, Tom looked the military man dead in the eye. "You will be my first, Colonel."

Leverton exhaled a thin, tight, blue stream of pollutants. "You sure you're man enough?"

"What have you done with Doctor Barrero?"

He shrugged. "That data hasn't reached me yet. I have no idea. That's the truth."

Tom believed him. PSOG had no reason to lie. These guys controlled everything, and besides, they didn't care about anything other than their own self-consumed interests.

"Okay, what about Foley Sellard?"

"He's on another flight to Andrews. They're going to give him a good going-over at Walter Reed. Eight lethal shots to the torso, and you brought him back. That's impressive, Senator. We're going to have a lot of use for you."

"I'll kill myself first."

"Oh, I don't think so," said Leverton. "You're too smart for that. Besides, much of what we intend is quite humanitarian."

"Yeah, and I'm John the Baptist."

Leverton looked at him, raised one eyebrow. "Actually, thoughts not so unlike that notion have occurred to us."

Tom shook his head. "You people are outrageous."

"Not really. Don't you remember that Bob Dylan song—'With God On Our Side'?" said Leverton with a mocking grin. "That's us."

"If there is a God, He doesn't want anything to do with the likes of Cobb and his crew."

Leverton looked at him through a cloud of smoke. Outside the plane, Tom heard voices. There were vibrations along the fuselage, the sound of hatches being sealed. "Senator, you used to have one of the most deceitful records on the Hill. Voted for all the government power-grabs for the last twenty years, and from what I can see, lived in the pockets of a lot of the big lobbyists and SIGs. Now, all of a sudden, you're acting like you just discovered a well-kept secret: power corrupts people. Who are you kidding?"

"No," said Tom in an embarrassed whisper. "Not just discovering it, just facing up to it."

Leverton chuckled. "You know, that's a real dangerous thing you've got there—that newly found conscience. If it shines any brighter, it's going to hurt your eyes."

"Yeah, well, you can let me worry about that."

The jet's engines kicked in, the characteristic warmup whine followed by a sudden movement off the chocks and a taxi out toward the runway.

"I thought you'd want to know what's on your agenda, but it doesn't sound like you're very interested."

Tom looked at him with as much disgust as he could muster. "Let me see if I can guess. You're breaking a story that will justify my disappearance and then you're going to salt me away under the Pentagon until you've sucked me dry of any utility. After that, I will probably be reported as missing or discovered dead or have a car accident on the Capital Beltway."

Leverton nodded. "Not bad for an amateur. I can assure you, we will try to be a little more creative for you. But I can promise you one thing—there won't be any more mistakes in dealing with you."

"Mistakes? I didn't know General Cobb was capable of making one."

"It was made before he was brought in," said Leverton.

"Something I should know about?"

The colonel shook his head. "It doesn't matter now. It's been dealt with."

Tom wondered what Leverton was talking about, and why he brought up a problem in the first place. It wasn't like these guys. Either he was getting pissed off and just talking out his ass, or the guy had some alternate motivation.

"Well, I can tell you right now," said Tom. "Until I find out what's happened to Doctor Barrero, I won't be cooperating with anybody."

Leverton affected a bad Nazi accent: "Ve haf *vays* of making you do vhat ve vant, Herr Flanagan!"

"Fuck you."

Leverton chuckled. "Is that why you're so worried about that doctor with the legs? That what she did for you—? Fuck *you*?"

"Colonel, you're making a big error."

"Look, Senator, I can tell you right now. If your little Carmen Miranda *is* still alive, she won't be for long, and you know why. And as for you cooperating, we can always make sure your little displaced Valley Girl daughter has a very bad car accident . . . so take that 'big error' bullshit and stick it up your ass!" Leverton jumped up from his seat and advanced to Tom menacingly. "You belong to *us*, now. You got that?"

Without thinking about it, Tom jabbed with his left, and caught the colonel squarely on his nose. Blood erupted all over his face, as if he'd squeezed a condiment pack at McDonalds, and Leverton was so stunned, he took no evasive action for the next instant—just long enough for Tom to leap out of his seat and ram his knee upward into his balls. It had happened so fast, Tom had shocked himself.

He watched what followed with complete fascination. Unlike guys in the movies, Leverton folded up like a cheap accordion after the impact. Before his jackknifed body could hit the deck, he was already puking up bilious, dark-green stuff.

"You got *that*, Colonel?!" he screamed. "Fuck you! I don't belong to anybody . . ."

The military man tried to push himself up on his elbows, tried to move his legs, but the slightest movement caused more puking, and he collapsed. Tom kicked him in the ribs with the hard toe of his wing-tipped brogue. It felt so good, he felt himself drawing back for another one. The sense of power and dominion threatened to take him over; so intoxicating, so *good* it made him feel.

For the first time in his life, he'd lashed out so physically, he had awed himself with the power of fury unleashed. He would have never imagined himself capable of it, and yet the urge to smash this bastard in the face one more time burned in him like a furnace with its doors blown off.

Suddenly the latch clicked loudly. The door opened and two of Cobb's shock troops barreled into the cabin. One of them smoothly subdued Tom and eased him to the carpet while the other checked Leverton.

"He's alive," said the grunt. Then, gesturing to Tom, "Don't hurt him. They want this guy in one piece."

The colonel turned his head, looked at him through the bloody mask staining his face. He was sucking for air, punctuating each breath with winces of exquisite pain. He looked pitiful as he lay there, and Tom could not stop staring at him as he entertained a thought he'd never imagined would ever give him such pure platinum excitement.

(I will *kill* you, you motherfucker. I *will* kill you.)

FORTY-THREE

Hawking

"Why haven't you helped him?"

A blade has no strength if it is not tempered first by a great flame.

"He's a man . . . not a sword."

Have you no sense for an appropriate metaphor?

"Of course not."

Then you know I speak the truth.

"I am sorry. It just seems as if he's endured more than enough."

His talent is special. No one knows what is required to force its development.

"Are you capable of intervening?"

Good question. Perhaps.

"Then, will you do it—will you help him?"

No. He is the one who must help us.

FORTY-FOUR

Barrero

The state highway stretched ahead of the pickup's hood like an endless ruler, measuring off the success of her escape. Estela had the accelerator on the floor, but the truck wouldn't notch past ninety. The engine had started to sound like an old sewing machine as soon as she reached sixty; and it sounded a lot worse now. The steering wheel had begun shimmying so badly, she had to hold it with a two-handed death grip. It was doubtful she was going to get terribly far, but she had no choice but to push the machine to its limits.

As long as the road ahead remained as straight, or until the truck decided to shake itself to pieces, she would flirt with ninety.

The town dwindled down to a smudge in the rearview mirror, and it was only then that she allowed herself to think about what had happened. Trying to remain rational, she kept telling herself that Tom would be fine. No matter what the feds had in mind, it wouldn't be killing him. They obviously needed him if they'd gone to all that trouble to track him down. She wished she understood the dynamics of government better. Tom's experience allowed him to anticipate the way others were thinking, to fully appreciate innuendo.

She would—

A series of loud backfires shook the truck down to its chassis—the engine sounding some serious alarms. It wasn't up for the panicked abuse Estela was dealing. The old Ford was getting ready to quit, and it was thoughtful enough to send her a message.

That meant she was going to have to ditch the truck before any of those soldiers might catch up with her.

But where?

Estela scanned the area on each side of the highway and it was typical Indiana topography—flat and featureless as a tabletop, other than the rare copse of trees surrounding a farmhouse and a barn. But up ahead, perhaps a mile or two distant, there loomed an intersection and a building.

As she kept the gas pedal flattened, the pickup began bucking and lurching forward in bursts of dying energy. The building resolved itself into a gas station with a small garage. A large tractor-trailer rig huddled at the pumps like a desert lizard taking in some sun. She smiled and began easing off the accelerator when a loud *whummp!* rattled the front end. Thick smoke forced its way through the seams of the hood; the engine let loose a wailing exhalation of machine death. Losing all power, she had no choice but to allow the smoking heap to coast into the station at high speed. Braking down as the engine rattled itself apart and the smoke almost obscured her windshield, she brought the Ford to a halt near the garage entrance.

The truck's driver, a large man wearing a Seattle Seahawks cap. His Grateful Dead T-shirt and jeans looked like a uniform—she'd seen so many variations on its theme. He smiled as he saw her desert the burning wreck.

"Looks like you've got trouble," he said loudly over the throaty rumble of his big engine.

"I've got to get to an airport—fast!"

Leaning down from the open door to his cab, he tipped back his cap, tried a little wider smile. He wouldn't have been too bad-looking if he lost his burgeoning beer gut, trimmed his scraggly hair, and decided against the Fu-Manchu mustache.

"No airports close by," he said. "But I'm headed in the general direction of a small field near the county line. Commercial."

"Charters?" she asked.

"Lots of cargo and freight lines use it, but yeah, I guess you could charter something—if you can afford it."

Not wanting to sound too desperate, she shrugged. "I'm willing to take a chance. Are you offering me a ride?"

Just then, the sound of a faraway helicopter tapped along the edge of the horizon. It would be catching up soon, and she was running out of time.

"Hey, lady?"

Turning, she saw a lanky kid of maybe twenty loping toward her from the office. "What's going on with your truck?"

"It's not running," she said as sweetly and as calmly as she could.

"Well, you sure as heck can't leave it there. It's blocking my pumps." He too wore a cap, but this one said something about fishing and a wife threatening to leave him.

She was glad she didn't have time to read it.

The drone of the chopper was growing louder. Estela was going to lose her cool if she didn't get things happening.

Reaching into her attaché, she pulled out a fifty-dollar bill and stuffed it quickly into the kid's hand. "Could you please move it for me?"

"Well, I guess I—"

Then turning back to the driver: "How about that ride?"

"Come on up, ma'am," he said. "The other door."

Running around to the passenger's door, Estela clambered aboard. Out of the corner of her eye, she saw the dragonfly shape of the helicopter, angling across the sky checking out the only sign of life on the highway.

Pulling the door shut, the driver eased out his clutch and rapidly chucked through a series of gears. Gradually, he goosed the rolling behemoth into motion. When they were getting up to cruising speed and had put maybe fifty yards between them and the station, the chopper overtook them, almost coming to a sudden stop in the sky and falling back toward the blue Ford pickup in front of the garage.

"Jesus!" said the driver as the chopper pinwheeled past them at a ridiculously low altitude. Estela had slid off her seat, below the cab's windowline.

"Hey, what's going on, ma'am? He ain't lookin' for you, is he?"

Before Estela could reply, an air-to-ground missile leapt away from the black craft and twisted its way downward toward the gas station. In the parking lot, the kid in the baseball hat was pushing her truck toward the garage when the missile corkscrewed a vapor trail right through the driver's-side window of the still smoking pickup. Estela had chanced a look out the side glass—just in time to see the truck, the attendant, and the entire station consumed in a brilliant blossom of flame. She saw it an instant before the sound and the shock wave of the explosion grabbed the rear end of the eighteen-wheeler and gave it a serious shaking.

"Holy Christ!" yelled the driver. "What was that?!"

"Keep driving!" said Estela, scanning the airspace above them to see if the chopper was readying another strike. The aircraft had cleared the truck and hovered over the burning debris of the gas station. The driver shifted up to his highest gear and the truck gradually pulled away from the site of the attack.

"Okay, lady, you're going to have to tell me what's going on—*now*."

Estela had been crouched down in the footwell of the cab, looking out the window. When she wriggled about, turned to face the driver, he was driving with his left hand; his right was holding a long-barreled six-shooter, and it was pointed at her face.

Estela did not even twitch a muscle in her face. Looking into the open end of the gun was like staring down the mouth of a well. "I can tell you everything."

Twenty minutes later, she sat comfortably in the passenger seat, drinking coffee from Rowdy's thermos. As she unfolded her story, he recognized her from the newscasts he'd caught at several diner and bar televisions. From that point on, he put away the Colt Special and listened with interest and sincerity.

He also volunteered plenty of information on himself. Rowdy (real name Roger) Harrigan had been a Desert Storm veteran, then bought his own truck with the pay he'd saved while in the Army. He'd been running coast-to-coast ever since. Two years of college at Southwest Texas State, two wives, two kids, and too much bad debt had taught him he was better off alone and on the road where he could listen to his stereo and do a lot of thinking. He was a very uncomplex man, who nevertheless seemed perceptive and more well-spoken than the average citizen.

"What made you want to be a doctor?" he asked when the conversation hit a lull. Outside, afternoon was leaning into evening, the flat Indiana farmland reaching for Illinois.

"I was always good in science. Medicine always interested me. It's something I think I wanted to do since I was a little girl."

Rowdy laughed. "Bet you never thought it would ever lead to this."

"No way," she said.

"You think they're looking for you?"

"If they find out I wasn't in that pickup, sure." Estela looked out the window, but there was little traffic on the road.

"I figured that, too," he said. "While we've been talking, I switched on and off a couple of the state roads, switched directions, too. Good thing my trailer didn't have any markings on it—million of 'em out here look just like mine. By the time we hooked back up to the interstate, they wouldn't have any idea what happened to us."

"I don't know," she said. "Flanagan says these guys are good."

Rowdy tapped himself on the chest. "Yeah, well, he never met Rowdy Harrigan."

She smiled, finished off her coffee. "How far to the airport?"

"*Field,*" he said "It's an air*field*. Just a couple of runways and cargo planes. One of my accounts sends comic books up to Canada, through Toronto, and they fly 'em out of

Lurton Field. It's on my route, so I make the drop-ship delivery for 'im."

"Comic books," said Estela softly. The phrase conjured up a host of images and memories of Flanagan and his Dr. Infinity character. An intense sadness lanced her. She had been too scared to realize how much she missed him until that moment. Until she thought of comic books. It was so eerie, so odd that words and sounds could have such power, such ability to key our thoughts and emotions so completely. She mouthed a silent prayer that he was safe.

"We're comin' up on it," said Rowdy. "Next exit, then about three miles on the state road."

"I really want to thank you," she said. "For being a good listener."

"First time anybody ever called me that." He smiled.

"No, I mean it."

"Well, I'm feelin' pretty bad about whipping out my pistol on you. Sorry about that."

"I understand why you did that. I would have been scared, too."

"Hey, I don't know if *scared*'s the right word. Maybe I just seen too many movies. . . ."

They exited the interstate without incident, although Estela kept expecting to see a roadblock looming into the foreground. Rowdy introduced her to the people at Louis Air Freight, and they connected her with a charter pilot who agreed to fly her back to Miami. She thought about going back to Washington, but the odds of hooking up with Flanagan in that city were practically impossible. Miami was the wise choice. She thanked Rowdy profusely for all his help, and he thanked her for injecting a little adventure and intrigue into his life. Although she tried to pay him for his efforts, he remained the gentleman by refusing the money.

Just after nightfall, she took off from Lurton Field in a Cessna Turbo-Prop Twin. Her pilot, an ex-surfer from California named Sandy, talked about how California's days were numbered, and how people were going to be taking their beach vacations just east of Provo, Utah, sooner or later. She listened with feigned interest for a while, then fell asleep in the reclining seat.

Her dreams were filled with visions of giant dragonflies and squads of men in hunting vests and shotguns trying to shoot them down.

It was the middle of the night when Sandy-the-pilot nudged her awake. The flight had taken more than eight hours. Their plane rested at the entrance to a nondescript hangar on the west end of Miami International in an area reserved for small air freight and cargo flights. The area was practically deserted and absolutely no one paid her the slightest attention other than Sandy, who probably considered himself quite a lady's man.

Estela had plenty of experience dealing with men like Sandy, and he didn't have a chance. He might have been a fine pilot, but she had no trouble making him crash and burn.

Rather than deal with his repertoire of bad lines, she walked away from the hangar and into the shadows beyond the buildings. As she walked past the deserted front gate, there was a service road leading to the Miami International Main Terminal. Sporadic traffic skimmed the blacktop bound for red-eye departures. She had no idea what would be the best course of action, but she was tired and not thinking very clearly. She walked toward the service road as a car approached her slowly.

Watch it, she thought, coming to a halt.

The car passed beneath a yellow sodium vapor light and she could see the word TAXI stenciled on a sign hanging from the open window on the driver's door. One of the thousands of "gypsy hacks" that roamed the airport and train stations looking for fares anywhere they could get. Totally unlicensed and unaffiliated, the gypsies—mostly driven by enterprising Cubans and Puerto Ricans—were the bane of all the big cab operations.

"Good evening, lady," said an accented male voice. "You need help? A ride somewhere."

"Yes," she said. "A ride somewhere."

"I can take you—cheap."

"Eso no importa. Le pagaré lo que cuesta."

"Argentina?" he said, obviously recognizing her accent. *"Sí."*

"*A su servicio, Señorita. . . .*" He spoke to her with just the correct amount of respect, and she knew she would be safe. Climbing into the backseat, she gave him the address.

The cab ride to her Turnberry neighborhood was negotiated as they rode along—and it *was* expensive, but with Flanagan's magic attaché, everything was exquisitely affordable. She was groggy from the uncomfortable flight, but she forced herself to think as clearly as possible. It wasn't until the driver was within a few miles of her house that she realized her home could be under surveillance.

The thought suddenly blinked and flashed in her mind like a bad neon sign. Panic surged up in her chest and she had to catch her breath.

"*Disculpa, señor,*" she said to the driver. "I gave you the wrong address."

"What's that?" he said.

She hastily explained that she hadn't realized how late it had become and that she would have to change her destination—giving him the street and number of Nelson Stanhouse's bachelor palace in West Palm Beach. He was probably her closest friend at the hospital, and he wouldn't care about being awakened in the middle of the night. She knew he'd always been attracted to her and had on occasion confided his interest, saying that if she ever decided they could be more than friends, it sounded like a fine idea to him. When he gave her a key to his house—ostensibly to care for his two golden retrievers whenever he was out of town—she knew he wanted it to eventually signify something more meaningful.

It never did. She had never considered anything beyond the friendship they currently enjoyed, but that never stopped her from going to his parties and taking care of Ginger and Cinnamon.

The cabby shrugged and redirected his route to Nelson's neighborhood. Even in the darkness, the moonlight crafted palms and shrubbery into pleasant, canopied sculpture. All the houses rested well off the streets, approached by sweeping lawns and landscaping. When she reached Nelson's driveway, she paid the driver with two fifties and let him keep the change.

As the taxi disappeared around the nearest corner, Estela became suddenly aware of the absolute silence. Her footsteps up the driveway sounded absurdly loud, despite her Timberland hiking boots. Up ahead, the hulking shape of Nelson's house blocked off a lighter night sky. No lights anywhere.

Not comfortable or all that secure in such complete darkness, she pushed onward only because of her familiarity with her location.

She searched her handbag for her keycase and the key to the door off the rear deck. It was very dark as she reached the carport and she had to move by memory, taking a left onto a flagstone walk that led away from the driveway, through a small garden, and up a small set of steps to the deck. When she reached the door, there was something stretched across the entrance, something slippery.

Recoiling from the touch of something so unexpected, Estela had almost cried out in surprise. Slowly she approached the door again, reaching out to examine the barrier. It was a wide band of plastic in either yellow or white. In the pale light of the rising moon, she could read the words in block capital letters:

FEDERAL CRIME SCENE NO ADMITTANCE

Oh God, what was going on here?

For a moment, she felt so paralyzed with shock and indecision, she just stood there, trying to make sense of what she'd found. It had never occurred to her that the government might be watching anyone else's property as well. But here, it looked as if Nelson had been arrested, or worse, that he might have been killed in his own home.

The thought of Nelson dead—because of her—chewed at the base of her stomach. It was the same feeling she'd been trying to suppress since she gave that poor boy at the Indiana gas station fifty dollars to handle the pickup. Even though she hadn't killed him, she'd been responsible for his death. Had she gotten Nelson Stanhouse killed as well?

Oh God, no. . . . Don't let that be true.

She remained standing in front of the police tape as other thoughts broke through the temporary wall of panic that had enclosed her. There was probably no sense in worrying about being caught by agents. If they had been staking out this location, she would have been caught already. Better to get inside and lie low. Not make any noise or use any lights.

Wriggling her small frame underneath the strands of plastic, she keyed the lock and entered Nelson's kitchen. There was no telltale *beep-beep* that would indicate his alarm system triggering, and she exhaled evenly. She had the disarming code memorized, but the stress of employing it at this moment was not exactly appealing to her.

Once inside the door, she left her bags by the door and steeled herself for any sign of disturbance or atrocity she might find. From room to room she moved, allowing her eyes to adjust to the darkness. It became obvious that Nelson's home had been thoroughly sacked. Everything that could contain anything had been tossed by a team of professionals. If her home had been similarly violated, she was going to cry.

But despite the evidence of a complete shakedown, there were no signs of violence, and that relieved her worst fears. Apparently Nelson had been arrested and his house investigated, but why? And where were Ginger and Cinnamon? Would they have carted him off without taking care of the dogs?

Too many questions to try to deal with in the middle of the night.

Estela had been through what was undoubtedly the most grueling and terrifying day in all her life. Her mind raced and revved, but her body was screaming for rest. It was time to crash, and worry about everything tomorrow.

Morning sun capering at the windows did not awaken her until almost 11:00 A.M., and when she did, she was ravenously hungry. After a quick, paranoid shower (being naked and alone in a strange place could not make you feel anything but vulnerable), she put together a breakfast from Nelson's pantry and refrigerator. As she sat at the kitchen table, she turned on the satellite news to see how the government had handled the events of the previous day.

It didn't take long before she was totally outraged by the story of Flanagan's plane going down in the Blue Ridge Mountains. She knew it was nonsense because she was listed among those missing. At noon, Senator Flanagan's campaign manager, Larry Constantino, would be handling a press conference concerning the event.

The nerve those people had was incredible!

And seeing this kind of thing made her wonder just *how much* of what is disseminated as fact is complete and utter lies.

To get a story of these proportions broadcast as fact would require the complicity of many people, and it scared Estela to think of what she and Tom were up against.

But things grew steadily worse and far more scary. The toxic waste accident in Broadview Valley was already in its followup mode, relegated to only a few seconds of reference. But there was a related story that told of an army helicopter involved in the government cleanup operations around the Indiana town that had lost control and accidentally launched one of its missiles, killing a man and destroying a gas station.

They had an answer for everything.

So they had done exactly what Flanagan had said they would. *An accident.* He said there would be a news release about some kind of accident in that small town.

As Estela finished her breakfast, she anticipated Constantino's press conference and wondered if he was in on the deception, or would be dealing with information he believed to be true. Despite the problems he'd caused Flanagan, he'd always seemed like a sincere, devoted man. If Constantino had not been corrupted, it was very possible he could be coerced. Estela had been a quick study on the tactics of the PSOG—they would do anything necessary to achieve their goals.

The satellite news continued through the major stories into smaller and presumably less important events. One of them involved the attempted hijacking of a truck in Illinois. The driver had been killed and the thugs had escaped after running their prize off Interstate 90 and into an overpass support.

As she watched the news commentator shuffle his papers and move on to a new story, Estela broke into tears.

Rowdy Harrigan.

Where was it going to end?

Had he told them anything?

Whatever sense of security she might have been feeling shattered like a cheap piece of glass. She half-expected agents to come bursting through the doors and windows at any instant. They were looking for her. No doubt about that.

And if they found her, she was in big trouble.

But who to trust?

The police could easily be involved or at least convinced by the federal people that she was a legitimate criminal. The media seemed like the logical choice, but again, who could she trust? There were so many levels of power and influence, how could she be sure the corporate levels of the information industry did not share the same interests as Big Government?

There must be somewhere to turn.

But where?

She took a quick walk around the house's interior, looking out random windows, wondering if a fleet of unmarked cars would be assaulting the premises at any moment. . . .

Her paranoia was red-lining and it was not a tolerable situation. She was not a big believer in drugs to control one's mood, emotion, or sensibilities, but she was tempted to find something in Nelson's stores of samples and freebies that would help her get through this attack against her rational side.

She kept telling herself that enough time had elapsed for them to have tracked her. In fact, on thinking back to the previous evening, the single event that might insulate her from discovery was the gypsy cab. They would be able to track her to the charter flight, but once she left the hangar, all official contact with her ended. The Cuban driver was virtually untraceable, belonging to no company, keeping no fare log, and being a member of a vast underground of pirate entrepreneurs.

She exhaled slowly, feeling instantly better. Thank God, the spirit of mercantilism still thrived in America.

Returning to the kitchen, she poured herself a second cup of coffee and sat back down to watch the noon press conference, which was about to start. Held in the briefing room of the Senate Office Building, the press conference had drawn an overflow crowd. If Senator Thomas Flanagan was not the biggest news of the week, then nothing was.

Estela watched as Larry Constantino, looking trim and handsome, approached the podium. He carried a sheaf of papers with him, and held up his hand to allay any premature questions.

"Good afternoon, everyone," he said in a somber voice. "I would like to read a prepared statement, and then I will entertain some questions."

A murmur coursed through the crowd as Constantino began reading. Estela was not as concerned with the content of the message as she was with trying to discern whether or not Larry believed what he was saying. The statement began with a vague description of an alliance between Senator Flanagan and the State Department to assist government agencies involved in national security. It detailed an "assignment" the senator had embarked upon on Sunday to an unspecified location, and ended with the pertinent data on his flight back to Washington via military air transport over the Blue Ridge range. Search crews had so far turned up nothing, but the statement ended with the admonition that the area was thickly forested and access to many areas of the mountainous woodland was difficult.

When he threw it open to questions, it became apparent that Constantino knew very little. No, he had not been briefed on the nature of the senator's assignment; no, he could not comment on the possibility of it requiring Flanagan's apparent ability to resurrect the dead; no, he had been given no statistics on the probability of survival based on the type of plane, terrain, and last known communication with the senator's aircraft.

The press conference was basically bullshit, as Flanagan would have said. Estela became so disgusted with the sham that she almost reached out to turn it off.

If she had, she would have missed an event that would be replayed endlessly on every network in the world, an event that would be forever archived as some of the most singular and spectacular video footage ever recorded.

A reporter for *Wired* had been given the floor, and had just asked Constantino if he could comment on speculations that the public was being hoaxed, that the events of the weekend were nothing more than an elaborate publicity maneuver to gain an overwhelming and unassailable sympathy vote for Senator Flanagan. Appearing to be angered by the question, Larry Constantino opened his mouth to address the journalist, when something happened.

At first, it appeared that he had gotten an object lodged in his throat because his jaw dropped, then locked wide open, curling his lips back from his teeth. His eyes bulged, like the halves of two boiled eggs, and he grabbed for his neck with both hands in a palsied, spastic motion disturbing to watch. A horrible sound escaped him, a rough, fluting, wheeze, and his complexion changed in an instant from his normal Mediterranean tan to that of an ashen and fragile piece of clay. One of the Senate Office aides advanced to the podium to help, but stopped just as he reached the man in distress.

Because it was obvious there was nothing he could do to help.

Larry Constantino staggered behind the podium, completing a full circle. By the time he was facing the cameras again, his skin had begun splitting apart all over his head, face and neck. His flesh was literally breaking up like a pie crust— dry and hard on the outside, but slippery on the inside.

Estela watched in horror, recognizing what was happening.

Constantino tried to scream as the fissures in his face deepened and spread. The audience, stunned until now, backed away from him as if they might catch the virulent condition that attacked him. The flesh on his skull and hands had ruptured like the blistering rind of rotten fruit, falling away from his bones like melted wax. Women screamed and men gagged as Constantino pitched forward and fell off the stage. When he impacted on the edge of the small stage and fell to the parquet floor, his body had almost completely disintegrated, reduced to a semiviscous substance leaking from the sleeves and legs of his suit.

No one approached what had only a moment previously been Larry Constantino. The media crowd had scattered in a terrified panic with their hands over mouths and noses as though escaping a charnel house. The camera view began to wander as if it had lost its operator, and the scene of abject horror lingered for another second before being replaced by a "technical difficulties" board.

Estela blinked her eyes and looked away from the screen. Her knees would hardly support her as she tried to turn and walk to the kitchen window. Nothing in all her years of medicine could have prepared her for what she had seen, and as she attempted to rationalize it, to identify what she had witnessed and therefore understand it, she felt herself unable to stop the urge to cry.

Oh, Tom . . . where are you? What have you done?

She needed him so much in that moment, and she cursed the circumstances that kept them apart. They had been sucked into a maelstrom of forces and mysteries beyond the grasp of anyone. But why? What did it all mean? And why them?

The news station broke her concentration with a return to a studio and a pair of commentators looking shell-shocked and ill-prepared. They had hastily rousted up a pathologist from Johns Hopkins Hospital in Baltimore and were speaking to him on a wall-screen behind their desk. Estela was only half-paying attention, already knowing what the man would be saying, and trying to reduce it down to layman's terms.

She shook her head at the irony.

Reducing it down.

That's exactly what had happened, all right. In a period of ten seconds, Larry Constantino's body accelerated through the complex process of tissue and cellular decomposition. Reducing it down to its basic elements.

Impossible. Yet, he'd shown a predisposition to the display of medical impossibilities before.

The pathologist rambled on, trying to make sense of something that refused the straightjacket of everyday logic. Estela listened to the questions and answers, and wondered when and if the commentators would make the connection she had made instantly—the connection with Senator Tom Flanagan.

To her, it was painfully obvious, but the point had yet to be made.

Larry Constantino had finally died.

Or maybe the reporter from *Wired* had been correct . . . maybe it had all been a very elaborate hoax, played by God or whoever might be in charge.

Maybe Larry Constantino had been dead all along?

All this time.

Four months' worth of decomposition. More than enough time to create the hideous nightmare that staggered and fell across the stage.

Whatever had happened to Constantino, the "power" of Tom Flanagan was directly involved. The idea touched off so many questions in her. What about the others? The little boy he'd healed of cancer, the man in Indiana, and his own son, Chip? Was the little boy safe because he hadn't been dead? Had Tom's power gotten stronger as he'd learned to control it? Strong enough to make its effect permanent?

And what really *was* the effect? Who controlled it?

Estela watched the screen, but heard nothing. She kept wondering what kind of mechanism had turned the universe on its side. The questions roiled through her mind like debris in a terrible dark storm, and she hoped that Constantino's spectacular death was not the harbinger of still greater dread.

She needed to be with Tom Flanagan.

Thinking of him so desperately made her wonder where they could have taken him. But worse, after seeing the true and lasting effect of Tom's special talent, they could decide his value to them had entered into a very rapid decline.

It would be so easy to cut their losses right here. It wouldn't be the first time a government scheme went awry and the plug was pulled. And this was an easy one, wasn't it? All the loose ends were right there in plain view, ready to be knotted up.

All but one.

Estela had become the wild card.

She was the only component they didn't control. Thinking like her opponents, she imagined it would be too risky to eliminate Thomas Flanagan until they were absolutely certain their story could *not* be told.

Until they had silenced Estela Barrero.

Constantino's death would accelerate their efforts to find her. If she thought she could just sit back in Nelson's place until things blew over, she was delusional. It was only a matter of time before they checked out every person she knew, and that trail would lead back to this house, on the off chance that she might be here. Estela might have slipped through their net, but not indefinitely.

She needed a plan, a way to reach someone or some institution that was clearly beyond the grasp of the powers that sought to consume them. She had no family in this country, no close friends other than people at the hospital, and after what had happened to Nelson, she was afraid to contact any of them.

Life and death.

The phrase was such a hackneyed part of our vocabulary, and yet it truly was the nexus about which everything else revolved. She'd always thought she'd thrown herself squarely into the center of that great dichotomy by becoming a doctor, but this was more central, more real.

Estela began pacing from the kitchen to the dining room, a habit she'd picked up from Flanagan, in the hopes it would engender the inspiration she would need. The television continued to re-run the story of Constantino's death, and she knew she could not concentrate on anything with such a distraction.

Walking back to the kitchen, she picked up the remote to shut down the set, and that's when it struck her. Unfamiliar with Nelson's remote, her thumb keyed the change button instead of the off switch, and when the channel changed, she discovered the answer to her problem.

FORTY-FIVE

Flanagan

He didn't even know where he was.

(Does it matter . . . ?)

After the incident with Colonel Leverton, they subdued him with some kind of injection. That had essentially put him on ice until the following morning, when he'd awakened in a room that could have been the Spartan surroundings of any college dormitory—: metal frame bed, chest of drawers, small study desk, all resting on black-and-white checkerboard tile, illuminated by a single bare bulb in the center of the ceiling. Probably sunk halfway to the center of the earth beneath the Pentagon. He'd been a visitor to some of the more mundane levels of the military hive, and he'd been surprised at how far underground the weasels had tunneled over the years. Regardless of how deep he might be, his door was locked, and he was certain there was an observation station or camera located behind the mirror over the dresser. Certain because it was bolted, riveted, or otherwise permanently secured to the wall.

(Fuck you!)

He waved at the mirror, smiled, and returned to sit on the edge of his bed. Earlier, they'd shown him a video of Larry's press conference—the one that would make all press conferences to come less than memorable. Tom had been as stunned and as shocked as everyone else when he first saw the tape, but afterward, he was not all that surprised. His life had been taking him on one sharp left turn after another, tossed him so many curves lately that he'd grown to expect the unexpected.

He had a vague memory of trying to be contacted by Infinity, but either his subconscious had lost interest in that psychic fabrication or the aftereffects of his drugging had removed the memory cleanly. That was the least of his problems.

(Larry . . .)

After trying to gauge his reaction to Constantino's death, they assaulted him with a new round of questions. But these were basically the same ones he'd already answered, except whether or not he had any knowledge of a "flaw" (their word) in his technique.

General Cobb even paid him a personal visit, which in itself was a barometer of their level of concern. It also told him they didn't have everything boxed up and neatly wrapped the way they preferred it.

Which, in turn, meant they hadn't been able to contain Estela—that she was most likely alive.

(I *knew* you could do it, Doc. . . .)

Smiling, he leaned back in the bed and tried to imagine where she was at that very moment, and how she had eluded them. Somehow, he knew she was going to hang tough on this one, that she would at least take care of herself. He wasn't worried about himself.

After seeing what happened to Larry, he couldn't stop thinking about his son. He wanted to see him, to be close to him and tell him everything would be okay. The kid was probably shaken, not knowing what to make of his situation. He needed to see Chip and Estela, but that was the last sentiment he could expose to his captors. They would seize upon any vulnerability and turn it against him if they could.

(If Estela—)

A buzzer sounded and a loud click signaled the unlocking of a magnetic latch in his door, which then swung outward. A detail of soldiers entered with a small table, two chairs, and a serving cart.

"Lunch for you, sir," said the soldier as he uncovered two plates containing steaks with baked potatoes and green beans.

"Our tax dollars at work," said Tom, taking a seat at the table. "Good to see we're spending it well."

As the food detail departed the small room, Colonel Leverton appeared in the threshold. His broken nose was emphasized by two large pieces of white tape criss-crossed over his cheekbones.

Looking up, Tom smiled. "I was wondering who my dinner companion might be. . . ."

"It's not who you think," said the military man.

For an instant, Tom's breath caught in his throat as he expected Estela to be ushered into the room

(No . . .)

At first he didn't recognize the man they brought to him. Tall, thin, his face pale and drawn. He looked like they'd been running him through some very rough interrogations. His expression was that of a beaten and scared puppy.

(Jesus, it's Stanhouse. . . .)

"Enjoy your meal, gentlemen," said the colonel as he pushed the door shut. Its closing was punctuated by the click and the alarm being set.

"Nelson, are you all right?" said Tom, jumping up and offering a steadying hand. "Here. Sit down."

"Thank you." The physician spoke with a level of vacuity that was scary.

"Try to eat something. Has it been awhile?"

"I—I haven't been eating much," he said.

Tom helped him with the baked potato and he cut up some meat into small bites. Stanhouse began to put the food into his mouth, slowly at first, then with more animation and gusto. The experience of eating and sharing time with a sympathetic companion seemed to revive him. Tom joined him and they ate in silence for several minutes. Just seeing the kind of damage these guys could do to a person psychologically as well as physically was making him even more angry. If there was any way, he vowed to himself he was going to make them pay.

Gradually, some color and personality leached back into Stanhouse's face. He appeared more in control and there was a familiar spark of recognition and intellect in his eyes.

"I'm sorry, Tom," he said finally. "They've kept me in Il Purgatorio for a few days."

"How long have you been here?"

Nelson shook his head. "Not sure. Three, four days. Before that, they had federal marshals arrest me at the hospital. They kept me in a Miami branch holding cell."

"I don't get it. Arrest you for *what*?"

"The official charges were destruction of federal property and intent to destroy physical evidence."

"I still don't get it," said Tom. "What did you *do*?"

Nelson provided a brief summary of his discovery in the labs, and how he panicked.

Tom shook his head. "Didn't you think you'd get caught?"

"Yeah, but I didn't want them to know anything." Nelson paused, looked around the room. "Do you think we should be talking like this?"

"They're counting on it," said Tom with a smile and wink toward the mirror.

"Well, shouldn't we be careful what we say?"

Tom shrugged. "If it's something you don't want them to know, either don't say it, or . . . use that secret code we used at the hospital."

He could see the blank look forming in Stanhouse's eyes, so Tom turned quickly and faced the mirror with a smile. "Thought that might fuck with your heads a little, guys. Now you're all sitting back there wondering if we have a code or is it just bullshit . . . ? Well, let me give you a little hint, numb-heads: be very suspicious if our conversation ever turns to Monopoly."

He laughed and turned back to Stanhouse, who was now smiling openly. "That reminds me," he said. "I have a *Get Out of Jail Free* card and I'm looking to buy *Marvin Gardens*."

They looked at one another and burst into uncontrollable laughter.

After a few minutes, they resumed their conversation. "Did you ever tell them about the animals being dead? That they'd decomposed like . . . like Constantino?"

"That they were dead. In a way. I lied—told them I killed them."

"And they believed you because . . ." Tom turned to face the mirror and smiled. " . . . they're stupid."

"Yes, that's right." Nelson smiled.

Tom nodded. "You know what the really funny thing is?"

"Sure," said Stanhouse. "That we've had the Reading Railroad all along."

Tom nodded and laughed again. He really liked the doc, and hoped they weren't going to kill him. It might be hard to do because his arrest was apparently well-known if they'd nailed him at the hospital. Of course, there were other terrible things that could happen to him, things worse than a quick and simple execution.

"Well, yeah, there's always that," said Tom. "But I was referring to their lack of understanding. You see, they think that deceit and lawlessness is going to work for them forever. You know how I know that, Doc? Because I used to think that way, too. But I was wrong. Just like they're wrong. They're going to wish they never fucked with me."

Suddenly the alarm sounded and the door barely clicked before it was yanked open. Two soldiers entered and grabbed Stanhouse, escorted him roughly from the room. Colonel Leverton reentered the room, stood in the doorway.

"You think you're so clever, don't you, Senator?"

"Well, let's put it this way—I *did* quit my day job."

"Actually, speaking of jobs, that's what I'm here for. We have some work for you."

The next seventy-two hours became a grueling series of "assignments" (their word). He was blindfolded, removed from his quarters, and flown to London's Scotland Yard, where he resurrected a man in his mid-thirties, who had recently died of unknown and not apparent causes. They told him nothing about the subject, but there was definitely great interest in finding out who or what had killed him.

The experience itself had become familiar enough that he could essentially will the ability into being. The actual interaction and hallucinatory aspects of the process had become diminished. Either Tom was growing accustomed to the activity, or his power was gradually leaving him.

He also noted that PSOG spent little time debriefing him or talking about any testing, validation, or experimentation. The current thinking was that he was a useful tool, but a tool with a bad manufacturing flaw. Although General Cobb and his minions weren't very talkative, Tom had to figure their intention was to use their tool as long and as often as possible. Until it broke or they found a better one.

Next stop was Riyadh, where the favorite nephew of the royal family had met an untimely end while astride a Harley-Davidson. In what could only be a State Department payback of some monumental favor, or the sealing wax for an upcoming agreement, they dragged Flanagan into one of the palace's back rooms to perform his magic. He wondered how the ruling sheiks were placated by the possible temporary nature of his gift, but no one offered an explanation and he didn't really care enough to ask.

Three more sessions within the next three days took him to Moscow, where an assassinated labor union leader was "reanimated" (the Russian's word); back to the States in Los Alamos, New Mexico, to bring back a weapons research physicist whose heart had kissed him off earlier in the week, then to nearby Albuquerque to revive a cattle rancher with strange burn marks on his palms and face.

Tom could only guess at the various motivations for his assignments, but even his captors realized he had limits and that they were pushing him rapidly toward them. He felt like a battery running on its last joules of power. So many deaths. So little time. As they drove him to a PSOG airbase, not found on any of the tourist maps, near the Mexican border, he became increasingly ill. His head was blazing from migraine-intensity headaches and his knees and legs felt so wobbly, he could not walk without assistance. By the time they reached the base infirmary, he must have looked particularly bad—judging from the distressed expressions on the faces of the staff.

After some serious tests, he was placed in bed in IC and was trying to get some much needed sleep, when his door opened to reveal General Cobb, wearing field fatigues and looking as dashing as possible.

"I'm really beat, General," he said in a heavy whisper. "This is going to have to wait—unless you're here to kill me."

"Come on now, Tom, why would I want to do that?"

"This round-the-world tour came close. Who do you think I am—the Rolling Stones?"

"We had no idea what the consequences might be. Sorry, but we had a few obligations . . . a few promises to keep."

"You and Robert Frost."

"Who's he?" said Cobb, taking a seat on the edge of the bed.

"You wouldn't like him—he wrote poetry."

"You're right," said Cobb, smirking. "Never interested in that faggot stuff."

"You're beautiful, General—you know that?"

"We're not here to play games, Senator. You belong to us now, and we need to take a little better care of you. They tell me you're going to be just fine, you're just exhausted."

Tom looked at him and started smiling, as wide and hard as he could manage. He said nothing; didn't have to. He knew his incongruous smile would do all the talking.

"What's going on?" said Cobb. "What's so funny?"

Tom said nothing for another minute or two. He wanted to watch the general squirm for as long as possible.

(Twitch, you bastard. . . .)

"She's going to take you down, you know that, don't you?"

Looking away for an instant, Cobb's eyes betrayed him. "She's dead, Flanagan."

(Yeah, right. . . .)

"You hadn't figured on her getting away. And that's going to be your only mistake. But it's the mistake that's going to sink you."

"You don't know what you're talking about. She's dead."

Tom laughed, sank back into the bed. "Cobb, I can tell you right now—she's not dead, and you're going *down*."

The general stood up and glared at him. "We can finish this later, Senator. You work for me now."

"Why do you think I'm cooperating with you, General? Do you really think I'm scared? Or cowed into submission?"

Cobb looked at him, but said nothing. He didn't have to—his features did all the talking. It was clearly a concept that had never occurred to him and he was snagged on it.

"Well," said Tom. "Let me give you the big picture—as you soldiers like to put it. I'm going along with the program because I've got something to live for. Doctor Estela Barrero."

"True love. . . . How inspiring." Cobb turned toward the door. "Goodnight, Senator."

The general left the room in long, defiant strides as Flanagan escorted him out with laughter.

As the door slammed shut, Flanagan closed his eyes and hoped he was right.

(C'mon, Estela . . . the good guys are counting on you. . . .)

FORTY-SIX

Barrero

Estela spent several hours compiling a careful reconstruction of all the events of the past week, being especially certain to include times, places, and names. She had always been a stickler for organization, and her note-taking skills had been the biggest single reason she breezed through medical school.

Then, she borrowed a piece of carry-on luggage from Nelson's closet, filled it with bathroom amenities, socks, T- and sweatshirts. She also found a fisherman's watch cap that would do a good job of concealing her hair. As she gathered the things she would need and packed them, she listened to CNN.

She found it more than interesting to see how quickly the world had begun to reject Thomas Flanagan. Only hours since the death of Larry Constantino, and already public figures and institutions were lining up to take their shots at the Maryland senator. Some of the more visible television preachers had already issued statements. Dr. Gerard Goodrop, founder of the Church of the God-Given Liberties, recanted his previous observation that Tom Flanagan's gift was clearly the handiwork of Archangel Michael: "As we careen steadily toward the Final Days, we must be aware of the Devil's deceitfulness. If even someone as vigilant as *myself* could have been fooled by this agent of corruption, then think how careful you of my flock must also be!" Deacon Bobby Calhoun of the Righteous Television Network used the incident as a springboard for one of his standard attacks on the Catholic Church: "This is just another part of the three-ring circus act from Rome! The horror of Tom Flanagan is proof positive, my brothers and sisters, that we have been duped by the Papist Conspiracy!" Freemason Cooper of the Church of the Holy Satellite Tabernacle employed a more subtle knockout punch: "It is certainly a tragedy to see the faith of hundreds of millions of people undermined by such a dramatic and conclusive statement from the Lord. For that is what this event surely means. The Creator has spoken and woe to those who shun His word!"

Estela was not terribly surprised by the reactions from the fringes, but she *was* angered by the official statement issued by the United Christian Leadership Council: "The appearance of figures like Thomas Flanagan validated the predictions of the book of Revelation. If these were the End Times, then Christians should expect to see more than one antichrist in their midst."

Reaction from the Vatican was terse, but equally damning: "The Roman Catholic Church has decided to withdraw from further investigation into the case for possible miraculous intervention by God." But the most incredible reaction to the story came from the parents of Bobby Marzano, who announced plans to file a two hundred and fifty million dollar lawsuit against Flanagan. Estela had become so enraged, she almost hurled a paperweight through the TV screen. There was no plumbing the true depths of venality when it came to human beings. Disgusted and sickened, she turned off the set, gathered up the travel bag, and included her journal in the attaché.

Outside, the sun was westering into the horizon. A few more minutes and dusk would be giving way to darkness. It was time to kick her plan into action. She dressed in her laundered jeans and L. L. Bean sweater, and Timberland hiking boots, then tucked her hair carefully into the watch cap. A pair of Nelson's aviator glasses and she looked sufficiently different to not be immediately recognizable.

When it was completely dark, she slowly slipped the lock of the patio doors and eased between the plastic barricade bands. Each step into the rapidly cooling evening air made her pulse jump a little higher. Estela would have never imagined she would be so excited merely to be outdoors, but the idea that she was unprotected filled her with a giddy fear.

Her plan was simple. Under cover of darkness, she would walk two miles through residential neighborhoods to the nearest suburban strip mall, catch a cab off the street, and head for the downtown area. As she walked along, ever watchful for anything out of the ordinary, her thoughts centered on Flanagan.

Where was he at this very moment?

Was he thinking of her? What she wanted more than anything was for him to know that she was safe and that she had a plan.

She had learned a lot from him about toughness, about not folding up your tents when things came at you from all sides. That's what she had tried to do when Antonio died, she knew that now. Got lost in her work, but otherwise cut herself off from everything else in the world that might hurt. But you didn't grow unless you reached out, made the stretch, and that's when you made yourself vulnerable. Precisely the time when people were waiting to apply the hurt. Flanagan understood the principle, but had never been afraid to take his lumps.

Not that she condoned the fat cat he'd once been, but she admired his aggressive nature, his toughness, and his willingness to stand up to whatever the world had ready for him. That he could take the heat, still look at himself in the mirror and realize changes were necessary, made him all the more admirable.

The time passed quickly as she moved through the darkened streets to emerge at a busy intersection off Ocean Boulevard. Standing by the traffic light, she waited patiently for a cab to appear, but the minutes passed and not one was to be seen.

The longer she stood there on the corner, the longer she felt exposed. She had never experienced the kind of paranoia that was inexorably overcoming her. Every person who approached and ultimately passed her on the sidewalk had become a predator, an enemy. Every car carried potential danger.

Half an hour dragged past her and still no taxis. She felt so naked, she felt like screaming. Had she been misleading herself to think that she had a real plan? Could everything she wanted to do be sabotaged so easily? She was carrying more than a hundred thousand dollars in her bags and she couldn't come up with a ten-dollar cab ride. She suddenly knew the desperation Shakespeare had created for Richard the Third when he offered his entire kingdom for a horse.

But wait . . . who said it *had* to be a cab? A bus would do just as well, but Estela had *no* idea which one to take. Riding a municipal bus had been one of those things she would have never contemplated in her everyday life. Not that it was beneath her, rather she never had a need of it. Looking up and down the busy boulevard, she was not even sure which direction along the bus routes would get her into the downtown district the fastest.

No matter. She would board the next one to pass by and get directions from the driver. The thought buoyed her spirits and her confidence once again. There was no room for doubt. She was just getting started and she had already felt herself starting to wilt under a little adversity. No way. No room for that kind of thinking. Confidence and ingenuity were going to get her through. There was no turning back and no—

A hand touched her shoulder, cutting off her thought abruptly. It was all she could do to keep from screaming and wheeling away from the touch. But she held her position, calmly turning as a sonorous male voice began speaking to her.

"Excuse me, Doctor Barrero, I think it's time you came with us."

FORTY-SEVEN

Barrero

It was over.

Just like that, everything she'd hoped to do would never happen.

The bottom of her stomach had dropped away and a sudden disequilibrium threatened to take her down.

The hand on her shoulder reached out to catch her, gently. Looking up, Estela stared into a familiar face. Thin, angular, handsome, and very Latin.

"Signor Oscaro!" she said, staggering away from him. She began sobbing, not knowing if this was a good or a bad encounter.

"Good evening, Doctor," said Domenico Oscaro. He was wearing his signature black ensemble, and looked as sophisticated and thoroughly continental as ever. "This way, please."

He escorted her to the open, rear door of a large, black Mercedes, helped her inside, then passed in her luggage. There was a broad-shouldered man sitting behind the wheel. Young and crew-cut, he continued to look through the front windshield, as if expecting something to happen. Oscaro closed the door, walked around the back of the car, and entered the front passenger side.

"*Avanti,*" he said, and the driver slipped the car into gear and glided from the convenience store parking lot. Then, he looked at her and smiled. "Comfortable, Signora Doctor?"

"I need to know right away," she said. "Am I in trouble?"

Oscaro chuckled, then translated for his driver, after which both men enjoyed a good manly laugh. That pissed her off, but discretion won out as she simply stared at them.

"Quite the contrary," said Oscaro. "We are here to help you."

The words were delivered so effortlessly in the man's suave and silky accent. It was a verbal seduction, and she knew she must be careful not to rush into their arms too quickly. The driver had entered the boulevard. Traffic swirled and eddied all around them.

"How do you know I need help?"

Oscaro nodded his head appreciatively. "Good question, Doctor Barrero."

"Do you have a good answer?"

"We have been one step behind you ever since our first meeting. We have seen everything, heard most of it."

The idea that she and Flanagan had been spied upon would have normally disturbed her, but at this point, in the apparent safety of the speeding sedan, she found the idea oddly consoling. "The football game, Indiana, everything?"

Oscaro nodded. "We do not take our orders from *Il Papa* lightly."

"But I don't get it," she said. "If you were going to help us, why didn't you do something before people started getting killed?"

Oscaro shrugged. "Death is a regrettable part of our affairs. You must understand that it is very important that my organization retain a *very* low profile."

"Because . . . ?"

"Because officially we do not exist."

The driver asked him something in Italian, and Oscaro gestured toward the road and to the right. Then, looking back to Estela: "Pardon me, Doctor, I have just realized I did not introduce my colleague, Arturo. His English is only passable, but he is also at your service."

"Where did you tell him to go?"

"To head for the interstate. I am assuming you are leaving the city, that you have some purpose, a plan of some sort."

Estela made every effort to conceal her surprise, but her eyes must have betrayed her. Oscaro smiled, held up his index finger in mock reprisal. "You should not be so surprised. This is my business, remember? But look at you—you are so obvious! You are certainly *dressed* for action and comfort, and that wretched hat was clearly intended to disguise you."

Feeling immediately self-conscious, she removed the hat, allowing her ponytailed hair to fall free.

"And your luggage—we did not even discuss what a giveaway that carry-on is."

"What would you have suggested?"

He shrugged. "A gym bag. Even a shopping bag, or a laundry bag. All of these would have been a good attempt."

"I was in a hurry. I didn't have access to whatever I wanted."

"Yes, you are a player in an unfamiliar game, granted, but you must always employ intelligence—that's how the game received its name."

"Where are we going?"

"That's what we must ask *you*."

"I don't underst—"

"Doctor, if we are going to help you, we will need to know your destination," said Oscaro with a deferential smile, " . . . and your plan, which we must assume you have."

"Yes, I have a plan." She hoped she didn't sound too defensive.

"A plan that will cost you a lot of money?"

She tensed, but her voice remained even as she spoke. "Why do you say that, signor?"

"Because you are carrying a very large quantity in one of your bags—in cash."

She chuckled. "You saw me packing it?"

He waved her off with a hand gesture. "No, Doctor, I can smell it—quite literally."

"You're not serious. . . ."

"Yes, it is a gift (and oftentimes a great curse) I have always had. My olfactory sense is probably ten times as acute as the average human."

"That's incredible."

Oscaro grinned. "Cash is one of those items with a very distinctive, detectable scent. Another instantly recognizable odor is gunpowder. My ability to tell if someone carries a concealed gun has saved my life on more than one occasion."

"I'm sure," she said. Oscaro was an interesting man. He had a gentle manner, but she suspected he could be deceptively deadly if necessary. She wanted to trust him, but was so unsure. Of course, riding into the night with two foreign strangers already transcended the boundaries of trust. She was at their mercy and she knew it.

"And so I can tell you—you carry no gun. But money, yes."

"You keep mentioning the money," she said. "Do you *want* it, signor? Is that what this is all about?"

Oscaro smiled. "Signora Doctor, I have access to all the cash I could *ever* hope to spend. You insult my intentions and my honor—I do not steal money from women or—how do you say—?—candy from infants."

Immediately she felt ashamed to have suggested such a thing. "I'm sorry," she said quickly. "I've been under a lot of stress and I guess I've been learning not to trust anybody."

"Understood," he said. "But you must believe me—we *are* here to help you."

"Okay," she said. "But before we get any farther, I need to ask you one more thing: *why?* Why would you want to do that?"

Arturo interrupted with a quick question. Oscaro looked at her. "Signora, we have reached the Interstate Highway Number 95. We must assume your plan includes heading north, unless you are going to Cuba, yes?"

"Yes, I was going north," she said.

Arturo nodded, accelerated the sedan onto the access ramp.

Oscaro looked at her again. Again the charming, disarming smile. "Now, you wanted to know why we would want to help you. . . ."

"That's right. It doesn't make sense."

Oscaro nodded, held an index finger to his forehead for a moment, as though in deep thought, then: "Despite what you may have heard, or believe about people like us—international agents, spies, whatever you want to call us—we are just like you. We are *people* who have likes and dislikes, feelings and fears, and little gray-haired mothers just like everyone else."

"Si, signora," said Arturo, giving the first indication that he was a part of the conversation.

"Now," Oscaro continued. "You most likely know that our superiors have closed the books on Senator Flanagan."

"Yes, it was on the news today."

Oscaro shrugged. "The decision comes as no surprise to us. The Vatican is very careful about what it decides to call a miracle. However, my colleagues and I can still be on the case if we so choose, do you follow, Signora Barrero?"

"Well, I think so."

Oscaro held up a single index finger. "Remember, the Vatican gives us, how do say?—a 'white card'—"

"Carte blanche," she said automatically.

"Yes, of course! We have carte blanche to handle every case as we see fit. And up until just a few hours ago, I was charged with your safety and complete surveillance."

"Do you mean if anybody had been waiting for me at Nelson's—"

"They would not have harmed you," said Oscaro. "Darkness and secrecy are our favorite allies. The times we work the best. In fact, we were expecting you to go straight to your home—where you would have disturbed a small nest of PSOG people waiting for you. We had planned for considerable trouble, but you fooled us completely by going to your associate's home."

"Completely an accident. I had no idea he'd been arrested."

"A perfect place to 'go to ground,' as they say."

"How close were they to catching up with me?"

Oscaro shrugged. "They had you marked all the way until you took the gypsy cab. They couldn't figure out *how* you left the airport, and when you never showed up at the hospital or your home, they knew they were in trouble."

"But they want me pretty bad." It was not a question.

Oscaro nodded, grinned. "Oh, yes, signora. *Very* badly. They were checking on every person you have *ever* had contact with and every place you have ever been known to go. Eventually they would have thought to recheck the Stanhouse residence, but it was not a priority since they had already nabbed him."

"What have they done with Nelson? Is he okay?"

"As far as we know, yes. For how long, we cannot be certain," said Oscaro. "But, we have wandered off the path. I was explaining our intentions, our motives."

"Yes, I'm sorry, it's just that I have so many questions," said Estela, ". . . and you seem to have the answers. Please, signor, go on."

"There is not that much more to tell. Truth be known, we have grown fond of you and your senator. We like you both, and we think you have been treated badly."

She couldn't believe what she was hearing, and could not help but smile. "That's it? That's why you're here, you 'like' us?"

Oscaro shrugged. "Basically, yes."

"Basically?" Estela knew there was more.

"Let's just say we have been asked to help you by . . . an interested party."

"Do I know them?"

Oscaro shrugged. "It is doubtful. But the party proved to us that he was in close touch with the senator. He knew things no one could know otherwise."

Estela's intuition suggested something too weird to mention. "Is there anything else you can tell me?" she said.

"And . . ." said Arturo, who was clearly the strong, silent kind of guy, "we think not much for Cobb and PSOG."

"What exactly *is* PSOG?" she asked. "I mean, I know what the letters stand for, but what do they do?"

"I will tell you all about them, my Doctor," said Oscaro. "But we need to know a few details. So that we may augment your plan, and coordinate your destination."

"That's right, I almost forgot," she said. "I haven't told you where I'm going."

"Or what you want to do," said Oscaro.

"All right, tell me what you think of this . . ."

As she explained to them what she had in mind, she realized that her plan was not as completely realized as she had thought, and when she outlined it, there wasn't all that much to tell. Oscaro and his driver listened with attention and respect. When she had finished, they remained silent, analyzing her ideas.

"Well, what do you think?"

Oscaro rubbed his chin dramatically. "Well, I think we must make some new arrangements. . . ."

Estela was crestfallen. They hated her plan. But she would not let them see the effect of such stinging defeat. With as much Latin haughtiness as she could muster, she pushed onward. "What is it you don't like?"

Oscaro smiled. "Who says we don't like it?"

"You said new arrangements. . . ."

"No, no, signora. I think what you have in mind is totally unique and *very* clever. It displays the kind of bravura only possible in America, and that is why it would not have occurred to me."

Estela smiled. "You mean you *like* it? You think it will work?"

"One never knows with this kind of thing. The best plans of men and rodents can well be ruined. . . ."

"Yes, I've heard that," she said, excitement glazing her heart. "But you'll help me?"

"Most certainly, but we cannot count on your actions being enough."

"What else do you have in mind?"

Oscaro waved off the question. "Plenty of time for that. We can work it out during the flight."

"Flight?"

"Signora, you don't expect us to *drive* a car all the way to Washington, do you?"

She felt silly, but not really embarrassed. Domenico Oscaro did not seek to make her feel badly. He spoke with comradely good humor, no offense intended or taken. "No, of course not, but you must remember, before I hooked up with you, I was planning to pay a gypsy cab the fare of his life!"

She shared a good laugh with both men, reflecting on how different things had become since they entered the equation. Suddenly her original plan seemed so primitive, so risky, even ill-conceived. But even as the thought passed through her, Estela wondered one last time if she had done the right thing by trusting them, by telling them literally *everything*.

She had no choice, really. They had either captured her or taken her into their alliance. She had been powerless to do anything but comply, and she kept telling herself there comes a time when you must simply pay your money and take your chance.

Arturo drove to a private airfield north of the city while Oscaro made several telephone calls in preparation for their flight. Each call was preceded by a series of codes punched into a small electronic unit in his briefcase. Explaining that it was a digital scrambler used in conjunction with the PCS phone system, he told her it was virtually impossible to steal a phone call. Impossible, he said with a smile, until somebody figured out how to do it.

When they arrived at the small field, three more Vatican agents—all looking chiseled and very Mediterranean—were waiting for them. They escorted Estela and Domenico onboard a Lear ExecuJet, and the pilot prepared for takeoff. The plane's interior proved to be a topological paradox, appearing to be twice as large as the plane's exterior space could define. The fixtures were modern and tasteful and designed as a mini-work/entertainment area.

"Doesn't this make it easy for them to track us down?" she asked after they were buckled into their seats in the lounge. "The FAA or something like that."

"Something like that is possible, but not on this flight."

"Why not?"

Oscaro smiled. "Because the FAA doesn't know we're onboard. This flight departs from this field every night. The plane is registered to a Japanese manufacturing company. An executive shuttle between their Baltimore and Miami offices. No passenger manifest necessary unless we go down and they need names to attach to the body parts they find."

"Such an elaborate ruse," she said as the others took their seats in the forward cabin.

"Oh no, signora. It is no ruse. The company and the flights are real. We have merely made arrangements at the highest corporate levels to use their flights. We have similar arrangements with more than two hundred companies throughout North America. Flights and schedules all updated daily by satellite and computer links. Instant access to almost limitless mobility. And we are completely invisible. No one asks any questions. We can literally arrange to be anywhere we wish in Mexico, the U.S.A., or Canada just by punching in a few codes in any notepad computer with a PCS modem uplink."

"You are very organized," she said, hoping that was the correct term.

"We are very small. We *have* to be. Some say the Israeli Mossad is the best. Some say MI6 in London. We like to think *we* are the best."

"Well, you're not what I would have expected. . . ."

Oscaro nodded. "I take that as a compliment."

She smiled. "As intended."

The conversation lagged for a moment, then she touched his arm. "Signor Oscaro, do you think Flanagan's all right?"

"We know he is."

She almost asked him how he could be so certain, but told herself she had to trust their access to information. "Where is he?"

"New Mexico. They are preparing to bring him back to PSOG HQ tonight or tomorrow, but that hasn't been confirmed yet."

She almost asked him if they had harmed him, but she controlled the impulse. She didn't even want to know what they'd been doing with him—she just wanted to know he was safe.

"You are in love with the senator," said Oscaro.

Estela paused. The direct statement, not a question, forced her to confront a notion she had not consciously faced. "Yes, I think so," she said after a pause. "I think I am."

Oscaro patted her hand and smiled. "We think you are also, signora. That is probably one of the reasons we like the both of you, and why we have decided to help you."

"Really?"

Oscaro nodded. "We Italians—it must be true what is said about us—we are hopelessly romantic."

She looked away for a moment, fighting back a burst of pure emotion. She missed Flanagan so much. "Then, get him back for me," she said softly.

"We will try. But don't forget, you will play a big part in that yourself."

"Thank you, signor."

After seeing that she was secured in her seat, Oscaro excused himself to the forward cab. Within several minutes the plane taxied to the end of a short runway and slipped smoothly into the sky. She reclined her seat and closed her eyes. It had been another long, complex day. She tried to relax, maybe get a few hours' sleep, but her mind refused to shut down, replaying the spectacularly gruesome death of Larry Constantino. It was something she had managed to keep from her conscious thoughts, was obviously embedded in another, deeper part of her mind. She knew it was something not easily forgotten, and she gradually realized it was a nightmare she would carry with her for a long time. As she drifted off to a less than restful sleep, she wondered what the decomposition really meant. Was it a sign—as the many institutions indicated—that there was something wrong, or even *evil*, regarding Thomas Flanagan? Or could it be some biological flaw in Constantino? She needed more information, and realized she probably wouldn't be getting it.

She missed Flanagan, and wanted to know he was safe, and the only way she could be sure of that was when she was holding him in her arms.

FORTY-EIGHT

Flanagan

It was very early in the morning when they came to get him, Colonel Leverton and a detail of grunts.

"The docs say you're good enough to travel," said the officer. "So we're heading back to HQ."

"So many corpses, so little time," said Tom as he finished getting dressed.

"Oh, they've got a few special items for you," said Leverton. "You'll see."

"I can't wait."

The colonel told the soldiers to wait outside the infirmary room, then wheeled on Tom, jaw to jaw. "But sooner or later they'll be *finished* with you, Flanagan. Because nobody lasts forever in this outfit. And when they're ready to put you on the scrap heap, that's when I get you."

"Oh, I'm soooo scared," said Tom, chuckling at him. Didn't this creep understand that nothing mattered anymore, that he was beyond cheap, macho threats like this?

Leverton backed away, his face twisted into a bulldog snarl. "Yeah, well you will be, mister. You will be."

Tom was so unmoved by the attempt to instill respect and fear into him, his thoughts had already raced away from the moment, into a place and time that had no fixed point, where he was with Estela and things were somehow different.

He found himself wishing like an adolescent boy that there could be such a thing as never-never land.

Estela remained allied with his every thought, and if he ever saw her again, he knew he would have to tell her he'd fallen deeply in love with her.

FORTY-NINE

Barrero

Excuse me, Doctor Barrero," said Oscaro. "We have arrived."

Blinking her eyes, she needed a moment to orient herself. She had been dreaming intensely, but had no memory of its content. "I'm sorry, I must have fallen into a very deep sleep."

"The sleep of exhaustion," he said. "I know it with great intimacy."

"Where are we?"

"We have landed at a private field northeast of Baltimore."

"What time is it?" She asked the questions automatically, but she was barely conscious yet. It was like dragging herself out of a bed of quicksand.

"Twelve forty-five in the morning."

"Oh God, what're we going to do now?" She knew she should be more aware, more awake, but it was so hard to focus on anything.

"We have a safe house in Columbia, Maryland—about forty minutes driving on the highway."

"A safe house, is it exactly what it sounds like?"

Oscaro nodded. "Yes, we operate a substantial number in and around various large cities throughout the world."

"Why aren't we going all the way to Washington tonight?"

"The location we wish to use is still being sanitized," said Oscaro. "It will not be ready in time for our launch—or yours. So we will use the Columbia station as our platform."

Finally, she felt together enough to stand. One of the other agents appeared carrying her bags. He and Oscaro escorted her out of the sleek plane and into the cool, early-winter air of the Maryland night. Just beyond the silent jet waited a black Lexus sedan. She was ushered into the luxurious backseat, while Oscaro took his customary place in the front passenger seat. The driver was one of the three from the plane, but the remaining pair did not join them. She was going to ask the usual why-and-where questions, but had by now realized they had everything worked out to their own schedule and plan.

Instead, she passed the time learning about PSOG and Jarmusch Gunnderson.

The Pentagon Special Operations Group had been in existence since the end of World War II—although under a variety of different names. The idea to change the name every so often had kept it from becoming a familiar, high-profile organization. In a bureaucracy as vast as Washington's, there have always existed a plethora of units, agencies, commissions, and military groups—forming, functioning, dissolving. It was easy for PSOG to get smokescreened.

Oscaro capsulized his presentation, but remained thorough. In essence, PSOG existed to *keep* information from the American public. Staffed by career military types and supported by a substratum of scientists and bureaucrats firmly embedded in the bedrock of government grants and slush funds, it was almost a closed system with few leaks, and few points of entry. PSOG's specialty was handling information in cases or events that were actually too large or too prevalent to hide, such as the entire UFO phenomenon, alien abductions, paranormal experiments, biological experiments, nuclear industry horror stories, etc. PSOG's propaganda machinery so dwarfed the resources and techniques of the Nazis at their peak, it was laughable. Their efforts to discredit sources was equaled only by their ability to "pollute" good data on the above phenomena with planted unreliable and unstable "witnesses," phony and staged events, and even the full-scale production of film and television documentaries skillfully created to appear to be exploring the secret phenomena while exposing the "true believers" as fruitcake ingredients. Their influence in the media was so pervasive that it had become very difficult for even the experts in various disciplines of study to determine when a piece of information was valid or planted by PSOG. An entity so encysted in the body of government it was practically unreachable, PSOG would always exist in various incarnations.

Jarmusch Gunnderson was another story.

Oscaro summarized the career of the man who had at one time been a CIA operative, who spent years gathering information on everyone in a position of power within his own government. When he took early retirement, ostensibly to work as a PAC/SIG lobbyist, he actually became what is known as a "repairman"—a guy with lots of connections who can fix up messes. But he took the job one important step further.

Gunnderson let it be known to the right people that he had compiled a dirty laundry database to rival J. Edgar Hoover's. Everyone was afraid to take Gunnderson down. He also leaked out reports that he'd planted what he called "information bombs" all over Washington, and unless he was around to "reset their timers" every now and then, some of them would go off. No one knew if these "bombs" actually existed, but no one was interested in finding out either. The result was a windfall for Gunnderson—he enjoyed a position wherein everyone was *forced* to turn to him, and he could deal or double-deal anyone without fear of reprisal. People all over Capitol Hill became anxious at the mention of Gunnderson's name, but no one *really* knew how dangerous an item he was.

Estela grew angry when she thought about the situation. Flanagan had thought he was getting real information from

Gunnderson, and trusted the man with his intentions and his whereabouts. According to Oscaro, they had been pawns in a larger game. And the worst part was Gunnderson's total amoral stance—he didn't care what confidence he breached as long as there was some kind of gain in it.

They arrived at the safe house under cover of the longest part of the night. It was a split level in a neighborhood called Owen Brown, enclosed by canopies of suburban trees. Manicured lawns and backyard swing sets were *de rigueur*, and the last place from which anyone might expect international intrigue to be launched.

They were escorted into the perfectly normal-looking home by a woman in her late thirties or early forties, who introduced herself as Sylvia. She was tall and model-thin, with long, straight ash-blond hair. She looked Nordic, but had almost oriental eyes, and was not as much a truly attractive woman as much as she was interesting and unique in appearance.

It didn't matter. Estela found herself simply happy to be in the company of another woman. There was an unexpected comfort to being in a woman's home. After what seemed like a lifetime of being surrounded by nothing but utterly masculine accessories and concepts, she welcomed the suggestion of an environment shaped or touched by a feminine hand. Even if this safe house was all smoke and mirrors, she found it a reassuring delusion.

Sylvia escorted her to an upstairs bedroom and whispered good night, leaving Estela to a warm, clean bed and what was left of a night of uncertain dreams.

The next morning she was awakened by the faint, unintelligible sound of masculine voices in the kitchen. The hour was approaching noon, and she was thankful for the chance to sleep until her body had decided her batteries were fully recharged. As soon as she was fully awake, a peak of excitement raced through her as she realized this would be the day she made a difference.

This would be the day she struck back against all the forces that had so threatened to reshape, or even end, her life.

After a quick shower and a change of clothes, she joined Oscaro and Sylvia in the kitchen. She exchanged pleasantries about the decorations and fixtures and the "hominess" of the place, but it was evident Oscaro had other things to discuss.

"I must leave you now, Signora Doctor."

She didn't hide her surprise. "Why?"

"Flanagan's jet will be arriving at Andrews at approximately seven o'clock and we will be waiting for him." Oscaro smiled knowingly. "But there is much coordination that must be accomplished before that hour. If all goes well, we will rendezvous with you and your subject at the appointed hour."

"Is there any way I could go with you?"

"Absolutely not. Please take no offense at this remark, Doctor Barrero, but there will be no place for spectators tonight."

"I understand, but what about me? How do I—?"

"Sylvia will be driving you to Washington, where you will meet Gino."

"Who is he?"

"He will provide the papers and ID that will get you into their offices. He will stay with you until you reach your objective." Oscaro took her hand, gave it a squeeze of confidence. "What happens after that will be up to you. But we *will* be counting on you to have prepared our own entrance."

"Just be there," she said.

"Have no doubts, signora." He stood up from the breakfast table. "Tonight. . . . Until then, *ciao!*"

FIFTY

Flanagan

It had been a rough flight, with an unscheduled stop outside of Topeka when an icestorm forced them down for a few hours. Delayed, but undamaged, the MATS jet touched down at Andrews and taxied to a hangar near the end of a little-used runway. The two grunts, who had said all of maybe five words since they detailed him out of the Los Alamos infirmary, escorted Tom and Leverton from the plane. Dusk was turning everything a temporary shade of gray as the ground crew swarmed over the jet.

No one spoke as he was guided past the hangar to a parking area where a commercial van awaited them. It was white, accented in orange, blue, and green lettering—POTOMAC CARPET CLEANING—plus the usual slogan, address, and prominently displayed phone numbers. There were two men sitting in the front seats wearing off-white workman's coveralls—which explained why they had dressed Tom in a like uniform. The driver wore an Orioles baseball cap, the other guy a set of headphones for a Walkman. Despite the poor lighting, Tom could tell they were broad-shouldered and young.

"Get in," said Leverton as one of the grunts opened the rear doors.

Looking inside, Tom was not surprised to see the bulkheads outfitted with rack-mounted electronic gear and miniconsoles with swivel armchairs. The claustrophobic area was sealed off by a steel partition from the driver's compartment, with only a small sliding panel, now closed, affording any access to the front cab.

As Tom climbed in, he took the chair farthest from the doors, and the colonel joined him. "Don't touch a motherfucking thing," he said.

As the grunts closed them inside, interior lights phased on, casting everything a soft, deep red. Tom felt like he was onboard a sub—an image that was shattered as soon as the driver keyed the ignition and the truck's engine rumbled. The van lurched forward, rolled away from the hangar area. When they had achieved cruising speed, Leverton flipped the switches on several of the rack-mounted pieces and spoke into a stationary microphone.

"Big Dog, this is Bravo Niner," he said. "Everything's nominal."

"*Confirmed, Bravo Niner. System Check at zero-three-zero.*"

"Affirmative, Big Dog. Bravo Niner out."

He flipped a few other switches, and a wide-angle view of the highway appeared on two small black-and-white TV monitors—one looking ahead, and one providing a rearview of the heavy traffic phalanxed across all the lanes of the Capital Beltway.

"Can you get Monday Night Football on that thing?" asked Tom.

"Fuck you, Senator," said Leverton. "I'm through talking to you till they've chewed you up down in Level Twelve. When they're ready to spit you out, then you're mine."

(You better hope nothing goes wrong. . . .)

Tom leaned forward, put his elbows on the edge of the workbench in front of him, and Leverton unholstered his 9mm semiautomatic.

"Uh-uh, Senator. Elbows off the table. Hands, too. Just fold 'em up in front of you where I can see them. You don't touch shit in here. I won't kill you, but you don't need both your knees to do what they want you to do."

Leaning back, Tom folded his arms and closed his eyes. He felt drained. Used up. The only thing he could think about was seeing Estela again. That was the single factor that kept him focused. He needed to at least *talk* to her and let her know he'd come to grips with his feelings. It had become important that she realize he'd fallen in love with her—deeply and hopelessly.

But it was quite possible he would never see her again.

(Where are you right now, Estela?)

He was fairly certain she was still at large. If they'd been able to track and net her, they would waste no time letting him in on that little piece of news. Nothing like bad news to crush morale and gain a firmer control of your prisoner.

However, the odds of her remaining out of their reach would go down the longer she eluded them. These guys, no matter how much he might despise them, were very slick, very proficient. If they wanted you found, they were going to find you. That was not admiration, simply a statement of fact.

He knew the situation was eventually—

"Christ on a fucking crutch . . . !" said Leverton, looking up at the rearview monitor into complete darkness.

Trying to appear disinterested, Tom did not move, but he tracked the focus of the colonel's attention. A Maryland state police cruiser had slipped in behind the van and turned on its flashers.

"How goddamned fast are those idiots going?"

The trooper hit his siren for a few seconds before the van's driver even noticed he was back there and started to slow down.

Leverton flipped a toggle on the radio unit. "Are you assholes on drugs, or what?" he said loudly into the microphone. "Didn't you see that yokel coming up our tailpipe?!"

"Jeez, sorry, Colonel. We had the radio on. . . ."

"Well, *stop* this fucking wagon before he gets his nuts twisted."

"Yessir, we're pulling over now, sir."

Flanagan watched the monitor with Leverton. The van jolted to a stop on the Beltway shoulder and the state police cruiser pulled up behind the rear doors. The car's high beams half-blinded the rearview camera, but when the trooper directed his spotlight across the back panel of the van, searching for the license plate number, the videocam went into total burn—whiting out the image on the monitor.

"Turn off that fucking spot, you whore!" said Leverton, who glanced quickly at Flanagan, then back at the monitor. His brow triple-furrowed as though a new thought had suddenly crash-landed there, and he almost leaped out of his chair to reach the sliding panel that opened onto the front cab.

Flanagan made no effort to get out of his way. They tangled into one another and went down in a twist of arms and legs.

"Get out of my way!" said Leverton, struggling to his feet. He threw the metal panel open just in time to see the state trooper emptying a silenced semiautomatic Sig-Sauer into the chests and foreheads of both men in the front seats. He slammed the panel shut, throwing the latch and locking it. Raising his own sidearm, Leverton turned toward the rear doors.

Simultaneously, recognizing the characteristic *Ffffftt! Ffffftt! Ffffftt!* of the silenced rounds, Tom uncoiled and launched himself at Leverton as soon as he turned away from him. Thudding into the colonel, Tom was not prepared for the *hardness* of the military man, the solid, banded-muscle feel to his back and shoulders. It was the difference between fitness training and power lunches. The shock of the impact stunned him and he fell to the deck of the van, whacking his elbow sharply.

No sucker punch this time. No lucky knee to the balls. He'd tried to match upper-body strength with Leverton and came away a poor second. Outside the van, someone attempted to spring the latch. Leverton readied his weapon and reached for the handle. When the door swung outward, he would be unloading his clip into whoever was in the way; they would in turn be filling the interior with flying slugs.

Not a prospect to want to sit around and wait for.

Tom tried to pick himself up off the floor, knowing he only had a second or two to act, or it would be too late. He didn't know who the cavalry was outside, but he didn't want Leverton evening the odds. Tucking his knees beneath his chest, he pushed himself upward and away from the deck as hard as he could. His joints screamed from the sudden exertion and extension. Something *popped* in his left thigh, but he managed to reach out with his right arm and hook Leverton's gun hand just as he'd popped the latch.

All at once the heavy rear doors burst outward, slamming into the state trooper. Someone yelled something in a foreign language as the flash of gun muzzles punctuated the blur of movement. There were two other men flanking the rear of the van, pointing weapons in the general direction of Tom and the colonel. Leverton, despite Tom's arm hooking him downward, still managed to squeeze off several rounds before they fell onto the rough surface of the highway's shoulder.

The points of gravel chewed into Tom's injured elbow like tiny teeth. Pain radiated up his arm, spiking into white-hot flashes before his eyes. Rolling away from the pressure, he realized he was still hooked up with Leverton, whose forehead, injured nose, and jaw had sandpapered across the gravel and were now a pulpy mess. The points of their chins threatened to jab each other's throats. Worse, Leverton's hand, and the weapon it held, were wedged in between them, only inches from Tom's eyes.

The colonel fired another shot as he struggled to push away from Tom, and the concussive force deadened all sound in Tom's left ear. Leverton surged upward, with his hand trying to direct the barrel toward the center of Tom's face.

(No way, you bastard. . . .)

Lunging, like a rabid dog, Tom attacked with the only thing he had left. Reduced to a reaction of pure and naked atavism, the senator from Maryland sank his teeth into the ravaged nose and cheek of his enemy. Feeling the flesh and cartilage collapse and separate beneath the sharpened pressure of his jaw and incisors created an unexpected spike of excitement in him. Like the frenzy created by the first burst of blood in a shark feeding, Tom felt his entire body resonate from the joy of the battle, the white-heat of the *kill*.

Leverton did more than just scream. An explosive wail of agony burst from him. His only reaction was to push Tom's jaws away from his savaged face. His grip on the gun shattered as his hands and fingers reached out to try to pry the attacker away from him.

There it was.

One.

Single.

Instant.

He seized it by grabbing the gun as it tumbled loosely between their chests. Its grip fell into Tom's palm and nestled there like an old friend, a familiar pet.

Without thinking, he tightened down, slipping his index finger against the trigger. Then he jammed the barrel upward, breaking off several of Leverton's teeth as it lodged against the roof of his mouth.

And suddenly everything stopped.

The screaming, the thrashing, the dull roar of passing traffic.

Leverton's breath hitched up in his throat like a broken gear, stopped.

His left eye was almost pressed against Tom's face, looking as wide and flat as a shark's, but radiating a knowledge that transcended shock or wonder. Tom stared into the stagnant pool of Leverton's eye, feasted on the fear bubbling up from its muddy floor.

If Leverton was calculating in that final moment whether or not Tom had the balls, he was not alone. But the equation could only be solved in one simple and direct manner.

Only one solution.

And it was delivered as he yanked on the trigger with all his strength. The enclosure of the colonel's skull muffled more of the muzzle blast than Tom would have imagined, and he hadn't expected the brief, rigidly spastic tap dance Leverton's body executed against the gravel.

But other than that, it felt . . . *good.*

And that scared him. The knowledge kind of numbed him as the body fell away from him and hands reached down to pull him up to his feet.

Tom tried to clear his thoughts and his vision the way you'd wipe a blackboard with a wet cloth, but the moment of execution kept replaying in his head like a tiny loop of film. There was a wedge of irony driven deep into the core of the experience, a truth he could not avoid. His gift of life had been so unwanted, so troubling, so full of its own freighted pain; but his gift of death had been so easy, almost effortless. The contrast was not lost on him, and it disturbed him.

He was only half-aware of the two men helping him toward a black sedan behind the state police cruiser. One of the men wore a trooper's uniform, the other all black, including a long, stylish topcoat.

"Are you injured, Senator?" asked the man in the police uniform, his accent definitely European.

"No . . . I think I'm okay."

"Very well," said the man, opening the rear door to the sedan. "Would you please wait here. We must attend to several final items."

Numbly, Tom nodded, his mind still replaying that tiny loop of film, while he watched them toss Leverton's corpse into the back of the van and slam the door. Another man in black climbed into the cab of the van, drove it quickly onto the Beltway. In a few seconds, Tom had lost track of it in the endless stream of passing taillights.

The trooper climbed into the back of the cruiser, disappeared for several moments, then reappeared wearing black shirt and pants. The other man carried a body to the back of the sedan, where he opened then quickly closed the trunk.

The man from the trunk climbed in behind the wheel, continued to stare straight ahead. The man from the police cruiser climbed into the front passenger seat.

"Presto!" he said to the driver, who was already accelerating away from the scene. Then turning to Tom, he said: "Senator Flanagan, good evening. My name is Mario DiCiancia."

"You are from the Vatican," said Tom.

"That is correct."

"What did you do to the state policeman?"

DiCiancia grinned. "He is sleeping. When he wakes up, he will remember nothing, and he will probably be very cold. But he will be fine."

"Why?"

"Our orders were to rescue you."

"I . . . I killed him, didn't I?"

"Yes, sir, you did."

The affirmation stamped the reality a little deeper into his head, with the impact of a hammer on an anvil. He wasn't sure how he really felt about what he'd done.

"What about Doctor Barrero? Do you know what's happened to her?"

"Oh, yes," said DiCiancia. "She is safe. In fact, we go to her now."

"What? You're kidding . . . !"

Suddenly, the steel gray shell enclosing his thoughts began to crack with little spiderweb fractures of hope. There might just be an end to this whole mess.

But *where*?

FIFTY-ONE

Barrero

During the drive to Washington in the Toyota, Estela tried to have a conversation with Sylvia, but the woman was not the type for small talk.

In fact, the only information she divulged during the entire trip was that she had been living in America for more than twenty years, all of them under the employ of the SSV, performing a variety of functions upon which she did not elaborate.

When she was turned over to the man named Gino at the Silver Spring Metro station, she was confronted by a totally different personality. Gregarious and talkative, Gino loved rambling on about his fascination with the United States—easily his most favorite assignment locale. Speaking without a trace of accent, and liberally coloring his language with American idioms and slang, he seemed the perfect spy. No one would ever suspect he was anything other than a suburban dad who loved Little League baseball and cutting his lawn. He was tall, broad-shouldered, but otherwise lean and formidable looking, even in a sport coat and black turtleneck. Dark aviator glasses accented a face so cratered with pockmarks, he would never be handsome, but he projected a rugged confidence that made him attractive anyway.

He took her to a late lunch at a small macaroni bistro off Dupont Circle, during which he finally detailed the plan to reach her objective. He also had complete sets of credentials prepared for both of them, which looked so authentic it was frightening. It made Estela wonder how she could ever trust anyone ever again. Having official documentation, she had learned, meant nothing.

Gino spent an hour briefing her on the procedures they would need to follow to get into the target building. As should be expected, security was very stringent and the personnel well trained.

"If you let me handle everything," he said. "Everything will be jake."

She did. And it was.

Gino assured her he would be there as they parked the big Chevrolet sedan right in front of the building at 820 First Street.

"Get out your ID now," he reminded her. Pulling it from her pocket, she was glad he'd said something, or she would have definitely forgotten it. You never wanted to have to go reaching into a pocket or purse when suspicious people with guns were going to be looking at you.

Jumping out of the vehicle, they crossed the sidewalk and pushed through the front doors into an expansive, tastefully decorated lobby. She moved with the quick, authoritative motions that Gino said would command respect. At all times, he'd said, they must give the appearance of being completely in control. They approached the receptionist at a large, computerized desk, and at the same time several security guards approached them, hands on their holsters.

Estela's heart was jackhammering in her chest, and she was glad she didn't have to say anything, because her mouth was as dry and sticky as a jar of old school paste.

"Can I help you?" said the guard, a man in his midthirties with eyes that bespoke a cautious intelligence.

"FBI," said Gino, producing his gold and plastic ID. Estela flashed hers, using the same professional posture he'd coached into her. The guards all looked immediately relieved, but still concerned.

"What's the problem, sir?" the first of the two approaching guards said. But Estela noticed his tone was now solicitous instead of threatening.

"We may have a situation in Studio Four," said Gino. "No alarms! No sign that anything is wrong—got that?"

"You want us to assist?"

"We have backup on the way. Just cover the front elevators!" Gino spoke in a harsh whisper that still commanded complete attention. "Don't let anyone leave the building you can't ID visually. Get us up the service stairs and then you cover that, too, okay?"

"You got it!" said the guard, signaling his partner to the front bay of elevators while he rushed them around the corner to the stairwell. Opening the door for them, he said: "Third floor, to the right!"

Gino nodded and ushered Estela in ahead of himself, and then both of them rushed up the stairs as quickly as possible.

When they reached the third level and stepped out into a carpeted area by the elevators, Gino tapped her shoulder and they turned right, pushing through a set of double smoked-glass doors to be confronted by a beautiful young woman behind an enormous desk. She looked genuinely surprised to see them, and hardly looked at their FBI credentials.

"FBI," said Gino. "We've got to see the Man—*now*!"

The woman couldn't get out of her chair fast enough. "This way," she said, and led them down a short hallway past smoked-glass window-walls, behind which technicians and studio staffers bent over their consoles.

Some little guy in a red bow tie looked up and saw them, then came rushing out one of the door behind them. "Hey! Marlene, who are these two? What's going—?"

Gino spun on the guy so fast it even startled her, and stuck gold in his face. "FBI—who are you?"

Bow Tie tried to smile. "Me? I'm nobody, man. . . ."

"That's what I thought," said Gino, turning and effectively dismissing him.

"In here," the young woman said, pointing to a door at the end of the hall, but not daring to open it herself.

Gino nodded, moved past her, knocked loudly on the door, then entered.

"What is it?" said the man seated behind a very large desk covered with books and papers. He was wearing a tattersall oxford button-down with a burgundy tie and matching suspenders. His hair was carefully styled and he wore expensive reading glasses.

"Are you Larry King?" said Gino.

"Yes, I am. Would you mind telling me who *you* are and what the hell's going on around here?"

Gino smiled. "I've got someone you're going to want on your show."

Turning to make way for her, he gestured for Estela to speak. "Hello, Mr. King. I'm Doctor Estela Barrero. The government says I'm missing in the Blue Ridge Mountains. . . ."

The expression on Mr. King's face displayed a combination of surprise, amusement, and admiration.

"Would you like to know why they're lying?"

"Ohmigod . . ." whispered King, then: "Please, sit down, Doctor. I would love to."

"Who is your scheduled guest tonight?"

Larry King smiled. "You mean *before* it was you?"

FIFTY-TWO

Flanagan

When they arrived at CNN's Washington studio, the security staff had been alerted to escort him upstairs. Despite efforts to keep things quiet, the lobby was filling up with CNN personnel trying to get a look at him as he was rushed through and into the building. Even a few journalists who happened to be in the area had brought their camcorders.

Life in the Information Age.

News didn't travel fast, it red-shifted.

"Is it true your plane didn't go down, Senator?"

"Do you blame the president as well?"

"Does this mean you're still in the race?"

"Will you dismantle PSOG if you win?"

Tom just waved and smiled as best he could as the SSV agents blazed a trail through the crowd. Tom wondered what they would think if they knew their celebrity of the hour had just blown a man's head into grapefruit pulp with his own gun.

The elevators accepted them as the building security screened off the questions and the anxious faces. When the

378 THOMAS F. MONTELEONE

doors opened three floors later, another smaller knot of people awaited him and followed his escort down a short corridor to a studio control room, where a tall woman in a beige business suit awaited them. She was flanked by a shorter man wearing a red bow tie. Beyond them, through a glass window, he could see the lighted edge of the set, where he knew Estela awaited him.

"Senator Flanagan, good evening. I'm Kate Margolis, this is my floor director, Steve Finley. . . ."

Tom nodded, turned to his guardian angels from the Vatican. "How do we work this, guys?"

"We will wait for you. Here."

"Sounds like a plan to me," said Tom.

"Larry's already on the air with your physician," said Margolis, looking at Tom with an undeniable air of disfavor. "But you're going to need to get cleaned up a bit. Get him down to makeup, Steve."

"No makeup," he said. "Just get me on the air."

"I'm sorry, Senator, but—"

Tom stepped forward, putting his jaw inches from hers, a grim reminder of the scene with Leverton. "You think I look like hell, lady?"

"Well, you—"

"Good. I want everybody to see what I've been through. No makeup. Are we clear on that?"

Steve Finley nodded. "I think I see his point, Kate."

"Then get me on the air. Now."

Finley turned to a control console behind him, flipped a toggle. "Jerry, give Larry a cue—the senator's here."

Kate Margolis gave Tom a look of complete deferral and backed away.

"This way," she said, and opened a glass door leading to the studio floor.

As Finley escorted him to the set, he could hear Larry King introducing his arrival and saw a stagehand slipping in an off-camera chair next to Estela's.

" . . . just escorted to the studio—Senator Thomas Flanagan from Maryland."

As Larry stood up to greet him, Estela launched herself from her chair and into his arms. Nothing had ever felt so good. The smell of her hair and her hands across his shoulders. Then, suddenly composing herself, she turned and said: "I thought I might never see him again. . . ."

"Understandable," said King. "Welcome to the show, Senator. I have to say, we've never been privileged to be on the edge of breaking such a fantastic story. . . ."

"Thank you, Larry," he said, taking a chair, pushing his sweaty and blood-matted hair from his forehead. He knew he looked rough and he wanted it that way. "Your audience needs to know what's happened to me."

King nodded, adjusted one of his suspenders. "Doctor Barrero has given us a summary of your incredible story. I am told that as we speak, the town of Broadview Valley is being 'liberated' by the president, and an attempt is being made to reach General Cobb of the Joint Chiefs for comment. In the meantime, can you tell us where you've been, Senator? And what this group called PSOG has been doing with you?"

Facing the camera, and for the first time in his political life not having to worry about enacting a demeanor that would "look" sincere, Tom told his story. There was no TelePrompTer showing him what to say. He didn't need it. He was eloquent, but spared no graphic detail. The time for euphemism and gloss was long over.

Larry King demonstrated why he is the uncontested master of the interview as he allowed Tom just enough room to tell the story, then backed everything up with cogent questions that always clarified and illuminated. But even King could not contain his surprise at some of the details. As the story of deceit and death unfolded, the studio's phone board looked like Times Square.

They handled the calls, interlacing them with late-breaking, related news, events which punctuated and underscored Tom's story with grim and final emphasis. General Cobb had shot himself in his Pentagon office. Jarmusch Gunnderson had been arrested by the FBI and implicated Senator Erskine Lattimore in the PSOG conspiracy.

Afterward, as they left the set, Larry King stopped in the relative privacy of the sound stage to speak to them. "What you've done was very smart, very brave."

"We couldn't have done it without you," said Tom. "You're the real hero here. I'll bet you're going to take a lot of heat in some circles for this."

King shrugged. "It's supposed to be a cold winter. I can use it. Besides, I can't see any better argument than what we've done to show why the government can never control the media. They can talk all they want about us having a political slant, but when you go on live, there is no agenda."

"That's right," said Estela. "Anything can happen."

"And thanks to you, it did." King shook her hand sincerely.

"This could have easily degenerated into something that looked like a campaign stunt," said Tom. "I learned a lot just watching you handle the callers."

"It's what they pay me for," said King, smiling.

Suddenly they were interrupted by Kate Margolis. "Mr. Turner wants to invite them to stay in the suite tonight," she said.

"Great idea," said King. "I usually take my guests out to dinner, but I have a feeling you want to be alone for a while."

"Actually, the first thing I want to do is thank some of the other people who helped us," said Estela, looking through the glass door at the Vatican agents standing in the control room. "Where's Oscaro?"

Tom looked at her, shook his head in the smallest manner, but said nothing.

"Oh, no . . ." She tried to hold back the tears, but they slowly tracked the angular contours of her face.

"Come with me, folks," said King, recognizing the awkwardness of the moment.

Tom shook his hand, thanked him again, and allowed some of his staff to escort them to the suite atop the First Street building.

When they were alone, she let all the pain and frustration and anger of the experience rush out of her in a cataclysmic, emotional release. It was one of the things women could do so well, and he admired her for it as he cradled her in his arms. He knew that she would feel much better when it was finally past her; just as he knew he might never be able to exorcise the demonic morality play staged between himself and Leverton on the side of a busy interstate. He never wanted to think that he enjoyed the act of killing, but he knew the experience would ghost through his memories for the rest of his life.

Together, they helped each other through the night, from an almost silent, privately catered dinner to a candle-light shower in which they helped each other wash away the stains of the spirit. Exhausted and spent, they still made love with a caring bred of understanding and respect. Setting the capstone on the most torturous day of his life, with Estela in his arms, he lapsed into a grateful sleep . . .

. . . until someone threw open a door at the end of the dream corridor.

The figure stood on the threshold, silhouetted by nova-like brilliance in the room beyond. It reached out a hand to him and spoke in a now-familiar voice. Tom knew he was dreaming, but it was more than a dream. There was a presence in the room, like holographic projection, but it also emanated from within his own body, within his own mind.

Thomas, you have done well.

(Not again. . . . Go away. I'm not crazy.)

No one said you were.

(I don't need you—whoever you are.)

Perhaps. But we may need you.

(Look, I can't *deal* with this kind of thing, don't you understand? If this keeps happening, I'm going to be some-body's fruit salad.)

You are Entropy.

(That's not going to work. It just proves you're from my subconscious. Not real.)

Could your subconscious know about your destiny?

(There's no such thing. . . .)

You saw Chip's helmet. I showed it to you. You knew you were moving toward that point.

(Don't remind me of him. He's doomed.)

Perhaps not.

(How could you know?)

Because a kind of veiled prescience is the gift of one of the others, and telepathy is my particular talent. Imperfect though it is—like your own.

(What are you talking about?)

My name is not Dr. Infinity.

(No kidding . . . ?)

I apologize for using those names from your childhood. My gift allowed me to pull them from your mind—I thought they would make you . . . accept me more easily.

(Well, it didn't work.)

My name is Hawking. Jefferson Hawking.

(Never heard of you.)

I was a cybernetics professor at Vanderbilt University. I was part of a cross-discipline team working on an artificial intelligence project.

(Was? What do you mean? Are you . . . dead now?)

Quite the contrary. I am more alive than ever before.

(I don't get it.)

More than two years ago, I was almost killed in an auto accident. Coma, brain damage. But I survived, recuperated, and was changed by it. Sound familiar?

(Go on . . .)

I discovered soon after that I had a . . . gift. I could reach out to people mind-to-mind, at first only in dreams, like this, later when I learned to control it, almost anytime.

(Okay, that makes sense. Maybe you *are* real. . . . What else? Why did you . . . find me?)

You found us.

(What?)

Let me explain. You can accept it now. Now that you have been through the ordeal of accepting and learning to use your gift. That you were a public figure made it all the more difficult, however. That is why we were so careful.

("We?" I'm losing you. . . .)

At first, I felt very alone with my gift. I misused it, became terrified by it. But it became a conduit, a means of allowing others like me to reach out and connect to share their fears and pain.

(What happened?)

Months passed, and I discovered through my dreams that there were others like me, like you, who have suddenly developed strange abilities and who were feeling lost and terribly afraid. Gradually we reached out to each other on an unconscious network, broadcast through our dreams. Believe me when I tell you it's the real information highway.

(What you're saying—it almost makes sense. It's like I want to believe you.)

I know you do. And you shall. Listen: we have come together. We have formed a group, a community where we are trying to learn what process is at work among us. There must be a reason why things are happening to people at this time.

(What do you want from me?)

Join us. With each new member, we advance that much closer to understanding.

(I couldn't. What about Estela?)

She is welcome. You are ready now.

The words struck him like a resonant chord being sounded. It almost yanked him from the false grave of sleep.

(I . . . I don't know. It sounds . . . almost silly.)

It is that, and it is the most serious adventure in the history of the human race. We believe that.

(Are you their leader?)

We have no leader. We are a group entity in that respect. An intellectual and spiritual hive, if you prefer an image.

(What have you discovered so far?)

That the human animal has the potential to be a truly superior being, but that we have barely left our infancy. That there may be some kind of cosmic clock ticking; that the hour that has come round at last, the one they call the millennium, may be some kind of evolutionary milestone, that, once passed, will signal changes for the entire race. Something is happening, Thomas, and we are a part of it. That is undeniable. You are ready for this knowledge now, and once ready, we believe there is no looking back.

The words impacted on him and he could feel their innate truth. There were so many questions that needed answers.

(I don't want to sound self-absorbed, but I need to know something.)

Your son.

(Yes. Why did you give me hope?)

It is possible your gift might be accepted better by bodies still in development. A prescient member of our group believes the Marzano child and your son will survive. But she cautions that time is the final arbiter.

(But you have given me hope.)

A fine gift in itself. Combine it with your own faith.

(If I could believe that, then I think I could . . . go with you. Help you find the answers.)

That is all we can hope for.

(How do I find you? Where are you?)

We will send for you. . . .

Epilogue

And they did.

   . . . but only after the loose ends were gathered and tied off.

   Following the celebration of media excess, in which press-funded investigations and Senate subcommittee hearings attempted to track down all the villains, Tom went about getting his life in order. The most important task was the reunion with his son, Chip, who had apparently survived his resurrection without qualification. Youth and health, as Hawking had suggested, had been on the boy's side, and he now looked forward to a career in professional football. More salient was the unspoken bond that had formed between Tom and his son because of the experience, and both knew they were far richer for it. It allowed Tom to see his political life in a more realistic perspective, making his subsequent decisions far less difficult. Not only did he officially and irrevocably withdraw from consideration for party candidacy to the presidency, he also resigned as the senator from Maryland.

Separating himself from Rebecca Quinn Flanagan, and effecting a divorce from her, was far more difficult.

In the end, Tom gave the woman everything she could ask for under the law, and he gave it freely because he only wanted to be free of her. He knew the meaningful things in his life could not be parceled or assigned by any legal papers or proclamations. And he walked away from Washington the way he had arrived more than twenty years ago—with nothing but his name and good intentions.

No, that wasn't quite true.

At this time in his life, he did not walk alone. For the first time, he knew he had a true partner. Estela had shared his most intimate thoughts as well as acts, and she had stood with him at the edge of life itself. Tom had finally gained wisdom, and had become transformed as well.

And so, six months after appearing on *Larry King Live*, they drove Estela's BMW into the Appalachian woodlands. Following Hawking's directions, they homed in on a settlement in West Virginia known as Drood's Peak. The colors of early summer covered them in soft, verdant shadows as the two-lane blacktop climbed higher along the spine of the mountain. When the road veered left, they left it to negotiate a gravel path to the top of the ridge and the gates to the settlement.

Neither one of them had expected to see the sophisticated fencing and security accessories, such as the infrared sensors and the intercom system. When they identified themselves, the gates slid back on motorized tracks and admitted their vehicle into an area that could only be called a "compound." Hangarlike buildings huddled around a central group of larger buildings. Beyond this central cluster radiated smaller groups of units that were probably living quarters. Everything looked very modern, well-kept, meticulously planned. There were pathways, landscaping, and plenty of the original mountain forest preserved wherever possible. It wasn't as attractive as it was striking and utilitarian. Estela thought the basic design persona of the buildings was a little too cold, a little too severe; Tom found the Bauhaus lines and thirties industrial gothic a refreshing change from the chrome and glass, marble and column stagnation of Washington, D.C. They saw only several casually dressed people as they drove toward the largest building in the center, and the pedestrians seemed to take little notice of them.

"Well," she said as she braked to a stop in front of a building with two garage doors in front. "We're here. . . . "

"Little weird, isn't it?" he said.

Estela smiled. "Yeah, right—like the rest of my life with you has been perfectly normal. Boring, even."

"Here comes somebody," said Tom as he pointed to a group of four people approaching the car. Two men. Two women. Thirties or forties except for a tall, thin man with wispy, gray hair and horn-rimmed glasses. He led the others to the BMW, smiling and gesturing for Tom and Estela to get out of the car.

"Welcome to Drood's Peak, Thomas . . . Doctor Barrero . . ." he said. "I'm Jefferson Hawking. These are members of our Gathering."

He introduced the two women and the other man, but Tom forgot their names as he was hearing them. It only happened when he was extremely nervous, and until that moment, he hadn't realized how anxious he must be. Estela was gracious and charming, and Tom counted on her memory being better suited to the introductions. As they were escorted off on a leisurely tour of the settlement, Tom tried to consciously calm himself and just take in the new environment.

What impressed him the most was the sheer size of their installation, much larger than first ascertained. He and Estela witnessed an entirely self-sufficient community, combining vanguard "green" technologies with classic and traditional methods to achieve all the amenities as well as the essentials of civilization. It was beautiful, impressive, but not self-inflated. From the way their tour guides spoke, and also the words of the various, working members of the "Gathering's" team, Tom could readily see these people were not engaging in any sappy visions of Eldorado or any other super-harmonious utopia.

This settlement, or compound, or whatever it was, had developed into a community. As the members of the Gathering gradually explained, it was not a place where everyone had run to escape, but rather a focal point where people with various Fortean "talents" could learn from each other and slowly achieve control and understanding over their newfound abilities. This was not an effort to withdraw from the mundane existence of humankind; it was an attempt to refine it and redirect it.

Tom realized the Gathering's proposition would be cause for occasional compromise and moral reappraisal—a point underscored when Estela asked Hawking where they'd acquired the money to create such an impressive, ambitious settlement.

The ex-professor smiled. "Some of our members are prescient," he said. "Others have number skills that make calculation, extrapolation, and prediction child's play. Against such lethal combinations of talent, the world's stock exchanges have no chance."

And so he could sense the confidence and the resolve of the people of this place. There was a comfort and a refuge in the knowledge that they were safe here, that they were free to expand, to reach outward as well as inward. As the tour ended, Tom's respect for the goals and purposes of the settlement soared ever higher. Drood's Peak was not a commune; it was a community. Of like minds and hearts. Of like souls.

He knew he could live here, if not indefinitely, at least long enough to learn who he had become, and to where he must travel next. The task of solving the timeless riddle of humankind's happy accident—its very existence—had been assigned to these people. And they wanted him and Estela to join in the struggle.

As they stopped in front of the settlement's administration building, Tom looked at Estela. With a smile and the subtlest of nods, she reached out to take his hand into hers. It was the sign he'd been waiting for.

Their new life—and that of all the world—had begun.

Here is an excerpt
from
Night of Broken Souls
by
Thomas F.
Monteleone

Coming in Hardcover
from
WARNER ASPECT
March 1997

ANNA SMITHSON

Chicago, Illinois

She'd forgotten to take her asthma medicine before leaving the house, but it was such a clear, clean day, Anna hoped it wouldn't matter. It was more of a bother than a serious condition, but sometimes she had the feeling that her asthma would cause her more trouble than anything else in her life.

But not today.

Asthma or not, it certainly was a pleasure to go into the city on a shopping spree, thought Anna as she parked her Riviera on the fourth floor of the parking garage off Dearborn. She locked her car and walked slowly to the elevators, being careful to adjust the blouse of her Donna Karan ensemble and accessorizing scarf so that everything fell just so. At forty-seven, she knew she still looked damned good, and still got whistles from passing cars and trucks when she was out jogging or walking. Watching her nutrition, exercising, and keeping abreast of the latest fashions had all contributed to her youthful body and face, her entire *look*.

She had paid an equal amount of attention to her mind and considered herself not only well read and widely cultured, but extremely interesting as well. Anna believed in herself, and it paid dividends every day. When the kids left the nest for college and their own lives, she started her own small mail-order catalog for one-of-a-kind dresses, and the business had grown into a substantial little company.

Good thing, too.

When they found Stephen face-down on the blotter of his executive desk, his brain and his life short-circuited from a stroke at age fifty, she discovered his terrible secret. He'd been borrowing against his life insurance policies to play games with penny stocks on the Vancouver Stock Exchange. Other than some Social Security benefits, he left her with nothing but a lot of debt. It had shocked her at first, actually angered her—that he would do something like that. He hadn't planned on the stroke, figuring he'd have plenty of time to funnel his "play money" back into the proper assets.

But time had just . . . run out. Nothing to take personally, although it was hard not to feel cheated at the time. And gradually Anna accepted it for what it was—Stephen had simply miscalculated. She loved him, missed him, and spoke of him as any respectful widow should. It had been several years now since she'd been on her own, and other than the occasional nightmare or migraine, she seemed to have survived all the stress and trauma associated with losing your husband and your security and your home all at the same time.

The migraines.

As she reached the street and began to idly search out the small shops and boutiques that featured not only the headline designer pieces but also the works of the up-and-comers, she found herself dwelling on those terrible, blinding headaches.

Sometimes Anna could not stop thinking about them, fearing them, and the way they would just burn into her head from out of nowhere.

And the nightmares.

Yes, go on and toss them in as well. Dark, grim, full of death-images. The doctors had told her the nightmares were a natural outgrowth of her situation.

Undefined fears and anxiety about being alone, about taking care of herself, all that sort of thing.

Maybe . . . she thought. Maybe that's what it was, but sometimes she felt convinced it had to be something else.

The notion began to nag at her as she turned a corner, but quickly left her as she found a place specializing in bolts of hand-painted and hand-dyed exotic fabrics. Oh, she thought, the gowns she could create from some of these would be matchless! One-of-a-kind specialties.

She spent the next several hours roaming around, searching for places that were off the familiar beat, where she could find items no one else had even considered. After lunch in an authentic kosher deli, she drifted into the frontiers of an older neighborhood known for its ethnic traditions. People on the street were dressed in subdued clothing, nothing fashionable as much as supremely functional. Everyone looked clean and neat, but certainly . . . different . . . and most assuredly they were not the type of people who would be her customers.

But Anna continued her stroll through their territory, following an instinct that she believed was telling her she would find exactly what she needed for her business. The afternoon grew as long as the shadows filling the narrow streets full of storefronts advertising basic services and trades that were becoming lost arts—hand laundries, shoemakers, woodcarvers, tile cutters, appliance repairs.

Then, as she slipped around another street corner, she was engulfed by the penumbral presence of a large building made of red stone with a slate-shingled roof. The architecture was austere, hard, functional, almost ugly. There was absolutely *nothing* to attract her interest or her sense of esthetics, but she found herself staring at the edifice, unable to break her trancelike gaze. And then she was moving, lugging both handfuls of shopping bags up a low case of wide, stone steps.

Halting for a moment in front of the building's double doors of thick, weatherworn oak, Anna blinked and almost caught herself acting so impulsively. What was she doing here? What was this place?

The thoughts passed through her quickly like invisible radiation and she reacted to them not at all. As though someone else was guiding her hand, she pushed open the door to the strange building and slipped within its cool, dim embrace.

For a moment, Anna could see nothing, but her eyes adjusted to the lack of light quickly, and she could see stained glass in the vaulted distance. Was she in a church? Her gaze shifting from place to random place, she caught glimpses of images familiar, blending together to form a particular motif. Images of multi-stemmed candelabra and six-pointed stars.

She *was* in a church, but not like any she'd ever seen before. This was a Jewish church.

A *synagogue*, thought Anna as she stepped more deeply into the place of worship. With each step, a feeling of déjà vu grew more intense within her, and as though she were walking ever inward to the center of a walk-in freezer, she began to shiver from the sensation that she'd been here before, that she'd walked down the aisle towards the altar where the holy Torah resided.

Where the *what*?

How did she know that? Her everyday, conscious mind was trying to push through the filmy skin that seemed to be encapsulating her, to make sense of her thoughts, her actions.

What was happening to her? Why was she here . . . and what did this mean?

The questions buzzed around her like insects, but they were less than an annoyance. They didn't matter. Something else was going on here, and Anna could feel it, in the core of her soul, something trolling down into that dark well of being, probing, grasping. It was an unsettling feeling, at once frightening and exciting, as if she were having sex with a total stranger. There came a subtle resonance in her head as though she had leaned close to a just-struck tuning fork. It grew in power until it became like the sound of the sea in a shell, then louder still to be an actual sussuration, a gentle but persistent *roaring* in her inner ear. The sound evolved and changed so that it was now becoming a kind of chorus of human voices, all twined together in a kind of atonal harmony.

But there was no suggestion of real harmony in the sound. Moreover, a rising statement of pain, of anger, the confusion of prayers never answered.

Anna felt her legs growing weak, her breath shortening.

Got to sit down, she thought. Just for a minute. I've got to just relax.

But as she eased into the closest seat, the sensation of disequilibrium intensified, and the roaring in her ears grew louder, crowding out even the steady rhythm of her innermost thoughts. Leaning back, she looked up at the images in the stained glass where the indistinct figure of a man seemed to dominate the fractured mosaic. A total paralysis gripped her, as though she were having a seizure, and she could feel the muscles in her body straightening, lengthening, locking up. Anna's eyes began to flutter as she collapsed stiffly across the hard lines of the bench. She—

—blinked her eyes and looked out the doorway of the barracks. There was very little color in the world she surveyed. Grays and blacks and pale flesh. A sky like chiseled stone and a breeze edged with coming winter. Her breath danced and roiled in front of her as she held out her arm to see what she was wearing—a coarse pajama top of gray and black stripes, and a badge made of two sewn triangles, one yellow and one white, one over the other and opposed to form a Star of David.

She was looking out upon row after row of sooty, colorless barracks where open windows and doors gaped like hideous wounds. Within them, stacked like cordwood, lay the workers of the camp. Anna knew this as she stood looking out at the grim tableau of her daily life. But her name was not "Anna." Some disconnected part of her had used the name, but she knew it was a fantasy. Just like the rule that had come down in Germany, when she was living with her family in München, that all the Juden females would have the name "Sara" added to their passports. She knew that her real name was Ruth.

She and her sister, Hilda, had arrived at Dachau along with so many others from the villages around the city, and now they worked in road crews and teams for a factory that made the treads for Panzers and tires for the troop carriers. Each day they worked sixteen hours, living on one meal of soup and bread. The soup was usually half-boiled water with a piece of chicken bone, the bread like a chunk of quarry stone. But it had kept them alive for more than a year, when she had seen so many others die. Children were the weakest and died the fastest, but Anna/Ruth had seen others die in the fields working, along the roadways, and even on the factory floor, when they either collapsed or were shot by the guards in their crisp uniforms.

But today was something different, she somehow knew this.

Anna/Ruth stood at the threshold because the rumor mill had been grinding about a strange visitor coming to the camp. Someone from Poland, from a camp there. And now, as if on cue, following the stage directions of an unseen God, she saw the gates to the barracks yard swing back to reveal several camp guards and an armored car. The vehicle moved within the gates, its machine guns bristling like insect antennae, and rolled to a stop at the first of many long, low-slung buildings full of prisoners. Behind the armored car lumbered a troop truck, like a dog following its master. It stopped by the barracks, disgorging a handful of black uniforms, the Schutzstaffel, better known as the SS, who waited until their superiors emerged from the armored car. The SS were very mean, and everyone hated them. They were like vicious wolves.

An officer appeared, then a driver and a tall gaunt man wearing a long black coat. He looked to be totally bald with great sunken eye sockets. Even from the considerable distance of her vantage point, Anna could tell the man looked frightful, ghoulish. There was something about this scene that held her attention. Her intuition screamed: this visit by the SS would be the most important event in her teen-aged life. Time eddied around her in a gray whorl as *she continued to watch the officer, his soldiers and the one she began to think of as "the golem," after a folk-monster from her childhood. Several times the soldiers emerged from the endless rows of barracks with pairs of prisoners, who were roughly tossed into the back of the troop carrier. It was only when the soldiers exited the barracks only three down the line from her own that she realized what was going on, that she knew her instincts had been correct, and that she should fear these men.*

THOMAS F. MONTELEONE is the author of nineteen acclaimed novels and editor of the award-winning Borderlands anthology series. Mr. Monteleone and his family live in Brooklandville, Maryland.